SURVIVE =
= *THE NIGHT*

KATIE
RUGGLE

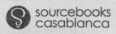

sourcebooks
casablanca

Published by Sourcebooks Casablanca, an imprint of Sourcebooks, Inc.
P.O. Box 4410, Naperville, Illinois 60567-4410
(630) 961-3900
Fax: (630) 961-2168
sourcebooks.com

Printed and bound in the United States of America.
OPM 10 9 8 7 6 5 4 3 2 1

EVERYONE IS TALKI

SEARCH & RESCU

IR

"I love Ruggle's characters. They're sharpl, vividly alive. I'm happy when they find each other. These are wonderful escapist books."
—**Charlaine Harris**, #1 *New York Times* Bestselling Author of the Sookie Stackhouse Series

"Gripping suspense, unique heroines, sexy heroes."
—**Christine Feehan**, #1 *New York Times* Bestselling Author

"Sexy and suspenseful, I couldn't turn the pages fast enough."
—**Julie Ann Walker**, *New York Times* and *USA Today* Bestselling Author, for *Hold Your Breath*

"Chills and thrills and a sexy, slow-burning romance from a terrific new voice."
—**D. D. Ayres**, Author of the K-9 Rescue Series, for *Hold Your Breath*

"Fast, funny read, and a promising start to a new series."
—*Smart Bitches, Trashy Books* for *Hold Your Breath*

" ...ries is off
t... s, 4 Stars
...ur Breath

ALSO BY KATIE RUGGLE

This one's for the dogs.

CHAPTER 1

"Alice!"

Jeb's shout made her jump, the tiny zipper tab slipping from her fingers. Alice glanced at the closed door. "Just a moment!"

"Hurry up." Jeb sounded tense, making Alice's fingers tremble in response. "Your brother is waiting."

Her gaze darted to the clock. It was just past eight, and Aaron had told her to be ready by eight thirty. It didn't matter that she wasn't actually late, though. The punishment would be the same. "I'm almost ready."

Alice fumbled for the zipper, only to have it slip from her fingers again. Gritting her teeth, she sucked a silent breath in through her nose and closed her eyes, willing her body to stop shaking. It would only delay her, and that would make everything worse. Opening her eyes again, she grasped the tab and slid it up until it touched the back of her neck.

Something scratched at her skin, and she frowned as she reached inside the collar. Had she forgotten to remove the dry cleaner's tag? Her fingers closed around a small piece of paper, and she tugged it free. Taking the two steps toward the small trash can next to her vanity, Alice absently glanced at the now-crumpled scrap. It wasn't the usual red tag the dry cleaner used, though.

Smoothing it out, she saw something written in a slashing, aggressive hand.

Be ready to escape. Soon.

Alice froze, staring at the words. What was this? A joke? Why had it been attached to her dress? It couldn't be meant for her, even though the wording made her desperately hope it was. How wonderful it would be to have a friend, one who would be willing to help her.

She didn't have any allies, though. Not in Aaron's world.

"Alice, for Christ's sake." Jeb swung open the door and stormed into the room. "It's like you're *trying* to piss off your brother."

Years of practice allowed her to keep the guilty anxiety from showing. Closing her fingers around the slip of paper in a way she hoped looked casual, Alice glanced at her bodyguard over her shoulder. "Almost ready." Her voice sounded calm, not revealing how hard her heart was pounding. "I just need to use the bathroom, and then we can leave."

"No time." Jeb grabbed her arm, his fingers pressing into old bruises, making it hard to hold back a wince. "You can go at the restaurant."

Alice twisted free, despite knowing that he would make her pay for that small act of disobedience. Still, whatever Jeb's punishment would be, it couldn't be as bad as what would happen if Aaron found that message. "I can't wait. I promise to be quick." Without hesitating, knowing it would be impossible to escape Jeb's grip if he caught her a second time, she darted for the bathroom.

The lock was something a five-year-old could unlatch with a piece of wire and some luck, but it would give her a few seconds, and that was all Alice needed. She allowed herself one last quick glance at the message, just long enough to convince herself that it was real. The words were still there, exactly the same as before, and her heart sped up again—this time, with hope.

Jeb's heavy fist pounded on the door. With sweaty fingers, Alice shredded the note, allowing the bits of paper to fall into the toilet. She flushed and watched the tiny pieces spin in circles until they were sucked down the drain. After a last check to make sure every bit of evidence was gone, she pulled up her sleeves and washed her hands.

As she dried them, the lock popped out, and the door opened. Alice adjusted her sleeves so they reached her wrists, hiding the faded and fresh oval bruises that dotted her forearms. She turned to Jeb, keeping her expression blank, but inside she braced for his anger.

"Let's go," he grunted, and she relaxed slightly. Obviously, Jeb wasn't willing to delay them any longer, even if he was irritated with her. He rushed her out of the bedroom and down the stairs, staying so close behind her that the thud of his footsteps was almost painfully loud.

"Alice!" The impatience in her brother's voice made her want to run back up to her room, but that would be futile. Not only would Jeb stop her, but her bedroom wasn't a sanctuary. There wasn't a safe place in the entire house—or in Alice's entire life.

The promise scrawled on that note flickered in her mind, but she quickly banished it. It could be a joke or a trick or meant for someone else or...who knew.

She couldn't get her hopes up. If she did, and whoever it was didn't come through, the disappointment would crush her.

As she reached the bottom of the steps, Aaron was already charging down the hall toward her. "Alice! Where is that… Oh, there you are." He stopped abruptly, frowning as he took in her appearance. Even though she knew he could find no fault—that he himself had chosen the blue dress for its nun-approved neckline and concealing sleeves—her stomach still soured with nerves. "What took you so long?"

She just stayed quiet. It was futile to protest, to tell him that she wasn't late, that she was, in fact, fifteen minutes early.

Besides, he wasn't really interested in what she had to say.

"Come on, then." He turned to the front entrance. "The car's waiting."

With Aaron in front of her and Jeb behind, Alice made her way out of the house. The driver holding open the car door was Chester, and he gave her a subtle wink as she slid into the back seat of the SUV. She raised her hand in a tiny return wave, hoping he saw it but not daring to do more. When she was younger, she'd spent as much time as she could with Chester and his wife, Gloria. He'd taught her how to drive and take care of the horses, and Gloria had taught her how to cook and take care of herself. Both of them had showed her how to be a decent human being. After her father died, right before she turned eighteen, Aaron took over as head of the family and assigned Alice full-time bodyguards. It became impossible to sneak away to the kitchen or the barn. Surreptitious waves were the closest she'd gotten to talking to Chester or Gloria in years.

Jeb circled the car to climb into the front passenger seat as Aaron sat next to her. Chester closed Aaron's door, and Alice had the almost irresistible urge to scramble out of the car and run. Only the knowledge that she'd barely get ten feet before Jeb tackled her stopped her from trying. *They said to be ready*, she reminded herself, fingers clutching the leather upholstery on the side away from Aaron, where her brother couldn't see her bone-white, desperate grip. *What if there really is a plan? I just need to wait a little longer.*

Aaron glanced at her sharply. For one terrified second, Alice thought she'd actually said the words out loud. Then reason returned, and she was able to smooth her expression into its usual placid lines.

"Best behavior, Alice," he warned, settling back in his seat. "This is an important meeting. First impressions matter. Make a good one, or there will be consequences."

Fire flared in her belly, working its way up to her cheeks. With a huge effort, she kept her rage locked inside and gave Aaron a small nod, hoping that he'd mistake her red face for embarrassment. Turning her head, she stared blindly out the window, not seeing the irrigated lawns or brassy, overdone homes they passed.

Just a little longer, she repeated, turning it into a chant in her head. *Just a little longer. If the note is real, if it's meant for me, if there's an escape plan...so many ifs. Wait and see and be prepared, just in case it's real. It won't kill me to wait a little longer.*

Why did it feel like she wouldn't survive another second?

When Chester pulled the SUV up to the entrance of Mod fifteen silent minutes later, Alice swallowed a groan. Of all the Dallas restaurants, they had to go to the most pretentious one? She shook off her annoyance. Of course they did. Aaron had chosen the place after all, and he was easily swayed by flash over substance.

"Miss?" Jeb held her door open. With a deep, soundless breath, she climbed out of the SUV.

"Thank you," she said quietly, waiting for Aaron to circle the vehicle and step to her side. Instead of offering an arm to her, he strode ahead. Alice hesitated, the temptation to turn and run so strong that it almost overwhelmed her. A nudge from Jeb brought her back to reality.

"Miss," he said again, gesturing for her to follow Aaron. Straightening her shoulders, Alice walked into the restaurant after her brother.

As she approached the hostess stand, she heard the tail end of his question. "…the Jovanovic party arrived yet?"

Her heart skipped at the name, and she sucked in a quiet, shocked breath. As shady and unethical as her father had been—and now Aaron was—the Blanchetts were angels compared to the Jovanovics. The Jovanovics, according to everything Alice had heard, were the worst of the worst.

Alice had always been quiet, even as a small child, and people tended to forget she was in the room. She'd heard dozens of horror stories about the Jovanovic family, and she wondered which of the demons they'd be meeting tonight. From what people said, Noah Jovanovic was the true head of the family now, although his uncle Martin was the false face of their empire.

She'd gotten a glimpse of Martin one day five years ago. Breathless and with bits of hay in her hair, Alice had been hurrying inside from the stables, hoping to clean up before her father caught her. She may as well not have bothered. Not only had he spotted her, but so had his guest. Her father had introduced them, and Martin had shaken her hand for a bit too long as he stared intently at her face. Alice had to fight not to yank her hand back, not to rip her captive fingers from his grip and run to her room. Even now, five years later, those eerily light-blue eyes were burned into her memory. His gaze had been cold, as calculating and predatory as a snake's. Even if she hadn't heard whispers about Martin Jovanovic and his family, Alice still would've recognized evil at a glance.

Now she was going to have to sit and have dinner with them. Alice briefly considered faking sick, but she was too afraid of the consequences. Aaron didn't like it when things didn't go as planned. It was either sit with the Jovanovics for a few hours or deal with the fallout. Her stomach churned until she thought she was going to vomit for real. Whatever she did, Alice knew it would be a lose-lose situation. Once again, she was trapped.

The hostess began to lead them into the dining area, making the decision for Alice. She'd endure dinner. At least this way, she knew it had to end. Aaron's anger never did. Alice flexed her shoulders, trying her best to stand straight and not cower as she followed the hostess into a private room that held a single round table surrounded by four chairs. Four men in dark suits stood around the room, and Alice knew they were most definitely armed to the teeth.

The two men who were seated at the table rose, and Alice's heart thumped in her throat. The elder of the pair wasn't Martin, thank God, but rather a somewhat older and more faded version. Despite his slightly cruel smile, he didn't have the same aura of menace.

Alice's muscles relaxed slightly. Dinner might not be quite as torturous as she'd expected.

"Judd," Aaron greeted the white-haired man, shaking his hand. "Good to see you again." He moved to greet the younger man, tall and gangly, with a sparse mustache, who looked to be in his late twenties. "Logan. This is my sister, Alice Blanchett."

The two strangers eyed Alice with a similar expression: smarmy avarice tinted with lust.

"Miss Blanchett," the older man—the one Aaron had called Judd—said, his voice low and smooth and much too slippery. "What a pleasure to meet you."

"Hello." Alice managed a slight smile as she shook his hand. "Please call me Alice."

The courtesy slipped out almost of its own volition. Manners had been drilled into her from the time she could speak, and it was as easy as breathing to go through the motions, even with Jovanovics. Then she turned to Logan, and the gross way he flicked his eyes up and down her body immediately made her stiffen. It wasn't even the rude, sexual perusal that bothered her. It was the possession in his gaze—as if he'd already paid the asking price and she was being delivered for his pleasure—that truly made her skin crawl.

After she shook Logan's hand and greeted him politely, her smile slipped away. He pulled out her chair, and she sat at the very edge of the seat, hoping to avoid any accidental touches. Logan slid the chair beneath her, brushing his fingers along her arms and shoulders as he straightened. Even through the fabric of her dress, Alice felt the sticky heat of his caress long after he'd moved back and taken his seat again.

"Any news on the case?" Aaron asked as soon as they were seated and a discreet server had poured their wine. Alice was careful not to let her interest show. There had been a few whispers about a raid on the Jovanovics' place—one that had led to several arrests—but this was the first time she would hear any of the details.

Judd made a face. "Nothing good. For the amount we pay the attorneys, you'd think they would've made these charges go away by now. Noah and Martin are getting…antsy."

"I'm sure they are." Aaron lifted his wineglass. "Here's to a quick dismissal of all charges, so that things can go back to business as usual."

The others lifted their glasses in response, and Alice followed suit, pretending to take a sip afterward. She'd always hated wine, but she knew better than to refuse with Aaron watching.

"Business as usual can't come soon enough," Judd agreed, sounding completely sincere. "I'm ready to hand the reins back to my nephew and brother."

Aaron raised his brows slightly, as if the idea of giving up power was inconceivable. "Any luck finding the witness?"

If the dinner continued to be this interesting, it would almost make up for the way Logan was staring at her. His gaze felt as if it left a sticky film on her skin wherever it touched. Alice felt a rare moment of appreciation for her Aaron-chosen, not-at-all-revealing dress. At least she had that thin layer of protection between Logan's slimy gaze and a good portion of her body.

Judd cast a quick glance at Alice, and Aaron waved a hand. "Don't worry about her. She's family." He gave Judd a knowing glance that Alice wasn't sure how to interpret before continuing. "She's aware of what the consequences would be if she ever even thought about betraying us."

The threat made Alice shiver, but his words seemed to convince Judd. "We're working on it. The witness met Noah in Denver, but she could've flown in from anywhere. Our guy in WITSEC can't find any mention of her, which is strange. Since the FBI was involved, we assumed she was in witness protection, but we're starting to wonder."

Aaron made a small, skeptical sound. "Isn't she just some nobody that Noah hooked up with a few times? How hard could it be to find one woman?"

"Harder than you might think." Although Judd's voice was still mild, he'd stiffened at the implied criticism.

"I'm sure it is," Aaron agreed quickly. "It's just surprising that a person without any connections can disappear so completely."

Although his frown remained, Judd settled back in his chair, partially soothed. "Even Logan hasn't heard anything."

Alice shot Logan a curious look.

"I'm a police officer in LA," Logan said, catching her glance. He brushed at the front of his jacket. The motion reminded Alice of a puffed-up rooster. "The information I collect is invaluable for the family."

With a small bob of her head, Alice searched for some way to respond. "I'm sure it is."

Leaving him to his preening, Alice turned her attention back to Judd. "We're watching a friend of hers," he was saying. "With Noah and Martin in jail, we're hoping she will relax and possibly contact her friend."

Noah and Martin Jovanovic are in jail? Alice felt her eyes widen. As hard as she tried to keep her face blank, this news was just too amazing. She sent a mental message of thanks and good luck to the missing witness who'd apparently had a hand in getting those monsters locked away.

"Alice." Hard fingers grabbed her chin, jerking her head around until she was looking at Logan's annoyed face. "Quit ignoring me."

His touch was so sudden, so rough, that she tried to pull away before she caught herself. "I wasn't ignoring you." Her voice sounded strained, and she tried to soften it. "I'm just…shy."

Still gripping her face, Logan studied her for a long moment. Alice stared back, clinging to her most earnest expression, not daring to let her fear show. Finally, he released her and sat back in his chair. "No need to be shy with me."

As he looked away, reaching for the bread basket, Alice risked darting a glance at the other two men. They were both watching, but their silence told her that there would be no help from Aaron or Judd.

"Bread?" Logan asked, his voice low and intimate. He leaned toward her, bread basket in hand.

"No, thank you." Despite her best efforts, her polite smile was stiff around the edges. All she wanted to do was listen to Judd and Aaron's fascinating conversation, but now she was afraid to take her eyes off Logan.

"No?" He placed the basket back on the table. "That's probably for the best, anyway. As small as you are, you probably can't eat too much without tubbing out."

"Tubbing...out?" she repeated, blinking at him.

"You know." Logan blew out his cheeks. "Getting fat."

"I knew what you meant. I just couldn't believe you said it."

"Alice," Aaron snapped, making her jump and turn toward him. "Don't be rude."

A rush of righteous indignation crashed through her, nearly burying her fear. She opened her mouth to protest, but the warning narrowing of Aaron's eyes made her close her mouth before she said anything at all.

"Apologize to Logan," Aaron ordered, as if she were a five-year-old who'd just kicked a fellow kindergartner in the shin.

She turned a blank face toward the man sitting next to her. "I apologize if I seemed rude."

"Alice..." Aaron said, low but sharp, and she had to hide a wince.

"I don't think you were rude," Logan said. "You just didn't understand what I said."

Forcing a smile, Alice said, "Thank you, Logan."

With a pleased grin, he reached over and patted her back. As he withdrew his hand, his fingers lingered, stroking down her arm. Clenching her teeth, Alice took back everything she'd thought about the dinner not being so bad. It was going to be horrid.

"That was disappointing," Aaron said after a chilly two minutes of silence.

"What was?" A cramping stomach told Alice that she knew perfectly well what was disappointing Aaron—she was. After he'd rebuked her, his conversation with the Jovanovics had taken a more general—and less interesting—turn. Alice had endured three hours of pretending to drink wine and eat overpriced, badly cooked food while attempting to evade Logan's groping hands. It had been hard to put him off when every movement had been monitored by Aaron. After Judd and Logan had left the table, Aaron hadn't said a word or even looked at her until they were in the SUV, heading toward home.

Aaron reached out, as quick as a striking snake, and backhanded her across the face. Her head jerked to the side, and she heard the slap of skin against skin before the pain registered, sharp and horribly familiar. "Don't play stupid. You know how to behave. You just chose not to."

Pressing her hand against her stinging cheek, Alice said nothing. Any attempt to defend herself would just enrage her brother more. Instead, she watched him warily, fighting the urge to press against the door. There was no way to escape. She was trapped. Her gaze met Chester's in the rearview mirror. The helpless fury in his eyes made her want to reassure him. If the driver tried to defend her, it would just make things so much worse for all of them.

"This is my chance," Aaron said, jerking her attention

back to him. "The Jovanovic family is in chaos right now. Eight people—eight!—were arrested, including Noah and Martin, and they'll be locked away for years. Judd is no leader. That's obvious. There's a huge power vacuum, and I'm going to fill it."

"So fill it!" Alice burst out. Enough was enough. Being stuck in the middle of Blanchett family power games was one thing. She was born into that. There was no way that Alice was going to get involved with the Jovanovics, though. Let Aaron wallow in all the power he could grab, but Alice didn't want any part of it. All she wanted was the freedom to do normal things—to choose her clothes and friends and meals and job and... everything. "What does any of this have to do with me?"

He grabbed her, his fingers wrapping around her throat, forcing up her chin so she had to meet his eyes. Alice's heart thundered in her chest, her breaths coming in short gasps. Although Aaron's grip wasn't tight enough to cut off air, the threat was there, that he could close his fingers and end her if he wanted to. His eyes were the exact same dark brown, same round shape as hers, but they were as cold and hard and pitiless as marbles. Alice tried to swallow and choked instead.

"This has everything to do with you," he said, fingertips digging in just a little more until Alice knew he was leaving small, round bruises. He'd put them there before. "You're my in."

"Me?" she tried to echo, although no sound emerged. All she could do was mouth the word.

"You." Aaron tightened his grip just enough that Alice couldn't breathe. She tried to hold back the panic by pretending she was underwater, that she was perfectly safe, that she could surface for air at any time. Eventually Aaron would let her go. He'd just said that he needed her. If he killed her, he wouldn't succeed.

Even so, she felt the panic rising as her lungs pinched, desperate for air. Her thoughts went fuzzy, fear creeping in until she couldn't focus on anything else.

She grabbed his wrist with both hands, instinct forcing her to fight. His arm was rock-hard under her grip, solid and unmovable. Despite knowing that it was futile, she yanked and pulled, trying to pry his hand off her throat. *Maybe he really will kill me this time.*

Just as her vision started to go dark around the edges, Aaron let go of her throat. Bending at the waist as far as her seat belt would allow, Alice sucked in deep breaths that rasped her throat and made her cough.

"What do you mean?" Her voice was hoarse and breathless as she forced herself to straighten, and she wished she were better at faking nonchalance. It felt like weakness to show her brother how much he'd hurt her.

"According to my sources, Logan is gaining something of a bad reputation with the California ladies." His mouth curled up at the corner—a mouth that looked just like Alice's. She hated that they looked so much alike, hated seeing bits of him when she looked in the mirror.

"What kind of bad reputation?" Her hands wanted to rub at her aching throat and rest against her swelling cheek, but she forced them to stay in her lap. This was important. She had to get all the information she could from Aaron. The more she knew, the easier it would be to figure out how to avoid falling in with his plan.

He waved a hand in a dismissive gesture, and Alice flinched before she could catch herself. "That doesn't matter. What does matter is that his dad—Judd—and the rest of the Jovanovics are sick of spending money paying off these women, not to mention the doctors and judges."

"Paying off doctors and judges?" Her stomach twisted as she tried to process his words. "Why? Did he hurt those women?"

"I said it doesn't matter."

Alice dropped her gaze, trying to force her brain past the idea that Logan—the same creep who'd just sat next to her all through dinner, who had touched her multiple times—had abused women in some way. He'd done something awful enough that the Jovanovics had been willing to pay off his victims and bribe the authorities. She swallowed, her sore throat complaining. "What do Logan's…issues have to do with me?"

"The Jovanovics are hoping he'll settle down with a nice woman." Aaron smiled, and it was terrible. "Someone that will keep him home, away from opportunistic whores."

Her pulse was going wild again. Aaron's plan was a simple one, but Alice was still having a hard time putting it together in her mind. It was just too horrific. "You…" she finally stammered. "You want me to date Logan?"

"No." For a second, his answer made her sag with relief, but Aaron wasn't finished. "You're going to marry him."

CHAPTER 2

EVER SINCE THAT NIGHT, ALICE HAD BEEN WAITING FOR rescue—hoping for it, praying desperately for it even as she searched for another way to escape. The days ticked by, and she fought to hold on to hope, keeping alert for any hint that her unknown friend had finally come through. When the first sign of rescue came, however, it took a form she hadn't expected.

She never dreamed they'd blow up her house.

The explosion knocked her out of bed, startling her out of an uneasy doze. Her insides felt battered, hurting more than her elbow or head where they'd connected with the hardwood floor. Her brain ran through crazy, illogical explanations—it had been an earthquake or a kick from Aaron or a poltergeist that had sent her flying.

She pushed up to her hands and knees while trying to sort out her thoughts. All the chaos made it hard, though. Alarms blared, shrill and ear-piercing, competing with shouts and heavy, running feet. Suddenly, it hit her—was this it? Was *this* the escape the note had promised?

Even as Alice climbed to her feet, she hesitated. What if this wasn't part of the plan? What if the house was on fire, and Alice was about to be burned to death because she'd waited for some mysterious savior to arrive? She sniffed. There was the smell of smoke hanging in the air, but it wasn't heavy—not yet, at least.

Either way, if it was a disaster or if someone had come to help her escape, she needed to be ready to run. Alice hurried over to the closet. Ever since she'd found the note, she'd been preparing for this. Shoving aside designer dresses hung on satin-lined hangers, Alice grabbed a full backpack and the stack of clothes that were sitting at the very back of her enormous closet. She yanked on jeans and a long-sleeved T-shirt, topping it off with a black hoodie while jamming her feet into hiking shoes.

Heaving the pack onto her back, she hurried out of the enormous closet, not feeling a single pang for all the expensive clothes she was leaving behind. They'd been chosen for her by her father and, over the past few years, her brother. To her, the clothes were just costly prison uniforms.

Back in her bedroom, Alice hesitated again, still not sure if she should try to escape or wait for someone to arrive. The smoke was thicker, and the voices were more urgent, although still muted, blocked by at least one level and the heavy door to her room. She moved to try the door, but it was locked from the outside, as always. Every night, from ten until six in the morning, she was bolted into her room.

Her already thrumming heartbeat picked up even more. What if her unknown friend didn't realize that she was locked in? What if they'd only been offering a distraction, an opportunity, and this was it? She could be missing the only chance she'd have to slip away, to escape from her brother and Logan and a future that was heartbreakingly close to her present.

Someone knocked.

Dropping her hand from the handle, Alice backed away, staring at the door in horror. Who was it—friend or foe or, even worse, family? The knock came again, a sharp *tap-tap-tap*, and she realized with a jolt of surprise that it wasn't coming from the door.

Whirling around, she stumbled back a step, swallowing a scream. A dark silhouette filled the window. Someone was outside, their dark-clad form just a few shades blacker than the night sky.

The lurker leaned closer, the dim light from the room illuminating his harsh features, and Alice recognized him. Shock gave way to disappointment mingled with fear. It was Mateo Espina, one of her brother's colleagues, a man who was as firmly entrenched as Aaron in their criminal empire. Alice berated herself for building so much hope on the shaky foundation of an anonymous note. Of course there was no one willing to help her, not in her tiny world of liars and thieves and abusive assholes.

Mr. Espina tapped again. Outside her room, the alarms still shrieked, and the shouts were getting closer and louder. The man outside the window watched her, still and serious, and Alice tried to figure out what was happening. Why was he outside? If he was on her brother's side, why sneak into her bedroom? She wondered if there was a chance, even a slight one, that Mr. Espina could be there to help her. Although she quickly shut down that thought, she moved toward the window. Dressed all in black, Mr. Espina stood on the ledge outside her window, over thirty feet from the ground.

"What do you want?" she asked.

"Didn't you get my note?"

With the window closed and the alarms blaring, she could barely hear him, but that didn't stop her heart from taking off at a gallop. She'd thought she'd beaten down all hope, but there it was again, trying to break through her doubt. With enormous effort, she kept her expression blank. "What note?"

"Do you want to get out of here?"

Yes! her brain screamed, and she took an automatic step closer to the window, to the freedom Mr. Espina was offering. She pulled herself up sharply. Knowing her brother, it could be an elaborate trick, a test of her loyalty and obedience.

"I'll get you out of here," Mr. Espina said.

"Why?" The word burst out of her, revealing too much, but Alice needed to know. "Why would you help me?"

He pressed a small, creased photo to the glass. In the low light, it was hard to make out many details, but Alice could see that it was a picture of a dark-haired, smiling girl. "The Jovanovics killed my sister."

Alice studied him, looking for any twitch, any tell that meant he was lying to her. There was nothing. He returned her gaze steadily, the picture still flattened against the window. In that moment, she made her decision. Maybe it was a trick, a cruel set-up engineered by Aaron. If it was, she'd take the punishment. It wasn't worth turning down this opportunity, this possibility of escape.

Alice fumbled to unlock the window but then paused. Opening it would cause an alarm to go off. Mr. Espina made a hurry-up gesture, and she shook herself. With all the alarms blaring, no one would notice another one...

she hoped. Taking a deep breath to steady herself, she jerked open the window.

There was a quiet, repetitive beep. Alice knew she had four minutes. After that, if the correct code wasn't entered into the keypad in Aaron's office, the alarm would start shrieking. It might be ignored, since all the other alarms were also going off. It might not. It could bring Jeb or Aaron tearing into her room, catching her and Mr. Espina in the middle of their escape.

"Let's go," Mr. Espina said, pulling her out of her frozen fear.

With jangling nerves that worsened with each shrill beep of warning, Alice swung a leg over the sill. She glanced down at the narrow ledge and immediately jerked her gaze back up to Mr. Espina's. The decorative molding protruded a mere six inches, not nearly wide enough for comfort.

"Hurry. We don't have much time."

Choking back her terror, she fumbled around with her foot until she had it planted as securely as possible on the too-small ledge. Inhaling a deep breath, she let it out in a rush as she swung her other leg over the sill. With both feet on the ledge, she felt a wave of dizziness rush over her, and she clung desperately to the edge of the window.

"Let's move." Mr. Espina covered her hands with his, detaching her desperate grip with ease. He shifted her hands over next to the window, where the stucco facade offered very little grip. Alice bit down on her tongue, holding back a sound of protest as she clutched at the too-smooth stone. Releasing Alice, Mr. Espina slid the window closed.

The dark made it harder for Alice to keep her balance. Flattening herself against the wall, she closed her eyes and prayed.

"Let's go."

She looked at him, confused. There was nowhere to go. Instead of answering her unspoken question, Mr. Espina wrapped his hands around her waist and lifted her up.

She stiffened as the ledge disappeared from under her feet and the rain gutter appeared right in front of her. Automatically, she grabbed it, needing to hold on to something to anchor herself.

"Up," he grunted, and she boosted herself onto the roof. A push from underneath sent her even higher, and she managed to get a knee onto the red clay tiles. Scrambling, she hauled her other knee onto the roof and crawled toward the peak. There was barely any sound over her shoulder, just the softest brush of fabric on tile, the quietest exhale. When she looked behind her, Mr. Espina was there, gesturing her forward.

The clay tiles were painfully hard under her knees, but she didn't try to stand. The roof was steep and slick, and crawling was hard enough. Thunder rumbled as she made her slow way toward the first peak, and she glanced at the dark sky. If it rained, this would all get that much harder.

A tile cracked under her knee. She jumped at the sound and started to slide. Grabbing for a handhold, she caught a metal exhaust flue, bringing her body to a jerky halt. Alice paused, trying to catch her breath, looking ahead at the mountain she still had to climb. The thought that she'd have to make up those painful feet she'd lost in her slip made her want to cry, but she'd learned long ago that tears didn't solve anything.

Clenching her teeth, she started to crawl again. Finally, she reached the peak. She hurried to throw a leg over before she started slipping backward again. Mr. Espina moved up beside her, turning so he was sitting with his feet out in front of him. Without hesitating, he pushed off and slid down the roof like it was a playground slide. As soon as he reached the valley between the peaks, he started climbing the next slope.

Breathing too fast, Alice forced herself to follow his lead. She turned so her feet were forward and slid down the slope. The tiles were painfully bumpy under her, especially as she started moving faster. By the time she reached the base of the next rise, Mr. Espina was nowhere to be seen. Fear built in her chest as she peered through the darkness, trying to spot his dark figure.

"This way," a voice whispered, and she gratefully started to climb toward where Mr. Espina lay on his stomach at the top of the next peak. As Alice scrambled over the top, she came to an abrupt halt. They were at the edge of the roof now. If she tried the sledding trick again, she'd go sailing off the edge and fall to the ground below—far below.

A hand on her arm made her jump and then freeze, terrified that she was going to lose her balance.

"Stand up," Mr. Espina whispered, and she stared at him. *Stand?* She could barely sit straddling the ridge without completely losing her nerve. He must've read her thoughts, since he urged her to move across the ridgeline to the spot where a stone chimney jutted out past red tile. Using it for support, Alice carefully stood on shaking legs. The weight of her pack pulled her backward, and she bent slightly at the waist to counter it.

As soon as she was upright, Mr. Espina buckled some sort of harness around her waist and each of her thighs. Hooking a cable to one of the front straps, he wrapped the line around the chimney and held the other end in both of his gloved hands. He gave her a nod.

Confused, she looked at him.

"Go."

"What?"

"*Go.*"

"Where?"

"Over the side."

"Over the side?" Alice knew she sounded like an idiot, but the idea was crazy. She was supposed to throw herself off the roof with just a thin cable and a moody all-but-stranger to keep her from hitting the ground like a mosquito on a windshield? It was insanity. "I'm sorry. I don't think I can do this."

Mr. Espina's hatchet-carved face softened ever so slightly as he moved closer to her. "You can." So quickly that she couldn't even brace herself, he gave her a tiny push.

It was hardly a shove, but it was enough to put her off-balance. She took a step backward to steady herself, but the roof sloped dramatically and her backpack didn't help matters. Her one step turned into two and then three, faster and faster until she was almost running backward off the roof. Alice knew that if she tried to stop, she'd pitch backward and slide the rest of the way on her back. The thought was too terrifying for words, so she continued her reverse, shuffling run until the roof ended and nothing was underneath her feet.

Time seemed to stop for a second. Alice felt like a cartoon character who'd run off the edge of a cliff, hesitating in midair while the realization of what was going to happen hit her. Then she dropped, free-falling for an infinite moment before the cable tightened and the harness caught her.

The tension tipped her back, and she swung toward the house. Just in time, she yanked her knees to her chest so that she didn't put her legs through the quickly approaching window to Aaron's study. It was located at the back of the house because, as her brother liked to say, it was far away from all distractions. Dizzy with adrenaline, Alice wondered if that was the real reason, or if it was isolated so that no one could hear people scream. She'd had several bad visits to that room.

Yanking back her wandering thoughts, Alice struggled to turn upright. She managed to straighten and get her feet underneath her as Mr. Espina lowered her slowly toward the ground. The alarms were suddenly silenced, and she couldn't hear voices shouting anymore. The quiet made her uneasy. If everyone was running around, trying to fix whatever Mr. Espina had done, then they most likely wouldn't be looking for her. The silence, though... Aaron could be checking on her right now.

As her feet touched down on the concrete patio bordering the pool, the cable hit the ground as well, coiling like a snake at her feet. Hitching her backpack higher on her shoulders, Alice gathered up the cable, looping it with shaking hands before clipping the coiled line to a carabiner on her harness. She unbuckled the belt and then the straps around her thighs, the dark and her fumbling, nervous fingers making it harder than it should've been.

By the time Alice had gotten free of the harness, Mr. Espina still wasn't next to her. Craning her head, she stared up at what she could see of the roof, although it wasn't much. Alice backed up several steps until she stood next to the pool, but there still was no sign of Mr. Espina. She wondered if he'd gone a different way. Now that she was out of her room, maybe his part was done, and she had to escape on her own.

If she waited here to find out, it may very well be too late.

She started to turn, to run around the pool toward the perimeter fence, when a loud boom rocked the ground. Alice crouched instinctually, her arms wrapping around her head. As two more blasts echoed through the night, a motion above her caught Alice's eye, making her flinch down again. It was Mr. Espina, flying through the air. Her first thought was that he'd been caught in the explosion, tossed off the roof like shrapnel, and fear for him made her lungs tight.

He hit the deep end of the pool just as yet another explosion shook the ground. When he began swimming toward the far side of the pool, Alice realized that he was fine. His leap must've been intentional, a quick way of getting off the roof. She had a brief moment of thankfulness that he hadn't made her jump with him. It would've been terrifying. Not only was she not a strong swimmer, but there was a long stretch of concrete between the house and the pool's edge. If she hadn't jumped far enough, she wouldn't have had to worry about escape—she would've been lying broken on the patio.

Shaking herself out of her shocked daze, she ran around to the other side of the pool, reaching the edge just as Mr. Espina was hauling himself out. He barely hesitated long enough to get his bearings before running toward the back perimeter fence. Alice followed, just as two more bangs echoed from inside the house. The silence afterward was terrifying. Everything sounded horribly loud—her pounding heart, her breaths tearing in and out of her lungs, her footsteps, the crack of every branch as she tore across the decorative landscaping. Even the harness buckles jangled as she ran, still clutching the assortment of straps in one hand.

Alice couldn't stop herself from checking over her shoulder, expecting at any second for Aaron and an army of guards to come tearing after them. Aaron would like that, to give her hope that she'd escaped before reeling her back in at the last moment. Alice wasn't the only one with something at stake, though. Aaron would make her life miserable, but at least he'd keep her alive and relatively undamaged. After all, he needed to use her to secure his entry into the Jovanovic family. If Aaron caught them, she might survive, but he'd kill Mr. Espina in the longest, slowest, most painful way possible.

When she tripped over a newly planted lacey oak, Alice forced herself to focus on the ground in front of her. Mr. Espina pulled ahead, the distance between them growing, and Alice had to hold back a plea for him to wait. She knew logically that he wouldn't abandon her at this point, but her anxiety was still thrumming through her. Without his help, there was no way she could get over the ten-foot wrought-iron fence.

He stopped at the fence and pulled something out of his small pack.

When Alice reached him, she saw that Mr. Espina was removing the bolts securing the brackets on the top and bottom crossbars of the fence. As she bent over, gasping for breath, he moved to the other post and did the same on that side.

A shout from the house made Alice twist around in panic. Someone with a flashlight stood right outside the French doors by the pool. The beam of light crossed the backyard and flickered over her. She hurried to turn her face away, but it didn't matter.

"Stop!" the man shouted. With sinking dread, Alice recognized Jeb's voice.

"Time to go." Mr. Espina gave the fence a shove, and the whole panel fell over with a heavy thud. Grabbing Alice's wrist, he ran across the panel and over the scrubby grass toward the wooded ravine that ran the length of the property.

There was an odd popping sound, and a clod of dirt kicked up a few feet away. It took her a moment to realize that Jeb was *shooting* at them. Mr. Espina pulled her to the side, leading her on a zigzagging trail. The ground was rough and uneven, and Alice caught her toe, but Mr. Espina pulled her right out of her stumble and back into a sprint. Jeb kept shooting, but Alice couldn't think about that, not when she was trying to breathe and run.

Fear kept her heart racing, and their mad dash made it beat faster and faster until she felt like her whole body was trembling with the effort. Lightning flickered overhead, making everything too bright for a second before plunging into darkness. Thunder rumbled, shaking the ground and blotting out the sound of her pounding heart and rasping breaths.

At first, Alice didn't realize that it was raining, that the droplets were pounding against her head and running down her neck to soak into her hoodie. Then it started to pour, falling in heavy sheets of rain, just as she and Mr. Espina entered the trees. The ground immediately fell away in front of them, dropping into a yawning ravine with a creek rushing along the bottom.

Alice tried to automatically brake, but Mr. Espina kept running, and his grip on her arm kept her in motion, as well. A cry escaped her as they flew off the edge, landing three feet down the slope. The dirt had already turned into mud, and they sank into the muck with each step. With Mr. Espina hauling her forward, Alice couldn't do anything but keep moving her feet, sprinting and sliding and only staying upright thanks to the hand on her arm and her continuous forward motion.

The rain was loud, too loud to hear if Jeb was still shooting. Alice couldn't look to see how close he was, though. She was too concerned with her high-speed downhill sprint. The slope started to level off, and Alice looked away from her footing for a moment. They'd reached the bottom, and she gave a gasping sob of relief. Splashing through the small creek, she risked a quick glance at the top of the ravine.

There were so many flashlights now—at least ten— bobbing and moving as Aaron's men climbed down after them. Jeb was the closest and closing the distance quickly. He grabbed a small tree, bringing himself to a sliding stop, and then lifted his gun.

Alice sucked in a breath, trying to force her legs to run even faster. They started to climb the other side of the ravine, but there wasn't anything close by that was big enough to hide behind, just brush and small trees and lots of weeds. Jeb had a clear shot.

The incline sloped up dramatically, and their run turned into more of a scrambling climb. Mr. Espina released her in order to use both hands. Alice grabbed a clumpy weed, but the plant pulled out of the ground. She started to slide down the slope, and she fumbled to grasp a half-exposed root. That one held, and she reached for the next handhold.

Every second, she expected to feel one of Jeb's bullets pierce her skin. Her breathing, already rough from fear and exertion, sped up even more. Closing her fingers around a thick vine, she shot a quick glance over her shoulder.

Jeb was standing in the same place she'd last seen him, his flashlight hand supporting his gun hand. The light turned the rest of Jeb's body into a silhouette, but Alice could clearly see the gun. The rain poured over him, but he stood perfectly still, his head cocked to the side as he aimed.

Then, the ground crumbled under Jeb's feet. The flashlight and gun went flying as he fell onto his back. He started to slide, traveling several feet before his body ran into a pair of tree trunks that brought him to a rough stop.

"Move!" Mr. Espina's command broke her paralysis, and she started climbing up the slope again. Temporary rivulets of water coursed down the side of the ravine, and

Alice's feet slid through the muck as she pushed herself forward and up. The tree coverage became heavier, and there were more saplings and roots to grab. Alice sped up, not wanting to look to see if Jeb had gotten up or if the other guards were closing in. She just climbed.

Alice didn't notice that she was at the top of the ravine until she reached for the next handhold and there was nothing there but grass and weeds. She looked up to see that Mr. Espina was already on his feet and jogging toward an older-model sedan parked on the shoulder. Alice stood and tried to run for the car, but her head spun and her stomach threatened to expel its contents.

Swallowing down bile, she had to settle for a shambling jog. It felt like it took forever to reach the passenger door of the car. She was sure that, any second, Jeb—or, worse, Aaron—would pop out of the ravine. That would be the end of any escape attempt. Aaron would never let her out of his sight until he'd married her off to Logan Jovanovic.

Her hand caught the handle, and she jerked open the car door. In the back of her mind, she mentally apologized to the car's owner, since she was head-to-toe mud, but that didn't slow her down. Alice threw herself into the seat as Mr. Espina shot them forward. The door swung shut, slamming with the force of their acceleration, and Alice wiggled out of her backpack, dropping it onto the floor by her feet as she grabbed for her seat belt. By the way Mr. Espina was driving, she had a feeling she'd need it.

She turned to face him as they flew down the road, the windshield wipers working at their fastest speed. "Thank you," she said.

His only response was a slight upward tilt of his chin.

"I dropped your harness." She glanced at her muddy hands as if she'd find the missing equipment hanging there. "Sorry."

The corner of his mouth quirked. "I have others."

"That doesn't surprise me." She settled back in the seat, her muscles easing slightly one by one, leaving her feeling limp and shaky. They were both still alive, though.

They were alive, and she was free.

CHAPTER 3

"She's up there."

Dee stood beneath the rickety frame of the ancient windmill, her head tipped back. Otto took a moment to catch his breath—Dee might be little, but she was *fast*, and their run through the woods had left him winded. The air left his lungs in visible puffs, despite the warm sun beaming down on them. It was late enough in the fall that the trees were bare and the sparse grass under their feet was brown, but it hadn't snowed yet, except at the highest mountain peaks he could see in the distance.

As his breathing slowed, Otto followed Dee's gaze and spotted the small shape wedged in a corner between two metal crossbeams. He resisted the urge to swear.

A familiar snort of laughter brought another slew of mental cursing. "What are you doing here?" Otto asked.

"How could I miss this?"

Otto glanced over his shoulder at a grinning Hugh. "You should go."

"Are you kidding?" Hugh rested his shoulders against a tree and took his weight off his injured leg. He was trying to be subtle about it, but Otto could see lines of tension and pain etched beneath the casual grin. "This is going to be awesome."

Having grown up with Hugh, Otto knew that, if

pushed, Hugh would only dig in even deeper. As jolly as Hugh appeared, there was a mountain of stubbornness behind his happy-go-lucky smile. With a resigned, silent sigh, Otto moved over to the metal skeleton. There was a ladder—well, most of a ladder, at least, since several rungs were missing—but it didn't start until about seven feet off the ground. The first step was going to be a doozy.

"Want me to call Fire?" Hugh asked.

"No." A part of him did. The firefighters would be able to get the cat down in minutes, but there'd be a price for convenience. Not only would the crew mock them for weeks, but the firefighters would get to play hero. Otto shot a quick glance at Dee, who was gazing at him as if he were a superhero combined with a god. He wasn't about to let some firefighter steal all the glory. They were conceited enough as it was. "I've got this."

"Sure?" Hugh asked, amusement clear in his voice.

"Otto's got this." The certainty in Dee's words made Otto even more determined. He'd get that cat down even if it killed him. From the looks of the ancient metal ladder, it very well might.

With a quick mental prayer, he grabbed the first rung with both hands. It creaked loudly but held. Pulling himself so that his shoulders were even with his tightly clenched fists, he reached up and grabbed the second bar. His muscles were shaking. Not for the first time, he wished he were just a little smaller. Most of his bulk was muscle, but it was still a lot to be hauling around.

Moving his other hand to join the first, he dragged himself high enough to grab the third rung. Just one more, and he'd be able to swing his feet onto the bottom bar.

"Otto's strong." Dee's admiring words brought a tiny

smile to Otto's lips as he latched on to the third rung with his other hand. There wasn't much he wouldn't do for Dee or her brothers. It was obvious they'd had it rough before Jules moved them to Monroe, but they were all sweet, smart kids, and Otto had a soft spot a mile wide for kids and animals—a soft spot that tended to get him into situations like this. *It won't be that bad*, he tried to convince himself. *Just get up there and grab the cat. Easy-pea—*

With a snap, the end of the metal bar popped free of its screw. Air rushed past Otto as his body dropped, his hands sliding down the now-vertical rung until there was nothing to grip but air. He grabbed at the ladder but missed, and his feet hit the ground with a jarring thud that vibrated painfully through his spine.

He didn't want to look, but he couldn't stop himself from glancing at his audience. Hugh, the bastard, was doubled over with laughter, while Dee appeared con-cerned…and slightly disappointed.

"Strong, yes," Hugh wheezed when he'd recovered enough to speak. "Needs to work on his coordination, though."

"The rung broke," Otto gritted out, even though he knew that would only encourage Hugh. He was tempted—so tempted—to ask if Hugh thought he could do better. The only thing that kept him silent was the knowledge that Hugh would take him up on the chal-lenge, despite his casted arm and the bullet hole in his leg. Hugh was supposed to take it easy—hell, he was still supposed to be on crutches—but he was incredibly bad at staying on the sidelines. He didn't need Otto's encouragement to be an idiot.

Turning back to the metal structure, Otto eyed the cat peering down at him. "How'd you manage to get up there?" he muttered, and the animal gave a plaintive cry in response. As much as Otto wished the cat could climb down on its own, it didn't look like that was going to happen. Setting his jaw and ignoring the sound of Hugh's snickers, Otto grabbed the bottom rung once again.

It was worse this time—so much worse. His muscles were tired, and he was wary about the strength of the rungs, sure each one would break as soon as his full weight was hanging from it. The new gap was an issue, too, and he had to haul himself up until the rung was at his chest before he could reach the next bar.

As soon as he had that rung in both hands, he bent his knees and found the bottom bar with his feet. It took some of the strain off of his aching shoulders and arms, but he was too aware of being so far off the ground. If he fell now, it would hurt—a lot.

Hugh had gone silent, and that added to his tension. Even his partner knew that things were serious now. As quickly as possible, Otto climbed the ladder, testing each rung before putting his weight on it. He was just below the cat now, with only five more rungs to go—five more chances to go plummeting to the ground. Firmly pushing away the pessimistic thought, Otto stepped onto the next rung. The bar shifted under him, and he quickly moved his foot to the one above it, making a mental note to avoid the unstable rung on the way down.

He reached an arm toward the skinny gray tabby as he drew level with the cat. "Come here, sweetheart," he crooned, inching his hand closer. The cat twitched its ears but didn't move otherwise. "Come on, kitten. Let's do this the easy way, okay?"

His fingers were almost close enough to brush the cat's fur, and Otto leaned closer, keeping his other hand locked around the ladder. The metal groaned ominously, and he hastily centered himself again, frowning. The cat, its gaze locked on Otto, hunched down into a crouch. It wasn't about to move from its perch, tucked in the junction of two supports.

Biting back a groan, Otto climbed another rung so he could step onto the crosspiece that looked like a skinny, metal balance beam. He shuffled sideways, not allowing himself to look down. The hushed tension of his small audience was enough to remind him of the life-and-death stakes—he didn't need to see the distance to the hard ground.

Why hadn't he wanted to call Fire again? His earlier reasons didn't seem so important now. Carefully reaching out toward the metal frame, he inched his boots closer to the cat. The distance between vertical handholds was too far. He was going to have to let go of one before grabbing the other.

Taking a deep breath, he blew it out in an even, calming stream. Pushing away from the ladder, he lunged for the other side…and caught it.

A cheer rose from below, and it sounded as if his audience had grown. Otto noted that fact absently, his curiosity not great enough to risk looking down. The cat had flinched back at his sudden movement, and Otto crouched—slowly, carefully—trying not to spook it. It would be bad if it took off. A mental image of him chasing the cat around the windmill's supports like some kind of insane carousel flashed through his mind, but Otto shoved it away.

"Hey, kitty," he said quietly, reaching out. The cat flattened its ears, and Otto paused, his hand in midair. *Don't run. Please don't run.* If they'd been on the ground, he would've sat down, talked to the cat, taken his time to earn its trust—but they were not on the ground. No, they were twenty-five feet in the air, on a rickety windmill. The entire structure swayed in the wind, creaking as if it was seconds from collapsing. He shifted his weight, and the metal beneath him shuddered.

There wasn't time for gentle persuasion. They needed to get down first, and then they could get to know each other. As quick as he'd been slow before, he grabbed the cat and pulled it in to his chest. The animal stiffened, but it didn't fight, and Otto blew out a relieved breath. This was not the place to have a pitched battle with a terrified, pissed-off feline.

Instead the cat latched on, hooking all its claws into Otto's jacket as he carefully straightened. Once he was up, he paused. With one hand supporting the cat, he was down to a single arm for climbing, and that was going to make things tricky. If he tried to tuck the cat inside his jacket, Otto was pretty sure it would climb right back out again.

As if in answer, the cat gave a miserable, warbling meow.

"Shh," Otto soothed. "I know. I'm not that excited about this either, but we just need to get down, and then everything will be much better for you." The wind gusted heavily, making the windmill shiver and groan. "Better for me, too."

A thump right below him startled Otto, and he jumped, remembering just in time not to step back to catch his balance. His hand tightened around the support instead, and he steadied. Glancing down, he saw Steve Springfield, the newest member of the Monroe Fire Department, bracing an extension ladder against the support Otto was standing on. It was the first time he was happy to see a firefighter. Hugh was helping Steve steady the ladder while Dee made anxious circles a short distance away, craning her neck to watch.

"Don't drop the cat!" she called when she noticed Otto was looking down at them. Then, a beat later, "Don't fall, either!"

If he'd had a free hand, Otto would've given Dee a reassuring wave.

"Come on down!" Hugh hollered, and Otto shuffled over to the top of the ladder. It was awkward with only one hand, but he managed to step first one foot and then the second on the top rung. The cat wiggled, and he made reassuring sounds even as he gripped it tighter to his chest. Otto hadn't risked his life just to have the darn thing leap to its death once safety was within reach.

Although still tense, the cat stopped squirming, and Otto moved down a step, and then another. After the precarious climb up the dilapidated windmill, descending this—even with only one usable arm—was a delight in comparison. The cat sank its claws deeper into his shirt, pricking his chest. With a grimace, Otto resisted the urge to detach the claws digging into his skin, knowing that it was not the time for readjusting his hold. Once he managed to get both of them to solid ground, then he could get a better, more comfortable grip on the cat.

Otto stepped down to the next rung, and the cat lunged to the side.

As the animal slipped from his grasp, Otto reached out, catching the cat mid-leap and hauling it back against his front. He was breathing hard, more from the scare than from exertion, and he took a second before starting down the ladder again. The cat gave a miserable yowl, and he made wordless soothing sounds. Ignoring Otto, the cat meowed again.

"Good catch," Hugh called, sounding subdued—and reassuringly close. Otto glanced down and saw that he was just six or so rungs from the ground. He blew out a hard, relieved breath as he hurried to descend the last few feet. He'd done it. The cat was safe, and Otto didn't have any broken bones. The rescue mission had been a success.

His foot touched the second-to-last rung, and he turned his head toward Dee, who was hovering right next to the ladder, her gaze locked on the cat.

"He's fine," Otto assured her. "A little scared, but that's understandable. He's had a hard day so far, but the bad part's over now." He smiled at her over his shoulder as he moved down to the final rung.

When his boot skidded off that bottom step and he stumbled off the ladder, Otto knew he'd spoken too soon. Dee was right next to him, and he would squash the tiny girl if he landed on her. Twisting away, he avoided crashing into her, but the dodge threw off his balance. There was no saving it—he was going down. He tumbled gracelessly to the ground, barely managing to turn in midair so as to land on his back and not flatten the cat.

The spectators gathered around to stare down at him.

"You okay?" Hugh asked, sounding suspiciously like he was about to laugh.

"Fine." Otto wasn't in any hurry to get up. Honestly, he was just relieved to be on solid ground, even if it was flat on his back.

"Thank you, Otto," Dee said, reaching down to take the cat.

"Careful," he warned, watching closely as he released it, ready to snatch it back if it tried to claw Dee to pieces in order to escape. The cat seemed only too happy to curl up in Dee's arms, though, purring loudly. Otto shot the animal an exasperated look. Why hadn't it been so well behaved when he was risking life and limb?

Laughing openly now, Hugh offered him a hand up. "Good work, Otto. You might want to work on sticking the landing next time, though."

"Seems like an okay place to fall, if you ask me," Steve said evenly, although the corners of his mouth twitched. "Better than up at the top."

"True." Otto brushed off the back of his pants, looking curiously at Steve's T-shirt and worn BDUs. "Off duty?"

The fireman nodded. "Our property is right over there." He pointed north. "Heard the commotion, saw you climbing, and figured you could use a ladder." They all looked at the rickety metal rungs barely clinging to the windmill. "A better ladder."

"Thank you," Otto said sincerely.

"If this is the extent of the excitement around here, I'll be happy," Steve said, folding the ladder. "I moved the kids here from Simpson because Monroe seemed like a safer place, but then all that craziness happened with the shootings and explosions. I'm glad things calmed down; I was starting to think I'd have to move us somewhere else."

Hugh snorted. "Yeah, they'll be calm until Dee brings that cat home. What are the chances Jules will ever let us babysit again?"

After taking a few days to recover from this adventure, Otto knew he could convince Jules to let him watch the kids again. After all, she allowed Hugh to babysit. Surely she'd forgive Otto for one small cat.

Before he could say as much, Theo charged out of the trees, striding through the clearing toward their little group.

"Uh-oh," Hugh muttered. "Theo must've sensed you were trying to throw yourself off a windmill."

Except for a pointed look, Otto ignored him, his gaze on Theo. The other cop looked even more aggravated than usual as he neared.

"This is my new cat!" Dee announced. "Isn't she beautiful? Or he, maybe. I don't know which yet."

Distracted, Theo eyed the cat curled in Dee's arms. "New cat?"

"Yes! Otto rescued her. I thought he was going to fall, especially when the ladder broke, or when he had to walk on the narrow metal thingy, way up in the air, but he didn't! Well, he didn't until he reached the bottom, and then he fell over. *Boom!* It was like a tree getting cut down."

Hugh started laughing again as Theo turned a narrowed gaze first toward the windmill and then at Otto. "You climbed that thing?"

Giving an affirmative shrug, Otto braced himself for the inevitable lecture.

"That was stupid. Why didn't you call Fire? Isn't getting cats out of high places pretty much the only thing they're good for?"

Steve gave a soft, amused cough.

With an abrupt shake of his head, Theo said, "Never mind. That's not why I tracked you down. This is an emergency."

"What is it?" Hugh pushed away from the tree, all traces of amusement gone. Otto took a step toward Theo, his body on alert. Theo's serious tone had both of them tense and ready to respond to the latest crisis.

"It's happening again." A muscle worked in Theo's jaw.

"What is?" Otto asked. Like Steve had said, it had been a rough few months—hell, a rough *year*—for the Monroe first responders, especially the K9 unit. From Theo's grim expression, whatever "it" was, it wasn't good.

"One of Jules's 'childhood friends' has arrived."

In unison, Otto and Hugh groaned.

"Another one?" Hugh asked. The twitch of Theo's right eye was answer enough, and Otto rubbed a hand over his head. Theo hadn't been exaggerating.

This was an emergency.

CHAPTER 4

"WHERE THE HELL IS SHE FINDING THESE WOMEN?" THEO grumbled after Dee had hurried ahead of them, the cat still clutched in her arms. Once Steve had realized that he couldn't help with Theo's "emergency," he'd taken his ladder and headed home.

Theo, Otto, and Hugh followed behind the little girl and her new pet. As Otto eyed the cat, he was just a tiny bit annoyed that the feline didn't look like he cared that he was being bounced up and down as Dee jogged toward her house. Otto couldn't even take a careful step down a ladder without the cat trying to leap out of his arms, but Dee could probably take the animal on a roller coaster, and it would be perfectly content.

"Beats me." Hugh's voice sounded a little tight, and Otto gave him a sideways glance. The walk through the woods was obviously not doing good things for his injured leg. "Grace told me pretty much everything about what happened with the Jovanovics, but she flat-out said she's not squealing on the person who helped her hide. She said that's not information I need to know." He snorted. "Such a bunch of bull. Grace should know by now that I need to know everything, or else it drives me nuts."

"Yeah, Jules told me this is another 'friend from school,'" Theo said.

Hugh gave a bark of laughter. "She's not even trying anymore."

"She doesn't have to," Theo admitted, and Otto could tell he was trying not to smile. "She knows that I know she's never met this woman before in her life. Saying that this new...houseguest is an old friend is Jules's way of asking me not to investigate her."

"I wouldn't care, except that someone's always trying to blow up these women," Hugh said with a dramatic sigh. "Jules still hasn't told you why she and the kids are running?"

"No."

Otto eyed Theo, a little surprised by his partner's lack of obvious annoyance. Theo was not known for being zen. "Doesn't it bother you?"

"I do want to know," Theo said. "It's harder to protect her if I'm in the dark. She's not withholding information because she doesn't trust me, though."

"Then why hasn't she told you?" Hugh asked. Now that they were in Jules's backyard, and the ground was relatively even, his limp was less pronounced. Otto relaxed slightly. It was hard not to yell at Hugh for abandoning his crutches so soon after he'd been shot, or for following them through the woods, or for the hundred other things he did every single day that aggravated his injury. It was much easier to deal with the wounded animals Otto rehabilitated on his ranch, rather than his stubborn-as-hell partners.

"As far as I can tell, she doesn't want to make me complicit in whatever crime she committed," Theo explained. "I know her, though. She'd do anything for those kids. If she did something illegal, it was to help them. When she's ready, she'll tell me. Whatever her secret is, it won't make me feel any differently about her."

They crossed the remainder of the yard quietly. Even Hugh didn't say a word. Otto wondered if he was shocked into silence by Theo's uncharacteristic loquaciousness.

"Officers Bosco, Murdoch, and Gunnersen." Jules stood in the back doorway with her hands fisted on her hips. Although she was attempting to scowl, it was obvious that she was amused. "A cat?"

"Don't include me in your lecture," Theo objected, taking the porch steps in a single stride. "I had nothing to do with it…this time." He slid past her into the kitchen, giving her temple a kiss and whispering something into her ear.

Jules immediately blushed and began to smile, although she tried to hold on to her frown as she eyed Hugh and Otto. "You are never babysitting again."

"See?" Hugh muttered under his breath, although not so far under his breath that Jules couldn't hear him clearly. "Told you it'd work."

Jules laughed, her hands falling to her sides. "A cat?" she repeated. "Really?"

"We couldn't leave it there," Hugh said, clomping up the steps with much less grace than Theo had shown. "What kind of horrible people would we be to leave a defenseless cat trapped on a windmill? Worse, if we'd left the poor cat to the mercy of the *fire department*? They'd be standing around, flexing, posing for calendar shots. By the time they got around to saving it, the poor thing would've died of starvation."

"Hey," Otto objected mildly. "Fireman Steve's okay. I appreciated that ladder."

Stepping back so Hugh and Otto could go inside, Jules looked back and forth between the two. "I have to hear this story. All I got from Dee was something about superheroes and how strong Otto is and how we need to go buy cat supplies. Oh, and something about a tree falling over?"

Hugh laughed as Otto groaned. He already knew he was going to hear about this for years. Stepping into the crowded kitchen, he glanced around, wondering where the newest houseguest was. Jules's three teenage brothers were sitting around the table showing Theo their homemade remote-controlled airplane that, to Otto, looked too much like a drone for comfort. Hugh had pulled out a chair and was lounging in it, trying to hide his sheer relief at sitting down and doing a crap job of it.

"Where's your friend?" Hugh asked Jules, and the kitchen went quiet.

Jules's mouth firmed into a straight line. "Nope."

"Nope, what?" Hugh asked, widening his eyes innocently. No one who knew him believed that look for a second.

"Nope, you're not going to do this again."

"Do what?" Hugh widened his eyes more.

"Every time someone new shows up in town, you grill that person until she wants to run away and never come back." Crossing her arms, she leaned against the counter. "It's the worst welcome wagon I've ever seen, and you're not doing that to Sarah."

"Her name's Sarah?" Theo asked, trying to sound offhand. "Sarah what?"

Otto resisted the urge to groan. Theo was worse than

Hugh at playing innocent. Judging by the way Jules narrowed her eyes, she felt the same way.

"None of your business, *Mr. Cop*."

Theo frowned at Jules, and she met him glare for glare. Even when he stood up and crossed the kitchen, crowding her against the counter, she held her ground. Theo's mouth quirked up, and then he kissed her.

Otto did groan that time, as did every occupant of the kitchen, except for Theo and Jules. Although the kiss had ended, they were staring at each other in their sappy, only-two-people-in-the-room way.

"Are they at it again?" Grace said as she walked in from the hallway.

"Yes." Ty, one of the twins, covered his eyes. "You guys shouldn't do this in front of me and Tio. We're still children."

"You two kiss so often, I'm surprised your lips haven't permanently fused together," Grace said as Hugh grabbed her hand, reeling her toward him and pulling her into his lap.

"I'd like my lips to become permanently fused to yours." Hugh teasingly nuzzled Grace's neck, making her laugh.

Tio looked at Hugh, his forehead creased. "That's not possible. Besides, it would be extremely inconvenient to be conjoined at the mouth. How would you eat?"

"I wouldn't need to eat," Hugh answered in a melodramatic tone. "Who needs food when I have Grace?"

Looking increasingly bothered, Tio said, "That doesn't make any sense."

"That's Hugh." Jules had managed to break out of her

Theo trance, although he was still standing very close to her. "He never makes any sense."

"Hey!" Hugh protested, sounding amused. "Occasionally, I make a lot of sense."

Patting him on the head, Grace gave Jules a look. "Sure you do, sweetness."

As Hugh pretended to bite Grace's hand, Otto glanced away. Seeing his two partners so happy in their relationships was gratifying, but it also made him feel...odd. He unintentionally caught Sam's gaze, and the two shared a look of mutual discomfort. Otto liked Sam, the oldest of Jules's brothers. Although the teen was still jumpy and suspicious around people who weren't his siblings, Sam had settled in a lot since the family had moved to town. He worked at the kennel where one of Otto's projects was staying, and Sam was great with the dogs. Otto could sympathize with someone who found the company of animals easier than the company of people.

"So, my love, my beauty, my goddess," Hugh was saying to Grace, catching Otto's attention. That amount of flattery was guaranteed to lead to something big.

"Yes?" Grace sounded suspicious, and Otto had to hide his smile. She was starting to know Hugh as well as his partners did.

"Heard you have a new roommate."

Grace hopped out of his lap, crossing the kitchen to get a glass from the cupboard. "We do, indeed. She's very nice."

"Yeah?" Hugh sounded hopeful that Grace was going to spill some details, but Otto had a feeling he was about to be disappointed.

"Yeah. Too bad you're never going to meet her."

Hugh, who'd sat forward in anticipation, flopped against the back of his chair. "What? Why? Do I embarrass you? Are you embarrassed for me to meet your friends?"

As she filled her glass from the tap, Grace gave a small shrug, shooting Hugh a sideways look. "Of course you do, and of course I am, but that's not why you're not meeting Sarah. You guys will pick on her."

"Will not."

"Will too."

"Will not."

Otto cleared his throat, knowing from experience that Hugh and Grace could go on like that for hours. "Can I meet her?"

The kitchen grew quiet again. Grace and Jules had a silent conversation involving meaningful stares and contorted eyebrows and a few scrunched noses.

"Fine," Jules finally said, and Theo and Hugh made protesting sounds. "Otto only."

"Why Otto and not us?" Hugh asked.

"Because Otto's nice." Putting her glass on the counter, Grace moved toward the doorway. "Come on, Otto."

"Get her name," Theo said, not looking pleased to be excluded.

"A driver's license number would be nice," Hugh added. "Maybe she could stop by the station sometime, and you could get a full set of prints." He laughed as Grace raised a mock-threatening fist.

With a neutral grunt, Otto followed Grace out of the kitchen. If this houseguest was anything like Jules and Grace, she was running from something. Theo and Hugh were blinded by the need to protect Grace, Jules, and the whole horde, but Otto didn't see the value in interrogating their newest arrival. He'd get an impression and trust his instincts to lead him well. If his gut told him the stranger was someone to worry about, then he'd worry. Until then, he'd ignore Hugh's and Theo's meddling.

"Pay no attention to them," Grace muttered as they headed for the stairs. "Sarah is a sweetheart."

"We'll see."

Glancing over her shoulder, Grace gave him a hard look and then snorted. "It's good that you've had years of practice ignoring those two."

Otto made a noncommittal sound. Even though she wasn't wrong, he wasn't about to say anything negative about his partners, even to Grace, who was head over heels for one of them. Having known Hugh since they were kids, Otto had rescued his friend from too many badly-thought-out plans to count. Theo was more even-headed, although the past year had been a rough one for him. The effort of keeping his partners and their new loved ones safe, especially over the past few months, had been exhausting, and Otto hoped that the upcoming season would be as boring and uneventful as winter in Monroe tended to be. The arrival of this new "old friend" of Jules's wasn't a good sign, however.

As they moved down the hall, Otto looked around with interest. He'd never been to this part of Jules's house before. The floor groaned under his steps, but Otto was pretty sure it was solid enough to hold his weight. The doorways weren't standard, smaller than in modern houses, and the knobs were many-faceted crystal. The walls had been recently painted. For as quaint and character-filled as Jules's house was, Otto knew it was a rickety money pit. It didn't help that Jules's absentee landlord never seemed to fix a thing. Theo helped, but Jules and her siblings did most of the repairs…with mixed results. Otto had to smile at the sight of a hall light fixture held together with duct tape.

Grace stopped at the last door on the left and knocked.

The door swung open so suddenly that Grace jumped back, startled, as Dee darted out of the room.

"Sorry, Grace!" she yelled as she ran for the stairs. "I'm in a hurry. Jules and I have to go to the store for cat things. My new kitty must be *starving*."

A soft laugh came from inside the room. "Hey, Grace. Did you need something? I hope it's nothing that involves moving. I've been enlisted as a cat-sitter, and he—or she—has taken that very literally."

Otto moved around Grace and pushed the door open all the way so he could see the mysterious new houseguest. As he took in the woman sitting cross-legged on the bed, the cat sprawled bonelessly across her lap, Otto suddenly found it hard to breathe.

She was beautiful. Light-brown hair loosely curled over her shoulders, just a few shades darker than her olive complexion. Something about her slight, fine-boned frame and delicate features reminded Otto of a fairy, a woodland creature who would disappear if he looked at her too hard. He blinked several times, confused and a little alarmed at the unusually whimsical path his brain had taken. The stranger's head was tipped down as she looked at the cat, but then she glanced up at Grace—and saw Otto.

Her sweet smile dropped away, and her already huge dark-brown eyes widened even more. Immediately all expression disappeared, and her face smoothed into a polite mask. Her gaze only wavered for a second, when she darted a look toward the window. With the door blocked, Otto assumed she was checking for another escape route.

Otto knew that look. That was the look of someone who was terrified. Worse, that was the look of someone who was so used to being terrified that she'd learned to hide it. This woman was obviously an expert at masking her fear. She tugged at her shirtsleeves, pulling the material so far over her wrists that half of her hands were covered. Otto had seen that gesture before. He'd be willing to bet money that those long sleeves hid bruises.

Damn it.

The sight of this beautiful, frightened woman kicked his protective instincts into high gear. The intensity of his reaction startled him. Although he was a sucker for animals in need, there weren't many people he allowed into his life. This fist-to-the-gut attraction—this instant magnetic draw—was unfamiliar...and uncomfortable. He'd just met Monroe's newest and most mysterious resident, and he already wanted to be near her, to help her. The longer he looked at her, the stronger the urge grew to protect her, to reassure her, until her fists unclenched and the tight muscles in her neck and shoulders relaxed.

He wanted to make her smile again.

Unwillingly fascinated, Otto took in every detail, from her clenched jaw to the tiny twitch of her left eyelid to the rogue strand of silky hair that had slid forward to frame her face. Her mouth was full and pink and completely distracting...and with a sinking feeling, Otto realized that he'd been staring *much* too long.

Grace cleared her throat, dragging his attention away from the house's newest resident. Looking back and forth between the two of them, Grace said, "Sarah, this is Otto Gunnersen. He's a cop. In his spare time, he rescues stray cats from windmills. Otto, this is Sarah. She's an old friend who will be staying here for an indeterminate amount of time. You, Theo, and Hugh are not to bother her about insignificant details, including her full name, criminal history, date of birth, or anything else along that line."

Otto couldn't speak.

It wasn't just that he couldn't get the words out. The words were just…gone. In social situations, he tended to get quiet, but this was different. He'd never had this strong a reaction to anyone. This feeling was so intense that his brain had just given up. His thoughts had come to a screeching halt, and he had to concentrate on breathing. Words were simply not going to happen.

Sarah stared at him, quiet as well, her neutral expression not giving him any clues about what she was thinking. The longer the silence continued, the more frantically Otto tried to come up with something to say and the blanker his mind became. He had the terrible thought that something completely inappropriate would pop out, something about how pretty she was or how scared or how he wanted to keep her safe.

Otto stopped worrying about *not* saying something and started worrying that he *would* say something mortally embarrassing that would make her hate him forever. The seconds ticked by, the faint chatter coming from the kitchen and the low hum of the wind outside pressing against the house the only sounds. Neither looked away.

"Wow. This is awkward," Grace said. "Otto, when I said you weren't allowed to interrogate her, I didn't mean to ban all polite conversation. You can, you know, tell her it's nice to meet her or make some comment about the weather."

She paused, and silence dropped over them again.

Otto tried to stop staring, but he couldn't seem to pull his gaze away. He felt like he'd been kicked in the stomach, but not in a painful way, just hard enough to steal his breath—and apparently all higher brain function.

"That's it." Grace turned and headed for the stairs. "I'm getting Hugh. There are never any weird silences when he's around."

The mention of his partner finally knocked Otto's brain back into gear. If Hugh saw him now, he'd never, ever, ever let it go. Hugh would tease him to the point of torture, and it would be Otto's fault. He was acting like an idiot, all because he'd been introduced to an attractive, frightened, oddly fascinating woman.

Turning instinctively to follow, Otto realized that he hadn't said a word to Sarah. He twisted around, but he couldn't think of anything *to* say, so he just raised a hand in an awkward, clumsy wave that embarrassed him even as he was doing it. Sarah blinked and then slowly, cautiously, lifted a hand in response.

Unsure whether she was returning his greeting or mocking him, Otto spun around and practically bolted after Grace.

"What in the holy hell was that?" she whispered once they were on the stairs, hopefully out of earshot of both Sarah and the group in the kitchen.

Otto gave a small shrug. He honestly had no idea.

What he did know was that the new arrival had burned her image into his brain. His gut gave a twinge, telling him what he already knew—his life was going to change.

CHAPTER 5

ALICE—*NO, SHE REMINDED HERSELF, IT'S SARAH NOW*—stared at the ceiling of her new bedroom. She'd startled awake in the predawn darkness, her heart thumping and her body clammy with sweat from a forgotten nightmare. Falling back asleep wasn't going to happen. Even though she'd been living in her new home for four days now, the bed felt strange and the night sounds were different. The wind never stopped blowing here, constantly groaning and whistling as it slipped around the old house. It should've been soothing, that constant noise, but it made Sarah nervous. It covered all other sounds, like possible footsteps on the stairs or the creak of her door or the squeak of the floorboard right next to her bed. If someone broke in, they could use the wind as cover. She might never even know they were there until they grabbed her.

Sitting up abruptly, Sarah fumbled for her bedside lamp. Her heart beat quickly as the bulb finally flickered on, and she peered around the room, checking all of the shadowy corners for any sign of danger.

The room was empty.

Gradually, her breathing slowed, but she was reluctant to turn off the light. She glanced at the stack of library books she'd checked out the day before, but

she felt too twitchy and restless to read. She needed
to move.

Sliding out of bed, she shivered as her bare feet made
contact with the cold hardwood floor. She moved over to
the window, looking out over the side yard and the trees
that stretched beyond it. It was dark outside, though, the
moon not bright enough to illuminate much of anything.

It was too easy to see frightening shapes in the blackness, so she backed away from her window. Looking
outside had made her feel more trapped, rather than less.
She cast a longing look toward the closed bedroom door,
wishing she could leave.

Why couldn't she leave?

As the realization sank in—that she was free now, that
she could walk out of her room if she wanted, that she
could do pretty much anything—a flutter of excitement
shot through her stomach, drowning out the lingering
fear. She hurried to dress in jeans and a hoodie, pulling
the clothes on over the leggings and long-sleeved shirt
she was wearing as pajamas. After tugging on socks, she
slid her feet into her athletic shoes.

Despite knowing that she wasn't doing anything
wrong, a bubbling, slightly anxious thrill warmed her
blood as she reached for the doorknob. Ever since she
could remember, she'd been locked in her bedroom at
night. Sarah had never taken a nighttime stroll before,
and her hand trembled as she pulled open the door.

More darkness awaited her, the gloom barely lifted
by a couple of hallway night-lights. Although Jules
had said that the small lights were for the kids, in case
they needed to use the bathroom in the middle of the
night, Sarah already knew that her new landlady had

issues with the dark. Sarah understood. She had her own demons.

She made her way toward the stairs, walking as quietly as she could. The floor creaked and groaned with every step, making her grateful—for once—for the steady drone of the wind. She didn't want to disturb any of her housemates, and she also didn't want any company. Jules, Grace, and the kids were wonderful, and Sarah was grateful to Mr. Espina for sending her to them, but she needed to start doing things on her own. After all, this house and this town were just a temporary stopping place, somewhere to hide from Aaron and get her wobbly legs steady underneath her.

No one had popped out of their room as Sarah made her careful way down the stairs and to the coatrack by the front door. She hadn't had a chance to shop for winter things yet, but Ty and Tio were happy to share their winter clothes with her. It was a little embarrassing to wear the same size as the thirteen-year-old boys, but she was grateful for the loan. It hadn't snowed yet, but the wind was fierce, and it would have cut right through her hoodie.

As she reached for the front doorknob, her hand paused. Was she being dumb? Were her nerves jangling a warning because she'd been too sheltered in Texas, or were her instincts warning her of some real danger? A surge of anger at her father and Aaron zapped through her. It wasn't normal for someone her age—an adult—to be so anxious about going for a walk alone. The sun would be rising soon, and her stomach was still turning somersaults at the thought of stepping outside.

Her resentment blazed through her, warming her and

pushing her through the doorway. Once she was on the porch, she paused again, taking in her surroundings. The night was cold, the wind whipping around her. The evergreens surrounding the property shadowed the yard, making everything look even darker.

Now that she was actually outside, Sarah wasn't sure where to walk. She glanced at the forest and immediately shivered. There was no way she was going to wander around the dark woods. She might be naive and sheltered, but she wasn't dumb. The only other option was walking down the driveway, so she descended the porch steps and set off along the narrow dirt path.

As she followed it through the woods, she was tempted to turn around and return to the safety of the house. Sheer stubbornness kept her feet moving.

"I'll walk to the end of the driveway," she muttered to herself, her words sounding loud despite the howling wind. The sound of her voice gave her courage, though, and her pace picked up. She'd get to the street, turn around, and head back to the house. No one would even know she'd gone.

The thought was supposed to be reassuring, but she crossed her arms over her stomach. What if Aaron found her? He could snatch her right off the road, and no one would ever know what had happened. She should've left a note, or taken a buddy, or done anything except walking by herself before the sun was even up.

Stop, she ordered her overactive brain. All she was doing was scaring herself. If she locked herself inside because she was too afraid of Aaron tracking her down, she should've stayed in Texas. It made no sense to create a new prison when she'd just escaped one. Despite her fear, she needed to live.

As she mentally argued with herself, she rounded the last curve of the driveway. In the gray morning light, she could see the silhouette of the mailbox, which listed so far to the right it seemed that one heavy envelope would send it crashing to the ground. The ramshackle homeyness of it made Sarah smile. She'd seen too many attempts at perfection in her old life. Here in Monroe, she was quickly falling in love with every shabby detail about the mountain town.

With every step, she gained confidence, especially since the sky was lightening in the east. Instead of returning to the house once she reached the end of the driveway, she turned left and headed into town. Sarah was used to isolation. Her father's—and then her brother's—house was centered on hundreds of acres, as were all the neighboring houses. Monroe, on the other hand, was cluttered and charming, the homes getting closer and closer together the nearer she got to the center of town.

It was cute and felt welcoming, and Sarah wished she could stay, could make her home in Monroe, but she knew that wasn't realistic. She had to be careful not to get too attached to the place or the people, since she needed to be ready to leave on a moment's notice if Aaron found her.

When Aaron finds me, she mentally amended. What Aaron wanted, he took, no matter how much others were hurt. He'd always been that way. She swallowed a bitter laugh. *Nice family I ha—*

A dark shape stood in the middle of the road.

Startled, Sarah sucked in a nearly silent breath and stopped, peering through the gloom. She couldn't tell who it was—or even if it was human. Whatever it was, though, it was moving closer to her. She took an abrupt step backward, wondering if she should turn and run. The thing got closer, looking larger and larger, and Sarah was rooted in place with fear. What on earth was it? It wasn't human, she was pretty sure now, and it was too big to be a dog.

A part of her wanted to bolt away from it, but she hesitated. It was the size of a horse or cow, and not bulky enough to be a bear. Since it most likely wasn't anything that would rip her head off, she made herself stand still. After all, how silly would she feel if she ran from a gentle farm animal? It moved closer to her, until finally it was near enough that she could see it more clearly.

All the tension seeped out of her, and her body sagged. It looked like a deer of some sort, with a rack of impressive antlers. It wasn't Aaron, wasn't anyone from her old life. It was just a four-legged woodland creature, and a harmless one at that—at least, she was pretty sure it was harmless.

Its head came up, and she froze again. Sarah was almost certain that it wouldn't hurt her, that it only ate grass and other green stuff that didn't include transplanted Texans. At the thought, Sarah gave a nervous giggle, and the animal's head rose even higher. Its mouth opened, and the strangest sound came out. It was like a loud, high-pitched whistle with a grunt at the end. Sarah stared at it, amazed.

An answering whistle-grunt came from behind her, and Sarah whirled around. Another of the deer-looking things was approaching her from the other direction. She could see its rounded muzzle and the way the fur darkened on its legs and neck. They were elk, she realized, remembering images from TV. She should've figured it out earlier, but they looked so different in real life.

The wind died for a minute, and silence settled over the street, broken only by a strange hissing noise. Sarah looked back and forth between the two elk, her body turned so that she could see them both, and she realized that the hissing was coming from the one to her right. She had a feeling that it wasn't a good omen.

The one on her left bugled again, making her jump. She started backing toward the side of the road, but a tall wooden fence blocked her escape route. The elk were getting closer and closer to each other—and to her. The road was narrow, and there was little room on either side of the elk to slip past. Sarah gave the fence behind her a nervous glance, wondering if she could climb it. It looked smooth and tall, with no available handholds. Unless she turned into Spider-Man in the next five seconds, scaling the fence was out.

The bulls were close now, so close that she could smell their wild-animal musk. One bugled, and she leapt back, smacking her shoulder blades against the fence. She didn't know much about elk, but she had a pretty strong suspicion that the two were about to fight—and she was right in the middle of their battlefield. She started to shift sideways, trying not to catch their attention, when the two ran at each other, their heads lowered.

Their antlers crashed together, the sound ringing through the silent morning, and Sarah couldn't hold back a yelp. The fence felt unyielding behind her, and her gaze darted around, looking for an escape route. Why hadn't she thought to bring her new cell phone or a bullhorn or *something*? The houses were all dark, and Sarah didn't know if they were empty or if the residents were just sleeping, unfazed by the sound of fighting elk.

At the end of the fence line was a slightly sagging carport, but she'd have to run right past the elk to get to it. Besides, it didn't look like it'd be much protection, unless she managed to get on top of it, and she wasn't sure how she'd accomplish that. Maybe she'd be better off sticking next to the fence and hoping that this wildlife nightmare ended quickly.

The elk, each struggling to hold his ground, pressed their antlers together and skittered sideways—right toward Sarah. Her indrawn breath would've been a scream if she'd let it. Before she even knew what she planned to do, her legs were moving. She dodged the elk, trying not to notice how close they were, how loud their grunts and whistles were, how strong their smell had gotten, how close she was to being trampled, and made a beeline toward an ancient-looking car parked next to the carport. Jumping onto the trunk, she ran to the roof of the car, reaching it just as the bull elk smashed their antlers together again with a thunderous crash.

One elk seemed to have the upper hand and was driving the other backward—right toward the car she was on. Grabbing the edge of the carport roof, Sarah thought of her frantic escape less than a week ago. If she could climb onto the huge, steep, slick roof of her former home, then she could most definitely climb this. Boosting herself up, she scrambled off the car roof and onto the carport, ignoring the way her knees burned as they rubbed against the asphalt shingles. Even through two pairs of pants, she knew they were scraped.

Air dragged in and out of her lungs as she twisted around, half expecting the elk to give up their fight for dominance and run directly at her hiding spot. When she spotted them, though, she saw they were still focused on each other. Her arms started trembling, and she lowered herself to sit on the roof.

The antlers hit together again, the sound of the crash echoing around the sleeping town. One elk drove the other back and sideways, right toward the carport—and Sarah's hiding place. The losing elk swung his haunches at the last moment before he ran into the car, and his massive hip struck one of the support beams.

The carport shook, and Sarah clung to the edge of the roof as the entire structure vibrated. It didn't look very structurally sound, and she wondered if it was going to collapse on top of the elk—bringing her down with it. She couldn't imagine which would hurt worse—the fall or the elk trampling her.

To her surprised relief, the carport stood despite the blow, and the losing elk ducked away, moving back to the center of the road before he turned to face the winner again. The bigger one followed, taking three running steps toward the other elk. Sarah braced, ready for the next crash of colliding antlers, but the first one dodged. The two stared at each other for what felt like an eternity before the winner bugled loudly.

The defeated bull finally turned and trotted down the road. The elk remaining gave a final bugle, staring after the retreating bull. His sides steamed with heat in the chilly air, and he stood as still as a statue until Sarah began to think he'd never leave. She was going to be stuck on the carport for the rest of her life.

Eventually, though, he turned in the opposite direction and moved slowly away, finally disappearing between two houses. Sarah watched him until he was out of sight.

Even with both elk gone, she didn't want to get off the garage, just in case they came back. Bending her legs, she drew her knees to her chest and wrapped her arms around them. Suddenly, she felt very alone on her rooftop perch, here in this strange, cold mountain town where wildlife fought in the street. Tears pressed against her eyes, wanting release, but she forced them back. Crying wouldn't help. She needed to get off the roof and walk home, but her limbs felt shaky and useless. What if they came back? What if there was an entire herd right around the corner, waiting to stampede her to death? What if there was something worse?

Sarah knew she was being silly, that anyone else would've been thrilled to be that close to nature, but she couldn't stop playing out the worst-case scenarios in her head. The wind seemed stronger up on the roof, and Sarah didn't want to move. If she tried to stand, she was afraid that she'd be blown right off the edge.

A different sound caught her attention, and she went still, straining her ears. It was a car engine, she realized, and a new type of panic rose out of the ashes of her fear. Had Aaron found her?

Even as the logical part of her brain reminded her that the car could be driven by many other people, she rose to a crouch, frantically trying to decide whether she should jump down from the roof and run or stay still and hope that the person—*please don't be Aaron*—drove by without seeing her.

A car turned onto the street, and her heart sank even further when she saw the light bar on top of the vehicle. Logan was a police officer. Had Aaron sent him after her? During that horrible dinner, Judd had mentioned that Logan had contacts. Did they include anyone at the Monroe Police Department?

As her brain raced, she'd frozen for a few seconds, long enough for the squad car to pull up to the curb in front of the carport. It was too late to run and pointless to hide. As close as the squad car was, the cop had to have seen her on the carport. A strong gust of wind pushed her off-balance, and Sarah sat abruptly. There might be no escaping him, but at least she wouldn't be blown off the roof.

As the police officer swung open the driver's door and got out, unfolding his large frame, Sarah felt her throat tightening. It was Otto, the tall, burly cop she'd met after she'd just arrived, the one who was so terrifyingly handsome that it was a struggle to look at him—like a cross between a Viking and a lumberjack. The one who'd watched her steadily and silently with light-blue eyes until he'd quietly left her room. The way he'd looked at her made her illogically worried that he could read all of her secrets and was just waiting for her to confess.

Once Grace had introduced him as a cop, Sarah had sealed her lips together, afraid that something incriminating would tumble out of her mouth. It didn't matter that she'd done nothing wrong, that she was an adult and legally couldn't be forced to stay with her brother—much less marry creepy Logan. There was something about him that still made her…not nervous, but jittery. *No*, she thought, *jittery isn't right, either*. He made her feel too aware of him.

He immediately looked up at her, confirming her suspicion that he'd known she was on the roof even before he pulled up. As he walked closer, he held her gaze, silently as he had before. Rather than ordering her off the roof or yelling at her to get down, as she'd expected, he circled around to the side of the carport. Instead of climbing on the car, as she had, he reached up and grasped the edge of the roof and hauled himself up with an ease that Sarah envied. Once he was up, he sat a few feet away from her.

She eyed his profile as he looked out over the street. What was he doing? If he was going to arrest her, to take her into custody and hand her over to Logan, she wished he'd just get it over with. Sitting next to him, waiting for him to do something, was making her muscles painfully tight.

When he hadn't said anything for several minutes, Sarah knew she had to break the silence. If one of them didn't talk, her head was going to pop like an over-inflated tire.

"Sorry." The word came out too softly, and it squeaked in the middle. "There were elk."

He turned his head to look at her.

"They were fighting?" Clearing her throat, she tried to make her words sound more definite. It was hard, though. His continued silence was freaking her out. "I was afraid of getting caught in the middle, so I climbed up here. Did someone call you?"

His chin dipped down in a nod. Even though he

hadn't actually said anything out loud, the gesture was a huge relief.

"I was going to get down, but I was worried they'd come back. Then I heard your car engine, and...well, you arrived."

It was a weak finish, she knew, but there was no way to explain her terror at hearing a car, not without telling him too much about her former life. After all, she still didn't know if he was one of Logan's contacts. Even if he wasn't, if a fellow cop arrived and said something awful—like that she wasn't mentally sound or that she'd committed a crime—Otto would believe the police officer over some woman he'd just met. Sarah had been sheltered, but she'd read books and watched TV. She knew that cops were loyal to each other.

"Is it strange?" Now that she'd started talking, she didn't want to return to that unnerving silence, the one that made her think he was reading her thoughts with some magical, gorgeous-cop superpower. He cocked his head slightly, as if in question. "Strange that the elk are in town, fighting in the middle of the street? I'm new to the mountains, but it seems weird to me. I mean, squirrels can hang out in town, or rabbits, but elk right here next to all these houses? That seems wrong."

His lips twitched in something that might have been a start of a smile. There was another pause, long enough for Sarah to think he wasn't going to answer. Was this some strange interrogation technique? He refused to talk until she spilled all of her secrets? If so, it was surprisingly effective. His silence made her want to open her mouth and let everything inside her head spill out. Quickly, she sealed her lips together. Sharing her thoughts with this cop would be dangerous—very, very dangerous.

He cleared his throat and she jumped. "It's not strange. Not here, at least." His voice was a bass rumble, not loud but big and full. It fit him.

"Oh." Relief flowed through her when he finally spoke. For some reason, hearing his voice made her warm and brought that same not-quite-jittery feeling she'd experienced before. Not able to hold his gaze, she glanced down at his car. "I probably should've just stayed where I was, then. If it's normal and all. Those antlers crashing together were just very…loud."

There was another pause, although it wasn't quite so long this time. "You were smart to move out of the way."

"Good. I mean, thank you." Silence settled over them again. "Why are you here, then?"

"We got a call that you were up here." He met her gaze, and she couldn't manage to look away. "I, ah, wanted to make sure you were okay."

It wasn't what she'd expected, and it wasn't what she was used to. No one ever worried that she was okay. His concern sparked a warm glow in her belly. She smiled, and his gaze dropped to her mouth. "Thank you. I'm okay."

His eyes snapped back to hers. "Good." There was a short silence. "Do you need help to get down?"

"Yes, please." She glanced at the ground below. Now that the scare was over, she wouldn't feel right climbing onto the car, and it was a long drop for her five-foot-nothing self. "Just a hand down, though. Don't call the fire department or anything. That could be embarrassing."

His mouth quirked again. "I won't."

Moving over to the edge of the roof, he swung his legs off the side and lowered himself down. Once again, he made it look so effortless that Sarah felt a little silly asking for help. She followed, turning onto her belly and letting her legs slide over the edge. His hands steadied her, sliding from her calves to her thighs and then gripping her waist. It was a strange sensation, his firm grip both comforting and slightly dizzying, and it made her pause.

"I've got you," he said in his low, steady way, his fingers wrapped almost all the way around her middle.

It was crazy to trust this stranger—this *cop*—but Sarah couldn't help herself. Just from their short conversation, her gut told her that he was nothing like Aaron or Logan or any of the petty, vicious people who had populated her previous life. Maybe he was conning her, but Sarah suspected he was honestly *good*.

Closing her eyes, she let go of the roof. Just as he'd promised, Otto carefully lowered her down. Even after her feet were securely on the ground and he'd released her, Sarah could still feel the warm impression of his hands pressing into her skin.

"Would you like a ride home?" he asked, and she realized that she'd been staring at him.

Ripping her gaze from his face, she glanced around. "I think I'll finish my walk. It looks like the road is elk-free. They probably went to the diner for breakfast."

That almost-smile came and went quickly, but it still gave Sarah a charge that she'd caused it. As she started to walk back toward Jules's driveway, she expected to hear the squad car engine roar to life, but the morning stayed quiet. The wind had dropped to a gentle breeze, and the rising sun warmed her. When she reached the turnoff for her driveway, she couldn't resist—she glanced behind her.

Otto was still parked by the carport. She wondered if he was watching to make sure that she made it home safely. The thought gave her a warm thrill, but she quickly quashed it. Monroe was just a temporary stop on her road to freedom. She needed to focus on building her new life, not on a Viking–lumberjack cop with steady blue eyes and huge, warm hands.

At the memory of his firm grip, another frisson of excitement whirled through her. This time, she let it stay. She'd enjoy it for a few moments, she promised herself, but then she would do her best to avoid Officer Otto Gunnersen. With a final glance at the surprisingly intriguing man behind her, she strode up the rutted dirt driveway, smiling.

CHAPTER 6

"Can't decide?" Jules asked.

"No." Sarah looked back and forth between the two pairs of winter boots. "They're both so amazing."

Grace chuckled, but her laughter died as she looked at Sarah. "Oh. You're serious."

"Yes." Grace's dismayed expression didn't bother Sarah. Even though she knew they weren't fashionable, Sarah still loved the boots. They were functional and soft inside and would keep her feet warm in the snow. The thought of snow gave her a thrill. The ground was still uncovered now, but her new housemates had assured her that snow was expected any day. The boots, the idea of snow, even her new name—everything was so different from her life under her family's thumb.

She was in Colorado now, and she was free.

"Get the green ones," Tio offered, and Sarah looked at him in surprise. Of all of her six shopping companions, she'd thought that he'd be the least likely to offer fashion advice—well, maybe least likely after Sam.

"The green?" She looked back and forth between the pairs again. Now that she was able to make choices, she found the process to be wonderful but hard. She didn't trust herself, even with the simplest decisions.

"Yes. The green ones don't have laces, so you won't get snow or water in them."

"Oh!" Sarah put the blue boots back on the shelf. "That makes sense. Thank you, Tio."

As Sarah carefully placed her chosen boots back in their oversized box, Grace gave her a teasing nudge. "We're going to have to go to Denver and do some real shopping."

"Sure." Sarah forced a smile but cringed inwardly. Monroe felt like a safe haven. She really didn't want to leave yet, especially to go to a big city like Denver.

As if she could read Sarah's mind, Jules frowned and said in a quiet voice, "It's too early for that. It'd be safer to shop online right now."

"Right." Grace wrapped an arm around Sarah and gave her a side hug. "Sorry. I forgot."

"That's okay." Now that the threat of having to show her face in Denver was off the table, Sarah's smile felt more genuine. "Can we look at coats next?"

Jules's siblings headed for the small sporting goods section as Sarah, Grace, and Jules moved toward women's outerwear. As she walked through the aisles, Sarah knew she was beaming like an idiot. She couldn't help it. This place was amazing. It was part farm supply, part hardware store, part department store. According to Jules, it was one of the few businesses in Monroe that stayed open all year round. Most of the shops and services closed for the winter.

They cut through a car parts aisle. Rounding the corner, Sarah sucked in a sharp breath.

"What?" Jules grabbed her arm and yanked her back into the aisle they'd just left. Grace followed, her expression concerned. "Is it someone you know? Do we need to go out the back?"

"No," Sarah said hastily, embarrassed by her overreaction. "Sorry. I just saw…" *Otto*. The name rang in her head, but she didn't want to admit that she remembered it. She hadn't shared the details of her eventful morning walk three days earlier. Since Grace and Jules weren't aware of the garage roof conversation, Sarah knowing Otto's name after so brief an introduction seemed like evidence of her budding, illogical crush. Her cheeks got hot, but she tried very hard to ignore that she was blushing—and the reason for her red face. "I just saw that cop I met last week. It was dumb. I just overreacted."

"Otto?" Grace asked, and Sarah nodded, feeling her face heat even more at the sound of his name. Seriously, something was wrong with her. "Oh, he's harmless. Really. I mean, so are Hugh and Theo, but they just come off a little more…harshly?" Grace gave Jules a *help me* look before turning back to Sarah. "You don't need to be afraid of any of the cops here. We just didn't want to overwhelm you by introducing you to all of them. They can be…" She looked at Jules again.

"Intimidating," Jules supplied helpfully, and Grace nodded. "Otto really is the easiest to get along with of all three of them. You'll love him once you get to know him." Sarah tried not to grimace at the phrasing. She couldn't admit that was why she was so nervous around Otto. The big cop was already in her thoughts much too often, and they'd exchanged just a few words. If she got to know him, she had a feeling she'd be in serious trouble.

Linking arms with Sarah, Grace started to lead her

out of the aisle. Even though she was freaking out at the thought of talking with Otto again, Sarah tried to hide it. Her feet wanted to drag, but she forced her body to cooperate. She'd only known Grace and Jules a week, and they'd been nicer to her than anyone she'd ever known before. She didn't want to admit her weird issues to them...not yet, at least.

"Otto!" Jules forged ahead, waving as she hurried over to the cop. He gave her a small smile before looking past her. When his gaze locked on Sarah, his expression stilled.

What does that mean? Why is he looking at me like that? she asked herself frantically. Unfortunately, she didn't have an answer. Her previous life had kept her isolated, her social interactions limited to employees and business associates of first her father and then her brother. Sarah wasn't sure how to read the big, blond cop, but she guessed that the frozen look was not a good sign.

He didn't look away as they approached. Sarah couldn't hold his gaze and dropped her eyes to the floor. It was impossible not to look at him, though, and she kept darting furtive glances in his direction. His hair was nearly white-blond, cut short in a no-nonsense style. He wasn't just a Viking lumberjack; he was like a Viking and a lumberjack had a baby, and that baby grew up to serve in the army and then become a Monroe police officer.

"Milk replacer? What orphans are you feeding now?" Jules asked, breaking what was turning into another awkward silence.

He finally looked away from Sarah to focus on

Jules. "Puppies. Curtis Trammel's shepherd was hit by a car."

"He brought them to you?" Before he answered, Grace spoke again. "Of course he did. You're the Dr. Dolittle around here, after all."

Otto gave an uncomfortable half shrug, but Sarah had stopped pretending not to stare at him. He was a Viking lumberjack cop who bottle-fed orphaned puppies? If he'd spent years trying to think of the most effective punch to the ovaries, he couldn't have come up with a better plan.

"Juju!" Ty called from across the store. "We're going to get these guns, okay?"

"What? What guns? No, not okay." Jules immediately charged toward the sporting goods section.

Grace grinned. Following after a stressed-looking Jules, she said over her shoulder, "This should be good. They probably want to mount them on their homemade drone."

The two women disappeared around the corner of an aisle, and the realization hit Sarah—she and Otto were alone. Together. Sure, they weren't really alone, since it was a public place with several people, including children, nearby, but…still. Alone. Together. Again. Her scalp prickled with sweat.

She tried desperately to think of something to talk about, but her mind was blank. There wasn't a nearby herd of elk to supply a handy topic of conversation. It had been the same every time they'd met. Otto seemed to be a huge walking magnet, wiping her brain's hard drive whenever he got near. "Um…how many puppies?"

He just stared at her, and uncertainty started to set

in. Her question had made sense, hadn't it? Maybe she should've clarified. But Sarah was afraid that, if she spoke again, she'd rush into a waterfall of babbly explanation, and that would just make her seem even more unbalanced.

"Your mouth…" He trailed off, his eyes fixed on her lips.

"My mouth…?" she echoed, and then horror hit her. There had to be something on her mouth. They had all just eaten lunch at the VFW-turned-diner where Jules worked. Was there something green and slimy in her teeth? Did she have residual barbeque sauce on her face? If so, she was going to kill Jules, Grace, and every last one of the kids for not telling her before she came face-to-face with a lumberjack Viking puppy rescuer. Sarah wiped frantically at her lips, feeling her cheeks heat. "What about my mouth?"

"It's pretty." His tanned face flushed to the color of brick. Abruptly, he turned and walked away.

Sarah went still, her hand still over her lips. There was a strange feeling in her stomach. It wasn't the anxious dread she was used to, though. This was more of a hopeful fluttering, a funny little squeeze of happiness. Dropping her hand to her side, she smiled at Otto's broad, quickly departing back.

He thinks I'm pretty.

Your mouth is pretty?! Otto groaned. The only thing that kept him from thumping his forehead against the steering wheel of his pickup was the fact that driving on the curvy mountain roads took focus, especially in the predawn darkness. He'd meant to tell her she had a nice smile, but it had come out so, so, *so* wrong. Of all the things he could've said, he'd chosen a line from a horror movie? From the *villain* in a horror movie? What was wrong with him?

He knew perfectly well what was wrong with him. Whenever he found a woman attractive, he turned into a bumbling thirteen-year-old. No, that wasn't right. Most thirteen-year-olds had more game than Otto did. For three days now, his idiotic statement had been running through his head, and he'd cursed himself out every single time. He'd managed to speak and not embarrass himself the second time they'd met, when he'd helped her off the carport roof, but he hadn't expected to see her at the store. It'd thrown him off guard. Still, why hadn't he just asked her out or, at the very least, said something innocuous? She'd just asked him a question about the puppies, for Christ's sake. It'd been a simple answer, too. All he needed to say was that there were four of them, and they could've continued having a perfectly normal, civil conversation.

But no. Otto had to pull out the creepiest, most unnerving line possible instead. "Four," he muttered, pulling into the VFW-turned-diner—otherwise known as the viner—parking lot. "That's all you would've had to say. Four. It's one syllable, you moron."

Scrubbing a hand over his head, Otto took a deep breath. He had to let it go. Dwelling on it was just making him crazy and giving him a stomachache. Letting out all the air in his lungs, he reached for the door handle. So he'd ruined any possibility of a chance with a woman he was hugely attracted to, all in four words. Things could be worse.

No. He couldn't think of how things could be worse, unless he had accidentally dowsed her in chemical spray or tased her or something.

With a quiet groan, he got out of his pickup and walked toward the viner entrance. Theo and Hugh were already there, Otto noticed. Both of their K9s, Viggy and Lexi, barked at him from their respective vehicles, and he gave them a small wave. He walked past Theo's squad car, going out of his way to check on Viggy. The dog had been in a rough way just a few months ago, right after his former partner, Officer Don Baker, had committed suicide. The dog had lost all of his confidence, and it didn't help that his new partner, Theo, had been wrecked by grief. The two were coming along, though, and the dog had been making huge strides.

Even now, Viggy was standing up in the back seat, his tail waving slightly as he recognized Otto. He looked like a different dog from the huddled mess he'd been just a couple of months ago. It gave Otto hope for Xena, the dog he was currently attempting to rehabilitate. They still had a long way to go, though, and his lieutenant was making noises about buying a trained K9 for the department—a K9 that would be Otto's new partner. His last K9 was retired and living a life of luxury chasing rabbits on Otto's ranch.

Breaking out of his thoughts, Otto strode to the viner entrance. Even at that early hour, it was starting to fill up with customers. Giving Jules a nod of greeting, he made his way to the table that had become their usual meeting spot after the diner had been blown up two months ago.

Hugh saw him and swiveled around, attempting to prop his leg on the chair next to him, but Otto was already there, sliding into the seat.

"Quit swinging your leg around," Otto grumbled, flipping his coffee mug right side up. "It'll never heal if you keep abusing it."

"I'm not abusing my leg. You're thinking of another body part." Waggling his eyebrows comically, Hugh returned his foot to the chair across from him.

Otto didn't laugh. "Your broken arm?"

"No, my..." Hugh's reply trailed off as Otto gave him a stern look. "You know, I liked it better when you were obsessing over Theo, rather than me."

"I didn't." Theo leaned back in his chair, his normally severe expression amused.

"Maybe if you'd quit getting shot and breaking bones, then I could 'obsess' less," Otto suggested. Sometimes he felt like the ground crew for two reckless acrobats, running around trying to catch them before they hit the ground.

Jules hurried over to their table and poured him some coffee. "How are you, Otto?"

He couldn't honestly say "good," since he was living in a hot swamp of still-fresh humiliation after his last encounter with Sarah, plus he'd had to wake up every three hours to bottle-feed puppies, but any response other than "fine" would awaken Jules's curiosity, and he didn't want to deal with the interrogation that would follow. Instead, he raised a shoulder and grunted.

"Uh-oh," Jules said, meeting Theo's gaze. The two exchanged a look that Otto knew boded poorly for him. "There's a story here. Hang on. Let me get the Lynches their breakfast platters, and then I'll be back to hear the whole thing."

"There is no 'whole thing,'" Otto protested, but Jules was already gone. From Hugh's laughter, his huffy mood had disappeared as well.

Theo leaned toward them. "Before she gets back, what did you learn?"

"About what?" Otto's brain felt foggy from lack of sleep.

"The newest houseguest," Hugh prodded. "We haven't had a chance to talk about it yet, and Grace *still* won't let me near her. You're the only one with access. Did you manage to get a look at her driver's license?"

It seemed like he couldn't escape from reminders of Sarah. A fresh wave of humiliation flooded him. "No." Otto didn't just mean he didn't see her license; he meant that there'd be no discussion about Sarah... not until he could forget what he'd said, which probably meant they could *never* talk about her. Otto would be okay with that.

"You didn't?" Hugh sat back, wincing slightly and reaching his good arm to reposition his leg. "I knew I should've followed you up there, but Jules threatened my life if I did. What's her last name?"

Pressing his lips together, Otto gave a single, sharp shake of his head.

"Are you blushing?" Hugh asked. "Holy monkey balls, you are! Why are you blushing, Ninja Paul Bunyan?"

"I'm not." *Shit*.

"You are." Theo eyed him from across the table. "Why?"

"What did you do?" Hugh gave him a feigned look of horror, and Otto resisted the urge to punch him.

"What could we have done?" he scoffed instead, staring down at his untouched coffee. "It was two minutes. Grace was there."

Theo was still studying him. "You like her?"

Opening his mouth to deny it, to say he felt nothing, Otto found he couldn't get the words out. Instead, he gave the same half-assed shrug he'd offered earlier.

"Yeah?" Hugh sounded fascinated, and Otto had to resist the urge to roll his eyes. It wasn't *that* uncommon. "You have a thing for her? The last time you had a thing for someone, it was that dispatcher who moved to Cleveland right after you got up the nerve to ask her out. What was that—two years ago?"

"Three," Theo corrected, his gaze not leaving Otto's face. "Consider doing a background check before you get in too deep." Otto gazed at him evenly, and Theo gave a half smile and a shrug. "Do as I say, not as I do."

"If you like her," Hugh said, "you're not the right one to be investigating her. Things get fuzzy when there are emotions involved. I should know. Want me to dig around for you?"

"There will be no digging," Jules stated as she pulled a chair from a nearby table and plopped down next to Theo. "Hey, sweetness. I'm on break so you can kiss me now."

Theo gave her a smile and obliged. Otto focused on his coffee until they came up for air.

"Okay." Jules sounded a little breathless. "Now what's this about digging?"

"We were talking about gardening," Hugh lied easily, and Otto held back a snort.

"Uh-huh." Jules sounded as skeptical as she should be. "Gardening. In November."

Hugh gave her a sweet smile. "Never too early to start planning."

"Right." After giving Hugh a suspicious look, she turned to Theo. "What were you really talking about?"

"Otto likes Sarah."

Mouth open, Otto stared at Theo. He'd expected Hugh to spill the beans, but Theo? "What the hell?"

Looking completely unrepentant, Theo laid an arm over the back of Jules's chair and picked up his coffee mug with his free hand. "I would've just told her later."

"That's true," Jules said, leaning forward with the same gossip-loving expression as Hugh. "He knows better than to withhold juicy tidbits. It'll be useful to have me in the loop, though. I can talk you up to her, arrange 'coincidental' meetings, let you know her date preferences, and all that."

Otto groaned, tipping his head back and closing his eyes. Why had he even bothered getting out of bed that morning? He could be wallowing in embarrassment with puppies sleeping on him, rather than wallowing in embarrassment with a growing crowd of amused, overly helpful friends.

"I'll find out today what she thinks about you." Jules was still talking.

"Please don't."

Hugh was snickering. "Fair warning, buddy. I have to tell Grace, too."

Opening his eyes, Otto turned his best glare—one that transformed even the surliest suspect into a compliant heap of goo—on his partner, but it only made Hugh grin wider.

"Sorry, but if she found out that she was the last

to know, my life wouldn't be worth living anymore. Grace would make sure of that." Hugh made a mock-terrified face.

"I'm not interested in Sarah." Otto held back a wince. It sounded like a lie, even to him.

It didn't help when Jules and Hugh started laughing. Even Theo looked amused.

His only hope was to change the subject. "Jules, I need a favor."

She bounced a little in her chair. "Do you want me to ask Sarah what her favorite flower is?"

"No. Can you take care of the puppies tonight during my shift?"

"Puppies?" Jules still looked excited, even though he'd shut down her matchmaking. "Of course. Dee is going to be out-of-her-mind thrilled."

At the mention of the little girl, Otto managed a smile. "How's the cat?"

"He's great. Turtle is quickly becoming the king of the house."

"Turtle?" Hugh repeated. "Interesting name for a cat."

Jules shrugged. "It involved about eight hours of discussion over two days. Once everyone agreed on a name, I wasn't about to argue."

"Jules!" Megan, the diner owner, yelled from her spot by the window. "Break's over. The Silver Fork Casino bus just pulled up."

Making a face, Jules pressed a quick kiss to Theo's cheek before standing. As she returned her chair to its rightful spot at the neighboring table, she said, "See y'all later." She winked at Otto. "Drop the puppies off anytime this afternoon. I'll make sure we're *all* home."

The emphasis reminded Otto that Sarah would be at Jules's house, and he almost groaned. A part of him was eager to see her again, but facing her after his super-creep act the other day would be uncomfortable. He gave Jules a slight nod, hiding his apprehension, and then turned back to his partners.

When he saw their smirks, he braced himself. Breakfast was going to be rough.

CHAPTER 7

HE WAS THERE, AT HER HOUSE, AND HE HAD PUPPIES.

Sarah leaned against the wall outside the living room, frantically fanning her face. She needed to cool her hot cheeks, or he'd instantly know how much he affected her. Dee chattered about the puppies, and listening to her calmed Sarah down. Blowing out a silent breath, she squared her shoulders. *Stop being silly and get in there.*

Pivoting around the doorjamb, she ran straight into what felt like a wall. Bouncing off a hard body, she started to fall backward, but Otto caught her arms in an iron grip and held her upright. Sarah swallowed a groan. Of course she had to run into Otto. A dignified entrance was too much to ask.

"Sorry," she said as he released his grip. Even after he moved his hands, she could still feel the ghost of his fingers warming her skin.

He dipped his chin, not saying a word. Sarah had run their encounter at the store through her brain a thousand times, until she worried that she'd just made the whole thing up, that the trauma of escaping her brother had forced her into some fantasy land where beautiful, dog-loving Viking lumberjacks thought she was *pretty*. Tearing her eyes from the way his tanned skin stretched over his cheekbones and jaw, where a hint of stubble marred the smooth texture, Sarah turned toward the puppies. She desperately needed a distraction from the man in front of her.

"Oh!" she exclaimed when she saw them, moving over to where Jules, Grace, and the kids sat on the floor. Each one of Jules's siblings held a puppy, although Jules and Grace looked as if they wanted to steal one of their own. Sarah sat on the floor between Dee and Jules, reaching out a finger to stroke the puppy Dee was holding. "They're like little furry sausages."

Dee's puppy blindly rooted against her middle, making squeaky grunting sounds. The little girl laughed, tucking the puppy closer. "I think this one's hungry, Otto."

"They're almost due for their next feeding," he said, and Sarah felt heat bloom in her belly at the sound of his gravelly voice. He had a distinctive way of speaking, as if picking each word carefully, and it made her want to listen to him for hours. He could read the dictionary to her, she decided. She'd expand her vocabulary and get to hear that wonderful voice at the same time. "They eat about every three hours."

"Can they sleep with me tonight?" Dee asked Jules.

Tipping her head toward the cat that was perched on the back of the couch, looking affronted at the entire situation, Jules said, "Don't you think Turtle might be a little hurt?"

Dee gave the cat a sheepish look. "Sorry, Turtle."

"I'll k-keep them," Sam offered. "That w-w-way they w-won't w-wake anyone d-downstairs."

"Sure?" Jules sounded concerned.

"Yeah. N-no school tom-morrow."

Not looking convinced, Jules absently started petting

the puppy sleeping in Ty's lap. "You have to get up early to work at the kennel, though."

"I'll do it." Sarah was surprised to hear herself volunteer—what did she know about taking care of dogs? It wasn't as if she'd ever been allowed to keep one. "I don't have to go anywhere tomorrow, so I can sleep after Otto picks up the puppies." She glanced at him, unable to keep her gaze off his face. Even *puppies* couldn't keep her attention when Otto was in the room. "You'll need to show me what to do, though."

Otto walked all of them through preparing the formula in the tiniest bottles Sarah had ever seen. They looked like something that would come with a doll. After Otto fed one of the puppies for a minute, he handed the dog and bottle over to Sarah. She felt oddly nervous that she wouldn't do it right, especially in front of Otto, who was so incredibly competent. It was trickier to bottle-feed than she'd expected, and the puppy flailed, searching blindly after the nipple slipped out of his mouth for the third time.

"Here." Otto reached around her, his chest to her back, and put his hands over hers. Sarah stopped breathing as he guided her hands, one on the bottle and one on the puppy. "Rub the sides of his head like this." His breath brushed her cheek, warming her skin. Exhaling in a rush, she forced herself to concentrate on what he was showing her. The puppy was sucking enthusiastically, and she gave a wondering laugh.

"This is amazing."

"Yeah. It doesn't seem that way at two in the morning, though."

Sarah huffed another quiet laugh. Even though she had gotten the hang of feeding the puppy, Otto didn't move away. Instead, he shifted his hands so they were wrapped around her forearms. It reminded her vividly of the feel of him gripping her waist, the way he held her with such care and strength, as if she was something precious. Looking down at his hands, at the way they covered almost her entire arm from elbow to wrist, she knew that it was too late to save herself from hurt—she was already addicted to his touch.

The puppy grunted as he ate, drawing her attention. Even as she marveled at the tiny creature eating so voraciously, milky bubbles forming around his nose and mouth, Sarah was hyperaware of Otto's warmth, of the way his body wrapped around hers. Unable to resist, she allowed herself to subtly lean against his chest. He was so hard and warm against her back that she shivered a little, delighting in how amazing it felt to be in his arms. His grip on her tightened for just a moment, as if he'd felt her tremble, as if he knew how much touching him affected her. Her heart thundered so hard in her chest that she wondered if he felt that, too.

"Otto," Dee said, and Sarah was brought back to reality with a snap. "Could you help me?"

He moved away, and Sarah's back and arms felt cold. She couldn't help but sneak glances at Otto, at the gentle way he taught Dee how to hold the puppy and the bottle. She shivered a little—from disappointment rather than pleasure that time. He was so careful and patient with Dee. It made Sarah like him even more, but it also made her wonder if she'd imagined his response. What if he'd just been teaching her how to feed the puppy? The heat, the attraction… Had he felt it, too, or was he just being kind to a friend of Jules's?

Sarah glanced over at Jules and saw that the other woman was grinning at her. Raising her eyebrows in question, she gave Jules a *what?* look, but she only got a wider smile in response. Something about the look made her blush, though. When she looked over at Otto again, she saw him quickly turn his head away.

That speedy movement made Sarah's insides do a little jump. Had he been sneaking glances at her? It could've been that he was simply curious about the newcomer, or that he found her odd, but a tiny bubble of hope still formed inside her.

Could her lumberjack Viking with a soft spot for puppies possibly have a soft spot for her, too?

The grunts and squeaks woke her before her alarm did, and Sarah groaned into her pillow before squinting at the clock. She'd only gotten to sleep for fifty-two minutes that time. Why had she volunteered to take the night shift?

The puppies' tiny noises increased in volume, and Sarah sighed as she rolled out of her warm nest of a bed. She'd volunteered because she'd been entranced by Otto and the furry sausages. That golden glow had dimmed after the ten p.m. feeding, been tarnished even more by the next one, and now, at just after four a.m., all warm and fuzzy feelings were pretty much gone.

Grabbing the handle on the top of their crate, she unplugged the heating pad and carried them down to the kitchen. She tried to mix and warm the formula with her eyes closed, but Sarah quickly found out that was a bad idea when she spilled milk replacer all over the counter.

"Shoot," she whispered, reaching for a paper towel to mop it up.

"Want a hand?"

Sarah jumped a foot and knocked over the bottle, spilling the little bit of formula remaining.

"Sorry." Grace gave her a sleepy smile as she crossed the kitchen to where the puppies were frantically paddling their uncoordinated limbs, trying to find the source of their breakfast.

Cleaning up the last of the mess, Sarah smiled back. "No need to be sorry. I'm just…jumpy."

"Understandable." Folding her long legs beneath her, Grace sat on the floor in front of the puppies. "You should've seen me my first week or so here. I was scared to leave the house."

As she prepped more milk replacer, Sarah gave Grace a curious glance, not able to imagine the other woman living in fear. She seemed too confident, too self-assured, to be anything other than majorly kick-ass. "Really?"

"Oh, yeah." Grabbing an old but clean towel from the pile Sarah had put on top of the dog crate, Grace spread it over her lap. "It took a pep talk from Sam before I managed to go into the yard."

"From Sam?" Sarah laughed, incredulous. The teen was so guarded and quiet that she couldn't imagine him giving a pep talk.

Grace looked up from the pile of puppies she'd pulled into her lap, where they squirmed and crawled, still searching for their food. "I know, right? I think it shocked the fear right out of me."

As Sarah laughed softly, Jules walked into the kitchen, a huge yawn taking up her entire face. "Hey, Sarah. Oh, hi, Grace. Didn't see you down there."

"Good morning, sunshine," Grace said.

"Sorry, Jules." Four bottles in hand, Sarah sat down next to Grace. She'd found it easier to prep four separate bottles. That way, she didn't have to worry about how much each puppy got. They could suck down the whole thing and, as long as she didn't double up and give one puppy two bottles, it worked pretty smoothly. "I didn't mean to wake you."

"You didn't." Jules took a seat on the other side of Grace. "A very annoying alarm clock did. I'm opening today."

"Does it bother you? Opening?" Grace accepted a bottle and started feeding one of the puppies.

"A little, but it helps that my stalker hangs out in the parking lot until Vicki or Megan arrives." Jules also grabbed a bottle and a puppy, and Sarah gave an internal sigh of relief. With three of them feeding, this would go faster. She might even manage to get an hour and a half of sleep before she was woken up again. Picking up the largest of the puppies—whom she'd mentally been calling Bruce—Sarah popped the nipple in his mouth.

Belatedly, Jules's words registered in her sleep-deprived brain. "Wait. Your stalker?" Her voice shot up in alarm, and the puppy startled. Sarah rubbed his head in silent apology, and he concentrated on sucking down as much milk replacer as possible in the shortest amount of time.

"I'm kidding." Jules gave her a smile. "I'm just talking about Theo."

"Oh." Sarah felt a little silly for not immediately getting the joke, but she knew that everyone living at the house had been sent there by Mr. Espina. That meant that Sarah wasn't the only one who'd had something bad happen to her, something that forced her to run away from everything she knew. Still, she asked, "Why would opening bother you?"

Jules grimaced. "Some really bad things happened when I opened for the first time."

"Oh." That answer just made Sarah more curious, but she didn't want to push if Jules didn't want to share. After all, it wasn't really her business.

With a dry laugh, Grace said, "Bad? Yeah, I'd call getting locked in the walk-in cooler and almost getting blown up pretty bad."

"Wait. *What?*" Forget any of that not-her-business nonsense; this sounded too interesting not to hear.

Jules waved a hand in dismissal. "I'll tell you the whole story sometime. Right now, though, I want to talk about Otto."

"Oh yes! We do want to talk about Otto," Grace echoed as Sarah felt her face heat.

"I saw some interesting looks going back and forth between the two of you yesterday." Jules looked like she was holding back a smile. "What's the story there?"

"No story." Sarah pretended to concentrate on Bruce, although he didn't need any help eating. After a second of silence, though, she couldn't stand it and peeked at Jules. "What looks?"

Jules's grin broke free. "I'm pretty darn sure the big guy is smitten."

"He's not." Now Sarah couldn't hold back her own smile. "Is he?"

"Hugh thinks so, too." Grace leaned forward until her puppy squeaked in protest. "Sorry, sweetie. It's just a very interesting bit of gossip." Once the dog was eating happily again, she looked at Sarah, her eyes alight. "Do you and Otto have a thing?"

"Oh no." Her face was so hot she could've warmed the puppies' formula on it. "We're not… I mean, it's not a thing, really."

"Do you *want* it to be a thing?" Jules asked.

"Yes." The truth was out before she thought, and she blushed even hotter. "No. I don't know. I was pretty sheltered in my old life. There wasn't really any opportunity to meet…well, anyone. This is all new to me. I don't really know how I feel. Plus, I'll be leaving eventually—or sooner than eventually—so I shouldn't get involved, right?"

Jules met Grace's gaze and both women made the same rueful face. "You're asking the wrong people," Jules said. "I knew I shouldn't get involved with Theo, but I didn't have any choice. It just…happened."

"Same. Only with Hugh, of course." Grace looked at Sarah. "If you were planning to stick around, would you be interested?"

"In Otto?" She dropped her gaze to the puppy again. "He's really sweet."

"Yeah, he is," Grace and Jules said in unison, and then laughed.

"And he's gentle." Sarah realized that she was smiling. Just the thought of Otto made her happy. "And he's so beautiful. And *big*."

When Grace and Jules started giggling, Sarah couldn't help but join them.

"Morning." Theo's grumbly greeting distracted them as he made his way into the kitchen, followed by his K9 partner, Viggy. Sarah jumped and immediately blushed, wondering how much of the Otto conversation he'd overheard. He seemed like his usual mildly grumpy self, so she hoped they'd been talking quietly enough that he'd missed the juicy parts. Sarah assumed his shift started early like Jules's, since he was already dressed in uniform. Leaning down, he kissed the top of Jules's head. "You should've woken me."

Tipping her head up, Jules accepted another kiss, this one on her lips. "How you can sleep through my obnoxiously loud alarm is beyond me. Puppy?"

"Sure." Settling down on the floor, Theo accepted the last puppy and bottle.

Sarah's pup had finished eating, so she put him on Grace's lap with his littermate so she could get some warm, wet paper towels. As she massaged Bruce's belly, simulating the mother dog's tongue to get him to go to the bathroom, Sarah made a face. "This is my least favorite part."

With a snicker, Grace said, "At least human babies don't need any help with that. They just go freely."

"Ew!" Jules giggled, scrunching her nose. "There'd be a lot fewer people willing to have babies if we had to lick them."

At Theo's disgusted expression, Sarah joined the other two women in laughter. Joy bubbled up inside her. What a difference Mr. Espina and a few days had made. She couldn't remember the last time, in her old life, when she'd truly belly-laughed. It felt good to be happy.

━━━━━━━━━━━━━━━

Later that morning, the knock on the door made Sarah smile. She hurried into the entry, feeling giddy despite her sleep-deprived state. The previous night had been brutal. By the time she'd fed and cleaned all four puppies and tucked them back into their heating-pad-warmed crate, she'd only managed to get an hour or two of sleep before the alarm went off and she'd had to start the whole process over again. After the four a.m. feeding, when Jules, Grace, and Theo had helped, things had gotten easier. Grace, a visiting Hugh, and the kids had assisted with the next two, but Sarah still hadn't been able to do more than grab quick naps. The prospect of seeing Otto woke up her clouded, sleepy brain, though. It also created an entire herd of butterflies in her belly.

They'd be pretty much alone, too. Sam had gone to work at his kennel job, Grace was running errands with Hugh, and Jules had dragged the rest of the kids outside for a Saturday home improvement project, despite their complaints. Jules was unsympathetic to their pleas. It was supposed to snow any day, and she was determined to clear away the remains of the old burned-out barn before everything was covered in a blanket of white.

The idea of being alone with Otto was both nerve-racking and glorious. The last time hadn't gone so smoothly, but Sarah was hopeful that this time would be different. After all, the ice had been broken. Jules and Grace seemed certain he liked her. Maybe he'd even ask her out. The thought made her swallow back an excited sound as she hurried to the front door.

Her fingers fumbled a little with the locks, but she finally managed to get the dead bolts and chain unlatched. Swinging open the door, she felt her smile fall away.

Aaron stood on the porch.

No. *No, no, no, no, no!* The word echoed over and over in her head. It wasn't supposed to happen this way. She'd just broken free, just started a new life. It couldn't end already.

"Alice." Her brother's mouth curled up in a smile that wasn't reflected in his flat, cold eyes. "You've put me to a lot of troub—"

She slammed the door. Her hands were clumsy on the lock, slipping against metal, as an angry shout from outside made her joints go weak and loose, like a marionette. Finally, though, she managed to turn the dead bolt, giving a quiet sob of relief at the *click* as it seated itself. The second lock was easier, but she left the chain hanging where it was. She had to get *away*.

Turning, she sprinted down the hallway, yanking the phone Mr. Espina had given her out of her pocket. Her sweating fingers fumbled on the screen, but Sarah finally managed to hit Send.

"Why are you calling me, you nutball?" Jules laughed as she answered. *"I'm in the backyard. You could've just yelled out the back door."*

"Jules! My brother's at the front door." Fear made her voice thick. Sarah dashed through the kitchen toward the back door. "He found me. Oh God, he's found me already."

"*Ty, Tio*," Jules said. Her voice was hushed and muffled, as if she'd lowered the phone slightly, but Sarah could still hear her urgent words. "*Take Dee into the woods. Sarah, get out here. I'll wait for you.*"

"No!" Despite her protest, Sarah was so tempted to run out and let Jules help her, but that would only put Jules and her family in danger. She locked the single dead bolt on the back door and hoped that would hold—at least for a little while—if Aaron came around back. "Run, Jules! Get the kids away from here. I've locked myself inside."

"*That won't stop him for long.*"

Sarah knew that, but hearing it out loud was still terrifying. Her heart thundered in her chest, so hard that her pulse throbbed. "It won't need to. As soon as you promise to hide in the woods with the kids, I'll hang up and call the po—"

The sound of breaking glass made her flinch, almost dropping the phone. Sarah sucked in a ragged breath. It had come from the front of the house. Jules had been all too right when she'd said the locked door wouldn't stop Aaron for long.

He'd broken in.

"*Sarah? Sarah!*" Even though Sarah knew Jules's voice couldn't be heard all the way across the house, she still winced at how loud it sounded in her ear. "*I'm calling Theo.*"

The phone went silent, knocking Sarah out of her terrified paralysis. She ran for the back door again, automatically dropping her cell in her hoodie pocket. As she fumbled with the dead bolt, desperately wishing she hadn't locked it moments earlier, she saw movement outside. Someone was walking between the trees bordering the backyard.

No! Go back! she mentally shouted, sure that it was Jules heading back to the house to help her. The dead bolt opened with a *thunk*, and Sarah yanked open the door. Before she could cross the threshold, Logan Jovanovic stepped into the open, heading toward the house—and directly toward her.

With an indrawn gasp, Sarah jerked backward, silently closing the door before he spotted her. Aaron was at the front of the house, and Logan was coming through the back. She was trapped.

Stop! A commanding voice in her brain broke through her panic. It wasn't over. There were other options. If she couldn't go out the doors, then she'd have to find a window. The police were coming. Otto's face flashed in her mind, and it gave her courage. She just needed to keep herself safe until Otto arrived. He'd never let Aaron or Logan take her.

Locking the back door again, Sarah forced herself to move to the kitchen doorway. Her heart was racing, and air felt thick in her lungs, making it hard to breathe. She was certain that Aaron was standing right outside the door, waiting for her, but she couldn't stay in the kitchen. There was no place to hide, and Logan was coming.

Gritting her teeth, she peeked through the doorway. No one was in the hallway, but the front door was wide open, one of its beautiful stained-glass windows shattered.

Moving silently, Sarah darted into the dining room, feeling hunted. It was almost worse that Aaron wasn't standing there, waiting. Now, she had no idea where he was. He could be around any corner, through any doorway. Her heart rate sped up until the beats started to blur together, and it was a struggle not to gasp for air.

Knock it off, the stern mental voice scolded. *Get to a window and get out. Otto will be here soon.* She clung to that thought. She'd dealt with Aaron and Logan before, and she'd survived—and escaped. Now, she had friends. She had *help*, something she'd never had before Mr. Espina had offered to help her. She just needed to hide or escape until her new friends arrived.

The windows in the dining room were the crank-open type, and she knew she couldn't fit through the opening—even if she wasn't caught trying to open it. She needed to get into the library. There were two windows in there with sashes that slid up. She'd be able to squeeze through one of those.

"Alice."

Aaron's raised voice echoed through the house, freezing her in place.

"You're just making this worse for yourself, Alice."

The dining room went gray around the edges as she struggled to breathe. His voice was getting closer. It sounded like he was right outside. Her frantic gaze darted around the dining room, but there weren't any hiding places, just an uncovered table and chairs.

She was trapped.

CHAPTER 8

"I'M NOT HAPPY WITH YOU, ALICE."

Aaron sounded like he was even closer. Any second, he'd come through the dining room door and find her. "Do you know how much of my time and money you've wasted with your little stunt?"

She spotted the small, waist-high door in the wall that Dee called an *elf door*. Silently, Sarah darted over to it and pulled the small, glass knob. The old wood stuck, and she had to hold back a frightened sob. There was a creak of a floorboard right outside the dining room door, and Sarah gave the knob a desperate yank. The small door popped open, revealing a serving hatch that opened into the kitchen.

Boosting herself up, she folded herself into the hatch, pulling the small door closed behind her just as the door to the dining room swung open. Scared that Aaron had spotted her, she didn't try to hide there, but shoved through the other side. Even as the small door leading to the kitchen swung open, her breath caught. What if Logan was in there?

As the opening widened, revealing an empty kitchen, Sarah sucked in a breath. Turning so she could swing her legs down, she lightly thumped her knee against the side of the hatch. The sound seemed so loud, even over her heartbeat drumming in her ears. He'd be rushing in at any second, Sarah knew, and she slid out of her hiding place as quickly and silently as she could.

She held back a terrified, frustrated sob. Now she was trapped in the kitchen again. Her only other options were the hallway where Aaron was, the back door where Logan was, and the basement.

Even as she thought it, her feet were already moving. The door was warped, and she tugged at it, her fingers slipping on the glass knob. It finally popped open with a *thunk* that sounded much too loud. With a frantic glance behind her, Sarah slipped through the doorway.

Standing on the first wooden step, she carefully pulled the door closed, stopping when it rubbed the frame with a squeak. Even though it wasn't latched, Sarah left it, hoping it wouldn't swing open and that Aaron wouldn't notice the door wasn't completely shut. She paused for a moment, listening. All she could hear was her own heartbeat and the rasp of her frantic breaths.

Her right hand automatically reached to the side and felt for a light switch, but she only found rough, unpainted wood and something fragile and sticky that she figured were spiderwebs. A faint sound through the door made her go still, her breathing loud inside her head. Had she imagined it, or was Aaron in the kitchen? He could pull open the door at any second.

Swallowing as much of her panic as she could, Sarah searched for the second step with her foot. As she eased her weight onto it, it gave a low creak, and she went still again. When the basement door stayed closed, she started breathing again in short, hard pants. She lowered her other foot onto the step. Her fuzzy socks caught on the rough wood of the step, and she wished she'd worn shoes. Why would she have, though, since she was going to go back to bed immediately after Otto picked up the puppies?

The puppies. Content with their full bellies, they'd been sleeping in their crate, which she'd placed on the living room floor under an end table. If they stayed asleep and silent while Aaron was searching for her, maybe he'd miss them. She'd never seen him be cruel to animals, but then again, she'd never seen him around animals. Sarah'd had a kitten for a few weeks when she was younger, but her father had taken it away from her after she'd broken one of his rules. After that, she'd never asked for another pet.

Aaron was carelessly cruel to people, though. Sarah knew this well, and her stomach churned with worry. She forced herself to focus. If she couldn't save herself, then she'd be no help to anyone or anything else.

Step by blind step, she crept down the stairs, one hand trailing down the exposed studs of the unfinished wall. The stairs were steep and uneven, some risers narrow and some wider, and the distance between them varied wildly. Her eyes started to adjust to the near-blackness, although she wasn't sure if the shapes she could barely make out were really there or just her wishful thinking. It would be infinitely less terrifying to be able to see where she was going.

Her foot dangled in space, and she had a moment of panic. What if the stairway ended, and she was going to fall off the edge onto a hard concrete floor below? Her toes finally made contact, and she blew out a relieved, silent breath. The next step was shallower than she expected, and her foot thumped against the wood.

Sarah froze, holding her breath as she listened for any sign that Aaron had heard her misstep. All she could hear was the blood thumping through her ears, and she started to breathe again.

As she stepped down again, the surface her socked foot came into contact with felt different. It was slightly uneven and cool. When she tried to descend another step, her body jarred when her foot connected too soon with that same bumpy surface, and she realized that she'd reached the bottom. It was a relief to be off the untrustworthy stairs and farther from Aaron, but the basement was an unknown. Sarah had no idea which way she should go or what she might run into.

She extended her hands, hoping to feel any obstacles before she crashed into them, and her fingers bumped into a wood surface. Flattening her palms against it, she ran her hands up and down, trying to figure out what it was—a wall? A large piece of furniture?—when she found the doorknob. That was why it was so dark—there was a door at the bottom of the stairs.

Turning the knob, she pushed it open, hoping it would be lighter on the other side. She only stepped into more blackness, however. She closed the door behind her, cringing at the click as it latched but wanting as many barriers between her and Aaron as possible. Although she felt for a lock, the door was smooth except for the round knob. Giving up on locking it, she turned to face the pitch-black room. With her arms stretched out in front of her, she took a shuffling step forward and then another. The dark was so complete that it was dizzying.

Something brushed her face. Sarah sucked in a hard breath through her nose, barely preventing a scream from escaping. She batted at the air, trying to swat away whatever had touched her, but it didn't work. The light tap against her cheek repeated once, twice, and a third time before she realized that she'd walked into a hanging string.

With a ragged gasp of relief that it hadn't been a giant, fanged spider or a rabid bat or a serial killer or whatever else might hang out in a dark basement, Sarah grasped the string and tugged. A lightbulb clicked on, blinding her for a few moments until her eyes adjusted.

She looked around, taking in the shadowy space. Antique-looking things were stacked against the walls, some broken and some not, some older than others, but all dirty, cobweb-covered, and very creepy. The floor was packed dirt, and the walls were unfinished with exposed, battered-looking insulation filling in the areas between the studs. There were suspicious rustling noises and the musty smell of rodents.

Hoping that nothing furry—or scaly or slimy or... well, anything—ran out in front of her, she crept forward, trying to see around the piles to a possible exit—a door or window or anything that would give her a chance to escape. There was nothing—no convenient outside door into the root cellar, no window. The bare bulb was dim, though, and threw a harsh, white light that distorted shapes more and more the farther from the bulb she went.

What she wouldn't give for a flashlight. Sarah promised herself that she'd start carrying one at all times. A flashlight, and a utility knife, and a gun would've come in handy at the door earlier.

A wave of guilt swept over her. Could she have actually shot her brother?

Then she remembered that he was planning on basically selling her to *Logan Jovanovic*. Her flash of guilt disappeared, replaced by the burn of anger. Aaron was the one who should feel guilty. He'd locked her up, hurt her, driven her to escape, and now he'd just ruined the first place she'd ever been uncomplicatedly happy. Rage built until it was pounding against her insides, wanting out. At that moment, if she'd really had a gun in her hands, Sarah would've shot him without remorse... although she'd probably have aimed for his foot.

There was a shadowy alcove behind an old dresser stacked with dusty picture frames. Sarah's heart rate sped up with hope that she'd found a way out—one that didn't involve backtracking and running into Aaron. The large dresser mirror blocked her view, hiding the nook. Was there a door there? Could she be that lucky?

Sarah picked her way around some scattered scrap lumber and wire hangers so that she could wedge herself between the dresser and the wall. She held her breath as she brushed against both surfaces, unable to stop thinking about what was rubbing off onto her—dirt and dust and spiders and... She forced herself to quit obsessing before she completely lost her nerve.

From her new angle, she could see behind the mirror, but it was too dark, the shadows too deep, to make out any details. Carefully, Sarah climbed onto the top of the dresser, making sure not to knock any of the picture frames off onto the floor. Peering over the top of the mirror, she could see into the nook. Disappointment struck as she saw the alcove was lined with solid rock.

Tipping her head back as she closed her eyes in anxious frustration, Sarah forced herself to think. She had to find a way out of the basement, a way that didn't involve going back upstairs where Aaron was. She opened her eyes and spotted a wedge of light illuminating the wall beneath a piece of plywood, above and to the right of the dresser.

Looking closer, she saw it was sunlight. Her breath caught with hope as she realized that there was a window behind the wood. She carefully made her way to the side of the dresser. From that position, she could just reach the top of the board. She grabbed the upper edge and hooked her fingertips behind it, struggling not to cringe away as her nails penetrated the thick layer of spiderwebs between the plywood and the window frame.

Sarah pulled at the board, praying that the age of the wood and the nails holding it to the window frame would work in her favor, weakening it enough that she could yank it free. The wood creaked and tipped toward her, and Sarah's heart jumped with excitement. It was working. She redoubled her efforts, leaning back to use her weight as she hauled on the edge of the board.

With a crack, the nails holding the plywood pulled loose. Sarah lost her balance, toppling back off the dresser. Her arms flailed as she fell, smacking against the piled lumber and sending pieces flying across the dirt floor. She landed on her back with enough force to drive the air out of her lungs.

For a moment, she lay stunned and gasping for breath. Light from the newly uncovered window poured into the basement, blinding her. There was a squeak and a thump from the top of the stairs, and Sarah recognized the sound: someone had just opened the door to the basement.

Suddenly, her lack of air wasn't from her fall but

from sheer terror instead. Sarah scrambled to her feet and climbed onto the dresser again, her hands shaking as she grabbed the mirror for balance. When she heard heavy footsteps on the stairs, Sarah quit caring about staying quiet, knocking all the picture frames to the ground as she moved over next to the window.

The glass had been knocked out long ago. Although the window wasn't big, Sarah was pretty sure she could fit. For once, she was thankful for her small frame. Grasping the bottom of the window, she boosted herself up. Sarah managed to get her head and shoulders out of the opening before her arms started to shake. Her feet scrabbled against the stone wall, trying to find leverage.

A laugh, horribly familiar and humorless, came from behind and beneath her. "What are you doing, Alice?" her brother asked. He was close—too close—and terror gave her a surge of strength. She hauled herself up and out of the window until she was halfway through. Just her legs remained in the basement, but that was still too much. She was vulnerable, exposed.

Sarah arched her back, struggling to see over the window well into the front yard. If she screamed, would it bring help, or just Logan? Her frantic gaze scanned the area as she strained to get the rest of the way through the window. The sound of boots on gravel made her whip her head around. If Logan came at her, she'd be trapped. Her wonderful taste of freedom would be over.

It wasn't Logan, though. Instead, she saw Otto rushing from his parked squad car toward the front porch. Relief and gratitude and something else, something new, poured through her. It wasn't just that someone had come to help her, it was *Otto*. She knew he would keep her safe, and here he was, proving it. At that moment, her small crush grew, solidifying into something real and amazing.

"Otto!" she yelled, her voice breaking with fear and wonder that he was actually there when she needed him most. "Help me!"

His head whipped around, and his gaze locked on her. He headed toward her just as Aaron's iron-tight grip wrapped around both of her ankles. Releasing the frame, Sarah grabbed the metal edge of the window well, but its smooth, rounded edge didn't offer anything to grip. Aaron gave a yank, and her shoulders shrieked in protest as she was stretched between her hold on the window and her brother.

"*Otto!*" she yelped in panic, knowing she wouldn't be able to hang on for very long. In fact, one more good pull would bring her back into the basement, to face the wrath of her brother.

Suddenly, Otto was there. He grabbed her, wrapping his huge hands around her lower arms, and Sarah had never felt so relieved. Releasing the edge of the window well, she grasped his wrists as he hauled her toward him. "I've got you," he said.

"No, you don't," Aaron snarled, his grip on her ankles tightening until Sarah could almost feel the bones grinding against each other. She gave a gasping sob of pain as her brother yanked on her legs, trying to pull her back into the basement.

"Who's there?" Otto barked in a tone so sharp and commanding that Sarah flinched, even though she knew it wasn't directed toward her. "Police. Let her go now!"

Either Aaron was surprised that Otto was a cop, or he

obeyed automatically without thinking about it, but her brother's hold loosened for a second. It was just long enough that, when Otto hauled on her arms, her legs pulled loose of Aaron's grip. Sarah heard him swear as Otto dragged her through the window, her knee banging painfully against the frame.

As soon as she was clear, Otto grabbed her around the waist and lifted her. The world spun as he turned and ran. She locked her arms around his neck, marveling that he'd come, that he'd actually saved her. Even now, with Aaron and Logan still close by, Sarah felt like it would be okay. Otto was here, and he was holding her. They'd keep each other safe.

He carried her to his squad car, and shifted her weight to one arm so he could open the front passenger-side door. Placing her in the seat, he cupped the side of her face.

"Okay?" he asked, his gaze running over her in a fast, intent appraisal.

As soon as she gave a slight nod, he said, "Lock the doors." He swung the door closed and ran back to the window, crouching to look inside. She immediately pressed the door-lock button, feeling a flash of relief at the comforting click.

With a quick glance at where she sat in his car, Otto moved swiftly toward the side of the house. When he disappeared around the corner, Sarah immediately began to panic again. She huddled in her seat, wondering if she should stay in the car or be ready to run when Aaron came out the front door or around the other side of the house.

She swiveled her head, trying to see where Logan

was, but the yard and what she could see of the house were quiet. It was impossible to see beyond the first row of trees. The pines and aspens grew so closely together that the rest of the forest disappeared into shadow. Aaron or one of his men could be thirty feet away from her, and Sarah wouldn't know. She shivered and started chewing on her thumbnail.

Instead of making her feel better, the quiet just scared her more. Were Aaron and Logan ganging up on Otto? He was a strong guy and a cop, but could he take on two armed criminals? She stared at the empty windows, wishing desperately to know what was happening. Did he need her help? She wasn't a trained fighter, but she couldn't leave him to the mercy of Aaron and Logan.

Her hand inched toward the door handle, but she froze at movement inside the opened front door. Logan ran out, a gun in his hand. After a paralyzed moment, Sarah slid down in her seat, attempting to hide, but it was too late. He'd spotted her.

He strode toward her, getting closer and closer until she could see his cocky, cold grin. She shrank away, pushing back in her seat, unable to tear her gaze from the man she'd been ordered to marry. All she could see was evil. She'd thought Otto had saved her, but it had only been a short reprieve. Logan was there, and he was going to either kill her or force her to return to her prison in Texas.

Her jaw set so firmly that her teeth clicked together. *No.* She'd barely gotten a taste of freedom, barely experienced the joy of making friends and feeding orphaned puppies and having a crush on a guy, and she wasn't about to go back without a fight.

She ripped her gaze away from Logan's and looked under the steering column. The keys weren't in it, and Sarah felt her tiny hope that she could just drive away extinguish. She grabbed for the radio mic, instead.

When Logan saw her holding it, his smug smile disappeared, and he raised his gun. Sarah quickly pushed the only button on the side of the mic. "Hello? We need help. I'm calling from Otto Gunnersen's ca—"

Logan pulled the trigger. There was a loud crack, and then the side window turned from transparent to opaque and covered in cobwebbing cracks. With a yelp, she flinched, dropping the mic as her arms flew up to cover her head. She heard Logan laugh, and her entire body felt cold.

"Caller, what is your location? Caller, are you there? Please respond."

She fumbled to grab the mic from where it was dangling just above the floor in front of the driver's seat. With another bone-chilling laugh, Logan raised his gun again. How many shots before the glass broke completely, leaving nothing but air between her and a bullet?

Logan's finger started to pull back on the trigger.

Frantic, Sarah looked down at the panel and pushed a button. The siren screamed, and Logan, startled, jerked the gun down as he fired. The car rocked as the bullet hit the door. He was scowling now, obviously furious that she'd made him flinch. This time, he aimed right for the already damaged window.

Sarah grabbed for the mic as the bullet struck the window. The sound was more of a crunch that time, and she couldn't keep herself from cowering at the sound. There was a clatter that was barely audible over the still-blaring siren, and Sarah looked up.

The remains of the glass had fallen. A jagged, empty hole framed Logan's grinning face. He pointed the gun at her.

"Out of the car, *fiancée*." She clutched the mic tighter, her gaze darting around as she looked for something that would save her. Did squad cars have guns in their glove compartments? A hand grenade, maybe? "Get out now, or I'll shoot you. I don't like to lose."

Desperately trying to think of a way out, Sarah reached a shaking hand toward the unlock button.

"Turn that noise off first," he said, sounding annoyed. Grateful for any delay, she pushed the button. With a final whoop, it went silent...but then immediately started up again.

"I said turn it off!" Logan yelled.

"I did!" Even as she stared at the button, she realized that the siren wasn't coming from Otto's car. Another squad car, its overhead lights flashing, raced around the final curve of the driveway.

"Fuck!" Logan gave her a final hard glare before he took off, heading for the trees. The newly arrived squad car stopped at the edge of the yard, and Theo jumped out. Still running, Logan fired off several shots behind him, and Theo ducked behind his opened door. He returned fire, but Logan disappeared into the trees.

As Theo started to give chase, Sarah fumbled with the handle. The door finally opened so abruptly that she almost fell out. "Theo! Otto went after Aaron! He needs help!"

Theo immediately pulled up, although he kept a close eye on the spot where Logan had been. "Where?"

"Aaron was in the basement, but I don't know where they ended up."

Theo headed for the open front door, just as Otto came around the corner. He had a firm grip on a hand-cuffed Aaron's arm. When Sarah saw them, a wall of emotions slammed into her, but relief was by far the strongest. Otto was okay. Her knees went wobbly, and she sank back down on the seat, ignoring the bits of safety glass scattered around her.

Aaron was being arrested. Logan had run away. Could it actually be over?

Once Theo saw Otto and Aaron, he turned and jogged back to his squad car. He leashed Viggy, who was already wearing a bulletproof vest, and the two headed into the woods after Logan.

Hugh's truck barreled around the turn, coming to a halt behind Theo's car. Lexi, Hugh's K9, followed him out of the pickup cab. She tore toward the house, but a sharp word from Hugh made her turn around and return to his side. Another squad car flew up the driveway, and then a marked SUV arrived. Soon, there seemed to be cops everywhere. As soon as her legs were semi-steady, Sarah stood and moved toward the hood of Otto's squad car. She couldn't look at the ruined window anymore. It made her think of how close she'd been to getting shot—or taken.

Otto walked Aaron toward one of the other squad cars. As they crossed the yard, Aaron's gaze was fixed on Sarah. His face was expressionless, but she knew he was coldly, deadly furious. She started to shrink back but then caught herself. There was no reason to be scared of her brother anymore. He'd been arrested. She was finally safe…for now, at least.

Otto sat Aaron in the back of the squad car and then hurried over to Sarah. He stood close, but not close enough. She fought back the temptation to throw herself into his arms, to hide her face against him and let him keep her safe.

"You okay?" he asked, his gaze scanning her body, as if checking for injuries.

Sarah took a mental inventory. Besides being a little shaky and sore, she was fine. "Yes."

"Would you be up to telling us what happened?" The way he spoke, so softly and gently, was soothing. His tone, paired with his reassuring strength, made Sarah calm down, bit by bit. She sucked in the first deep breath she'd taken since she'd opened the door to find Aaron on the porch.

"Of course." As the panic ebbed, her thoughts rushed in. "Jules! She and the kids are in the woods!" Sarah lunged away from the car. She had to go find them, help them. Logan was still out there… All the terror that had faded roared to life again.

Otto made a shushing sound, a kind of soft hiss through his teeth that reminded Sarah of something Chester—her brother's driver and one of the only two kind people in her old life—would do to calm a startled horse. It worked on Sarah, as well. To her surprise, she found herself settling back against the side of the car, close to him. "Jules and the kids are fine. She let the dispatcher know that they ran to Steve's house."

"Oh. Good." As relief flowed through her, so did exhaustion, and her head dropped back. A strand of hair escaped her ponytail and tangled in her eyelashes. Otto reached out and brushed it to the side, tucking it carefully behind her ear. She blinked at him, startled by how good that small touch had felt. His hands were so big—all of Otto was so big—but he was the gentlest person Sarah had ever met. She felt her heart expanding like a balloon, filling until it pressed almost painfully against her ribs.

"You sure you're okay to tell us what happened?" he asked.

"Yes." She took a breath. "I'm fine."

Sarah pushed away from the car, but Otto didn't move. She paused, looking at him uncertainly, and realized that their faces were just inches apart. They stared at each other, frozen, until Hugh clearing his throat made both of them jump.

"Any day, lovebirds," he called. "Grace and a *Tattered Hearts* marathon are waiting for me at home. If I'm not back soon, I know she's going to start without me. She's rude like that."

"I don't think she's starting without you," Theo said, looking at the driveway. When Sarah followed his gaze, she spotted Grace pulling up behind Hugh's truck. As soon as she climbed out of her car, Hugh was right next to her, frowning. Otto had stepped back, so Sarah moved away from the squad car absently, watching Grace and Hugh with fascination. Hugh was always smiling, so his ferocious scowl looked strange on him.

"Why is he so upset?" Sarah whispered to Otto.

"Pretty sure he told her to stay at his place," Otto murmured, leaning down so that he could speak quietly right into her ear. His breath brushed against the side of her neck as he spoke, and Sarah shivered.

"I'm not Lexi," Grace said as she faced off against

Hugh, her hands on her hips. "You can't tell me to stay. Well, you can, but I won't."

"Obviously." Hugh leaned in closer. "If you'd stayed at home, like I asked you to do, you wouldn't be here, in the middle of a dangerous situation."

Grace barked a laugh. "If it's so dangerous, why are you standing here yelling at me? Shouldn't you secure the perimeter or arrest a perp or somehow make it *less* dangerous?"

Although he made an attempt to hold on to his peeved expression, Sarah could tell that Hugh was amused. Even after meeting him just a few times, she recognized the way his mouth tucked in at the corners. Sarah was pretty sure he was just a few seconds away from laughing. "It's under control now, but you didn't know that. You could've walked into a really bad scene."

"This is my home." Grace's tone had softened a little, though. "Jules, Sarah, and the kids were here. I needed to find out what was happening, to help if I could."

"You need to stay safe."

"Your definition of keeping me safe involves locking me in a tower lined with bubble wrap," Grace shot back, although she sounded more fond than annoyed now. Sarah, though, flinched at her words. Were all men like Aaron, wanting to lock away the women they loved, needing to keep them safe to the point of making them prisoners?

Even as the thought crossed her mind, Sarah dismissed it. If she'd said to Aaron what Grace had just said to Hugh, Sarah would've been on the floor, bleeding. Aaron wasn't normal. Most guys were nothing like her brother. Sarah sent a quick glance toward Otto.

Some guys were his exact opposite, in fact. Otto had saved her from her brother, and then he'd arrested him. Thanks to Otto, she was finally safe. He'd given her back her freedom.

CHAPTER 9

THEO WAS PACING AGAIN.

As he sprawled in a chair in Jules's kitchen, Otto watched his partner stride back and forth, crossing from the back door to the hallway entrance and then angrily retracing his steps again. It wasn't as if Theo was doing anything especially interesting. Pacing was his usual response to a stressful situation, and Otto had seen him do it hundreds of times. Watching Theo, however, was keeping Otto's eyes away from Sarah—no, *Alice*. If he let his gaze stray, it kept turning toward her.

"So, Alice, you were hiding from your brother?" Hugh asked. He was also sitting, but his chair was arranged right next to Grace's, close enough that he could keep an arm around her. Grace didn't seem to mind. Otto glanced at Sarah despite himself. They were seated on the same side of the table, although there was an empty chair between them. Even with that wooden chaperone, they were still close enough that sweat beaded on the back of Otto's neck. He resisted the urge to wipe it away, knowing that eagle-eyed Hugh would notice his nervous tic. Sometimes, it was hard to work with people who knew him as well as Hugh and Theo did.

"Call me Sarah. I don't want to be Alice anymore. And yes. My mom passed away when I was a baby. I don't remember her. My father wasn't a good man, and my brother's even worse. They didn't share details of the business with me, but I lived in the middle of it. It wasn't too hard to figure out. Both my father and Aaron were very controlling and cruel. A...friend helped me escape." Although she was sitting, Sarah wasn't still. She shifted in her chair, leaning forward and back, occasionally chewing on her thumbnail before jerkily returning her hand to her lap. Otto fought the urge to reach across the chair and put a soothing hand on her arm or rub her back or... The back of his neck prickled, and he rubbed at it instead.

"What's wrong with you?" Hugh asked.

Otto jerked his hand back down, but it was too late. Hugh was starting to smile. He looked from Sarah to Otto, his gaze a little bit knowing and a whole lot devilish.

"What?" Sarah asked faintly.

Hugh laughed. "Oh, I didn't mean you. I was talking to the offspring of Paul Bunyan over there."

"Hugh," Theo said sharply, pausing in his pacing to give Hugh a glare. "Focus." He looked at Sarah. "How old are you?"

"Twenty-three." She sounded a little confused by the question, but Otto knew where Theo was going.

"Why did you have to run?" Theo asked, glancing out the window as he passed the sink. "You're an adult. Why not just move out? Your brother doesn't have any legal authority over you."

"He doesn't seem to care about that." Although his words came out mildly, Otto was seething on the inside, remembering the pain on her face as her brother tried to yank her back into the basement.

Sarah shot him a grateful look that warmed Otto's belly. "He doesn't. If I'd told him I was moving out, he would've locked me in my room until I was eighty—no"—she corrected herself—"until my wedding day."

Needing something to do with his hands, Otto picked up a spoon that was sitting on the table. Even as he did so, he marveled at his strange behavior. He wasn't a fidgety person. Something about Sarah, though, made him as twitchy as Bean, the horse that was his newest rescue project.

"Your wedding day?" Grace repeated. "If you're locked in your room, how are you going to find a groom?"

Sarah's face tightened in a way that made Otto want to go to the police department, corner Aaron in his holding cell, and choke the life out of him. It was a good thing that Aaron wouldn't be in Monroe for much longer. The FBI had been very excited to hear that the Monroe police had arrested Aaron Blanchett, and they were sending agents to pick him up as soon as they could arrange a transfer. The entire Monroe Police Department—what was left of it, at least, since three quarters of the officers left for the winter—had joined Theo in searching for Logan. There'd been no trace. The Texas authorities were notified, but Logan hadn't been spotted yet. Otto wasn't too hopeful that they'd find the fugitive. He had a feeling Logan would disappear.

"Aaron's already found the groom," Sarah said, and Otto's whole body went stiff. "Logan Jovanovic."

"Ugh!" Grace groaned. "I met him briefly at the police station where he tried to kill me."

Sarah stared at Grace, but everyone else had heard the story, so she was the only one shocked. Otto did notice that Hugh scowled and tucked Grace closer to his side, though. "Logan Jovanovic tried to kill you, too?"

"What?" Jules stood in the entrance to the hallway, her face chalk white. Theo immediately strode over to wrap an arm around her. She leaned in to him but kept her gaze locked on Sarah. "What about Logan Jovanovic?" Her voice shook a little as she said the name.

"He tried to kill Grace," Sarah said.

"I know that part." Jules still looked too pale, although her voice was fairly even. "How do *you* know Logan Jovanovic?"

"He shot out Otto's car window today, and I'm supposed to marry him." Sarah was trying to sound brave, but her voice quavered. "Aaron thought that giving me to Logan would give him an opportunity to take over the Jovanovics' business. Supposedly, the Jovanovic family is a mess right now, with Noah and Martin in jail."

"What the hell did you just do to that spoon?" Hugh asked, looking at Otto's hands.

Otto glanced down, staring blankly at the twisted metal clutched in his white-knuckled grip. He looked at Jules. "Sorry."

"What?" She waved a hand. "It's just a spoon. Don't worry about it." Still pale, Jules turned back to Sarah. "Your brother's name is Aaron? Aaron what?"

"Blanchett."

At the name, Jules leaned against Theo. He wrapped his arms around her. "Do you know him?"

"Yeah, I know him—well, of him. I wanted to work for him at one point."

"Why?" Sarah said, sounding bewildered. "He's not a good person to work for...at all."

"I know." Straightening and turning to face Theo, Jules said, "I tried to keep this a secret. It wasn't that I didn't trust you, but I didn't want to put you in a bad spot. I mean, I broke the law. I'm still breaking the law, and not in a jaywalking, take-the-tag-off-the-mattress way. It's serious, and I didn't want you to have to decide between your duty as a cop and how you felt about me."

"Jules." Theo cupped her face in his hands, speaking directly to her, as if no one else was in the room. "No matter what you did, I'm on your side—yours and the kids. Are they here?" He glanced toward the hall, as if expecting Jules's siblings to be listening in.

"They're still at Steve's. Dee and the twins are friends with his kids."

"Good," Theo said. "Tell us what happened. I'm pretty sure I've figured out most of it, anyway."

Curling her fingers around Theo's wrists, Jules leaned in to kiss him lightly. "I love you."

"Okay, okay, okay." Hugh broke into the tender moment. "You both love each other and complete each other and would climb every mountain for each other. We get it. Enough with the kissy-kissy. Tell us what happened."

Jules looked a little startled, as if she'd also forgotten about the spectators to her and Theo's tender scene. "Oh. Okay. Um…my stepmother is a horrible person, and my dad has early-onset Alzheimer's. I've been trying to get custody of my siblings, but I lost my CPA license after being questioned by the FBI, so I had no way to pay for attorney fees. I went to Mr. Es—uh, a slightly shady contact of mine and asked for a reference so I could work as an accountant for the Jovanovics or Blanchetts—"

There was a collective, audible inhale from everyone in the kitchen, and Jules put up a hand. "I know, I know. It was stupid, but I was desperate, and no one legitimate would hire me after the FBI thing. The contact wouldn't give me the reference, but he gave me money and the name of someone who would set up new identities for me and the kids. So…I kidnapped them and drove from Florida to Colorado."

There was a pause before Hugh repeated, "Kidnapped them?"

"Sam, Tio, Ty, and Dee. They wanted to be kidnapped, though, so that made it less evil than it sounds." Jules kept her gaze focused on an expressionless Theo. Otto recognized his partner's "thinking" face, the one he got when he was processing information.

"Why wasn't there a huge police response?" Hugh asked. "Four kids—including twins—are pretty distinctive, and I don't remember an Amber Alert."

"Mr.…the slightly shady contact has evidence of the worst of my stepmother's abuse." Jules's mouth pulled tight, and her eyes were glossy as she wrapped her arms around her middle. "He told her that he'd release it to the police if she reported the kidnapping. I'm sure she has private investigators working on it, though."

Theo reached out and gently tugged Jules toward him. As she rested her head against his chest, he wrapped his arms around her.

"Do you hate me?" she asked in a small voice.

Theo cupped the back of her head with his hand. "I could never hate you, especially not for this."

"I'm a felon."

"You're a good sister." Her body jerked with a single sob, and her hands clutched the sides of his shirt as Theo kissed the top of her head. "We'll figure this out, Jules. Together."

"I love you." The words were clear, despite her tears.

"I love you, too."

"Why not just turn in the evidence immediately?" Hugh asked, interrupting their sweet moment. "She'd be arrested, and you'd get custody. Problem solved."

"Sam was her main victim." Jules turned her head so that her voice wasn't muffled against Theo's chest. There were tears streaming down her cheeks. "He doesn't want anyone to know. He's so ashamed. I tell him over and over it wasn't his fault, but he doesn't believe that. If he had to testify…" She trailed off, her mouth drawing down at the corners. "He wouldn't be able to do it. If he tried, for us, her lawyers would tear him to pieces. It would destroy him."

Otto realized that he was torturing the twisted spoon again, and he set it carefully on the table. He'd known that Sam had been abused. The signs were all there—his stutter, his wariness, his whole demeanor. It was still hard to hear it confirmed.

"Now that we're finally all sharing, how did you end up here?" Hugh asked Grace. Before she could answer, he spoke again. "I know that you were dating Jovanovic—"

"Barely dating," Grace interrupted to clarify. "Noah and I had been on, like, three dates."

"You were dating Noah Jovanovic?" Sarah asked in a hushed voice. "He completely freaks me out—his uncle Martin, too."

"Until Grace met me," Hugh said with pretend pompousness, "her taste in men was…well, a little sad."

Grace pinched Hugh's thigh, making him yelp. "I'll have you know, I'm still questioning my judgment." She gave him a teasing, sideways glance when he protested. "Yes, all the Jovanovics turned out to be scary. At least Noah and Martin and some of their other top guys are in jail now."

"I wish Logan was," Sarah said.

Theo looked at her with a frown. "Sorry we didn't get him. Viggy tracked him through the trees, and then his trail ended. We're assuming he ran to where he'd parked a car earlier. There's a nationwide BOLO out for him. He'll be picked up soon."

"Why did you both come here, though?" Hugh repeated, returning to the earlier conversation. "Why were you—and then Sarah—sent to Jules?"

The three women exchanged a glance that told Otto he and the other cops were not going to get that information. "He asked for a favor," Jules finally non-answered.

"He who?" Theo asked.

"The slightly shady guy I know."

"Name?"

Widening her eyes, Jules gave Theo an innocent look. "I can't remember. I'm sure it was a fake one anyway."

With a disbelieving snort, Hugh nudged Grace. "You must've worked with this 'shady guy,' too. What's his name?"

"No clue." Grace spread her hands in such a dramatic way that Otto wanted to laugh. It was obvious that the women were protecting the person who helped them escape. He couldn't blame them.

Theo and Hugh silently turned their gazes to Sarah.
As she shrank back in her chair, Otto had the urge to
stand in front of her to block the other men's intimidating
glares. "I forget?" Sarah said in a tiny voice. "I just hope
Aaron didn't find him." Otto saw her widen her eyes at
Jules, who gave the tiniest shake of her head as she pulled
her phone out of her pocket, wiggling it meaningfully.
By the way Sarah's shoulders relaxed, Otto assumed that
gesture meant that the mystery man had texted Jules and
assured her that he was alive and well.

"Oh, for Pete's sake!" Hugh sounded like he was
trying not to laugh. "You all are the absolute worst at
trying to be sneaky."

Faint, squeaking protests came from the other room,
and Otto stood, even as Sarah jumped to her feet, looking relieved. "The puppies!" She hurried toward the
hallway. "They must be hungry."

Otto followed her out as the others continued their
discussion in the kitchen. Sarah glanced over her shoulder and slowed, allowing him to catch up. When they
were walking side by side, alone, he immediately lost
his ability to talk. Ideas for different topics of conversation bounced around in his head, but it didn't matter. He
couldn't force any words out of his mouth.

"Thank you," she said, jerking him out of his mental
scramble.

"For what?" His voice sounded gritty, but at least
he'd managed to speak.

Sarah smiled at him. "For saving me. If you hadn't
been there, Aaron would've pulled me right back into the
basement, and who knows where I would be right now."

Anger rushed through him at the thought of Aaron

stealing Sarah away, of hurting her and forcing her to marry that asshole Jovanovic against her will. Otto's rage was strong enough that he forgot his nervousness and wrapped an arm around Sarah's shoulders. She stiffened at the contact but didn't move away. Her bones felt fragile and prominent under his hand, reminding him of the orphaned baby hawk he'd once cared for.

Clearing her throat, Sarah spoke again. "So...um, thank you."

"You're welcome." They were standing in the living room, right next to the puppies' crate, but Otto didn't want to let go. "Sorry we didn't get Jovanovic."

"That's not your fault, or Theo's. I told him to help you first. I was so terrified that Aaron would hurt you. I shouldn't have pulled you into my mess. You could've been killed." She stared up at him, her brown eyes earnest and soft, and Otto couldn't look away. He'd come so close to losing her, and he hadn't even had a chance to really get to know her yet. It didn't matter that they'd met just a couple of weeks earlier. She was already important to him.

Her lips parted slightly, and his gaze focused on her mouth. She was so beautiful and so sweet. Without thinking, he found himself leaning closer. Sarah didn't move away, and he stopped breathing. Up close, she was even more perfect. It felt like she was drawing him in, pulling him closer without even having to touch him.

One of the puppies gave an especially loud, warbling cry, and Otto jerked back, startled.

"Sorry, puppies," Sarah said, crouching down to open their crate. "You must be starving. I was so worried you'd wake up and Aaron would find you. I'm putting everyone in danger. The sooner I leave town, the better it will be for everyone." She pulled out two wriggling, grunting bodies and offered them to Otto. Once he accepted them, she picked up the last two and stood. Sarah looked down at the puppies in her arms, a worried frown on her face. Otto wished his hands weren't full so that he could give her a comforting hug.

"Don't leave town. Come stay with me," he blurted out, shocking himself—and Sarah, from her expression.

"With you?" she repeated faintly, and he could feel the back of his neck begin to itch again.

"Just till we find Logan Jovanovic and bring him in. It's safer there." Otto resisted the urge to rub his neck. "There's a bunker with…ah, tunnels. And food." He closed his eyes for a moment in self-annoyance. He'd just told Sarah that she should come stay with him because of tunnels and food. He was hopeless.

She made a noncommittal sound, but she didn't agree—or disagree—with his plan. A tiny spark of hope glowed in his belly. If she stayed at his place, she wouldn't leave town. In fact, she'd be around him all the time. Heat from that small fire began to spread, filling him with something a lot warmer than hope.

They returned to the kitchen in silence, although he couldn't stop himself from shooting quick glances at her profile. She looked thoughtful and conflicted and so pretty that he found it hard to look away. One of the puppies he was holding made a disgruntled sound, wiggling in his hold, and he absently soothed it with his thumb.

As they entered the kitchen, both Otto and Sarah ducked when the spoon Otto had mangled flew through the air, hitting the stove with a clatter.

"Sorry!" Grace said, standing and crossing to where the spoon still spun on the floor. "That wasn't aimed at you. I actually threw it at Hugh's stupid head, but he plays really good defense, so it deflected off his hand and that's when you two walked in."

"Why were you throwing a spoon at Hugh?" Sarah asked. Obviously, she hadn't been around Hugh and Grace very much. It seemed to Otto that something was always flying between them, whether it was words or pillows or random spoons. They made up as quickly as they started a fight, and that part was almost as awkward for everyone else involved.

"Apparently," Grace said, stretching out the word with a long glare at Hugh, "I'm supposed to marry him and move into his house like a good little woman."

"Oh." Sarah blinked several times, and Otto had to hold back a laugh. He could've warned her that the answer would be something like that. He noticed that Theo and Jules were also eyeing each other in a way that meant they were in the middle of a disagreement.

Grace reached for one of the puppies in Otto's hand, and he relinquished it. When Hugh held out his hands, though, Otto pivoted away, blocking him with his body. "Get your own puppy."

Hugh turned to Sarah, but she held her hands up, showing that they were empty, before moving to the counter to mix the milk replacer. Theo and Jules, both cuddling a puppy, smirked at Hugh, who huffed. "Don't you have to go back to work?"

Theo glanced at his watch and frowned. Giving Jules a kiss on the cheek, he handed his puppy off to Hugh. "How can you even feed it with a cast on?"

"Even with only one-and-a-quarter arms, I'm very... agile." He gave Grace a wink, making her giggle.

Turning back to Jules, he said, "I'll be back after five. Think about what I said."

She made a face at him, but then smiled. "Be safe."

Once he left the kitchen, Otto looked at Hugh, Grace, and Jules. All were focusing much too hard on their respective puppies. "What?" he asked.

"Nothing," Jules replied too quickly. "Just Theo and Hugh are being overprotective freaks again."

At Hugh's unhappy-sounding grunt, Sarah turned from where she was filling bottles. As she took in their various expressions, her face fell. "This is about me staying here, isn't it?"

During the beat of silence before Grace spoke, Sarah looked even more miserable. "Don't worry about that," Grace said. "Having your brother and fake fiancé come after you is nothing. I mean, Hugh's stalker blew up the diner—and shot at us."

"So did mine," Jules added quickly. "We're all running from something."

"No." Sarah screwed the tops on the bottles, her gaze fixed on her task. Otto wanted to hug her again. "They're right. What if Jules and the kids hadn't been outside? What if they hadn't gotten away? I need to leave."

"He's in jail," Otto said, hating how sad she looked. "He can't get to you anymore. Every cop in the country is watching for Jovanovic. If he shows his face, he'll be arrested. You're safe now."

She offered him a towel, a bottle, and a bittersweet smile. "Thanks, Otto, but what if he gets out on bail or something? I don't trust Aaron. He doesn't care what or who he has to destroy to get what he wants. I shouldn't drag any of you—and especially not the kids—into this mess with me." She studied Otto's face, her expression serious. "Does your offer still stand?"

"What offer?" Grace and Hugh chorused.

"Yes." Otto's heart rate quickened.

"Then I'd love to stay with you and your bunker and your tunnels." She gave him a smile that didn't quite work. "At least I can help with the puppies when you're on duty."

Despite the grave situation, excitement buzzed through Otto's veins. She'd be staying with him, living in his house, sleeping just a room away. It was almost too good to be true.

What am I doing?

It was the hundredth time Sarah had asked herself that question. She eyed Otto's broad back as he led her on a tour of his house. It was beautiful, an old farmhouse in much, much better condition than Jules's place, and animals seemed to be everywhere. A one-eared gray tabby blinked at them from his spot on the top of the couch, and a fawn-and-black Belgian Malinois with a graying muzzle thumped his tail against the hardwood floor without getting up from his spot next to a heating vent. Outside, a lanky bay gelding shared a paddock with a goat, and a rainbow variety of chickens scratched in the expansive run attached to the coop.

They'd driven for miles of twisting mountain roads before arriving. Otto's property was set in a valley surrounded by bluffs. It looked as though a giant had pressed his thumb into the mountain. Rock rose on all sides of the property, creating a huge hollow for Otto's house to nestle in.

The moment Sarah had gotten out of Otto's squad car, his property felt like home. She'd taken the first deep breath she'd had in weeks as she'd looked around, feeling the tension seeping out of her as the peace of the place settled deep inside. Otto's home fit him. She felt an echo of the same security and reassurance that the man himself emanated.

It was beautiful and safe and already felt like home, but what was she doing there? Otto had barely spoken to her, and she'd seized on his offer like a desperate person…which she was. When the reality of her situation had struck her, along with the knowledge that Jules or Grace or Sam or Ty or Tio or Dee could be hurt the next time that someone from her past came for her, Sarah knew she couldn't allow that to happen. Aaron was in jail. That was the only reason she wasn't already on the road out of town. Logan barely knew her. Without Aaron to prod him, he would most likely leave her alone. Logically, she knew that no one else would be chasing after her, but it was still terrifying to stay. What if she was wrong?

Otto was looking at her expectantly, like he was waiting for an answer, and Sarah felt heat creep up her neck to her cheeks. "Sorry," she said. "I was distracted. What did you ask?"

"Would you like to sleep upstairs or in the bunker?"

"Upstairs," she answered immediately, without having to consider it. A bunker sounded too close to being locked in for her own safety. She'd move out of Jules's house to keep them safe, but she wouldn't lock herself away, not even to hide from her past. After all, her main reason for leaving had been to gain her freedom. If she remained in Otto's basement bunker like some kind of human/mole hybrid, she might as well have stayed locked up in her childhood home.

"I'll show you how to get to the bunker," he said, crossing the living room to what looked like a closet. "Just in case."

Curious, she followed him into the closet and watched as he pushed aside hanging coats and opened a hidden door at the back. Sarah peeked around him as he flicked a light switch.

"Wow," she said, peering down the flight of stairs. "This is great."

He gave her a small, pleased smile as he led the way down into the bunker. It was bigger than she'd expected, with what looked like years' worth of food and water stacked on shelves that circled the room. There were several bunks along one side, and she was glad she'd chosen to sleep upstairs—the beds didn't look that comfortable. The bunker was brighter and bigger and less prison-like than she'd expected, though.

She peered down a corridor on the opposite side as the stairs. "Where does this go?"

"If you go left, it'll take you into the barn," he said. "Stay straight, and it connects with the old mining tunnels. I like having a lot of possible exits."

"I get it." After the terrifying game of hide-and-seek she'd just played with Aaron, she understood all too well.

"There are packs here," he said, nodding toward several camping backpacks hanging on the wall. "If you need to leave the house, even if you're not planning on going far, always bring basic supplies. Water, food, matches, a folding knife, extra layers." He pointed at each item as he named it.

"Water, food, knife, layers," she repeated.

"Matches."

"And matches. Got it." It was sweet, how he was so intent on keeping her safe. She didn't plan to wander into the wilderness without him, but it was still good information to have.

He frowned at her. "Are you warm enough?"

"Right now?" When he just continued to eye her, as if using X-ray vision to determine how many layers she was wearing, she answered, "I'm fine. Thank you."

"There's long underwear here if you need it."

Long underwear, she'd found out recently, was not sexy. At all. For some reason, though, his offer made her blush. "Thank you."

"There are coats, gloves, hats—if you need anything, just take it."

"I will. Thank you."

He held out a stocking hat, and she accepted it automatically. The knit was warm where his hand had been. "It's important to keep your head warm."

She smiled at him, holding the hat. His gaze dropped to her mouth and then he looked at the floor as he cleared his throat. "Want to see your bedroom?"

"Sure." As they left the bunker, she gave a last, quick glance at the mysterious tunnels. She'd love to explore them, but that could wait. After all, she'd be living here now. An excited shiver coursed through her, and Otto frowned at her again.

"You're cold," he said. "You should put on your hat."

Rather than explain her true reason for shivering, she pulled on the hat and followed Otto up to the main level. As they crossed the living room and started up the second set of stairs, she couldn't help but admire the way his muscles moved under the material of his uniform pants.

Pervert, she scolded herself, pulling her gaze away. For as big of a guy as he was, she was amazed that he didn't seem to have any fat on him. It was all muscle. She remembered how his corded wrists had felt under her grip while he pulled her through the basement window, and she shivered again. He was sweet and strong, and she needed to stop this crush immediately.

Even as she cut off her Otto-related thoughts abruptly, though, she wondered why she had to. Maybe it wasn't a one-sided silly crush. He'd told her that she was pretty—well, that her mouth was pretty—and he'd put his arm around her, and he'd invited her to live with him. Plus, at Jules's, she'd been almost positive that he was about to kiss her before they'd been interrupted. As isolated as she'd been in Texas, Sarah was still pretty certain that a guy wouldn't do all those things if he didn't like her—or if he wasn't at least attracted to her a little.

"Is this okay?" Otto asked, and Sarah had to yank herself out of her obsessive thoughts yet again.

She looked around the bedroom. "Oh yes. It's beautiful."

"Bathroom's across the hall." Clearing his throat, he glanced away. "We'll have to share. Hope that's okay."

At the word *share*, the image of sharing the shower with him popped into Sarah's head, making her blush. Other less lustful ideas followed—of brushing their teeth together and dodging around each other as they hurried to get ready in the morning. Those thoughts, where they were happy and settled and together, were even more seductive than the first ones. She'd never had anything like that. She'd never really thought she'd get to. "That's fine," she hurried to say when she realized he was waiting for a response.

"Are you tired?" he asked after a short silence.

"No." Sarah wondered if she should've said she was, just to be polite. They'd been together since he'd saved her from her brother. He might need a break from her.

"Want me to show you around outside?"

"Yes," she answered, too quickly. Even if he needed some time away from her, she wasn't ready to let him go.

He looked pleased, though, rather than annoyed or harassed, as he led the way back down the stairs and through the kitchen. The old dog pushed to his feet with a low groan as they passed and followed them to the door.

"Is it okay if he goes with us?" she asked, petting the dog's head.

"Sure." Otto held the door for both of them to pass through. "That's Mort. He was my partner, but he's retired now."

Sarah watched the dog trot down the steps. "You haven't replaced him yet?"

"Not yet." He put his hand at the small of her back, steady but barely touching, as they walked toward the paddock holding the horse and goat. Sarah could feel the heat of him through her shirt and hoodie. "It's expensive and time-consuming to buy and train a new dog. We've been…busy lately."

Shooting him a sideways glance, Sarah remembered the conversation they'd all had in the kitchen earlier that morning. "All the explosions?"

He scowled, as if remembering. "Yes, and the shootings. Hugh kept getting hurt. Hopefully, that's over, and we can have our usual quiet winter."

"Things do seem really quiet in town," she said, trying to distract herself from the fact that even Otto's cranky face fascinated her. Clouds slipped across the sun, blocking it for a few moments, just as the breeze kicked up. Sarah shivered, and Otto's hand moved from her back to her hip, tucking her closer against him as if sheltering her against the wind. She decided she liked that even more than the hand on her back.

"Most people leave Monroe in the winter," he said, keeping her close as they walked. Sarah basked in his heat and nearness, as well as his unusual chattiness. It was nice not to have the stilted silences. "About three-quarters of the people, in fact."

"Why?" she asked. To her, Monroe seemed like a paradise. She couldn't imagine anyone wanting to leave.

"It gets cold, and it snows—a lot." He opened the paddock gate and held it for her as she moved through. Mort stayed out, sniffing around a tree ten feet away. "There's no ski resort here, and the highway gets closed down often, especially over the passes."

"And that's the only way through town." It finally clicked how isolated Monroe was. The only way in or out was east or west on the highway, and there was a mountain pass on either side. If they were closed down frequently, like Otto was explaining, then the people in Monroe were stuck—possibly for weeks on end. Sarah wasn't sure if she found the idea reassuring or terrifying.

The goat trotted up to greet them, and Otto pulled something out of his pocket—a treat, judging by the goat's enthusiastic chewing.

"This is Hortense," Otto said, scratching the goat on her neck as she leaned into the caress. "The horse is Bean. He's still not sure about people, but he's more timid than aggressive."

Sarah studied the horse, who was staring back at them, his ears flicking back and forth with uncertain interest. He was tall and lean, with long legs and a veiny, sensitive face. His ribs showed, but not overly much, and he gave the impression of nerves and speed with a mane and tail tacked on. "Where'd he come from?"

"The racetrack outside Denver, originally." Otto gave Hortense another treat. "Bean wasn't very fast, so he was sold a couple of years ago. He went through a few more homes before he ended up with a rancher southwest of here, in a stall right next to a couple of wild boars the rancher was raising. Poor Bean was scared out of his mind. He tried to climb right out of there a couple of times, and the rancher had no idea what to do with a spooky, timid Thoroughbred. I traded a few bales of alfalfa hay for him."

As Otto talked, Bean had been slowly making his way closer until he was just a few feet away. Sarah kept her attention on Otto, not wanting to startle the horse away. "He's right behind you," she said quietly.

"I know." Otto stood, calm and relaxed, as Bean

stretched out, blowing out a puff of air against the back
of Otto's neck. Sarah held her breath, waiting to see
what the horse would do. After another exhale, Bean
snorted and shied, dodging away from them. Once he
was a safe distance away, he turned to watch them again.

Sarah smiled. "He almost seems like he's playing."

With a shrug, Otto gave Hortense a final pat before
moving toward the gate. "Part of him is scared, and
part of him is curious. Every time I don't give him anything to be scared about, that part gets smaller. He'll
come around."

As she walked through the gate, Sarah gave Bean one
last glance. "I like horses. The person who took care of
my father's horses let me help with them."

"Did you have any pets?"

"No." She paused before admitting, "When I was
small, I had a kitten, Laila, but only for a few weeks."

"What happened?"

"My father was angry with me, so he took her away.
After that, I didn't want any more pets." She studied
the rocky ground in front of her. "It hurt too much to
lose her." Sarah didn't want to meet Otto's gaze. She
was too afraid there'd be pity in his eyes, and she didn't
want to be pitiful, especially to Otto. "Now that I'm free,
though, I'm going to have a lot of pets—well, once I
move out of Jules's place." The reality of her situation
hit her once again. "If I ever go back to Jules's. If I ever
really can stop running."

"You will." His huge, warm hand was back, this
time resting over her shoulder blade. "Your brother
will be locked up for a long time, and Jovanovic won't
return, not with everyone looking for him." The firm,

commanding way he spoke—as if every word was the complete and total truth—almost made Sarah believe that it could be so simple.

She knew her brother, though. He didn't play by the rules, and he wouldn't consider the skeleton staff of a small-town police force to be any deterrent to getting what he wanted. Sarah was the key to infiltrating the Jovanovics' business, and Aaron would get out and snatch her back—or kill a lot of people trying.

She glanced at Otto. He was so good, and all of his animals depended on him. Was she being selfish to stay? As much as she hated to leave her new town, it might be the smartest thing to do. The only thing was that Sarah didn't know if she could do it. Leaving Otto, even if she knew it was the right thing to do, would hurt more than anything Aaron had ever done to her.

CHAPTER 10

Sᴀʀᴀʜ sᴛᴀʀᴇᴅ ᴀᴛ ᴛʜᴇ ꜰᴇᴡ ᴄʟᴏᴛʜᴇs ʜᴀɴɢɪɴɢ ɪɴ Oᴛᴛᴏ's guest-room closet. That was the extent of her wardrobe, but it looked so skimpy, almost pitifully so. It had taken her five minutes to unpack, and she'd moved slowly, trying to give Otto some time alone after he'd given up most of his day for her. She thought back to the enormous room that had housed her clothes at her brother's house, and her face scrunched at the memory. She closed the closet door, suddenly very happy. This was much better than her life before.

A tap on the door made her spin around. "Yes?" she said tentatively. The knock had reminded her of Aaron's appearance on Jules's front porch that morning.

"Do you eat meat?" Otto asked through the door.

"Yes."

"Bread?"

"Yes."

"Vegetables?"

With a small laugh, Sarah walked over and opened the door. He shifted back, obviously taken off guard. "Yes, and I want to help make lunch."

"You don't have to," he started to protest, but she moved toward him, determined not to be a burden.

Just like when she'd gotten out of his squad car earlier

that day, he didn't give way as she shifted forward, so they ended up just inches apart. Tipping her head back, Sarah stared up at him. From that angle, he seemed like a giant—a beautiful, Nordic giant—but she didn't feel any nervousness around him. She understood why Bean had felt safe enough to get close to Otto. The man radiated security and steadiness. She felt completely safe and utterly attracted to him at the same time.

He looked down at her, his light-blue eyes oddly warm. It was hard to read him. Sarah knew that wasn't just because of his excellent poker face. Her lack of experience was working against her as well. She wanted to kiss him. In fact, there wasn't anything she would rather do in that moment than kiss him, but she lacked the nerve to reach up, grab him by the ears, and pull his head down so she could plant one on him. Just the thought made nervous giggles bubble up in her throat.

Her impending laughter was smothered as he shifted closer. In fact, Sarah couldn't breathe at all as she waited to see what he was about to do. Raising a hand, Otto brushed his knuckles lightly across her cheek. His skin was rough, but he was so careful that it didn't hurt at all. Her cheek warmed under his touch, and she leaned into the caress, understanding why every animal seemed to gravitate toward Otto, why they groaned with pleasure when he petted them. It was the best feeling in the world to be touched by Otto Gunnersen.

He cupped her face with both hands, still with that infinite gentleness that made her want to smile and burst into tears at the same time. He leaned toward her, slowly, every move careful and easy, as if he didn't want to startle her. The light blue of his eyes was as hot as blue flames, and an answering fire leapt to life inside her chest. The heat spread through her, warming her down to her toes. She didn't need the hat he'd given her to stay warm. He just needed to touch her, and she ignited.

As he got nearer, her heart sped up in anticipation. She could barely breathe as he leaned closer...and then paused when their lips were just an inch apart. Sarah wanted to cry. They were so close, and she wanted him to kiss her so badly, and she hoped desperately for all interruptions to wait just a few more minutes.

"Is this okay?" he asked.

The air from his words brushed her mouth, distracting her. When she didn't answer, Otto pulled back slightly.

"Yes!" Her answer came out so fervently that she would've been embarrassed if she hadn't been so frantically, enormously eager. "It's fine. It's good, in fact. I mean, it will be good, or I'm pretty sure it will. You need to kiss me now so that I'll stop talking."

His chuckle came from deep in his chest, so low it was almost soundless, but Sarah heard it and felt an intense pleasure at making him laugh. Then his mouth was on hers, and any thoughts of laughter or babbling awkwardness—or even possessive, sociopathic brothers—washed away. She'd been right. It was good...very, very good.

The kiss started softly. It wasn't tentative, just gentle. It lured Sarah, made her want to get as close as possible. Otto kissed like he lived: soft and sweet and wonderfully caring.

As she moved closer, the kiss deepened, intensified. Otto groaned, another chest-deep sound, and shifted forward, pressing her back against the doorframe.

Sarah clutched two handfuls of his shirt, pulling him even more tightly against her. She lost track of time, distracted by the feel of his mouth on hers. When he eventually eased away, she blinked, trying to return to reality. Her brain was telling her that barely any time had passed, but her lips were swollen and a little sore, which meant that they'd been kissing for a while.

Otto smiled at her, slow and sweet, and she had to restrain herself from lunging at him and capturing his mouth again. Instead, she forced her hands to release the flannel balled in her grip. Sarah smoothed his shirt, flattening the wrinkles she'd caused. His chest was as solid as wood beneath the fabric, and she stroked again, this time for a different reason.

Chuckling, he put his hands over hers, stilling them. "Lunch?"

Even though she'd rather have kept kissing him, Sarah was too unsure about what was happening to say that out loud. Instead, she nodded and then followed him down the glossy hardwood stairs. Running her hand lightly along the carved banister, she marveled at how beautiful and well-kept the house was, even though it had obviously been built around the same time as Jules's place.

"I love your house," she said as they entered the spacious kitchen. "Did you grow up here?"

"No." His tone was a little short as he started pulling food out of the refrigerator, and Sarah was worried that she'd overstepped until he spoke again. "I bought this place five years ago."

"Who used to live here?" Sarah moved over to stand next to him, leaning against the counter as he began assembling sandwiches. From that position, she could watch his face. She would've loved to ask more questions about his childhood, about him, but she didn't feel that she knew him well enough to go poking around in possible sore spots. They'd kissed, but they'd only had a handful of conversations. Officer Otto Gunnersen was still a huge, gorgeous, animal-loving mystery to her.

"An older couple." A small smile tilted up the corners of his mouth, and Sarah desperately wanted to kiss him again. Apparently, the taste she'd gotten earlier had just whetted her appetite for more. "Monroe was getting too crowded for them. They moved west to a remote spot in the mountains."

"Too crowded?" she repeated. "I've seen fewer than a dozen people in town."

"The Branigans were…independent. They were the ones who connected the basement to the old mining tunnels so that they'd have an escape route if something happened."

Sarah felt her eyes get round. "Does this house have other secret passageways?"

"One…well, two, if you count the tunnel that leads to the barn."

"That counts." Sarah resisted the urge to go back and check out the tunnels immediately. She felt like she was in the middle of an old *Scooby-Doo* episode. Even in the sprawling mansion she'd escaped, there weren't any interesting quirks. It was just a lot of rooms in an expensive shell. "Can we explore them later?"

He darted a quick glance at her as his smile grew. "If you like."

"I would most definitely like." Sarah gave an

exaggerated nod to emphasize how very much she would enjoy exploring the hidden secrets of his home. Their gazes met and held, and his smile faded, replaced by an intent stare that warmed her all over.

A whine broke the spell, and they both looked down to see Mort and the cat—named Bob, Sarah had learned—sitting side by side, looking at Otto with pleading eyes. Otto sent Sarah a sideways glance that held a little guilt before giving both animals a tiny bit of the sliced turkey he was using to make their sandwiches. "They're a little spoiled," Otto admitted, giving her another sheepish look.

Sarah couldn't stop the smile that spread over her face, even though she knew she must look like the sappiest person who'd ever lived. It was just that Otto proved over and over again how kind a person he was, and Sarah's previous life had not been full of kind people—just the opposite, in fact. She was used to ambition and casual cruelty. Kindness was new—new and enormously attractive.

She realized that she was staring at him again, but he'd busied himself with putting the sandwich fixings away and didn't appear to have noticed her obsession. Dragging her gaze away, she gave herself a mental lecture. She needed to be careful, to guard her heart. She'd be leaving soon, after all. Besides, one kiss did not mean that he was head over heels in love with her. With every gentle, caring gesture he made—whether it was directed at her or some other person, or animal—Sarah got a little bit more attached. That kiss... She blew out a hard breath. That had pushed her over the edge. She was falling for someone she barely knew, who barely knew her, but she couldn't stop herself. She'd been doomed from the second he'd shown her how to feed an orphaned puppy.

Shaking off her distraction while promising she'd work harder to ignore Otto's finer qualities, Sarah realized that he was watching her, a quizzical look on his face. "Sorry, did you ask me something?"

"Just if everything's okay," he said, placing two filled plates on the table. "You looked…anxious."

Her brain blanked as she struggled to find an explanation that did not include her actual thoughts. If he knew what she was thinking, it would be horribly embarrassing—and would probably send him running hard and fast away from her clingy self. Sarah sat down at the table, using that as an excuse to delay her answer. With a groan, Mort settled onto the heat vent again, and she seized on the first non-sappy thought that occurred to her. "Oh. Um…just thinking about the puppies. It's strange not having them around. It's been less than a day, but I keep getting that feeling like I'm forgetting to do something, you know?"

With an amused sound, Otto sat down next to her. The chairs weren't that close together, but he was so big that his knee brushed hers. Heat radiated from the spot where they touched, and she was inordinately happy when he didn't shift away. It was just a small bit of contact, but she felt as if every nerve in her body was focused on that spot. "I'm doing that same thing," he said, and it took a moment for Sarah to remember what they were talking about. That tiny touch of his knee against hers was just too distracting. "I keep thinking I'm late feeding them."

"I'm pretty sure Dee would've wrestled you down and taken the puppies by force if you hadn't agreed to let them stay there for the weekend. Theo didn't look that excited about two days of puppy-sitting, though." She took a bite of her sandwich and barely resisted letting her eyes roll back in ecstasy. Even though she'd grown up eating food made by a professional chef, this simple sandwich tasted better than anything she'd ever eaten. "Wow. This is so good. No, better than good... This is amazing!"

His small smile was even better than the sandwich. "Thanks. I like to cook. Not that making sandwiches counts as cooking."

"Well, you're incredible at it." She took another bite, closing her eyes as she chewed. "I've never had a simple sandwich that tasted so good."

Otto waved at her slightly awkwardly, carrot stick in hand, as if dismissing her praise. He looked pleased, though. They ate quietly for a few minutes, and Sarah savored each bite. Living with Otto in his beautiful, animal-filled home, eating his delicious food... It was easy to forget everything that had just happened with Aaron and Logan when everything else was so wonderful.

Careful, she warned herself. Sarah knew she couldn't fall into believing this peaceful fairy-tale existence could last. The most she could hope for was that Aaron would be locked up for a very long time. If not, and he was able to get her back, he'd never give her another chance to escape.

Sarah huddled deeper in her new coat. The sky was gray, and the wind was picking up, sweeping down the north mountain face and cutting across Otto's property. He'd crashed after lunch and headed for bed. She'd felt guilty for keeping him up. She'd forgotten that, while she'd managed to grab some sleep between feedings, Otto had worked all night. Sarah had considered taking a nap, but she'd felt too wired. With the terrifying encounter with Aaron, and revealing why she was in Monroe, and moving to Otto's, and the kiss—and then the lack of discussion about the kiss, her brain was still spinning. She knew that sleep would be impossible.

Otto had told her to feel free to explore his house while he slept, but doing that felt intrusive and strange. Instead, Sarah had put on her new outerwear and wandered outside.

As she looked at the rocky slopes circling the house, Sarah shivered. There was something watchful about those towering cliffs. Even though she knew it was her imagination, goose bumps prickled her skin. Without Otto there, she felt very alone. Everything was too quiet, except for the rising and falling hum of the wind.

Ducking her face, Sarah hurried toward the barn. She tried to push away the uneasy feeling of strange and hostile eyes on her, but it still lurked in the back of her mind. Anyone could be out there, watching her. Maybe Logan hadn't gone far. As much as she believed that he'd save himself before he'd obsess about her, she still felt…unsettled.

It was a relief to reach the barn door, not only to be sheltered from the wind, but also to be hidden from spying eyes. She hurried to latch the door behind her, locating the handle by feel, since her eyes hadn't adjusted to the dim interior yet. It smelled of hay and grain, and Sarah smiled. Those were good scents, ones that reminded her of the rare happy times in her childhood when she'd helped Chester with the horses.

The single large horse stall was empty, the barn appearing to serve more for storage than for housing animals at the moment. There were various enclosures, made with different fencing and configurations. Sarah examined them, wondering what rescue animal Otto had housed in each one. As she moved around the space, the floor creaked under her weight, and she remembered the secret tunnel that Otto had said led to the barn. She searched but couldn't find the entrance to it.

Sarah left the barn through a door on the opposite side from the one she'd entered, and the wind immediately hit her hard. Her eyes watered from the blast, and she turned her face away as she hurried around the corner of the building. Her blurry eyes made it hard to see where she was going, and Sarah blinked away the wind-burned tears as she ducked into the three-sided run-in shed attached to the side of the barn.

She halted abruptly when she came face-to-face with a startled horse. Bean tossed his head high and blew a loud, nervous breath through his nostrils. Hortense started at the sound. Once she saw Sarah, the goat ambled over to check her hands and pockets for treats.

"Sorry, Hortense," Sarah said quietly, offering both hands palms up. "I'll bring you something next time." Hortense investigated her fingers thoroughly, as if Sarah were a magician who could make carrot chunks appear out of nowhere. Once the goat had decided that Sarah was of no use as a vending machine, she wandered back to her original spot on the other side of the shelter.

Bean had watched the interaction with wary eyes, although he hadn't bolted for the pasture, as Sarah had suspected he would. Instead, his head came down slowly. His legs were splayed slightly, frozen in place but ready to take off at a second's notice if she made any move that was even slightly threatening.

"Hey, Bean." She kept her voice low and soft, trying to channel Otto's calm manner. "I heard about your experience. I'm from Texas, so I've seen some of those wild boars, and I don't blame you for being freaked out of your mind. I mean, if they were living right next to me, I know I'd be completely terrified."

He huffed out another breath, but it wasn't as loud or tense as his first one.

"I've got to tell you something, Bean," Sarah continued, taking heart in the fact that he didn't go tearing across the pasture. "You've lucked out here. With Otto, you'll get nothing but kindness. Oh, and good food— you'll get fed really well. I'm sure you're more interested in hay and grain and maybe peppermint candy, but Otto makes a mean sandwich, too."

Although the wrinkles over his eyes showed that he was still anxious, his head came down another few inches as she spoke. Encouraged, Sarah kept talking.

"He's a really good kisser, too. I mean, I'm not that experienced—trying to date anyone when Jeb was always lurking in the background was not easy—but I'm still smart enough to know a good kisser when I run into one...with my lips." She giggled, and Bean jerked back, startled. "Sorry. Bad joke, I know. Anyway, Otto is incredible. I completely forgot about everything while we were kissing. All we needed was a romantic soundtrack playing in the background, and it could've been something from a movie. It was amazing." She paused, and Bean breathed through widened nostrils. "There's just one thing."

The wind howled louder, an eddy sweeping into the run-in shelter, tossing bits of hay and grit at Sarah. She twisted away, screwing her eyes shut, until it subsided and she wasn't being sandblasted any longer. When she opened her eyes, she fully expected Bean to be gone, spooked by her sudden twist away from the pounding wind, but he was still standing in the same place, watching her with a mix of curiosity and wariness.

"So, we kissed, right?" Bean flicked an ear forward and then to the side. "I know, I already told you that part. Anyway, after that, he didn't say anything. It was like it never happened, except that my brain kept replaying it, so I'm sure I sounded like an idiot during lunch when I kept missing his questions and zoning out of the conversation. Is that normal, though? To kiss and then ignore it? I don't want to have a full postmortem or anything, but a mention would've been nice. More kissing would've been even nicer."

Bean studied her, his eyes still wide but missing the ring of white they'd had when she'd first startled him.

"You're a very good listener, Bean." Sarah was tempted to reach out to pat him, but she didn't want to scare him off. "I'm sorry for being whiny. With everything happening with Aaron, I shouldn't be obsessing over a kiss. I'll stop now. If something happens with Otto, then it happens. I'm not going to build up my hopes, though, especially since I'll be leaving town eventually. I'll just enjoy being with him while I can. Sound like a plan?"

After eyeing her in silence for a long moment, Bean stretched out his neck. Sarah held her breath as the horse's head got closer. Even though Otto had said that Bean was more timid than aggressive, Sarah still felt a twinge of worry. Horses were unpredictable. What if he was about to take a bite out of her middle?

When Bean was close enough to touch her belly, he lipped at a stray strand of hay that was stuck to her coat. Sarah laughed out loud, a mix of elation and relief bubbling through her. This time, the sound didn't startle the horse. He just dropped his head and started to eat hay off the ground.

"You're going to be fine, Bean," she said. Sarah just hoped she would be, too.

Later that night, with Otto at work, the house seemed empty. Sarah lay in the guest bed, trying to sleep, but the wind was too loud. It reminded Sarah of that awful—yet amazing—night when Mr. Espina had blown up part of her home so that she could escape. There wasn't any rain, though, just the wind and the dark and the creaks of a mostly empty house. She didn't want to endanger Jules or Grace or any of the kids, but she had a moment when she wished she was back in the tiny bedroom at Jules's house. At least there were other people to distract her and make her feel less alone.

She turned onto her side and squeezed her eyes closed. *Stop*, she ordered her brain. She was perfectly safe and just needed to quit dwelling on the fact that the wind was so loud it would drown out any sound of Logan breaking in and creeping up the stairs. She wouldn't even know he was in the house until he grabbed her—

"Stop!" Sarah sat up abruptly. Grabbing her pillow and the blanket folded over the foot of her bed, she slipped out of the room and tiptoed down the stairs. The windows were uncovered, and the moonlight poured through the glass, illuminating everything with an eerie blue-white light…until clouds covered the moon, and all at once the room went dark.

Her heart pounding at the sudden blackness, Sarah clutched the banister and rushed down the rest of the steps. The clouds passed as she reached the main level, lighting her way to the closet door. She pushed aside the coats and felt her way to the back of the tiny space. When Otto had shown this to her earlier, Sarah had been entranced, loving the secret door to the hidden stairway.

Now, though, her hands were shaking as she fumbled to open the door. What had looked so simple when Otto unlatched it now seemed impossibly hard. She almost sobbed with relief when the back of the closet finally swung open to reveal descending stairs.

Something brushed against her leg, and she jumped, biting her lip to hold back a startled scream. Sarah hurried to find the light switch on the wall next to the stairs, smacking it hard enough to hurt her hand.

The fluorescent bulb flickered to life gradually, revealing Mort sitting next to her. Her relieved exhale came out as a shaky laugh.

"Want to hang out in the bunker with me?" she asked in a quiet voice that still sounded too loud in the empty house.

As if in response, Mort trotted down the stairs.

Sarah turned to close the closet door behind her and tripped over something—something that gave an indignant yowl.

Pressing her hand against her chest, Sarah closed her eyes, trying to recover from her second near-heart-attack in less than a minute. "Bob? You nearly scared me to death!"

The cat didn't seem at all contrite, zooming down the stairs after Mort.

As Sarah closed the hidden door and followed the animals down the stairs, she could feel her nerves settling. The three of them would stay in the bunker for the night. Tomorrow night, she'd be brave enough to sleep in the guest room.

Maybe.

CHAPTER 11

"THEO." OTTO TOOK THE LAST OF THE STAIRS AT A LOPE SO he could catch up to his partner. Viggy, Theo's K9, glanced back at Otto and wagged his tail. Theo was not so happy to see him. After one look at Theo's scowl, Otto's original reason for chasing him got pushed back. "What's wrong?"

Theo's frown grew even more ferocious. "What's wrong? Are you kidding me right now?"

"What?" Otto wondered if he'd missed some big news. It was possible, although he'd just returned to the police station at the end of a quiet night shift, and he hadn't heard anything announced over the radio. Had Jovanovic been spotted in the area? Otto's heart rate sped up, and he mentally cursed himself for leaving Sarah on her own at his place. He'd shown her how to get into the basement bunker, though. She was smart. If something happened, she'd hide. "Did something happen?"

"Yeah, something happened." Theo's sarcastic tone calmed Otto. If there'd been a serious incident, Theo would've been direct and to the point. "Some asshole left four puppies at Jules's house. Apparently, she's able to sleep through their hungry squeaking—I have no idea how, since they're as loud as a fire alarm—so I was the one who got up with them. Every. Three. Hours."

His disgruntled expression almost made Otto smile, although he could definitely sympathize. Getting woken up every few hours had left him feeling like he'd been run over by a truck, which had then backed over him for good measure. He'd slept like a baby that afternoon—except that the dreams he'd had about Sarah had been more of the adult variety. "Sorry. Why didn't you wake up Jules so she could help?"

Theo suddenly appeared to find the hallway ahead of them so fascinating that he couldn't look away. "She had an early shift this morning. She needed her sleep."

"You had the early shift, too."

Theo's scowl was back as he abruptly changed the subject. "Shouldn't you be getting home?"

The mention of "home" reminded Otto of what he'd originally needed to talk to Theo about. He looked around and then jerked his head toward the roll call room. Even though it didn't look like anyone else was nearby, it was better to be safe than sorry. The cops he worked with could be brutal with their teasing, and Otto knew he'd be handing them solid-gold gossip fodder if they overheard what he was about to ask Theo. "You have a few minutes?"

"Yeah." Theo glanced at his watch as he followed him into the room. "You only have six minutes before roll call, though, so you'd better talk fast."

Otto closed the door behind them, and then turned back to see Theo eyeing him curiously. "Thanks. I have…well, a question."

"Okay. Ask." Theo half sat on the table behind him, crossing his arms over his chest. Viggy lay down next to him, his head resting on his front paws. Theo's smirk looked a little too Hugh-ish for Otto's liking. There was a reason he'd gone to Theo with this and not Hugh. "Well?"

Otto stared at Theo for several seconds, but the words wouldn't come. "Never mind."

As he started to turn away, planning to leave the room and take his potential humiliation with him, Theo grabbed his arm. "Hang on. Ask your question. You already stuck me with bottle-feeding your puppies. You can't drop that teaser and leave. I'm curious now."

"Fine." Otto really did want to get someone else's take on the situation, and he only trusted Theo and Hugh to keep their mouths shut. Since Hugh would torment him unmercifully, that meant he was stuck with Theo. Taking a deep breath, he forced out the words. "I kissed Sarah."

Theo's brows shot up. After a moment of uncomfortable silence, he said, "That wasn't a question."

"Right." Otto cleared his throat, his gaze bouncing around the room before finally settling on the whiteboard in the corner. "She's staying at my place so that she'll be safe from Jovanovic. What if she thinks…? How do I let her know that she doesn't have to…?" He trailed off again with a grunt of frustration.

"You don't want her to think that she has to put out as payment for staying with you," Theo said baldly, and Otto winced. It sounded as bad out loud as it had in his head.

"Yes."

"Just tell her."

Otto shifted uncomfortably. "I tried. It doesn't come out right."

"You don't want me to—"

"No!" Otto raised his hands in horror, cutting Theo off in mid-sentence. "No. I'll do it. I'll talk to her." He'd figure out how to get the words out somehow, no matter how awkward it got. "I just want to know, was it wrong for me to kiss her? I mean, I don't want to take advantage, and she's so…" He stopped again, annoyed with how hard it was to articulate how he felt about Sarah. She was beautiful and sweet and brave. But she'd managed to escape from her controlling brother, and Otto was worried he was taking advantage of her vulnerable state. He didn't want her to kiss him out of gratitude for saving her or for letting her stay with him. He wanted her to kiss him because she felt like she'd die if she didn't—just like Otto had felt outside the guest bedroom yesterday.

"Otto." Theo pushed off the table, bringing Otto out of his thoughts. "You're not taking advantage. You're the least-likely person to ever take advantage of anyone. Tell Sarah you like her, ask her out, and tell her she's free to say no without any repercussions. If she does say no, then accept it and do your best to move on, so that things aren't weird for her while she stays at your place."

"Okay." Otto blew out a long breath. It was painfully awkward to discuss this with Theo, but hearing it laid out like that helped clarify things in his mind. Otto had a clear plan now. He didn't have to rehash it over and over until he wanted to smack his head against his squad car steering wheel anymore. "Thank you."

With a brisk nod, Theo pulled out a chair at the nearest table and sat. Viggy shifted so he was lying closer to Theo's boots, and Otto had a pleased moment that the dog was doing so well now. It reminded him that, thanks to the recent excitement, he hadn't been to the kennel to work with his project dog lately, and he made a mental note to stop by on his way home.

"Any sign of Jovanovic?" Theo asked, stretching out his legs under the table.

"Yeah, but not around here. California State Patrol reported a possible sighting, but they lost track of his vehicle before they could confirm." Otto had a strong urge to hunt Logan Jovanovic down and teach him a lesson. What made it worse was that he was—or had been—a cop. "It's been a quiet night here." Too quiet. There'd been way too much time for Otto to stew about the whole situation with Sarah.

"Welcome to winter in Monroe," Theo said as the door opened behind Otto. He moved out of the way so that Lieutenant Blessard could enter.

"What are you still doing here, Gunnersen?" Blessard demanded.

"I'm on my way out," Otto said, giving Theo a final nod of thanks. "Just telling Theo there weren't many calls last night."

"Good," the lieutenant said, dumping a stack of folders on the desk at the front of the room. "The chief took eight officers to crisis intervention training in Colorado Springs for the week. Figured it'd be quiet now that most of the town has left for the winter."

"Eight?" Theo repeated as Sergeant Wesley Gibson walked in and sat at the table across from Theo's. "With Hugh still out, that just leaves…"

"The four of us." Blessard gestured around the room, as if it were full of officers. Otto met Theo's concerned gaze. "We're down to bare bones here, gentlemen. Now would be the wrong time to get sick."

"This is a bad idea," Theo said, and Otto grunted agreement, moving to stand next to his partner. "We're already down officers. Blanchett just tried to kidnap his sister—"

"And we arrested him," Blessard said, cutting him off. "The FBI agents will be here in a few days to pick him up, as soon as the judge signs off on his transfer paperwork, and then we won't even need to feed him. That situation is taken care of."

"Jovanovic is still out there." Just the thought of Sarah being at risk—even if that risk was small—made Otto feel sick. He'd been planning to ask some of the other officers to keep an eye on his place while he was at work, but there wouldn't be any help until they returned from training.

The lieutenant narrowed his eyes, looking back and forth between the two of them. "Jovanovic wasn't even back in California for a full day before he was spotted. Things are too hot for him. I'm guessing he'll make a beeline to the Mexican border. If you're worried about Blanchett's sister, though, talk to the FBI about protective custody when they're here."

Otto was torn. He wanted Sarah to be safe, but he also wanted her close by. "That's days from now."

"Enough." Blessard's tone was final. "It is what it is. File a complaint with the chief when he returns. Gunnersen, go home and get some sleep. It's going to be a shitty week."

Otto was in a bad mood by the time he got to Nan's. After Blanchett's attack, he was wired and on edge. Despite the lieutenant's reassurance, Otto still felt like it was a bad time for two-thirds of the police force to be sitting in a classroom several hours away.

It made him twitchy. He'd be the only cop on duty for the next four nights, so Sarah would be alone out at his place. It had been hard to leave her the previous night, and he'd been toying with the idea of using some of his personal days. Since he didn't tend to get sick and didn't take vacations, he'd racked up quite a bit of unused leave. Now, though, there was no one to take his place. He'd be leaving Sarah unguarded each night whether he liked it or not.

He slammed the door of his squad car a little harder than necessary, and he made himself pause and breathe for a second. It wouldn't help Xena, the dog he was working with, if he was angry. Putting the whole situation in the back of his mind, Otto calmed his thoughts.

Once his annoyance and worry settled, he walked toward the building where Nan kept the rescue dogs. When she'd bought the property and built the kennels, she'd planned to board and groom dogs. The Monroe K9 unit used her facility when they needed to house a dog, since it was a better setup, with exercise yards and indoor training areas, than the small kennel next to the PD parking garage. Nan had never intended to house an animal shelter, but the closest humane society was almost an hour away, so people started bringing strays and unwanted dogs to Nan. Soft-hearted Nan could never turn them away.

"Hey, Sam," Otto said as he stepped inside the

building. It was only when he was in the warmth of the heated building that he realized how cold it was getting outside. The first big snow of the season was supposed to hit in a few days, and Otto had felt the bite of winter in the air. Jules's brother, Sam, gave Otto an unsmiling nod without pausing in his work spraying down kennels with the pressure washer. Sam had worked for Nan since his family had moved to town a few months ago. He hadn't had any experience when he'd started, but he'd learned quickly and was good with the dogs.

A quick glance showed that all the kennels were empty. Zipping his jacket a little higher, Otto stepped back into the cold. The wind had picked up, and it pushed against his back and legs as if hurrying him along. He moved quickly, wanting to get back into the warmth—or at least find a windbreak—soon.

Xena had the same instinct, since she was tucked into her shelter. Holding back a groan, Otto lowered himself to the ground, patiently rewarding her with a tiny treat every time she poked her nose in his direction. The pit bull–Lab mix had gained quite a bit of weight since being rescued in a raid of a suspected dogfighter's home, but Xena's ribs were still visible under her short coat. Her muzzle and head were crisscrossed with old scars, and she was missing part of her right ear.

By the time he'd succeeded in luring her out with treats, Otto was half-frozen. He gave her a final, gentle ear rub and slowly shifted away before standing, so as not to startle her. When he reached the gate, Nan was there, waiting for him. She was tall, her rangy frame disguised by multiple heavy layers. Her graying hair was covered in a colorful stocking hat.

"Brrr!" She gave an exaggerated shiver as he approached. "Xena's coat is too short for this kind of weather. I asked Sam to bring in all the dogs, so Xena will be back inside soon. This wind is ridiculous. I'm nowhere near ready for summer to end."

"Summer's been over for a while," Otto said, glancing at Xena as he closed the gate behind him. The dog watched him go, and her tail wagged slightly before she retreated back into her shelter. "Now fall is done."

Nan arched her eyebrows so high they disappeared under her hat. "Thank you for that, Mr. Depressing."

Otto just offered a small shrug of apology. It might not be cheery, but it was true. Winter was well and truly there, and he had the frozen ass to prove it.

"Do you have a minute?"

The words, so close to what he'd asked Theo such a short time ago, worried Otto. Nan had never asked Otto for romantic advice, and he would be very happy if she kept it that way. They'd discuss dogs, the weather, and occasional town happenings, and that was it. Otto really didn't want to expand their conversational subjects, especially if it meant hearing about Nan's love life. She was watching him, though, waiting for an answer.

Trapped, he gave a silent sigh and a slight tip of his head before following her to the main building where her office was. As they crossed in front of the kennels toward the office door, barking echoed and reverberated, bouncing off the ceilings and walls, painfully loud.

Once inside Nan's small, untidy office, Otto hurried to close the door and muffle some of the noise. Nan moved a stack of papers off the lone visitor's chair, but he waved her off, preferring to stand. If she was going to

ask some extraordinarily awkward question, he wanted
to be able to make a quick getaway.

After sitting in her own chair, Nan didn't seem to be
in any hurry to speak. Instead, she picked up a pen and
focused on it as she rolled it between her fingers. Otto
watched her, curious, but not curious enough to prompt
her. If this was about something that was going to be
vastly uncomfortable, he'd rather stay in ignorant bliss
for a little longer.

"Otto, about Xena…"

"Xena?" He hadn't expected the dog to be the topic
of conversation.

"She's been here almost three months."

Otto's stomach clenched. He knew where this conversation was leading. Suddenly, Nan's reluctance to
speak made sense.

"I know you've been working with her a lot—almost
daily—but she's just not making much progress." Nan's
voice was gentle, but her words still made Otto stiffen.

"She is making progress," Otto said, keeping his
voice even with some difficulty. "She wouldn't even
look at me when she first arrived, much less take any
food out of my hand. Now, she's coming out of her shelter willingly, and we're working on her touching her
nose to my hand. She just wagged her tail at me!"

Despite his best effort, his voice rose on the last words.
Immediately clamping his mouth closed, Otto gave
himself a mental lecture. He needed to stay calm and
rational. Xena was special to him, though. She reminded
him of a much-younger Otto, before he'd been fostered
by the Lopez family—an Otto who'd learned to keep his
head down and who'd gotten very good at dodging fists.

"I know she's making some progress." Nan's expression was apologetic. "It's just not enough progress. There are two malamutes coming in tomorrow that got left in a foreclosed house after the owners moved away, and I need that space. I just don't have the room for Xena anymore, not when it's probably going to take another year to get her to the point where she can be adopted. I called the pit bull rescue in Fort Collins, but they have a waiting list. I'm stuck, Otto."

Otto looked at her resolute face and knew that she'd made up her mind. Nothing he said was going to budge her. He knew, though, that he couldn't abandon Xena when she had nowhere else to go. "I'll take her."

"What?" Nan looked surprised, as if she hadn't been expecting him to offer. "Are you sure?"

He wasn't sure whether taking home a fearful pit bull mix was a smart idea, not when he had the puppies to bottle-feed and Sarah to guard and skeleton-staffed night shifts to cover, but it was the only option. He wasn't about to give up on Xena. "Yes."

After Nan eyed him for several moments, her shoulders sagged and she leaned back in her seat. "I'm so relieved. I hate turning any dog away, but there are just so many kennels and only so much time."

Otto dipped his head in acknowledgment, but he was anxious to go. The thought of Sarah had awakened the anxiety he'd pushed back before working with Xena. He needed to get home, to check on her, to make sure everything—and everyone—was okay. Now, he needed to get Xena to her new home, too.

"Leash?" he asked, reaching for the doorknob.

"Here." Nan pulled one off a peg on the wall and

handed it over. "Sorry about this, Otto. If there was any other way…"

"Not your fault, Nan," he said truthfully. "Like you said, there's only so much room."

Leash in hand, he made his way through the kennel, not even hearing the volley of barking this time. Otto was too busy trying to figure out how he was going to save everyone he was now responsible for. If he screwed up and dropped one of the many balls he was juggling, someone could get hurt—or killed.

———

It was hard for Sarah not to run out to greet Otto when he got home, but she managed…barely. It had been a long night. She'd slept a little in the safety of the bunker, but the cot had been hard and narrow—especially since she was sharing it with Mort and Bob.

Instead, she focused on scooping the egg mixture into tortillas. She'd gathered eggs out of the nesting boxes in the chicken coop earlier, getting a thrill with each egg she'd found. It was such a simple thing, but it felt so much more rewarding than pulling a carton of store-bought eggs from the fridge.

Otto's kitchen was well-stocked, and she'd had no problem finding all the ingredients for breakfast burritos, plus fresh fruit she'd cut up. Sarah had always enjoyed cooking. It centered her and calmed her racing thoughts. Now, though, with everything that was going on, she knew it'd take a lot more than just throwing together some breakfast burritos to give her peace.

"Morning," Otto said, standing right at her elbow.

Sarah jumped, bumping the plate on the counter in front of her. Even though she'd seen Otto's truck pull up and knew he was there, she'd expected to hear him walk in. "Oh! Wow, you're stealthy."

"Yeah." Otto snuck a piece of orange and popped it into his mouth. "Hugh tells me that all the time. Says I'm part Paul Bunyan and part ninja."

Sarah smiled. "That's actually a really good description. Are you?"

"Am I what?" he asked absently, his attention focused on stealing another piece of fruit.

Sarah put the plates on the table. "Part Paul Bunyan and part ninja." When he just shrugged slightly, she asked, "What were your parents like?"

"Not sure." Although his words lit a fire under her curiosity, she had a feeling she shouldn't push any further. "Breakfast looks great. You didn't have to cook, though."

She accepted the subject change easily as they both started eating. She of all people understood not wanting to talk about family. "Figured I'd pay you back for lunch and dinner yesterday—well, partially pay you back." Everything was made from his groceries, after all. "I'm going to town tomorrow to do some shopping and look for a job."

Otto paused, his forkful of food halfway to his mouth. "To town? That's not safe."

"Why?" It was Sarah's turn to stop eating as she stared at him, worried. "Did someone see Logan? Has he been hanging around?"

"No, but it's better if you stay here, just in case." He resumed eating, but Sarah laid her fork carefully on her plate.

"All the time?" She hadn't left one prison just to live in a second. "I can't do that. I sold some of my jewelry, so I have a little money, but it's not much. I need to find a job."

His brows drew together as his mouth tightened with resolve. Even his chewing was resolute. "You don't need money. Whatever you need, I'll get it for you. It's safer here."

Sarah knew Otto was just looking out for her, but the restriction chafed. "Thank you, but I need to start working. Aaron's been arrested, and Logan's long gone. It's safe enough in town, especially with you, Theo, and Hugh right there if I need help. I'll go crazy without anything to do all day, and I can't mooch off you until I leave Monroe." The idea made her cringe.

"You wouldn't be mooching," he argued. "You can help with the animals and…" He paused, looking around as if searching for something else to suggest. "Cooking. This is really good."

"Thank you, but I need to be independent. It's important." Her tone was firm, shaking just slightly, even though her stomach churned. She'd never stood up to her father or her brother. Despite Otto's gentle manner, it was still terrifying to hold her ground.

He frowned at her before stabbing another bite of burrito with his fork. "Fine, but I'm going with you."

"To work? Every day?" Sarah stared at him. That sounded strange and uncomfortable and frankly unworkable. How would she tell a potential employer that she couldn't be separated from her bodyguard? It would be like trying to get a job with Jeb in tow, except that Otto was much more attractive, and kinder, and, Sarah assumed, a much better kisser.

At the thought, her face grew warm with what she was sure was a bright-red blush.

"No." His word came out grudgingly, as if Otto was wishing there was a way he could follow her around all the time. "Tomorrow. I'm going with you tomorrow. We'll work something out for the rest of the time. One of us needs to be able to get to you quickly if you need help."

"Okay." It was such a relief that she hadn't gained a new constant bodyguard that she didn't even argue. Honestly, she didn't really want to argue. It'd be reassuring to have Otto around as she ventured into public for the first time since Aaron had appeared, and she was perfectly happy having multiple cops close by. "We can go right after breakfast so we're back before your bedtime."

After Otto's grunt of agreement, they ate in silence for a few minutes. Finally he said, "There's a new dog in the barn. I'll introduce you after breakfast. If she does okay with you and the other animals, we'll move her into the house."

"A new dog? From where?"

"A rescue from Nan's. She's out of space and getting more dogs."

"It's sad that there are so many homeless dogs." Sarah was perfectly fine with having another companion for the lonely nights, although she'd have to push two cots together if they all ended up in the bunker again. It had been tight enough with only Mort and Bob joining her. "Are we going to pick up the puppies while we're in town, too?" As much work as they were, she'd missed them.

"Yeah." The word came out as a sigh. Otto looked

tired. "The kids have school tomorrow, and Theo and Jules probably want a full night's sleep."

As she finished her breakfast, a warm curl of excitement pushed away the nerves that had been wearing at Sarah's insides since fleeing Texas. It was fun—thrilling, even—to be staying with Otto and his ever-expanding collection of pets and the possibility of more kisses and the prospect of a job—her first ever. Best of all was that she'd stood up for herself, and he hadn't slapped her down or insisted she stay at home or anything.

Despite everything, her new life was starting to take shape, and it was amazing.

"She's very shy," Otto warned a little bit later as they walked toward the barn. "I've been working with her for a couple of months, and it still takes a lot of time and treats to get her to come to me. She'll let Sam approach her and leash her—Sam has a way with all the dogs— but she'll still try to run from Nan if she's able."

"Okay," Sarah said. "I'll try not to scare her."

"I don't want you to be upset or think that you're doing something wrong. It's just how Xena is. Her previous owner caused a lot of damage."

"What happened to her previous owner?" Sarah ducked into the barn with a shiver of relief. The wind seemed even sharper than it had the previous day.

"County jail." Otto closed the door behind him and flicked on the lights. Despite the multiple bulbs, it still took Sarah's eyes a moment to adjust to the dimness. "He was denied bail, since he's skipped out on it before, so he'll be locked up until his trial for dogfighting and a number of other charges. He's a..." He paused. "He's not a nice guy."

"At least he's paying for his crimes." Sarah peered at the opening to the wooden doghouse and saw the quick flash of a light-colored muzzle as Xena peeked at them and then disappeared back inside. "I imagine that doesn't happen often with these cases."

"No, it doesn't." Otto gestured toward a few hay bales stacked against the wall. "This might take a while. Want to sit?"

Although the top bale looked a bit prickly, Sarah settled on it. It was more comfortable than she'd expected, since her jeans protected her from the scratchy hay. Scooting back, she leaned against the wall while Otto sat next to her. With his leg just a few inches from hers, Sarah couldn't stop thinking about all the "roll in the hay" jokes. There was something wrong with her. Every time she got close to Otto, all her thoughts instantly went to sex. It was like he short-circuited her brain.

She cleared her throat, needing to change the direction of her thoughts before she overheated or blurted out something very, very inappropriate. "Do you think I'll have any luck finding a job? I know that a lot of places are closed for the winter."

He made a low humming sound. "True, but most of the employees have left. The places that stay open are short-handed. What kind of job are you looking for?"

"Anything really." Although she hated to sound like a spoiled princess, she wanted to be honest, especially with Otto. "I've never had a job before." She braced herself, waiting for his judgment, but he just made another of his humming sounds.

After a short pause, he said, "Since you're flexible about the type of job, that'll open up some options for you."

Sarah looked at him, studying his profile as she wondered why she'd ever been worried about Otto being rude or condescending to her. He just wasn't that way. Everything she'd heard him say had been thoughtful and kind. Even though she barely knew him, she felt like she could trust him. She understood why animals gravitated toward him. After all, she certainly felt his magnetic pull. "You're such a good person."

He glanced away. "Not really."

"Yes, really." When she saw how uncomfortable his shrug was, she changed the subject. "Have you always had a way with animals?"

"Pretty much." He was quiet for a few moments, long enough that she thought he was done talking. "Animals are…easier than people." He sent her a quick glance. "Most people."

"True." It was her turn to go quiet.

"Not you, though. You're easy." His face immediately flushed when she gave a choked laugh. "Not like that. You know what I mean."

"I know." She did know. After growing up the way she had, it was easy to believe that everyone hid an evil side. Meeting truly good people, like Otto and others she'd met in Monroe, was a shock—a good one, but still a shock. "I understand how hard it can be to trust people."

He was silent for a long moment. "I was left at a hospital when I was two." It surprised her when he spoke, especially when he shared something so personal. She stayed silent, not wanting to say the wrong thing and make him stop talking. "I went through a lot of foster homes. Some were bad."

Blinking away tears, Sarah studied the piece of hay between her fingers. She didn't want him to know that the thought of Otto as a hurt little boy made her want to cry, so she kept her head down as he continued.

"When I was eleven, I went to live with the Lopez family. They lived on a cattle ranch east of town."

"Were they nice?" She had to know, or her heart was going to break for him.

"Yes. They were good people. I learned a lot about animals while I was there. I met Hugh that year, too, and we became friends."

"Why did you become a cop, rather than a vet?" she asked.

"I knew I could do more good as a cop," he said. "Besides, I don't have the temperament to be a vet."

She laughed, tension leaving her in a rush. Later, she knew, she'd think about Otto as a sweet, quiet little boy in an awful place, and she'd cry. For now, though, she teased, "Too much talking?"

"Way too much."

When she snuck a glance at him, he was smiling at her. Instantly, she was caught and couldn't look away. As attractive as he was when he was serious, he was a hundred times more beautiful when he smiled.

Sarah knew she should look away and pretend she hadn't been staring at him like a creepy stalker, but she just couldn't. His eyes were so pale in his tan face. That light of blue should've been cool, almost frosty, but they were very, very warm instead, like the flame of a gas stove.

He slowly—almost shyly—raised his hand and ran his fingertips along the curve of her cheek, along her jaw to her ear, and then down the side of her neck. Sarah's shivers had nothing to do with the cold air. In fact, her skin prickled with heat. Otto leaned closer, his gaze locked on her mouth, and Sarah's stomach swooped like she was going through the loop-the-loop on a roller coaster.

His lips were close, so close that she closed her eyes, waiting for the kiss. The seconds ticked by, but the contact she wanted never came. She opened her eyes to see him watching her with a look she couldn't interpret.

"What's wrong?" she asked, although a big part of her didn't want to know if there was a problem. The selfish, shallow, needy part just wanted him to kiss her.

He opened his mouth and then closed it again, and Sarah started to worry. What was so bad that he couldn't say the words? All sorts of horrible scenarios trampled through her mind: he was married or he was dying or he didn't really want her or—

"I want you," he said baldly, and she jumped at the juxtaposition of her thought with his words. She had a nonsensically worried moment that he'd managed to read her mind. "I like you."

What's the right response to that? she wondered frantically. As the moment stretched awkwardly, she finally blurted out, "Thank you." As soon as the words were said, she wanted to smack her head against the barn wall. "I mean, I'm glad, since I do, too. Like you, that is." Desperately wishing she'd actually gone away to college and had managed to gain some social skills and experience in conversations like these, she shut her mouth firmly before any more nonsense could escape.

His smile came slowly, like his speech, curling up until the corners of his eyes wrinkled. Sarah was fascinated. He was so honest. He was smiling because he was truly happy. Growing up, everyone she'd met—including herself—had been hiding something. Their masks kept them alive, and Sarah had become so accustomed to hiding that she'd forgotten that not everyone was forced to live that way. Otto reminded her that people could actually mean what they said.

"Good." His fingers ghosted over her cheek again. "You don't have to, though."

Her forehead puckered with confusion. She hadn't said any of her thoughts out loud, had she? There was no way—she was an expert at hiding her feelings. "What?"

Otto's eyes closed for a moment before he looked at her again. "Sorry." Even in the low light, Sarah could see a slight reddening of his face under his tan, and it intrigued her as much as his slow and authentic smile had. "I'm making a mess of this."

"Not a mess," she hurried to say, although she still didn't know what he was talking about. "I'm just not sure what you're saying."

"Even if you aren't…interested. In me, I mean." His cheeks darkened even more. "You can stay here. I would never push you into something you didn't want."

"I know."

He still looked concerned, so Sarah caught his hand and squeezed it.

"I know," she repeated, meeting his gaze evenly so he

would understand that she was serious, that she wasn't just blowing off his warning. "I can see it."

"See it?" His fingers closed around hers, and she marveled at his gentleness. It was such a contrast to how rough his skin was and how large his hands were. They could crush hers, but she trusted that they never would.

"You bottle-feed puppies."

He paused, as if waiting for her to continue. "So?"

"Your skittish horse approaches you. Your retired K9 partner loves you. You climbed a collapsing windmill to rescue Dee's cat. Your human cop partners would die for you. Even Sam is comfortable around you, and from what I've seen, he's not comfortable around anyone."

Still he waited, looking at her without comprehension.

"I know when people are cold and hard." Her voice shook a little. "You, Otto, are not cold or hard. Your heart is huge and as squishy as a marshmallow."

"Squishy?" From his expression, Otto wasn't sure how to take that. Sarah had to laugh at his crinkled nose.

"It's a good thing." Feeling enormously brave, she leaned forward and kissed the corner of his mouth. The roughness of his stubble contrasted with the surprising softness of his lips, and she lingered there for a moment, lightly exploring. When she finally pulled away, his eyes had gone gas-flame hot again.

Otto slid a hand over the side of her neck and under her hair to cup her nape. As he leaned forward, her eyelids closed, her breathing speeding up in anticipation of his kiss. Kissing Otto was her favorite thing in her new life, and that was saying something, because she loved many, many things about her newly discovered freedom. His lips brushed her, touching the right corner of her mouth and then the left. Even those tiny kisses made heat blaze through her, as his gentleness created a softer—yet no less addicting—warmth.

He increased the pressure, deepening the kiss, and she leaned in to him, her hands going up to clutch his shoulders. She couldn't get close enough. Her hands slid up his neck and over his head, and she marveled at the silky softness of his hair, despite the short length. Soon, however, his kiss took over her thoughts, and she could only concentrate on how amazing his mouth felt on hers.

"Otto." She somehow managed to pull back just far enough to speak. "I want—"

Something pressed against the side of her calf.

Sarah jumped with a shocked yelp. As she turned her head to see what had just touched her, Otto made a surprised sound.

A pit bull–type dog was crouched next to her, huddled against the hay bale, her blocky head tucked behind Sarah's legs. "Hey," she said softly, slowly reaching toward the dog's ears. "You must be Xena."

Her fingers touched the dog's head, felt how much Xena was trembling, and her heart broke. Sarah knew what it was like to be that scared. Twisting around, she carefully lowered herself so she was sitting on the ground next to the dog. Xena turned her head and laid her muzzle on Sarah's thigh.

"Poor baby," she crooned, stroking the velvet ears, her fingers tracing the bumps of the dog's scars. Sarah wasn't sure how long they sat there before Otto broke the silence.

"Let's introduce her to Mort," he said quietly, standing up. Xena eyed him warily, although she didn't move her head off Sarah's leg. Otto handed Sarah a leash, and she clipped it on Xena's collar.

"Come on, sweet girl." Lifting the dog's heavy head off her leg, Sarah got slowly to her feet. "You'll like the house better than this chilly barn." Now that she was moving again, Sarah realized exactly how cold and stiff she'd gotten sitting on the hay and the ground.

As they made their way toward the barn door, Xena moving low to the ground with her tail tucked tightly, Otto put a hand lightly on Sarah's back. "Impressive," he said quietly. "She's never reacted like that to anyone else."

Sarah smiled, but it quickly dropped away. She had a feeling that Xena had approached her because they were common souls—both had been victims; both had needed to be rescued.

She sent a quick glance at Otto. They'd survived, though—survived and found this marshmallow-hearted man and his beautiful, safe home and his sandwiches and his secure bunker. And *freedom*. Freedom no one was ever going to take from them. Reaching down, she gave Xena's ears another rub.

They were both going to be fine.

CHAPTER 12

MORT HAD GREETED THE NEW ARRIVAL WITH A CASUAL WAG of his tail before stretching out on his heat vent again, while Bob had taken a more cautious approach, monitoring the situation from his perch on top of the refrigerator. Xena stayed close to Sarah's legs until she'd discovered a secure spot in the living room between the couch and the wall.

Sarah stood by the sofa, uncertain. "Should I try to coax her out?"

"No." Otto placed a hand on her back, and she marveled at how big it was. Otto's size should probably make her nervous, but it didn't. Not at all. Her father hadn't been a big guy—neither was her brother—and they'd managed to hurt her. It wasn't the size or the strength, but the intent. "She's had a stressful day. Let her have some time alone."

"Okay." Sarah didn't move, though, not wanting Otto to drop his hand. His touch was like water to a neglected houseplant. She sucked up everything he gave her and wanted more. They were both still for a few moments, but Sarah knew she couldn't just continue to stare at Otto's couch all day, mentally begging him to keep touching her. Still, though, she couldn't bring herself to be the one who broke the spell.

When Otto's hand slipped down her back and then fell away, she sighed silently in disappointment. "I should probably try to sleep," he said.

"Oh! That's right! I'm sorry for keeping you up." She snuck a glance at his profile to find him still staring at the sofa. Sarah felt a little guilty. The poor guy worked all night. He was probably exhausted, and she...well, she really didn't want him to go to sleep. Going to bed she was okay with, as long as he brought her along.

She blushed at the thought and didn't look away in time. He turned his head, catching her mid-stare.

Their gazes caught and locked together. "It'll be hard to sleep now." His voice was gritty, and his blue eyes were as hot as the gas flames they resembled.

She couldn't speak, couldn't get actual words to leave her mouth. All she could do was make a wordless, inquiring sound that squeaked at the end. Sarah resisted the urge to close her eyes in despair at her absolute lack of game. She was, and would always be, a hopeless dork.

By the way he was looking at her, though, that didn't seem to matter to Otto. "If I try, I'll just lie awake, thinking about you."

Sarah could only stare as her heart pounded and a whole flock of fluttery birds danced around in her stomach. Had he really said that? It was as if her fairy godmother had told Sarah to dream up the perfect man, waved a wand, and created Otto out of a redwood tree or something. "You're so perfect," she said, amazed she was able to breathe, much less talk.

"No." He blushed—he actually blushed—just proving her words all over again. "I'm not."

Instead of arguing, Sarah just enjoyed his rapt attention and being able to look at him as much as she wanted without seeming weird. It was blissful to be able to wallow in all things Otto.

Then he made it even better. Bringing his hands to her face, he leaned down and kissed her.

It was different from the other kisses. Right away, he took over. It was rough without being scary, and hard without being painful. He nipped at her bottom lip, making her gasp at the excited thrill that zipped through her body, and then he met her tongue with his own. Rather than intimidating her, though, his aggressive kiss freed her. She could respond as wildly as she wanted, because he was just as out of control as she was.

His hands slipped down her arms, landed on her hips, and then skimmed up her sides, burrowing beneath her layers. Her whole body lit up with heat and pleasure, everything in her straining toward where he touched her. She had to touch him in return. Sliding her hands up his arms, she didn't get any farther than his shoulders. His mouth worked against hers, and she clutched at him, holding on so she didn't melt into a puddle on the floor or float toward the ceiling. As the kiss turned from hungry to greedy and then back to tender, Sarah just knew: Otto was the one for her. Any other man would pale in comparison to his gentle strength and kindness, not to mention how he erased the rest of the world with one look.

It wasn't that simple, though—not for her. She couldn't get too attached to Monroe and her new friends and Otto—*especially* Otto. His rough palms smoothed up her sides as he kissed her more deeply, and she had the sinking feeling that it was too late. She was already attached.

She pulled back slightly, and he followed, seeking out her lips again when she withdrew. With a breathless laugh, she put a hand on his chest, putting a couple of inches between them.

"I don't want to stop—I mean, I really, really don't want to stop—but Xena's going to think we're exhibitionists."

He laughed softly, his breath hitting her lips. Suddenly, she didn't care if they were being watched. Sarah just wanted to kiss him again. When she leaned in, he lifted her by the waist and turned her in a half circle. The sudden movement made her give a laughing yelp and grab his shoulders. "Should we go upstairs?" he asked. "Xena won't be able to watch us up there."

Sarah was wonderfully, horribly tempted. *You're leaving soon*, the stern voice in her head warned, and her amusement died. *The closer you get to him, the harder it will be.* It was already going to be agonizing, and all they'd done so far was kiss. She needed to protect herself, but she felt so *good* when she was around him—talking to him, watching him, kissing him…

With a sigh that turned into a groan, she took a step back, her hands dropping to her sides. It took him several seconds to release her, but it wasn't in a frightening way. His hands just lingered, as if reluctant to lose contact with her skin.

"You should sleep."

"Yes." He didn't sound excited about the prospect, and his gaze ran over her hungrily, as if he was thinking about snatching her up and carrying her to his bedroom.

Excitement at the thought made her skin prickle, and she shivered in a way that had nothing to do with cold. It was tempting—so tempting—but the nagging voice in her head wouldn't stop reminding her of the heartache to come if she let herself be weak. "Join me?"

The words jolted through her, and she took a step closer to him before she caught herself. "I want to, but I shouldn't. I don't want to start something I can't finish." His brows drew together in a puzzled frown. "I mean, Monroe can only be a temporary safe house." Otto flinched, and she felt like a monster. "If I have to run again…" The thought was too terrible to finish out loud.

"Your brother's locked up," he said. "The judge denied bail, and the FBI will be picking him up later this week, as soon as the transfer paperwork goes through. He can't get to you."

"What if he gets off, though? What if he bribes the next judge or pays someone to grab me? Aaron's never been a good loser. I can't get comfortable here, because Aaron will ruin it for me. He always ruins everything."

Otto reached out, slow and easy, to cup her face again. "Just come sleep with me. Only sleep." He gave her a tiny smile, but his eyes were guarded. "I'll rest better knowing you're safe next to me."

She had to say no. She had to resist. "Okay." *Ugh*. She was such a soft touch. There was no way she could say no to Otto, not when he was holding her face so gently and looking at her so sweetly. "Yes."

They made their way up to the second floor quietly. Even though Otto had specified that they'd only be sleeping, bubbling tension crept up Sarah's spine. What if she couldn't hold back any longer and hurled herself onto his unconscious body? Her willpower seemed to be as strong as a bowl of overcooked oatmeal around him.

Automatically, she moved toward the guest bedroom where she'd been sleeping, but he took her hand and tugged her through the doorway across the hall. She looked around, not having seen his bedroom yet. It was just like him—big, but warm and cozy and a little old-fashioned. The bed was huge.

Wordlessly, he handed her a T-shirt before disappearing into the bathroom. She quickly changed, hugging the soft cotton against her and wallowing in the scent. It was a clean shirt, she could tell, but it still smelled like his detergent. As he walked back into the bedroom, she smiled at him, and he stopped dead in his tracks.

"Okay?" she asked, her grin starting to fade with concern.

"Yes." He started moving again, right toward her. She held her breath as he grew closer and closer, until he finally slid past her and walked to the enormous bed. Pulling down the covers, he stepped back and gestured for her to climb in first.

Her entire body heated from nerves and embarrassment and need as she slid into his bed—*Otto's* bed. The sheets were flannel and wonderfully soft, a small part of her noticed, even while the rest of her brain was occupied with watching Otto, dressed only in a T-shirt and loose exercise pants, get into bed next to her.

I'm in bed with Otto, she thought, delighted even as the voice in her head scolded her, telling her it was a mistake, that it was the first step on a slippery slope that ended in tears, but she tuned it out. *I'll give myself this*, she decided, turning onto her side so she faced Otto. *Tomorrow, I'll be smart.*

Otto smiled at her, and everything inside her loosened and warmed. His hand came up to stroke her cheek briefly. When he started to withdraw, Sarah grabbed his hand. Lacing her fingers with his, she tucked their conjoined hands under her chin, making him smile again. He kept his gaze on her until his eyes closed and his breath slowed and deepened.

Sarah held his hand tightly as she watched him sleep. Tiredness pulled at her, tempting her to close her eyes, but this was too precious. She wasn't about to waste even a second of it.

The night shift had been hellish. Between a domestic call, a car accident, and a propane leak, Otto had been running at full speed for twelve hours. On the bright side, no one had been hurt, the cars ended up with only minor damage, and nothing exploded, but Otto was bone-tired—too tired to even curse the chief for stealing away so many officers.

Despite the busy night, Otto hadn't been able to stop thinking about Sarah. She'd told him flat-out that she was leaving eventually. How could he expect her to stay? Monroe—especially in the winter—was dull and isolated. Just because he considered it home didn't mean that the woman he was fascinated with would want to stay. He kept telling himself to enjoy the time he had with her and quit thinking about how empty he'd feel when she was gone.

Finally, his shift ended, and he hurried home, pushing his speed, even around the hairpin turns. As he hurried up the stairs, he imagined finding her in his room, in his bed, and the mental image made him rush even faster. As he moved through the doorway, his smile faded. No one was there. Returning to the hall, he glanced in the guest room and saw it was empty, as well. Nerves started to buzz deep in his gut as he quickly checked the house. All of her things were still there, so she hadn't left yet—at least not voluntarily.

That thought had him tensing, adrenaline shooting through him as if preparing him to hunt down the person who'd snatched Sarah out of her bed and her new home. He rushed through the living room, peering through the windows to see if he could see her outside. It was still really early, but maybe she couldn't sleep.

His gaze fell on the coat closet leading to the bunker, and his pulse slowed slightly. Hurrying into the closet, he opened the door in the back wall and then took the stairs four at a time. As soon as he spotted her, curled on one of the bunks, surrounded by his animals, all the air left him in a relieved rush.

Otto stared for a few moments before he started to smile. Sarah was curled up on her side, sleeping on one third of the cot, with Mort, Xena, and Bob taking up the other two-thirds. Mort and Bob opened their eyes briefly, saw it was Otto, and then closed them again. Xena, on the other hand, watched him warily from where she was curled up behind Sarah's knees.

He had to admit that he was a little bothered that Xena had bonded so quickly to Sarah. It was a good thing she had, and Otto tried to brush off his slight jealousy, but it was hard when he thought about all those hours feeding the scared dog treats at Nan's. Xena gave a slight huff, as if she could read his thoughts and was laughing at his pettiness.

Otto checked on Sarah, wondering if the dog had disturbed her, but she was still solidly sleeping, her breathing deep and even, and her hair falling across her face. He hated to wake her, but he wanted her to know he was home. The night, as busy as it had been, had also felt incredibly long, with a rerun of the previous afternoon replaying over and over in his head. He was antsy to talk to her, to see how she was. Maybe she'd offer to make breakfast again. Yesterday's breakfast burritos had been incredible. Usually, when he was on night shift, he wasn't motivated to cook when he got home. He'd just grab something, do animal chores, and then crash in front of the TV until he went to bed.

With Sarah there, though, he was hopped up on adrenaline. He couldn't get their kisses out of his head, and he grinned every time he thought about her. The one good thing about being short-staffed at the station was that, if they'd been there, the other officers would've been mocking him relentlessly about his cheerfulness.

It wasn't just the attraction. Having someone else at his house was unexpectedly nice. Otto hadn't realized just how depressing coming home to an empty-except-for-animals house had been. It would be hard once she left. His stomach dropped at the thought, and he instantly chided himself. He couldn't get attached—well, more attached. She wouldn't be staying with him for long, and then he'd be alone again. That seemed to be the pattern of his life—people and animals stayed for a while, and then they left.

Shaking off his self-pity, Otto reached forward and

closed his hand around the foot that was sticking out from under the quilt. Her long, fuzzy, yellow-and-orange-striped socks fit her sunny personality so well that he had to grin when he saw them. "Sarah," he said quietly.

Her eyes popped open as soon as he touched her, coming awake and anxious in a fraction of a second. "What's wrong?" She sat up abruptly, the movement pulling her foot free of his grip.

"Nothing." Otto automatically used the calming voice that worked to soothe injured and frightened animals. "Unless you consider me having to cook my own eggs as wrong."

"Oh, I'm sorry." She got out of bed, swaying a little as she stood, and Otto hurried to catch her arm before she toppled over. "I'll cook something."

"No, I'm teasing," he said as she blinked up at him, still looking dazed from sleep. He felt guilty for waking her just because he didn't want to be alone. "You can go back to bed. I wanted to let you know I'm home, that's all."

To his surprise, she blushed. "Am I that obvious?"

"Obvious?"

"That I have a hard time sleeping when you're gone?" She dropped her gaze, and Otto wondered if she would've blurted that out if she hadn't just woken up.

He grimaced, torn by the need to stay home and take care of her and the responsibility he had to the police department. If only the chief hadn't picked that week to send everyone to training. "Sorry. I'd take time off, but—"

"Oh no," she interrupted, looking embarrassed. "I'm sorry I said that. I'm still half asleep, I think. Xena kept prodding me with her feet, and Mort has this way of half lying on me and jabbing me with his pointy… What is that joint? His elbow? His shoulder? Whatever it is, it's like the bone equivalent of a poker."

Otto groaned and laughed at the same time. "Yeah. I know what you mean. He does that to me, too."

"I'm glad you woke me up," she said, stretching, still rumpled with heavy-lidded eyes. He loved seeing her this way—although he loved seeing her any way. "You're always welcome to wake me if I'm sleeping when you get home. We don't get much time together, and I don't want to miss a minute."

His stomach warmed at her admission. "I will."

They made their way up the stairs. Mort and Bob stretched and yawned before ambling after them, and Xena slunk along right behind Sarah. She was close enough that it looked like the dog would crash into her legs if Sarah were to stop abruptly.

"Did you still want to go job-hunting today?" Otto asked reluctantly, holding open the door. It was hard not to wrap Sarah in bubble wrap and keep her safe at home, but Otto didn't want to turn into her jailer. She'd had too many of those.

"Yes!" Her face lit with excitement. "Can we go after breakfast?"

"Sure." Her happiness made him feel churlish. To make up for it, he insisted on making breakfast. It was just simple veggie omelets and fruit, but she thanked him as if he'd served her a five-course meal.

"Just let me do chores, and then we can go."

She tagged along, eager to help and surprisingly proficient with a manure fork.

"You're not what I expected." As soon as the words

were out, he wished them back in, knowing what her immediate question would be.

She finished putting several flakes of hay in one of the feeders before asking, "What did you expect?"

He paused, wanting to get the words right. It wasn't a bad thing, what he'd expected when he'd first saw her, and he didn't want his explanation to come out as an insult. "Your family has a lot of money. Money usually means that you can hire people to do things for you. Sometimes, when people don't have to do the messy jobs, they forget that those things exist. You don't, though. You know they exist, and you know how to do them. In fact, you seem happy to do them." Otto watched her carefully for any sign of offense, but she looked thoughtful instead.

"You're right." Turning away, she stacked hay in the other feeder. He wished he could watch her expression, since her voice was carefully even. "My father and brother hired people to do everything. Two of those people, Chester and Gloria, pretty much raised me. Chester taught me about horses and cars, and Gloria taught me how to cook and how to defend myself and basically all of the things that normal people know how to do. I was lucky. If I'd been a boy, my father would've taught me how to be like him. I'd much, much rather be like Gloria and Chester."

Her voice shook a little at the end, and Otto couldn't help himself. He reached out and stroked her back. When she leaned into his touch, he felt a deep satisfaction, more intense than anything he'd ever felt before. It startled him, the hugeness of that feeling, and he withdrew his hand, reminding himself that he needed to be careful. She could leave him in ruins if he wasn't.

Then Sarah turned her head and gave him a smile that was sweet and whole and knocked his caution right out of the water. It was too late. He was well and truly caught.

CHAPTER 13

SARAH CLUTCHED HER FALSIFIED RÉSUMÉ IN BOTH HANDS, hating how much she was shaking. She tried to force her feet to walk through the door, but they were not cooperating. She turned to face Otto, who was patiently standing next to her, waiting for her nerves to settle. "How do people do this?"

Otto chuckled, but it sounded more sympathetic than mean. "It'll get a little easier, once you've gotten through a few interviews, but I don't know anyone who actually enjoys job-hunting. When I applied to the Monroe PD, I was shaking in my boots, and I knew the chief."

"So, what's the secret?" She shook out one hand and then the other. Her hold on the résumé had been so tight that her fingers were cramping.

"Confidence?"

"You don't sound too confident about that."

He smiled at her, bumping her arm lightly with his fist. "You have to fake it at first."

"Okay. Fake it." She thought of all the dinners she'd sat through, all the horrible people she'd been polite to. "I can do that."

Squaring her shoulders, she marched into the store and up to the register, where an older man with a craggy face and a couple weeks of scruff was playing on his phone. He was wearing overalls. Sarah had never seen anyone over the age of four actually wear overalls before—not in real life, at least. It was a good sign, she decided, that the employees could dress casually.

"Hi. Is the manager here?"

He lifted his eyes from his phone without raising his chin, which was a slightly menacing look. *Fake it*, Sarah reminded herself, and she held his gaze. "What do you want?" he asked.

"I'd like to apply for a job…um, here." She gave herself a mental smack. *No stuttering. Project confidence! You can do it!* Her thoughts were the mental equivalent of inspirational posters.

He slipped his phone into his overall bib pocket. "You're new in town."

"Yes."

"Why'd you move?"

"My friend Jules lives here, and I've always wanted to live in Colorado." The line came out smoothly—as it should, since she'd practiced it over and over.

"Why'd you leave wherever you were from?"

"I graduated from college." She liked answers that weren't actually lies, since she was less likely to stumble over them, and there were no twinges of guilt.

"Where you staying?"

Her first instinct was to lie. For the past few weeks, she'd been so focused on hiding that it was hard to answer honestly. Aaron was in jail now, though, and soon he'd be with the FBI. For the moment, she was safe. "With Otto Gunnersen—for now." As she added the qualifier, she felt a pang, but she quickly pushed it away. It wasn't the time for moping. She had a job to secure.

"All winter?"

"Will I be staying with Otto all winter?"

"No," Overall Guy said, leaning back against the wall. "Will you be staying in Monroe all winter?"

"Oh. Yes." Unless her brother made her run again, but that wasn't a confidence-building thought, so she pushed it back.

"Sure about that? Gets pretty cold and snowy here."

"Yes."

Some of her determination must have shown on her face, since he pushed away from the wall. "What hours can you work?"

"Anytime." That sounded promising. Little sparklers of hope started fizzing in her belly, but she tried not to get excited. She didn't have the job yet. "Afternoons would be best, but I could do mornings, too." It would be nice to work while Otto was sleeping. Even after just a few days of settling into their routine, she'd miss their mornings together.

Pressing his lips together, he eyed her up and down. It wasn't a creepy look, but more of an assessment. "You're pretty small."

"I'm strong, though." *Confidence. Sell yourself.* Her brain was doing the motivational-poster thing again, and she quickly shut it down before she started laughing like a loon. "Smart, too. If something's too heavy for me to lift, I figure out a way to move it."

He hummed, and Sarah's palms prickled with sweat. She couldn't tell if that sound was thoughtful or skeptical or shorthand for "How do I get this woman out of the store?" She wondered if Overall Guy was the manager or owner. If she had to go through another interview with someone even more intimidating, she might end up curled up in a corner.

Her hands clenched, and paper rustled, reminding her of what she was holding. "Here's my résumé." She held it out, trying not to cringe at the rumpled edges where her nervous fingers had been clamped. Sarah hoped that he didn't ask her any questions about her pretend job history. Even though she'd studied it carefully for hours, her mind was currently a blank. She could barely remember her new last name.

Overall Guy glanced down briefly, but he didn't seem too interested in her résumé. Instead, he went back to studying her in that nerve-racking way. Finally, he spoke. "Come in tomorrow at noon. We'll give it a try."

"Really?" The sparklers in her stomach burst into full flame. "Thank you! I'll work very hard, I promise."

Overall Guy—her new boss—made a *humph* sound and fished out his phone. "We'll see."

"Yes. Thank you. I'll be here tomorrow. At noon. To work." Sarah closed her mouth, not wanting any more babble to spill out. It was just that she was so excited. Her first job…and she'd gotten it all on her own. She hadn't needed the Blanchett name to open doors or prove her worth or scare someone into giving her the position. She'd done it by herself, as Sarah Clifton.

She nearly skipped out the door. As soon as she emerged, she stopped short so she didn't crash headlong into Otto.

"Well?" he asked, looking almost as stressed as she'd felt earlier.

Sarah beamed, knowing that all of her excitement and pride must be obvious. "I start tomorrow."

With a whoop, Otto grabbed her in his arms, spinning her around. Laughing, Sarah hugged him back. Having him share her accomplishment made everything fifty times better. Her grip tightened as she pulled him closer, clinging to him. At that moment, she was almost unbearably happy.

"Want to go to the viner for lunch to celebrate your new job?" Otto asked, putting her down.

Sarah stepped back reluctantly. Although she knew it wouldn't be practical for her to spend all her time being hugged by Otto, it would be a nice way to live. "Sure. I haven't seen Jules in a few days."

As they walked the half block to the VFW-turned-diner, Sarah shivered, wrapping her arms around her. Her coat was thick, but the wind was cold, and it seemed to find all the vulnerable spots on her body, snaking into her collar and cuffs where a tiny bit of bare skin was exposed. Down the street, the spot where the diner used to be before it had been blown up was just a bare dirt lot, looking like a missing tooth in the line of shops. Everything looked so barren and abandoned, with the closed signs in almost every window. Sarah was looking forward to seeing Monroe in the summer, when it was warm and bustling with people.

The wind picked up, and Sarah twisted her head to the side. "Brrr! Do you think it's going to snow tonight?"

"Supposed to, but the weather site's been predicting snow for the last few days. I'll believe it when I'm trying to drive the squad car in it."

Sarah ducked under his arm as he held the viner door for her. Inside, warm air and a host of good food smells hit her at once, and she relaxed muscles she hadn't even realized she'd braced against the cold.

"Sarah!" Jules waved from across the room. "And Otto! Have a seat, and I'll be right with y'all."

Sarah smiled. She loved Jules's Southernisms and the way she stretched out words. Her accent sounded softer than the Texas twang Sarah was used to hearing. Spotting Grace and Hugh, Sarah wound her way through the tables until she reached them.

"Guess what?" Sarah slid into the chair Otto held out, giving him a smile of thanks. Before either Grace or Hugh could guess, she blurted out her news. "I got a job!"

"That's great!" Leaning over, Grace gave her a side hug. "Where is it? It's not at Nan's, is it? Because that was way too much poo for me. I'm much happier dealing with theoretical poo in my development job than the real stuff."

Sarah laughed, her happiness bubbling out again. "No, it's poo free—at least I hope it is. It's at Grady's."

"Congratulations." Hugh grinned at her from across the table as Otto settled into the chair next to him, stretching his long legs out in front of him.

"Thank you." Sarah looked back and forth between Grace and Hugh. "You two aren't fighting, are you?"

"*Fighting* fighting? No, although we're pretty much always arguing. It's a constant of our relationship," Grace said. "Why?"

Before Sarah could answer, Hugh broke in. "It's not arguing when we do it. It's flirting."

"Flirting with occasional yelling?" Grace asked skeptically.

Reaching across the table, Hugh caught her hand, looking very pleased with himself. "Not yelling. Loud flirting."

"Right." With an amused snort, Grace turned to Sarah. "Why did you think we were fighting?"

"You just seem more like a sit-on-the-same-side-of-the-table type of couple, that's all."

Otto laughed, and both Grace and Hugh stared at him, looking surprised. "What?" Otto asked.

"Did Sarah open Otto's laugh vault?" Hugh asked. "You're positively giddy today."

He is? Sarah wondered, eyeing him. Otto didn't look giddy to her. He had the stoic expression that he usually wore. His eyes might've been a little softer, and his mouth curled up a bit higher at the corners, but Sarah didn't see any dramatic changes. She figured Hugh was just exaggerating, as usual.

"We're not a same-side couple," Grace said, pulling the conversation back on track. "I refuse to be part of a same-side couple."

"We're more of a same-chair couple." Hugh gave Grace a look that Sarah could only describe as steamy.

Grace laughed, but she didn't deny it, and Hugh pushed out of his chair, leaning across the table so he could kiss her.

Blushing a little, Sarah looked away. Unfortunately, her gaze landed on Otto, who was watching her with a hungry expression. Her warm face got hotter, and she dropped her gaze to the menu in front of her.

"Hey." Jules bustled up to the table, saving Sarah from the awkward and heated moment. "Sorry that took me so long." She looked at Grace and then Hugh.

"If you two are here, and the kids are at school, who's watching the puppies?"

"We are." Hugh had settled back again. He discreetly pointed toward the floor by his chair. Everyone else, very indiscreetly, ducked to look under the table, where a soft-sided pet carrier was sitting.

"You brought them *here*?" Jules gave a hunted glance over her shoulder and lowered her voice. "Megan is so going to kill you if she finds out you brought dogs into her diner. If the health inspector saw that…"

"They're allowed." Hugh waved a hand, brushing off her concerns.

Jules stared. "They are not."

"Sure they are." Stretching his legs out in front of him, Hugh didn't look worried about the health inspector's wrath—or Megan's. "They're service animals."

"They're two-week-old puppies."

"Service animals in training."

Although Jules was obviously trying to cling to her indignation, Sarah could see her holding back a smile. "Fine. Just keep them quiet. If you're caught with them, I don't know a thing about any puppies. Got it?"

"Got it." Hugh didn't even try to contain his grin.

"That's amazing." Sarah didn't realize she'd said it out loud until everyone looked at her.

"What's amazing?" Grace asked.

"He just convinced Jules to let him keep the puppies in a diner. Does he get his way all the time?"

"Yes," Grace said, talking over Hugh's "No." "It's unbelievable what he gets away with."

"That's true," Otto chimed in, and Hugh turned his gravely offended expression toward his partner.

"I'm appalled that you would even think…" Hugh started, but Grace patted his arm, interrupting him.

"You are spoiled rotten. We all know it and love you anyway."

When Hugh opened his mouth to argue, Grace was the one who leaned over the table and gave him a peck. This time, Sarah was very careful not to look at Otto. They hadn't kissed since he'd left for work the previous evening, and Sarah was starting to get antsy and needy and a little desperate. How quickly he'd turned her into an Otto addict.

"We're never getting the puppies back, are we?" Otto asked.

"Never," Grace, Jules, and Hugh chorused.

Jules patted Otto's hand. "Sorry."

He gave her a small smile. Honestly, Sarah didn't think Otto was too torn up that the puppies had been confiscated. He had too much on his plate as it was, and getting up every three hours for feedings on top of all his other responsibilities would've been brutal.

"Thank you for taking care of them," Sarah said, looking around the table. "We miss them, but it's nice having sleep."

"We've been trading off." Grace took a sip of her coffee. "It's still rough, but they're cute, so that makes up for it."

"I think that's what new mothers say, too." Jules grinned until one of the other customers called her name. "Sorry. I'll get your food. Sarah, what would you like? I know everyone else's orders."

"The pancakes, please. With strawberries."

"Whipped cream?"

Her instinct was to say no, since her father or her brother would've made some comment about how she needed to be careful not to get fat, but then she remembered that she was free. She could eat whatever she wanted to eat. She could be whatever size she wanted to be. "Yes, please. Extra whipped cream."

As if she could read Sarah's thoughts, Jules's smile grew huge and supportive. "You've got it."

"You like pancakes?" Otto asked her.

"They're my favorite breakfast food." She noticed that everyone was quiet, listening to their exchange, and she looked around the table. In her previous life, she'd hated it when the focus was on her. It never turned out well. Now, though, her new friends all looked relaxed and interested in what she had to say. It was different from before, but she still shifted a little, unsure if she liked the attention or not. It was a lot to get used to.

"I'll make them for you," he said. "You'll like my pancakes."

"I'm sure I will." The words were out, thick with innuendo, before she could think twice. Hugh was grinning ear to ear, and Grace tossed a balled-up napkin at him.

"See? That's how normal people flirt," she said. "There's no yelling involved."

Hugh caught the napkin. "If I were normal, you wouldn't love me so much."

Eyeing him for a long moment, Grace finally shrugged. "Not a lie."

Theo, in uniform, pulled up a chair to the end of the table.

"Careful," Hugh warned, reaching down to shift the puppies' carrier away from Theo's feet.

"Of what?" After glancing under the table, he refocused on Hugh, his eyes narrow. "Are those the puppies?"

"Shh!" Everyone except Hugh shushed him.

"Why are they here?" Theo looked at the carrier again, and his frown deepened. "There's not an outlet down there. Don't they have their heating pad? They're going to get cold."

"We put a couple of hand warmers under their blankets," Hugh said. "They're fine. If they weren't fine, they wouldn't be quietly sleeping. They're not shy about letting us know when they're cold—or hungry or too warm or in any way not comfortable."

Although Theo's grunt sounded like grudging agreement, he still didn't look happy. "I should've taken them to work with me."

"You can't bring puppies on calls with you." Jules popped up next to him to pour a cup of coffee and kiss him on the cheek. "The puppies are fine with Hugh. We trust him to babysit the kids. The health inspector might close the viner down, but the puppies will be okay."

"I thought you weren't going to let me babysit the kids anymore after the cat incident," Hugh said.

"That's Otto," Jules corrected before rushing off to serve another table.

"Hey," Otto said mildly. "I didn't find the cat. If I hadn't gotten it down, Dee would've climbed up herself."

Theo shrugged slightly as he took a drink of his coffee. "She's just kidding. You're still our second pick after Grace."

"What about me?" Hugh complained.

After giving Hugh a flat look, Theo turned back to Otto. "Like I said, you're still our second pick."

Grace smirked at Hugh before saying to Sarah, "How have things been going at Otto's?"

Sarah opened her mouth to tell Grace everything, but then looked around and noticed the other interested faces around the table. There was even a bearded guy at the next table who appeared to be eavesdropping. Sarah swallowed back all of her news and just said, "Fine."

Giving the people around them a sweeping look, Grace obviously understood the situation. "I'm going to the bathroom." She stood up. "Sarah? You coming?"

Sarah popped out of her seat, falling in next to Grace, but Otto caught her hand, halting her. "You'll have to go one at a time," he told her. "There aren't any stalls. It's just a single bathroom."

Hugh started to laugh. "They're not going to the bathroom to actually use it," he said.

His forehead furrowing in the way it did when he didn't understand something, Otto looked at Hugh and then back at Sarah.

"They're going to the bathroom so they can have some privacy when they talk about us." Glancing at Sarah, Hugh amended his words. "You, buddy. They're going to the bathroom to talk about you."

Sarah felt her face heat as Otto released her hand, still looking confused. She wanted to say something, to assure him that they wouldn't be talking about him, but Grace tugged her away from the table. Besides, Sarah thought as she looked back over her shoulder while Grace towed her toward the bathroom, denying it would be a lie. They were going to talk, and it most likely was going to feature Otto.

"So?" Grace demanded once they were in the bathroom, even before the door latch clicked shut. "Tell me everything. What's been going on?"

Sarah hesitated. It wasn't that she wanted to hold back, but she wasn't sure where to start. "Well…a lot."

Grace's eyes got huge even as her voice lowered to a whisper. "Are you guys having sex?"

"Not yet."

"Not yet?" Grace's smile grew until it curved her mouth up wickedly. "So why are you blushing? Have you kissed?"

"Yes." Her face got even hotter, but she couldn't stop grinning.

"Is Otto a good kisser?"

"Really, really good." Her smile matched Grace's. "Amazing. The best. I don't think there are words good enough to explain just how incredible he is."

Grace gave a laughing squeal and caught Sarah in a hug. "Yay! Kisses! Good kisses!"

Laughing, Sarah hugged her back. Having a friend felt almost as nice as Otto's kisses. They turned in a circle, squeezing each other and laughing, until they finally quieted enough to talk again.

"Was it just kissing, or did he push the envelope? Otto's so quiet, and you know what they say about those quiet guys."

Sarah frowned in confusion. "What do they say?"

"I'm actually not sure." They laughed again. Sarah was more giddy than amused, but it didn't matter. Grace snickered right along with her. "So is he—"

The door handle rattled, interrupting her.

"Just a minute," Sarah called out, figuring it was

someone who needed to use the bathroom, but the knob shook again.

"Hugh," Grace said in a warning voice. "If you pick that lock again, I am going to kill you."

"Again?" Sarah whispered, her eyes on the knob. If it was Hugh, then Sarah had a feeling some of that "yelling flirting" was about to happen.

Grace waved a hand. "It's his thing," she said dismissively, while Sarah goggled at her. If her boyfriend— Otto's face jumped into her head when she thought the word *boyfriend*—had a "thing" that involved unlocking the doors to women's restrooms, Sarah was pretty sure she'd have a problem with that.

The knob kept turning from side to side. "Hugh?" Grace's voice grew less bossy and more uncertain when no response came from the other side of the door. The knob went still, but Sarah and Grace continued to stare. After a few seconds, Sarah's shoulders relaxed. It had just been someone needing to use the bathroom, like she'd first thought, and they hadn't heard her telling them that it would be a min—

The door flew open, crashing against the wall. Grace screamed, but Sarah's shout went the wrong direction, burning her throat as she sucked in a frightened breath. Jeb stalked into the bathroom, followed by Logan Jovanovic in a police officer's uniform.

"Your little rebellion's over. Time to go home," Jeb said, reaching out to grab Sarah's arm. The movement knocked her out of her paralysis, and she dodged, darting out of reach and backing away.

"What the hell?" Logan said, and Sarah's gaze flashed to him for just a second. He was staring at Grace, an unpleasant smile growing on his face. "You're here, too? It's a two-for-one special."

Sarah jerked her attention back to Jeb, but the distraction was enough to give him time to lunge. She twisted, trying to stay out of reach, but he managed to grab a handful of her coat and hauled her out of the bathroom into the VFW entryway. Panic wiped her brain clear, and she struggled like a kitten caught by the scruff until she started thinking again. Yanking her arms from the sleeves, she pulled out of her unzipped coat, falling to the floor once she was free.

The jarring impact drove a grunt out of her, and she remembered that she had a voice—and that there was a table of help only a few feet away. Sucking in a breath, she screamed.

Logan ran from the bathroom, blood running from his nose as he bounced off the doorjamb. He jumped over Sarah's legs on his way to the door. Yanking it open, Logan dashed outside.

"Shit," Jeb muttered, grabbing at her again. This time, Sarah was able to scramble away and dodge his grip. A nearby roar caught her attention.

Everyone in the viner was running toward them. The pack was led by Otto, whose face was pulled tight with rage. Jeb grabbed her, gripping both of her arms, but Sarah hardly felt it. All her attention was focused on the rampaging Viking lumberjack coming to her rescue.

Jeb's hands went slack, and he made a strange whimpering sound that told Sarah he'd spotted Otto. She grinned fiercely. Jeb was right to be scared. Otto, her gentle, kind giant, was about to kick his ass.

Then he was there, yanking Jeb off her. Otto's huge

fists smashed into him—once, twice, a third time—before Theo and Hugh were pulling him off.

"Leave us enough to arrest," Hugh said, his usual lighthearted tone just a thin overlay. Even shocked and battered, Sarah could hear Hugh's rage. His gaze raked the area, finally landing on Sarah. "Where's Grace?"

Her heart skipped and then started to pound. Grace! Before Sarah could scramble to her feet and run into the bathroom, Grace was standing in the doorway.

"I'm okay." Hugh loosened his hold on Otto and was at Grace's side in an instant. She gave him an only slightly wobbly smile. "Really, Hugh. I'm fine."

Sarah looked back at Otto, who was breathing hard, his hands clenched at his sides. Jeb was still on the ground, staring up at him. Blood trickled from a cut below his eye, which was what reminded Sarah of Logan.

"Logan was here," she said, and all three cops snapped their heads around to look at her. "Logan Jovanovic. He ran out that way."

Keeping his gaze locked on her, Otto shook free of Theo's hold and walked the few steps to where she was still sitting on the floor. He crouched down and cupped her cheek.

"I'm fine, too." She made a shooing gesture. "Hurry. He's getting away."

"You going to kill him if I leave him with you?" Theo asked Otto, quickly handcuffing a cowering Jeb.

There was a pause before Otto finally said, "No." Theo frowned, obviously not believing him.

"I'll watch him," Jules said, pushing through the gawking customers standing in a circle around the action. "Go get the other guy."

Theo still hesitated until Megan and then Vicki joined Jules. Apparently, since he rushed out the door, Theo thought that the three of them—four including Sarah— would be enough to keep Otto from dismembering Jeb.

"What happened?" Hugh asked, sliding an arm around Grace's shoulders. She leaned against his side.

"Jeb and Logan broke into the bathroom," Sarah said. She started to climb to her feet, mentally cursing her shaky limbs, and then Otto lifted her off the floor. Once she was up, he kept his hands on her shoulders until she felt steady. A part of her wished he would pull her into his arms so she could bury her face in his chest and forget about everything, but she knew she couldn't collapse yet. *Later*, she promised herself. She could cuddle him later. "At first, we thought it was Hugh—"

Hugh made a small sound of protest that drew everyone's attention. After a second, he shrugged, keeping the gesture small enough that it didn't jostle Grace. "Fair enough. Keep going."

"They kicked the door in." Sarah swallowed, willing her voice not to shake. "Jeb dragged me out by the coat, so I slipped out of it and screamed. By the time he grabbed me again, you were all here."

"I punched Logan in the face," Grace said baldly. "He started to come at me again, but then he heard Sarah scream, so he took off." Her voice caught as she looked up at Hugh. "He recognized me."

Hugh pulled her gently against his chest. "It's okay, Gracie. Theo and Viggy will run him down. We've got a bunch of the Jovanovic bastards already locked up. I'll keep you safe while we get the rest of them."

With her face still pressed against him, Grace shook her

head. Her voice came out muffled. "There are too many of them. I can't keep dragging you guys into my mess."

"I'm sorry." Sarah stared at the back of Grace's head as she realized what she'd done, what she'd brought on these people who she'd started to consider friends.

Otto slid his hands from her shoulders to her upper arms in a reassuring caress. "Not your fault."

"It is, though." She turned to meet his gaze. "I brought them here. Logan would've never even seen Grace if he hadn't been here for me. I should've left after he found me the first time, but I was selfish. I'm sorry, Grace. I'm sorry for pulling you all into this."

"It's not your fault," Otto said sharply, although his hands on her arms still glided up and down in gentle contrast to his abrupt tone. "It's not Grace's fault. It's your asshole brother's fault. It's this piece of garbage's fault." He flung a hand toward Jeb, who flinched back. "It's the fault of every single Jovanovic who works in the family business, doing evil things."

"But if I'd left—"

"You shouldn't have to leave." He cut her off. "We'll deal with this, with these people. Together. All of us. You have backup here. If you were running from strange town to strange town, you'd be alone."

The thought of that terrified Sarah, but she didn't want to be selfish. She didn't have the right to bring harm and possible death to these good people.

Otto's voice lowered until it was too quiet for anyone but her to hear. "Don't go, Sarah. Xena needs you here. I need you here. Don't let them chase you away. They're hoping you'll run so that you'll be easier to catch. See what just happened? Your brother sent two people after you. One ran off after Grace punched him, and the other is cowering on the floor in cuffs. If you stay here, we'll help you win. Your brother is not stronger than you, not when you have us here to help."

Sarah hesitated, still not completely convinced, but what Otto had just said... She wanted so badly for it to be reality. One by one, they could defeat her brother's allies. She could have allies of her own—friends—and her new job and live in this tiny town she was growing to love. The thought of it made a bubble of optimism start to grow inside her. "Okay."

Tipping his head down even closer to her ear, Otto repeated, "Okay?"

Her breath caught as the warmth of that question brushed her skin. "Yes. Okay."

Ever so gently, he gathered her against him in a hug.

She pulled away with a start when the outside door swung open, and Theo shoved a cuffed Logan inside. "Didn't even need Viggy. This moron was running down the middle of Main Street. If this is the brains of the Jovanovic crime family now, they're in serious trouble."

Logan glared at him but didn't say a word. Despite the handcuffs, Sarah's heart started pounding at the sight of him. As if he could sense her anxiety, Otto pulled her close again.

"What's that sound?" Megan asked, but Sarah didn't really pay attention. She was too busy wallowing in warmth and security, in the scent and feel that was all Otto.

When she pulled away and stepped back, she realized that everyone was watching. Blushing, she ducked, pressing her forehead against Otto's solid upper arm.

"So?" Grace asked from where she still stood tucked

against Hugh. "Are you staying with us, or are you going to let the bastards run you off?"

"I'm staying."

"Good." Grace gave her a fierce smile. "I'll punch a Jovanovic for you anytime. It's oddly satisfying."

"I'd like to try it sometime," Jules said. "I've heard it's nice."

Sarah's laugh was a little choked, but that hopeful bubble inside her grew even larger.

"What the hell?" Megan's roar came from the dining area. "Who brought dogs into my diner?"

CHAPTER 14

Stocking shelves was oddly soothing, Sarah found. She was glad, because her life at the moment needed some soothing. Taking the last spool of rope out of the box, she added it to the display and then sat back on her haunches.

"How's it going?" asked Grady—who, it ended up, both owned the store and wore overalls every day.

"Good." She stood, picking up the box and taking a final glance at the neat rows of various sizes and types of rope. "It's very satisfying."

At Grady's silence, she glanced over to see him looking at her oddly.

"What?"

"You're a strange one."

"Yes." It wasn't the first time she'd been told that.

"Need you to watch the register for a while."

"Okay." She headed for the front. Ringing people up wasn't as calming as stocking the shelves, but it was interesting. Just in the few days that she'd worked at Grady's, Sarah felt like she'd met everyone left in town. Grady had a habit of disappearing for an hour or so in the afternoons. Grace's theory was that he was watching *Tattered Hearts*. Sarah loved the idea that the crusty old guy was addicted to a soap opera.

Her first customer proved her wrong about having met everyone. The man was very nondescript-looking— average height, average weight, average brown hair and eyes—but Sarah was pretty sure that she hadn't seen him before.

"Hi." The bar code on the spool of wire wasn't wanting to scan, so she entered the numbers by hand. "I'm Sarah."

The man studied her for a long moment. "Norman Rounds."

"Nice to meet you."

"You, too." He was quiet while she finished scanning the rest of his items.

"That'll be forty-four dollars and two cents."

As he handed her the exact amount in cash, he spoke again. "Are you the Sarah staying out at the cop's place? The one with all the animals?"

An instinctual jolt of fear shot through her, and she caught herself right before she lied and denied it. Aaron, Jeb, and Logan were all locked up. They couldn't hurt her now. "That's me." She bit back the urge to clarify that she was only there temporarily. The longer she lived with Otto, the less she wanted to leave. Sarah wasn't sure how Otto felt about her staying, though. He hadn't kissed her since right before they'd slept—just slept— together, and she'd catch him staring at her with an odd expression. She knew she needed to talk to him, but she didn't want to know if he was just no longer interested. That would hurt. A lot.

She handed Norman Rounds his receipt, but he didn't leave. Instead, he asked, "Where are you from?"

"Iowa." For some reason, she'd never picked up a

Texas accent, so Mr. Espina had her pick her imaginary home state. To her, Iowa had always seemed like an ideal place to grow up. She pictured helping with the chores as part of a big farm family—kind of like a modern-day *Little House on the Prairie*. Now that the cops, Grace, and Jules knew her story, she supposed that she could've said Texas, but she liked pretending that happy farm upbringing had really happened.

"Hmm." He studied her for so long that she shifted uncomfortably.

"Can I get you anything else?"

"No." He picked up his bags, looking secretly amused. "I think I have everything I need for now."

As she watched him leave the store, Sarah felt a little shiver of unease ripple through her. "Stop it," she muttered. "You have enough real bad guys in your life. Don't be inventing more."

"Who are you talking to?"

Whipping her head around, she saw Otto leaning against the counter. Her heart did the usual hop, skip, and jump it always did around Otto, and she smiled. "Hey! I'm just mumbling to myself. Organizing the back room made me a little batty, I think."

He smiled back, that slow, honestly happy smile that always dazzled her.

"Shouldn't you be home sleeping?"

"I'm headed that way. I promised Theo I'd pick up more milk replacer for the puppies."

"How are they doing?" she asked. Sarah realized that she was leaning forward, bracing her hands on the edge of the counter, as if her body instinctively wanted to get as close as possible to Otto.

"Good. Fat." He rolled his eyes. "Theo and Hugh fight over them like a pair of fussy nannies."

"Mannies?"

The breathtaking smile came again. "I like it. How's your shift going?"

"A tiny bit boring and a whole lot satisfying."

"You've been stocking shelves again."

"Exactly." Her own smile faded. "Has the FBI picked up Aaron and the others yet?"

"Not yet. There's an issue with the paperwork that had to be ironed out. Lieutenant Blessard said it should just be a few more days, though."

Her stomach churned at the thought of Aaron being in the same town as her, even though he was behind bars. Jeb had admitted under questioning that Logan had come along so that they could use his police status to more easily kidnap her. Even though Aaron had been locked up, he'd still managed to get to her. If they hadn't been in Monroe, it probably would have worked, too.

Otto interrupted her gloomy thoughts. "I'm hoping they get them out of here before the snow hits."

Peering out the front windows into the gray parking lot, Sarah snorted. "If it ever snows. It keeps threatening, but I haven't seen a single flake."

"Be glad." Reaching over, he gave her a teasing poke in the ribs. "Once it snows here, it never seems to stop until June."

With a laughing yelp, she twisted away. When he dropped his hand, disappointment filled her, and she resolved to talk to him the next morning. She wanted—no, *needed*—more kissing.

Pushing that thought to the back of her mind, she

glanced through the window again. Her view of the parking lot was narrow, but she could see a sedan parked in front of the store. The engine was running, judging from the stream of exhaust drifting from the tailpipe into the cold air, and someone sat in the driver's seat. Her mind immediately went to Aaron, and she stiffened. Could he have called in someone else? Even with him, Logan, and Jeb locked up, she still didn't feel completely safe.

"What's wrong?" Otto moved around so he was between her and the window.

"I'm just being paranoid." Despite her effort to make her voice casual, her words had a tremor. "Who's in that car out there?"

Otto moved closer to the window, and Sarah's throat tightened. What if it was one of Aaron's lackeys, and he had a gun? Her stomach clamped as she imagined the bullet shattering the window and burying itself in Otto's massive chest.

"Wait…" she said, going after him.

"Huh." He sounded curious and much too casual for the driver to be a bad guy. Sarah's knees wobbled with relief, and she moved back to the register so she could lean back against the wall behind it. "I haven't seen him in a few months."

"Who?"

"Norman Rounds."

"Oh!" She instantly felt silly. Of course it was Norman. He'd just been shopping, so he'd gone out to warm up his car before driving away. Her paranoia was getting the best of her. "He was just in here."

"Was he?" Otto turned back to face her. "Did he say anything to you?"

"Just introduced himself. Oh, and he asked if I was the Sarah living with you." Heat crept into her cheeks. "I mean, staying with you."

"Hmm…" His face was serious, making her wonder if she should worry. "Did he say anything else?"

Sarah mentally ran through their conversation. "Not really. Why? What's his story?"

"He's involved with the local militia leader, Gordon Schwartz. For a while, Rounds was a suspect in an explosion that destroyed Jules's barn."

"Oh!" Her eyes rounded as she thought of the innocuous man who she'd just introduced herself to, and his purchases—wire and batteries and motor oil and wool socks—became much more sinister. Except maybe the socks. It was hard to think of any nefarious use for socks, unless he put a bunch of nickels in one or something. "He's a bad guy, then?"

"No, not a bad guy. He was cleared of the barn explosion, plus he almost died saving Jules's life. When we tried to question him about it, he denied all knowledge and then disappeared."

"So mostly good with a side of shady?"

Otto grinned. "I like how you put things."

A pleased flush heated her cheeks as she smiled back at him. They were quiet, just looking at each other for a long moment until Otto cleared his throat.

"I should get that milk replacer." His voice had a little more growl in it than usual.

"Right." Sarah shook her head to clear it. More and more lately, she'd been caught in an Otto-related daze. Once again, she resolved to talk to him about where they were headed. "You need to get home and get some sleep. When are the chief and the rest of the officers back from training?"

"Four days—well, nights." He yawned, covering his mouth with his hand, as if her mention of sleep had triggered it. "Then I get a week off. Can't wait."

"Me, either." Her own sleep was still sketchy, even in the bunker with a full squadron of animals. The house felt so isolated and empty at night without any other humans in it.

Nan, the kennel owner, approached the register with a couple heated water bowls, and Otto backed away. "I'll be right back." He paused, as if he was about to say something else, but then turned and walked away.

With a small smile, Nan looked back and forth between Otto's back and Sarah. "You and Otto, huh?"

Forcing a noncommittal smile, Sarah scanned the tags on the water bowls. She was hoping for a her-and-Otto, but they weren't there yet.

"That's great," Nan said, obviously misinterpreting Sarah's silence. "He has a huge heart. It's about time he fit a person in there along with all those animals."

Sarah's smile became more genuine. She liked the image of her squeezed into Otto's heart, surrounded by Xena and Mort and Bob and Bean and Hortense. What a wonderful place to be.

When Sarah got home that afternoon, she expected that Otto would be sleeping. Instead, he was waiting on the porch, Mort and Xena next to him. Her heart skipped when she saw him. That was the hardest part of her job—she didn't get to spend as much time with Otto. She parked next to Otto's truck, and then climbed out. The wind cut through her jacket and shirt, and she shivered. Mort trotted over to greet her, but Xena was more tentative, slipping around behind Sarah to poke her cold nose into her palm.

As Sarah headed toward the porch, she had to fight to keep from jogging toward Otto. It was hard. Otto seemed to have a strong magnetic pull that reeled her in whenever she was close to him.

"Hi," she said as she climbed the steps, the dogs close behind her. "I thought you'd be sleeping. Did you manage to get tonight off?"

He grimaced slightly. "No break for me until the other officers get back from training. I slept earlier."

"Oh." She took another step toward him and then paused. Any closer, and she'd be in his personal bubble. It wasn't that she would mind, but she wasn't sure how he'd feel about that. "Where are you headed?"

"I'm going to work with Bean. Want to help?"

"Yes." The word popped out quickly, but a sharp gust of wind reminded her of the cold. "Let me get a few more layers on, and I'll join you. I can meet you at the barn."

"I'll wait." He moved to the porch support and leaned against it. "Do you have enough warm clothes? I have a stack of things in the bunker. You could take some of those."

"I'm good." She smiled at him as she lingered by the door, taking him in. It was silly, since she'd just seen him earlier that afternoon, but she'd missed him. "Besides, your clothes would be huge on me. Remember the T-shirt I borrowed?"

"I remember." The blue flame in his eyes smoldered.

Her gaze was caught by the heat in his until another cold blast of wind hit her, and she was able look away. "I'll be right back." She slipped into the house before she could do something silly like hurl herself into his arms. For some reason, she was as breathless as if she'd sprinted around the house a few times. *For some reason*, the voice in her head mocked, and Sarah couldn't blame it. She knew perfectly well what—or who—had stolen her breath. It happened every time she got near Otto.

She hurried to her room and pulled on some layers. When Grace and Jules had encouraged her to buy long underwear and fleece-lined sweatshirts and thick wool socks the first time she'd visited Grady's, Sarah had thought they were exaggerating what she'd need. It hadn't been an exaggeration, though. She'd worn every piece of her new wardrobe, especially now that she was at Otto's, where buildings didn't block the worst of the wind like they did in town. If it was this cold already, then winter was going to be brutal. With a shiver at the thought, she zipped her jacket over her multiple layers and grabbed her hat before running back down the stairs.

As promised, Otto was waiting for her on the porch. His gaze ran over her in a way that overheated her, making her warm clothes unnecessary. He didn't say anything, just held out his hand.

She gripped it, loving the gesture, even if it was glove to glove rather than skin to skin. When they reached the barn, he released her in order to open the door, and Sarah felt instantly and illogically colder. As they cut through the barn, Otto grabbed a halter and lead rope off a hook next to the single, oversized stall.

"That's a huge stall," Sarah said as she followed him toward the paddock gate.

He gave her a slightly sheepish look over his shoulder. "It used to be two, but Bean and Hortense like to room together."

"Makes sense." It was hard to keep her tone even when her heart was squeezed so tightly. The idea that this burly man took out the connecting stall wall so that Bean wouldn't be as scared was so sweet that tears burned Sarah's eyes. She quickly blinked them back. "Was Hortense a rescue, too?"

"A couple of years ago, I went on a call for a stolen vehicle case we'd been working on with the sheriff's department. We found the stolen cars in the barn, and Hortense was in there, too. She was pretty much a mess—wormy, mangy, and so skinny you could see every one of her ribs, but she wasn't skittish or scared at all." He smiled as he held the gate for her. "She walked right up to me and started chewing on my jacket sleeve. Her owner was going to jail, and he said he didn't care if I took her. I just had a squad car there, though, so I convinced the deputy to let me load Hortense into the back of her SUV. Even now, when I see that deputy, she tells me that her squad car still smells like goat poop."

Sarah laughed at the image, feeling a surge of compassion toward the goat that was now trotting toward them. "You sure have a soft spot for animals in need." *And people*. She pushed away the thought that he might just be interested in her because of her situation. If that were true, though, he'd have gone after Jules or Grace. Her sad story paled in comparison to theirs.

He shrugged slightly as he dug in his pocket for a treat. "I think every animal deserves to feel safe."

That simple statement hit Sarah hard. Until she'd run to Monroe—no, until she'd moved in with Otto—she had never felt safe. Now that she'd gotten a taste of it, she knew that she would fight with everything she had to keep that feeling—for her, and for everyone she was coming to love. She couldn't think of how to respond to him, how to express her thoughts, so she stayed quiet. As she watched him feed Hortense, she leaned against his other side, wanting that contact, that connection. He put his arm around her, drawing her closer, and she wallowed in his touch, in his kind and protective nature. At that moment, she decided that she was going to enjoy every second she was given with him. Even if she was forced to run, if she was ripped away from the first place that had offered her security and friends and freedom, she didn't want to leave with regrets.

"I want to…" She trailed off, distracted by what she saw in his hand. "What on earth are you feeding Hortense?"

"Cheetos." He gave her a lopsided smile. "They're her favorite treat."

"Of course they are." Now that the mood had changed, she decided to keep her revelation to herself. "No one can resist that orange fake-cheese stuff. Wouldn't, I don't know, some kind of vegetable be healthier?"

"Probably. I figure a few won't hurt."

"That's true." A movement caught her eye. "Bean is very sneakily headed this way. Does he get Cheetos, too?"

"Carrots," he said without looking at the horse standing just six feet away from them. As Bean sidled a little closer, Otto put a chunk of carrot on his palm and extended his flat hand toward the horse. Stretching his neck so he could reach without stepping closer, Bean took the piece of carrot and then retreated several feet to chew it as he watched them warily.

"Is he rideable?" Sarah asked, leaning more heavily against Otto.

"Yes, but we're taking it slow. I want him to enjoy work, not to fear it. No reason to rush things. We've got time."

For some reason, that made her want to cry. Otto and Bean had time, but did she? Did they? Blinking, she focused on Bean, who'd started his sneaky sidle toward them again. Otto, occupied with giving Hortense a Cheeto, didn't have a carrot waiting, but Bean still stretched his neck out…and snatched Otto's hat. The horse, his prize dangling from his mouth, took off for the other side of the pasture.

"What?" Otto reached toward his now-bare head, looking startled. Sarah began to laugh. Still holding on to the hat, Bean trotted along the fence, head and tail up.

Sarah laughed harder until she had to bend over and hold her stomach. "Sorry!" she gasped between breaths. "He just looks so…proud." That set her off again.

"He does, doesn't he?" Otto didn't sound annoyed. He sounded…bemused. When she looked up at him, wiping tears of laughter from her face, she saw he was watching her with banked heat and something else in his gaze—something that looked a lot like affection.

By the time they got back inside, Sarah's nose was numb from the cold. She didn't care, though. She would've stayed outside all night if it meant she could keep Otto company. Unfortunately, that wasn't an option. He had to head in to work, and she had to quit clinging to him.

He walked out the door and then stuck his head back inside. "Lock the door after me."

"I will." The commanding tone made her shiver in a good way. Whether Otto was being sweet or bossy, she liked him. She *more* than liked him. Even though she knew she'd probably have to leave him, it was too late to protect her heart. It was already his.

She turned the dead bolt and then stayed there, staring at the closed door, long after the sound of Otto's truck engine faded. Her plan of playing it safe and guarding her emotions had failed. It was time for a new strategy. Now that Aaron, Jeb, and Logan were all in jail, she could move back in with Grace, Jules, and the kids, but the idea didn't have any appeal. As much as she was learning to love her new friends, everything inside her wanted to stay close to Otto.

Why did she have to run away from this? The thought sent a rush of terrified delight through her. She'd fallen for Otto. It was too late to stop it, so why not enjoy the time she had with him?

As the word *enjoy* echoed through her mind, she shivered in anticipation.

She'd do it. If she was forced to leave Monroe, then she would deal with it, but now… Now, she was going to soak up every single drop of joy she could. She started to smile. Otto was going to have a surprise waiting for him when he finished work the next morning. With a *whoop* that made Xena jump, she ran for the stairs. Her clothing options were limited, but she was going to find *something* that could pass as seduction-worthy.

───────────

Sarah lasted until almost midnight before an especially terrifying creaking sound sent her scrambling for the bunker, two dogs and one cat right behind her. She climbed into the bunk she'd been using, pulling the sheet and draped sleeping bag up to her chin. After reviewing her clothing options, she'd realized that nothing had been even close to sexy, so she'd grabbed an oversized T-shirt from Otto's room. He'd seemed to like seeing her in that when they'd slept next to each other.

Xena and Mort jumped onto the cot, settling into their usual spots behind her knees and against her waist. Although she knew the dogs would annoy her all night with their poky feet and poorly placed bodies, it was reassuring to feel them curl up against her, their warmth and size comforting. Bob tucked himself in the curve at the back of her neck, purring almost silently. He was the quietest cat Sarah had ever known—not that she'd known a lot of cats, but she'd never heard Bob meow or make any noise, except for the one time she'd been rushing to get into the bunker and had accidentally stepped on him. He'd yowled then, and who could blame him? She still felt terrible about doing that.

She snuggled into her warm nest, deciding to wake up early so she could go upstairs and be waiting for Otto in his bed like she'd planned. That was her last thought until she woke up to a tickling sensation on her right cheek. Without opening her eyes, she brushed at it, grumbling wordlessly. She was so warm and still tired, and she didn't want to wake yet.

A male chuckle woke her completely, and she lifted her eyelids to see Otto bent over the cot, his fingers lightly brushing her cheek and a sweetly smoldering look in his eyes.

"Hi," she said groggily, lifting her hand to return the gesture, stroking her fingers across his stubbly face. He smiled at her, and it was impossible not to smile back. "I meant to be waiting for you upstairs."

His smile disappeared, and he looked startled. "Upstairs?"

"Yes." She'd been nervous about this moment, but now that it was happening, she wasn't hesitant at all. This felt right. "In your bed."

He swallowed, and she watched his throat, loving that she could affect him so strongly. Instead of saying anything else, she slid her fingers to his jaw and down his neck. Once she got to his shirt collar, she paused, self-consciousness finally kicking in.

"Unless you don't want to?" Her hand dropped away from him at the thought. If he rejected her, or laughed, or did anything except grab on to her suggestion with both hands, she knew she would be completely mortified.

"I do." His firm words pulled her out of her panicky thoughts, and she relaxed. "If you're sure?"

"I'm sure." Ever since she'd decided to do this, she hadn't had a moment of doubt.

His smile was back, wider and brighter than before. "Let's go upstairs, then. If I try to join you here, the whole cot will collapse."

Pushing herself up onto her elbows, Sarah looked at the dogs and cat heaped on top of her. There wasn't a single inch of clear space on the cot. She laughed. "Good idea."

Her chuckle turned into a surprised squeak when Otto caught her under the arms and lifted her out from the heap of animals. Mort made a grumbly sound but didn't open his eyes. Xena jumped down and slunk under the cot, the sudden movement obviously too much for her. Bob gave them both a condemning look, but he didn't move except to twitch his tail in an annoyed fashion.

Placing Sarah on her feet, Otto pulled her against him. Immediately, her body temperature shot up as her muscles relaxed. It was a strange feeling to have two such opposite reactions simultaneously, but that was the Otto effect. He made her feel extremely safe and like she was about to jump off a cliff at the same time.

Leaning down, he kissed her, and Sarah quit thinking about dichotomies. Her lips parted and he accepted the invitation, deepening the embrace, using his lips and tongue and even his teeth to make her crazy with need. The world around them disappeared, and all she knew was Otto. When he withdrew, she made a sound of disappointment as she tried to follow his mouth.

"Upstairs." If his raspy voice was any indication, he was just as affected as she was. "This floor will not be comfortable."

"No," she said absently, worried less about comfort and more about touching him. She flattened her hands over his chest, marveling at the strength living underneath the layers of clothing and skin. Once her fingers landed, she didn't want to move them. He was so solid.

Suddenly, she was desperate to see him naked—or at least shirtless. Her face heated again. Sarah had never considered herself so…lustful before.

"What?" he asked, walking her backward toward the stairs.

"What?" she echoed, dazed and overwhelmed by everything she was feeling, by the amazingness that was Otto.

He smiled his usual slow smile, although it had a wicked edge she'd never seen before. Sarah was pretty sure she loved it. "You're blushing."

"Oh." She smiled back, and his eyes blazed with hunger. "I was thinking naughty thoughts." Her heels bumped the first step, and she turned around to climb up the stairs.

Crowding close behind her, so close that it felt like he surrounded her, Otto asked, "You going to share them?"

Having him so close should've made her feel claustrophobic. Back in her old life, if her guards got within four feet of her, she felt crowded and desperate for space. Having Otto against her back didn't bother her, though. In fact, it made her feel safe, because he was Otto, and he'd protect her. "Maybe."

"Maybe?"

She loved his teasing, husky tone. He was usually so serious, and each smile or laugh felt like she was receiving a gift. "Maybe. Depends on how good you are at convincing me."

"Oh, I'll convince you."

With a giggle, she slipped away and ducked through the closet, leaving the bunker door open so the animals could get out. He followed her across the living room, up the other flight of stairs, and into his bedroom. His silent, steady progress as he stayed just a step or two behind her made her heart quicken. It felt like she was being stalked, but there was no fear involved—just a thrilling anticipation.

"Your bed really is huge." It was the biggest bed she'd ever seen.

"So am I," he said with a shrug. Then he went still, and he gave her a sheepish look.

Sarah burst out laughing. "Thank you for the warning."

"I didn't mean…" He trailed off, waving it away. "You know what I meant."

"I do." Now that she wasn't being held against him, Sarah's insecurities were returning. "I'm…ah, I'm not that experienced."

"We'll take it slow." Reaching out, he took her hand and tugged her toward him.

She knew she needed to get it out before he kissed her, and her brain evaporated again. "I'm *really* not experienced." He studied her thoughtfully, and she kept talking, worried about the silence that might fall if she stopped. "Having full-time bodyguards around kind of killed my social life. I mean, I dated a little in high school, but there was no one… There was really no one."

There was another pause, but it didn't feel uncomfortable. Sarah got the impression that Otto was just taking his time, making sure that he chose the right words. "Thank you," he finally said, before pulling her toward him and kissing her.

It was hard, but so, so sweet. *Kind of like Otto is right now*, she thought, giggling against his mouth. His lips tilted up in response, and all of her nerves disappeared, brushed away by desire and Otto's smile and the complete perfection of the moment. This was right. She'd never been surer about anything.

It was all so natural. There was no awkwardness, no fumbling. Otto pulled off his shirt and eased her top over her head, and then they were kissing again. His hands on her breasts made her gasp against his mouth with wonder and delight.

He didn't stop kissing her as they toppled down onto that huge bed, didn't stop until he left a trail of kisses down her front. He slid her panties down her legs, leaving her naked and breathing hard and wanting more of him.

She couldn't stop touching him, amazed at the smoothness of his skin over all of that muscle—muscle that twitched and flexed under her fingers and mouth. He was huge and strong, but she could make him groan with a single light scratch of her fingernail. It was incredible and so very arousing.

He left her for a few moments to shuck his pants and don a condom. When he returned, Otto rolled them over so she was on top, and that was a whole amusement park of joys to explore. Sarah touched him everywhere with her fingers and lips and even her tongue, until he was slick with sweat and groaning with need.

Even then, he didn't push into her. Instead, he flipped them back over and did the same thing to her as she'd done to him—tortured her in the very best way until she was desperate. He kissed and lightly nipped her skin, his mouth and fingers discovering sensitive spots that she didn't even know she had.

"You're so beautiful," he said as his lips and the

air from his breath brushed against her bottom rib. "I couldn't even talk the first time I met you. All the words were knocked right out of me."

Her breath caught as he lightly scored her belly with his teeth. "I thought you looked like a Viking lumberjack."

His chuckle made her insides twist and swoop. "Can't decide if that's better or worse than Hugh's ninja-Paul-Bunyan comparison."

"Both are good—and accurate." She couldn't stop touching him. Her fingers ran over the back of his head and neck, scratching lightly at his scalp. He shifted so they were face-to-face, his body caging hers. It should've felt claustrophobic, but she felt free and safe at the same time. She reached up as she pulled his head down, and their mouths met in a kiss that was wild and almost savage—and so, so sweet.

Finally, he entered her, and it was heaven.

As he moved in her, Otto watched her face, holding her gaze, giving her that complete attention that was almost as addicting as his hands on her bare skin. She kept her eyes open as long as she could, until the pleasure built too high and she had to close her eyes and let go, let everything go except for the beautiful, beautiful man connected to her.

He came right after she did, and she was entranced. It was just like when he made a joke or laughed, only even more so. She was witnessing something that very few people got to see—the secret and best parts of Otto Gunnersen.

Afterward, they lay on their sides, gazing at each other. Sarah memorized what he looked like, the angles of his cheek and jaw, his full mouth, his gentle expression and warm eyes. If she had to leave, at least she'd have this amazing memory of him. He studied her just as intently, and she wondered if he was also taking a mental picture of her.

She liked the thought of that, and she smiled. In response, his lips tilted up at the corners until it grew into a grin. *There*. She took another imaginary photograph, wanting to remember him just like this—gorgeous and so, so happy.

CHAPTER 15

"Seriously, who uses a fax machine anymore?" Grace fumed.

"The scholarship committee that wants you to fax their forms back before they'll give those students a bunch of free money, apparently." Sarah dipped her head, pretending to focus on the boxes of ammunition that she was stacking in the case. Grace's annoyance was justified, but her wide gestures and pained expression were so dramatic that Sarah had to hide a smile.

Grace gave a drawn-out groan, and a small laugh escaped Sarah before she got it back under control. "But *why*? It's like using a mimeograph machine. We're beyond faxes as a civilization."

"Why not just scan it in and use a faxing app?" Sarah asked, topping off the stack with the last, surprisingly heavy box. Standing up, she stretched out the kinks from crouching next to the ammunition case for so long.

"I tried," Grace said gloomily, leaning against the wall. "It's not going through. Satellite internet is just a tiny bit better than dial-up."

"Where's the nearest fax machine?"

"Dresden, probably." As she spoke, Grace's eyes widened. "Oh, this could be good!"

"It could?" Sarah blinked, startled by Grace's

dramatic change in mood. She was starting to look almost giddy.

Grace grinned, as excited as she'd been frustrated just a minute earlier. "Yes! Do you know what Dresden has?"

"Ski slopes?"

"Yes. What else?"

"Rich people?"

"Yes, and what do rich people like to do?"

"Uh…" A number of possibilities ran through Sarah's mind—things that her father and Aaron had liked to do—but they were all slightly psychopathic. She tried to think of things that *normal* rich people liked to do. "Buy things?"

"Exactly!" Grace gave an excited bounce. "Dresden has shopping that doesn't involve buying clothes at the general store." Her gaze moved to a point behind Sarah. "No offense, Grady."

"None taken, but you, missy, need to leave so that Sarah here can get her work done." Grady spoke right behind her, making Sarah jump. She sent an apologetic look toward her friend, but Grace didn't look at all abashed by the mild scolding.

"I'm leaving," she said. "I'll be back at… What time are you done here?"

"Four."

"I'll be back at four, and then we'll go shopping in Dresden. We'll celebrate your brother and his minions getting picked up by the FBI today. By the time we get home, Monroe will be blessedly Blanchett- and Jovanovic-free." Blowing Sarah a kiss, Grace left the store, leaving Sarah feeling a little dazed, as if she'd been swept up in a tornado. It *would* be nice to shop somewhere besides Grady's, though. She thought about getting some pretty lingerie that would make Otto go all caveman on her again, and she flushed, giving Grady a guilty look, as if the man could read her wicked thoughts.

"Back to work, missy" was all he said.

To her disappointment, the shopping trip in Dresden was a bust. They'd barely gotten halfway there when the check-engine light had come on in Grace's car. Both of them agreed to turn around, since the sky was an ominous gunmetal gray and neither wanted to be stranded somewhere in the wilderness between Monroe and Dresden. They'd returned to town empty-handed.

One positive was that Grady admitted that he had an ancient—but functional—fax machine in his office that he grudgingly let them use. While muttering about obsolete technology, Grace had sent her fax. She'd wanted to wait until the scholarship committee signed the forms and faxed them back to her, so she had stayed in the office while Sarah headed home.

As Sarah drove, small hard pellets of snow smacked against the windshield. An inch had already fallen and was sweeping across the road in white, frozen eddies. It had gotten worse now that she was on the other side of the pass and had turned onto the twisting, uphill road to Otto's place. Everyone had been warned about the coming blizzard for so many days that it was almost a relief to finally have the snow arrive, except that she worried about Otto. It would make his job so much more difficult—and dangerous.

She glanced at the dashboard clock: it was just after six. Otto would be at work. She was tempted to call him, just to hear his voice and ask him to be careful, but she didn't want to bother him. Besides, he was a grown man and a cop; he already knew he needed to be careful in snow.

The wind whipped up, pressing on the side of the car and sending a flurry of snow pellets smacking against the windows. Sarah usually enjoyed driving the twisting, scenic road leading to Otto's, but tonight it felt as if she was going to get swept right off the side of the cliff.

The snow wasn't thick enough to block visibility, but the wind was brutal. It howled and groaned, pushing against the side of her car so hard it felt like a giant was trying to shove her off the road. She realized she was hunched forward, her hands clutching the wheel so hard her fingers ached, and she forced herself to sit back, taking one hand at a time off the steering wheel so she could stretch them out. *The car's too heavy to be blown sideways*, she reassured herself.

The wind screamed, a gust smacking against the car, and Sarah jerked forward, her hands squeezing the wheel again. The final curve before the turnoff onto Otto's driveway was approaching, and she blew out a breath in relief, although her hands remained clamped on the wheel. Almost home.

Boom! A crash drowned out the screaming wind, and the earth shook.

With a yelp, Sarah instinctively jerked the wheel and slammed on the brake, sending the car toward the edge of the road. She immediately corrected, turning toward the center, but the pellets of ice sent her sliding. The car plowed toward the sadly inadequate guardrail, and a long-ago driving lesson with Chester popped into her head.

Acceleration gives you control, Alice, he'd said in his gentle, patient way. Yanking her foot off the brake, she pressed the gas pedal. The tires caught, sending her back toward the center, and she straightened the car with jerky motions as she audibly gasped for breath.

Her fingers shook, and she tightened them around the wheel, as if she could stop the tremors if she just held on tightly enough. What had happened? An earthquake? An avalanche? A rockslide? She crawled through the final hairpin turn, desperate to get home safely so she could figure out what had happened and who might be hurt. As she crested the last hill, the view improved, and the side of the mountain stretched out to her left.

The road was on fire.

Her foot hit the brake pedal, so suddenly that the car went into another small slide before jerking to a stop. Sarah slammed the car into Park and fumbled for the door handle with shaking fingers. When she finally got the door open, she almost fell into the road. Her legs were trembling so much that standing was hard, but she managed to stay upright as she ran to the edge of the road.

The wind ripped at her, buffeting her first from one direction and then the next, and she gripped the top of the guardrail fence as she stared over the cliff. The fire glowed red, bright enough to illuminate a stretch of highway in front of and behind the flames. Black smoke billowed, backlit by the fire. Sarah wasn't sure how long she watched it, mesmerized by the horror of it and the terribly beautiful flames. She craned to see it more clearly, struggling between her need to know what had happened and the fear she'd be blown over the cliff. Was it a car or a truck that had just exploded? From the earlier sound, Sarah was pretty sure it had been an explosion and not just a fire. The conversation she'd had with Otto the day before about the militia guy and his friend—Norman Rounds, the man suspected of blowing up Jules's barn—resurfaced in her mind.

"He was cleared," she muttered to herself, even as she fumbled for her phone. "You don't know what that was. It was probably an accident."

Another, fainter boom echoed through the night, bouncing off the cliff faces until it sounded like a hundred small explosions. Her body jerked back, and the guardrail slipped form her fingers. The wind caught her, and she fought to keep her balance and her grip on her phone. She peered through the darkness in the direction of the latest explosion, but it was too far away. She couldn't see anything except the tiny, hard pellets of snow that drilled into any exposed skin.

She turned back to the original fire and saw that the red glow had shrunk. She still couldn't see anything except the short, lit ribbon of highway and the flames. Tearing her gaze off the burning spot on the road, Sarah stared at her phone. She stumbled back toward the car, wanting to call Otto, needing to know if he was okay. There had been two explosions, some distance apart. That was not an accident.

Her thumbs shook as she found Otto's cell number, but she finally managed to call. Immediately, there was a double beep, and the screen read "No Service." It took all of Sarah's willpower not to throw the phone across the road. She would need it later.

After a final glance at the still-burning explosion site, she climbed back in the car and put it into Drive. She slammed down on the accelerator. The car juddered sideways, and Sarah realized that quite a bit of snow had piled up on the road. The car drifted closer to the far side of the road, but then the tires finally caught.

Her gasp of relief was more of a sob. She almost missed Otto's driveway, since the snow already blanketed the area, hiding the gravel path. Wrenching the wheel, she made the turn, the car sliding diagonally toward a large aspen tree. She corrected the skid, straightening the car and concentrating on the faint dent that showed where the sides of the driveway were. She pulled into the garage automatically, feeling a huge sense of relief when the overhead door closed, shutting her safely inside.

Quickly, though, she remembered that it was just an illusion. Sarah didn't know who was safe—was Otto? Or Theo? Or Jules and her family, or Grace, or Hugh? She didn't know what the explosions had been or why they'd been set off, but she knew, deep in her gut, that Aaron Blanchett was behind it. He always got what he wanted, and, right now, he wanted his sister back, even if he had to destroy a town to get her.

At the thought, her stomach tried to turn itself inside out. Hurrying to climb out of the car, she swallowed down bile as she ran for the door. This was no time to be fussing over how she felt. She needed information. To get information, she needed a way to communicate.

Mort and Xena came to greet her as Sarah rushed inside the house, smacking the hall light on as she entered. With a quick apology to the dogs, she dodged around them, running for the house phone. It was a satellite phone, rather than a landline, but it would have to do. She grabbed it, and, with her cell phone in one hand and the satellite phone in the other, she entered Otto's mobile number into the home phone.

Nothing happened. Sarah looked at the screen, hitting the Call button again and again, but the satellite phone stayed silent. With a frustrated shriek, she pressed her hands—still holding the phones—against her head and tried to think. How could she reach Otto? Phones were out, so what was next? To reach someone, she could call, text, email... Email!

Pivoting around, she dropped the satellite phone, shoved her cell phone in her pocket, and ran for Otto's office. The dogs and Bob followed close behind.

Otto's computer was on the desk of his study. He'd given her the satellite internet password on the first day she'd moved in. Sitting in front of the computer, she pushed the power button and waited impatiently for it to boot up. Unable to just wait there, she got up and paced.

As she'd entered the office, Sarah had flicked on the overhead light. Her reflection looked back at her from the large window, and she had a sudden, paranoid feeling that someone was out there...watching her. She hurried over to the light switch and turned it off, standing still until her eyes adjusted to the darkness.

Moving over to the window, she peered through the thick sheet of snow. The flakes were coming down so hard that she could barely make out the dark shape of the barn. Sarah tried to take heart in the fact that anyone trying to watch her would have visibility as bad as she had, but that thought didn't really help. It still felt like they could see her, and she couldn't see anything *except* snow.

Xena whined, breaking the thick silence.

"It's okay, sweet pea," Sarah said. Even though she spoke quietly, it still sounded much too loud. She stroked Xena's blocky, silky-soft head as the dog pressed her muzzle against the side of her thigh. Mort was silent, but he was alert, standing in the middle of the room, dividing his attention between the doorway and the window. With the dimness hiding his gray hairs, he looked like a poster for an on-duty K9, readiness vibrating through every muscle. It was slightly reassuring knowing that she had a trained cop on her side. Bob hid under the desk.

There was another sound, faint and mostly lost under the howls of the wind. Tipping her head closer to the window, Sarah listened, trying to decide if she was just imagining it. The wind quieted for a moment, and the sound became clear—a faint, rapid *whump-whump-whump*. Mort started to bark.

Sarah wasn't about to ignore the trained law enforcement officer in the room. Leaving the computer still booting up, she ran for the door. Mort bounded out first, and Xena followed right behind Sarah. In the doorway, Sarah paused and started to turn around, intending to grab Bob. He beat her to the punch, though, streaking by her and flying down the hall after Mort.

Taking off after the animals, she ran for the closet in the living room, frantically turning off lights as she went. The *whump-whump* was getting loud, obvious now, even over the screaming wind. Mort and Bob waited for her in front of the closet, and Xena stayed glued to the back of her legs. She was grateful that the animals seemed to have a strong sense of self-preservation.

Shoving to the back of the closet, Sarah fumbled as she tried to work the hidden latch free, and she remembered having the same problem several nights ago. Her nerves had been so pointless then, just silly late-night jitters. As the door finally swung open, Sarah swore that she'd never be scared without reason ever again.

Mort and Bob took the lead again, darting down the stairs into the bunker. Securing the door behind her, Sarah, with Xena close behind her, turned on the light and followed the animals, taking the steps three at a time. Just as she reached the bottom, there was a thunderous boom. Everything shook, and Sarah was knocked off her feet, falling painfully onto her hip and her arm.

She pushed herself to sitting, feeling too vulnerable sprawled on the bunker floor, as the walls and ceiling and the ground itself trembled around her. Xena climbed onto Sarah's lap, eighty-plus pounds of knobby joints and poky feet, and Sarah didn't have the heart to push her away. Instead, she wrapped her arms around the quivering dog, hugging her tightly until the room around them went still.

When it finally did, when everything was eerily silent, Sarah didn't want to move. Moving required making decisions, and she was a little too freaked out for that. That sound, those tremors, were becoming uncomfortably familiar. Something above them had just blown up. By the force that had radiated all the way down into the secure bunker, it had to have been big. Sarah wondered with a sick twist of fear whether Otto's entire house was gone.

Grief hit her at the thought. What if that elegant, well-preserved house that had withstood everything the Rockies had thrown at it for over a century was now destroyed, all by her stupid, sociopathic brother?

The thought of Aaron brought anger, and that sent a surge of determination through her. He wasn't going to win. He might have the helicopters and the bombs and a whole mercenary army he could direct from a jail cell, but she had...

She looked around, taking a tally. She had a terrified pit bull mix and an elderly K9, plus a chubby cat currently wedged under a cot. A spark of fear hit her at the thought of being responsible for these animals—for any lives, including her own—but she shoved it away. She dug for confidence, picturing Otto's face as he told her to fake it until she made it. The thought of him both gave her courage and added another surge of terror. There'd been at least two explosions in town. What if he'd been hit by one of them?

Her anxiety swelled, blocking out everything else as she imagined all sorts of nightmare scenarios. The room blurred around her, and Xena whined as she pressed against Sarah's legs. Swaying, Sarah dropped a hand onto Xena's back. The feel of warm, hard muscle under the dog's slick fur steadied her.

Forcing away any and all thoughts of Otto being injured—or worse—Sarah tried to come up with a plan.

"Okay," she said, and then jumped at the sound of her voice. Feeling sheepish that she'd scared herself, she spoke again, just to prove she wasn't afraid. "What do we need?"

First, they needed to get to safety. The bunker felt

secure, but it wouldn't be if one of Aaron's people discovered the door in the back of the closet. She glanced at the entrance to the tunnels.

"Okay, guys. Let's make an escape, then."

Sarah looked around. Her brain was still racing at a hundred miles an hour, and worry about Otto and the others was still nibbling holes in her control, despite her determination to stay focused. The memory of that first tour of the bunker echoed in her mind. In his calm, deep voice, Otto had explained what was there and why it was important to have certain things in an emergency. She started digging through the storage containers, pulling out a camping backpack and filling it with water bottles, food—Otto even had dog- and cat-food stores—a lighter, a folding knife, a flashlight, and some rope. She thought about taking the tent and sleeping bag, but decided against it. It was less than ten miles into town. They should make it there in about three hours, even moving slowly. There shouldn't be any need to camp, and the extra weight would just slow her down.

She turned to the container holding clothes next. Stripping off her shoes, coat, long-sleeved T-shirt, and khakis that she'd worn to work, she pulled on some long underwear. It was meant for someone much bigger than her. Next, she pulled on her khakis and T-shirt, followed by some snow pants, a fleece top, two pairs of socks, and her coat. The snow pants were much too big, but she was able to tuck all the extra into her boots, and the waist had a drawstring. The crotch hung down around her thighs, which made walking awkward, but she figured she'd get used to it. Staying dry and warm was what was important now. Pulling on her hat and grabbing mittens—and then throwing extra hats, mittens, and socks into her pack—Sarah called it good.

A sense of urgency pushed her to move, to leave before Aaron's goons found her. If they'd blown up Otto's house, not caring that she might have died—or maybe hoping for exactly that—then Aaron wasn't worried about getting her back alive anymore. Now, it was all about revenge and damage control.

Her mind went to Grace, and she wondered if the Jovanovics were involved in the attack. Aaron had resources, but that was a lot of money to spend just to kill an uncooperative sister.

After wrestling her mind back under control, she took one last look around. There were a lot of things that looked useful—camp stoves and a huge first-aid kit and a wicked-looking ax and sledgehammer combo—but Sarah decided to just leave with what she had in her pack. After all, Bob was going to have to fit in there, too.

As she approached the cot, the cat gave a tiny, pitiful meow.

"I know," Sarah crooned. "That's how I feel, too. Once we get to town, though, you can hang out with Dee's cat. You'll get along great. If you don't, then that's okay. Their house is huge. There very possibly could be mice, too, so that's a bonus." As she kept up her soothing commentary, she moved closer and closer, not wanting to spook Bob into darting for another, less-accessible hiding place.

Except for another nearly soundless meow, however, the cat was docile, allowing her to scoop him up and carry him over to the backpack. Sarah tucked him in the large front pocket, which had mesh sides.

"It's a little like one of those purse pet carriers," she said, as Bob growled, a steady, continuous rumble that made the whole pack shake. "This'll be over soon." Sarah zipped the cat in and looked at the two dogs crowded around her legs.

I hope.

Hoisting the pack onto her back while trying not to jostle Bob too much, Sarah looked around one last time, wondering if she should try to hunt down leashes—or make some out of rope, if necessary. She glanced at the ceiling. There was no telling if anyone was up there, or if the helicopter had just dropped the bomb and then flown away.

The thought made her antsy, and she started for the tunnel entrance. She had rope and could leash the dogs later, if necessary. So far, they had stuck closely to her. If something did happen to her, she wanted the dogs to be able to run away. She quickly shook off that morbid thought before it could make her start trembling again, and opened the door to the tunnels.

Tunnels was the wrong word for it, Sarah thought as she turned on the light. It was more of a series of hallways than the cave-like hole that the word *tunnel* brought to mind. As she came to the spot where one passageway branched off from the main one, she stopped so abruptly that Xena's head bumped the back of her knees.

Bean and Hortense. How could she have forgotten the horse and goat? Bile rose in her throat as she thought about the way the ground shook after the blast. Had it taken out the barn, too? Her stomach twisted, and she retched.

She couldn't leave without seeing if they were okay. As

much as she wanted to run through the tunnel and down the mountain, not stopping until she reached town and Otto, she had to find out if Bean and Hortense were still alive. If they were, she had to get them out…somehow.

Hurrying down the hallway hopefully leading to the barn, she eyed the ceiling worriedly. It was fairly low, but was it too low for Bean to walk through? The ground started to slope upward. Feeling like she was getting close, Sarah started to jog, even as she worried about what she'd find in the barn…if there was a barn anymore.

The tunnel ended at a set of double doors, and Sarah unlocked them with shaking hands. Mort made a sound deep in his chest—not quite a growl but more than a whine—and Sarah sucked in a quick breath, bracing for what she might see.

Although she wanted to fling the doors open, to move as quickly as she could to save the animals, Sarah turned off the tunnel light and made herself hold her hand close to the door, checking for heat. It was cool, almost cold, so she slowly cracked one door. The light was strange, red and orange and flickering, and her lungs seized. Was the barn on fire? Her eyes adjusted to the eerie, uneven glow, and she saw the interior of the barn. Everything was still in place and unburned. The breath she'd taken escaped in a silent rush. The barn was still standing.

Peering into the structure, Sarah didn't see anyone, and she pushed the door open a little more. Mort tried to wiggle his way in front of her, but she used her legs to block him.

"Sit," she said in an almost inaudible voice. Mort must've heard, since he settled onto his haunches behind her. She slipped out, debating whether to leave the dogs in the tunnel. She was worried that they'd bark and howl, though, so she let them exit with her and closed the tunnel entrance behind her. The main barn door was closed, so Mort couldn't go running out into danger.

Sarah moved toward Bean's stall, but she couldn't help but peek out of one of the dusty windows. Her breath caught. The flickering red and orange light that filled the barn was coming from a huge fire—a fire that was destroying the blackened and flattened skeleton of Otto's house. The wind whipped the flames to higher and higher peaks, both painfully loud.

Her throat tightened, but she turned her head away from the charred remains and rushed to the oversized stall that Bean shared with Hortense. For a moment, Sarah was grateful for the bad weather, since it meant that Otto had put the animals in the barn for the night. If she'd had to chase Bean down in the pasture, this would've been almost impossible.

The wind slowed for a few moments, and the roar of the fire softened with it. In the sudden slight hush, Sarah heard a shout. She froze as the wind whipped to life again, burying any follow-up. Had she really heard a male voice, or had it just been her imagination? Her stomach jumping anxiously, she grabbed a halter and lead rope off the hook and slid open the stall door.

Hortense was right there, looking for treats. Nudging the goat to the side, Sarah slid into the stall. Xena followed her in, and Sarah watched Bean, hoping that he wasn't scared of dogs. The horse's coat was dark with nervous sweat in patches on his neck and barrel, and his head was high, the whites of his eyes reflecting the red light in an eerie way. He didn't seem to even notice the dog, though, too concerned with the fire outside to worry about who—and what—was in the stall with him.

As if testing the theory, Mort pushed his way inside. Sarah moved toward Bean, trying to look as calm and unthreatening as possible. The horse's muscles twitched with tension as he stood slightly splay-legged. Although he flicked an ear toward her, Bean didn't look at her. His attention was fixed on the entrance. Sarah followed the horse's gaze to the closed main doors, and her muscles tightened in warning.

Mort growled, startling Sarah. Ripping her attention away from the barn doors, she looked down at the dog. Mort's ears were just as focused as Bean's—on the main doors. Staring at the entrance again, Sarah tried to swallow, her mouth suddenly dry. All of her instincts were screaming that something bad was coming. Mort had saved their lives earlier. Sarah knew better than to ignore the dog's warning.

Choking back creeping panic, she moved toward the stall door. She and the dogs needed to get to the tunnel. In there, they'd be safe until whatever—whoever—was on the other side of the doors left. Then, they could come back for Hortense and Bean. Sarah took a step, her gaze locked on the entrance.

The door swung open.

Sarah quickly ducked down. Grabbing both dogs by the collars, she hauled them to the front of the stall, pushing them into a sitting position right under Bean's hay feeder. Slipping out of the backpack straps, Sarah pressed her back against the wood and pulled her backpack in next to her. If someone didn't get too close, Sarah, both dogs, and the cat would be hidden.

It was a long shot, though. If Aaron's thugs were searching the barn, they wouldn't just glance inside the stall and then wander away. At the very least, they'd open the door and look. Sarah thought about covering them in the wood shavings that blanketed the stall floor, but then she heard the howl of the wind cut off as the door was pulled shut with a thud.

Too late.

CHAPTER 16

OTTO CRUISED DOWN MAIN STREET, WATCHING FOR ANY activity in the closed businesses. Monroe generally didn't have a problem with theft or vandalism during the winter, but he liked to keep an eye out, just in case. The building snowstorm had cleared things out even more than usual. Even the gas station had closed early. The town felt abandoned, and Otto wished that he still had Mort in the squad car with him. Not only had he been a good partner, but the dog had been good company, too.

Lieutenant Blessard was hopeful about getting the funding for a new K9 for Otto in January, but Otto was leaning toward training his own rescue dog. When he first started working with Xena, he was hopeful that she could progress to detection training, but she was still so timid. Confidence was crucial in a K9.

Thanks to their current officer shortage, the lieutenant had to stay late to meet with the FBI agents who were finally picking up the three occupants of the jail: Aaron Blanchett, Logan Jovanovic, and Jeb Hopp. If Otto had had to do it, there wouldn't have been anyone available to take calls. Besides, he tried to limit how much time he spent with the trio of prisoners. Every time he saw them, Otto was tempted to punch them in their cruel, smug faces for what they'd done to Sarah.

A hazy figure outside the general store waved at him, and Otto turned into the lot. As he drew closer, he recognized Grady, the owner and Sarah's new boss.

"Hey, Otto," Grady said as Otto rolled down his window. Small, sharp snowflakes immediately pelted his face. "My truck won't start. Mind giving me a jump?"

Otto climbed out, heading to the trunk to get the cables. The wind grabbed the edges of his department-issue coat, making it flap. The promised blizzard was finally here, and it was going to be a rough one. Otto hoped Sarah and Grace would make it home safely. He glanced at his watch, noting that they should be in Dresden by now. He decided that, as soon as he'd gotten Grady's truck started, he'd send Sarah a text suggesting that they stay there overnight. The drive back would be much better tomorrow, after the snow had stopped and the plows had cleared the highway.

As he clamped the cables onto the battery terminals, Grady leaned against his truck and watched. "Your girl is doing a fine job at the store."

"Good." A warm sensation spread through Otto at Sarah being referred to as "his girl." It felt like she was. He wanted her to be. Just the thought of her leaving made him feel like his insides were being ripped out. Otto didn't want to push too much, though. Her life had been filled with so many people who tried to coerce and bully Sarah. He didn't want to be one of them.

"Never seen someone so excited about stocking shelves before." Grady chuckled. "Every time we get a shipment in, she acts like it's a present for her."

Otto smiled. "Yeah, she enjoys that part."

"Customers like her, too."

The mention of customers reminded Otto of something Sarah had told him. "She mentioned meeting Norman Rounds."

Grady's laughter died as suspicion filled his expression. "Could've been. I wasn't there at the time."

"He come in your store a lot?" Otto asked.

"Wouldn't say a lot."

"How about Gordon Schwartz?"

"Don't really keep tabs on all my customers." Grady sounded surly now, making Otto pretty sure that he'd hit a nerve. Grady was likely covering for Gordon, the militia leader who was wanted for skipping bail after being arrested for weapons violations.

Without responding, Otto went to fire up his squad car engine. It gave him a moment to think about where he wanted to take his questioning. Grady was pretty close to shutting down completely, and Otto didn't want to miss out on the opportunity to get any information on Gordon. Norman, he wasn't worried about as much, because he'd proven himself to have some kind of moral code. Gordon, on the other hand, had an impressive cache of explosives and weapons, he very likely bore a grudge against the MPD after his girlfriend had been killed a few months ago, and he was one conspiracy theory away from waging war against the world.

"Didn't mean to make you uncomfortable," Otto said once he'd returned. "I wouldn't want to pit you against your customers."

"Then don't." Although Grady's voice was sharp, he didn't look as tense as he had a minute earlier. "Just because your girl works for me doesn't mean I'm your informant."

"Of course not." Taking a faux-casual pose, Otto kept his words slow and even. "I just worry about Sarah. She's too trusting. Rounds is one thing, but Gordon's skipped bail. He's being hunted. Desperation makes people do things they normally wouldn't, and I don't want Sarah in the middle of that."

"Understood." Moving to the driver's door, Grady reached in and fired up his truck. After cranking slowly a few times, the engine caught. As Grady straightened, he said, "No one's going to get in a shoot-out—or even a brawl—in my store. They know that I'd kick their asses from here to Dresden if they tried anything. Your girl is safe there."

"Good to know." Otto didn't believe it, though. Trouble could start anywhere, especially when Gordon Schwartz was around. "Think you're good?"

"Yeah. That should do it."

Otto detached the cables and put them back in his trunk. He noted that the snow shovel was missing, and he made a mental note to get it back from Hugh's squad car. Whenever equipment went missing, it was always Hugh behind the "theft." Even though Hugh had been on medical leave since September, he seemed to be a constant presence at the station. Otto wasn't sure why Hugh needed his snow shovel, though.

Climbing back in his squad car, Otto raised a hand to Grady and left the lot. As he slowly made his way down the otherwise empty street, he kept an eye on the rearview mirror to make sure that Grady managed to get off okay. He'd told Grady to get a new battery a hundred times, but the guy never listened. He just said it had lasted him twenty years. Why would he change it now?

Otto had given up lecturing Grady. Now, he just gave him a jump, watched him drive off, and then swung by Grady's house a little later to make sure that he'd made it home okay. Since Sarah had started working at the store, Otto had started feeling more positive about Grady. He was odd and cranky, but he seemed to be a good boss. Otto was happy to give daily battery jumps to someone who was nice to Sarah.

With a snort, he slowed, nearing the end of town. "You've got it bad," he muttered to himself. "You'd do pretty much anything to keep her happy." It was true. He was completely smitten.

As he braked, preparing to turn onto Case Street, Otto glanced in his rearview mirror again and watched with satisfaction as Grady's truck taillights got smaller as he drove in the opposite direction. Just as Otto was about to look away, a huge, red fireball lit up the sky.

Otto's head jerked back in shock. He craned his head around to see it straight on rather than in a reflection. It was real. Yellow and red lights bounced off the rocks, lighting up what should've been a dark section of the highway. The boom came a few seconds later, shaking the ground with the force of the explosion. Jolted into action, Otto whipped the squad car around, turning 180 degrees and taking off toward the fire. He couldn't wrap his head around it, couldn't believe there had actually been an explosion. Watching it in his rearview mirror had given it a surreal quality, made it seem like he was watching fiction on a small screen. He fumbled for his radio even as the dispatcher said his unit number. Grady had stopped in the middle of the road, and Otto steered around his truck.

Impatiently, Otto held the radio mike, waiting for the dispatcher to tell him about a report of the explosion. When it finally went quiet, he said, "Copy the explosion. I saw it. It looks to be just south of the pass. I'm en route."

"*Copy*," the dispatcher said. "*I'll notify Fire.*"

"Fire copies," a different voice responded. "We're coming from Borr, so we're about five miles west. What kind of explosion was this? Any idea of the cause? Do we need to have the hazmat team on standby?"

"Give me two minutes." Otto pushed a little harder on the gas. The car shot forward, fishtailing slightly in the deepening snow. The rear-wheel-drive squad car was pursuit-rated, which meant it was fast, but it wasn't great in winter weather. The chief was gradually replacing their cars with SUVs, but money for the department was always an issue. For now, Otto just had to work with what he had. "I'll get you some answers as soon as I'm on scene—or close to the scene." If it had been a chemical explosion, Otto knew to stay back until hazmat cleared it.

"*Otto.*" Theo's voice was rough with sleep, but sharp. "*I'm responding now. I'll be on scene in fifteen minutes.*"

"*Same.*" Hugh was the next one to speak over the radio.

Just as Otto raised the mic to tell Hugh that he was to keep his ass at home, the lieutenant spoke. "*Murdoch. Keep your broken arm and bullet-hole-ridden carcass at home, do you hear me?*"

"*Breaking…kkkk…up. Can't…kk…understand. Can you…please…kkk…repeat?*"

"*Knock it off with the fake broken transmission, Murdoch,*" Lieutenant Blessard growled. "*Stay. Home. Is that clear enough for you?*"

There was a long pause, and Otto could picture the conflict on Hugh's face. "*Copy*," Hugh said finally, sounding defeated. Otto didn't believe it for a second. Hugh would be there as usual, dodging the lieutenant.

Otto reached for the phone clipped to his belt. Sarah and Grace would've been long past the pass by the time the explosion occurred, but he still needed to hear Sarah's voice, to have her assure him that she was okay. His brain was running through possible causes as he called her—a vehicle explosion? If so, by the size of it, it would have to be a semi. There weren't any homes on the pass, so that limited the options.

When the call went straight to Sarah's voicemail, Otto swore under his breath. Ending the call, he put the phone away. The snow was starting to come down hard, and the wind was taking it sideways as well. Visibility was poor, plus the curve of the road and the rocky bluffs hid the explosion site. The only sign was the fire glowing as it burned the surrounding trees. Even that was just a faint orange haze through the veil of snow.

As he passed the last building in town, Otto increased his speed. Even though logic told him that it had been a vehicle explosion, that a truck driver hauling some kind of explosive material had slipped off the side of the pass, his gut was worried. Something was happening, and it wasn't good.

The dispatcher's voice said his unit number over the radio. "*I'm getting reports of…*" She paused, and Otto's interest picked up. Usually, Cleo was one of the most experienced and professional dispatchers they had. In emergency situations, she was so calm that she seemed almost robotic. Her hesitation was unusual, to say the least. "*I'm getting multiple reports of a low-flying helicopter in the area.*"

"Who's reporting it?" Otto slowed as he reached a switchback. There were certain people in town who reported low-flying aircraft of all kinds on a regular basis. Multiple reports of the same aircraft were unusual, though.

"*Branson Burr and Nan Villela.*"

Nan? Branson was on the fringe of Gordon Schwartz's militia group, and he tended toward paranoia, but Otto trusted Nan.

"*I've contacted Flight for Life, DNR, County, State — it's not with any of them.*"

"Copy," Otto said. He copied, but he was still baffled. Why was there a helicopter buzzing the town? "LT, are you hearing this?"

"*Yeah, I copied.*" The lieutenant sounded grim. As Blessard started to speak again, Otto rounded the last turn before the top of the pass. Blackened rock, dirt, and trees covered the road in a thirty-foot pile. It looked as though a new cliff had sprouted in the middle of the road.

Otto braked hard. His squad car slid over the slick pavement, the back end skidding to the side. The tires squealed in protest as the antilock brakes shuddered, pushing against the pressure of his right foot. The pile of rocks and debris grew larger, making it feel as if he was going to plow right into the side of a small mountain. The tail of the car swung farther to the side, rotating until the vehicle careened diagonally toward the mound of boulders. His foot pressed harder as he held tight to the wheel. It felt as if he was trying to stop the car with brute strength alone, and his leg vibrated with effort as he stomped on the brake. The car still headed toward the rocks, but it finally started to slow, sliding to a stop just a few feet from an enormous boulder sitting in the middle of the road.

Ignoring the way his hand shook with residual adrenaline, Otto grabbed for the radio mic. "The highway at the top of the pass is completely blocked." His voice was rough as he tried to get his breathing calmed. Everything was okay. He hadn't plowed his car into a huge rock. He'd survived. Gradually, his breaths came slower, and the sheer enormity of the damage the explosion had caused began to sink in.

Otto peered through the snow whipping around his squad car. The top and side of the rock wall bordering the highway appeared to have been sheared off and dumped on the pavement. The few trees that remained on the cliff were still burning, like torches glowing in the snowstorm. With the small mountain on the highway, a drop-off on the left, and the rock wall on the right, there was no way to get through. Otto blew out a long breath. This was going to be a huge mess to clear. In the meantime, he and Sarah would have to take another route to get back and forth between home and Monroe. The drive would take three times as long.

Glancing at the radio mic in his hand, Otto realized that no one had responded to his last transmission. "Dispatch, did you copy about the rockslide?"

Silence. When he reached to change the radio channel, he realized that the display was blank. His squad car radio was completely dead. With a grunt of annoyance, he took his portable radio off his belt and turned it on. Once he heard the faint beep indicating that it had power, Otto repeated the information about the rocks and debris blocking the road.

There was no response.

Grabbing his phone, that feeling from earlier—the one telling him that something was very, very wrong—hit him again, a hundred times stronger that time. He called the number for dispatch, but his phone gave a beep and displayed *No Service*.

"What?" He always got service in Monroe, even this close to the pass. There were a few locations on the way to his place where cell service was sketchy, but he hadn't discovered a dead spot—until now. Otto wondered if the rockslide had blocked the signal. He turned in his seat, moving his phone around, trying to improve the reception. The *no service* message didn't change.

With a huff of irritation, he lowered his phone, but a light to the east caught his eye—a light that seemed to be moving. He squinted through the passenger-side window, trying to make it out. At first, he thought it was headlights, but it was too high in the air. Was this the mystery helicopter Nan and Branson had been talking about?

He peered through the snowstorm, trying to see more than that faint, moving light. As he watched, there was a bright flash. Otto knew what it was even before the crash of sound caught up to the light, so loud that it shook the ground and his car with it. Otto felt as if time was looping around on him, that he was watching that first explosion over again, but then logic returned, and Otto knew that it was on the other side of town. He knew in his gut that the east mountain pass—the only other way out of Monroe besides the blocked west pass Otto had just left—was blown.

If a helicopter was bombing the passes on either side of Monroe, that meant that someone—a "friend" of Sarah's brother, Aaron Blanchett, came immediately to mind—was knocking out highway access to the town. Had the FBI arrived to pick up Aaron and the other two men yet? Were they trapped in town, or had they gotten clear before the bombs were dropped? It seemed like a huge coincidence that all this was happening around the same time the men were supposed to have been picked up by the FBI. Otto sent a quick glance at the still-blank radio display. What if they were knocking out communications as well? The idea seemed crazy—although not as crazy as the thought that two random, unrelated explosions happened at opposite sides of town within minutes of each other.

Moving the car so his headlights pointed straight at the rockslide, he took some—admittedly blurry—pictures. He tried texting one of them to Blessard, Theo, and Hugh, but it wouldn't send. Putting his phone away, he did a three-point turn and drove back toward Monroe.

The wind hit the side of his car, and Otto fought to stay in his lane. Snow flew across his windshield, making it seem like his squad car was spinning around in a circle. As he retraced his route, he noted that his tire tracks had already been erased by the vicious wind. Normally, after going around the first curve, he could see the entire town of Monroe stretched out in front of him. Tonight, the snow was obscuring the view. Nothing was visible except for a few of the brighter lights, and a slight lightening of the area compared to when he looked at the darkness to the west.

The snow was getting thicker. He slowed even more

as he curved around the side of the mountain, despite his intense need to slam his foot down on the accelerator. He had to find the lieutenant to see what the status of the FBI pickup was. Once again, he was grateful that Sarah and Grace were in Dresden. Whatever was happening, Monroe was not a safe place to be tonight.

As Otto followed the next hairpin turn, his back wheels spun for a second before finding traction. He needed to stop by the station, figure out what was going on with their communications, check in with the lieutenant, and get his four-wheel-drive vehicle. He briefly wondered how Sarah was and whether she and Grace would try to make it back before the danger had passed, but he shoved the question out of his head. That thought led to panic, and he didn't have time for that.

His mouth set grimly, he concentrated on making his way down the hill and around the last curve. After that, it was a direct shot into town. As he came out of the final turn, Otto straightened the wheel—but the car didn't straighten. It slid sideways, barreling toward the side of the road and a row of evergreens. Otto fought the car, hauling the wheel to the left as hard as he could, but it skidded toward the trees. He braced for the hit as they neared the edge of the road. The right two wheels slipped off the shoulder and into the drift collected at the edge of the road. The car tilted as the right side sank lower, the spinning wheels sending up a spray of white powder as he tried unsuccessfully to drive out of the snowy ditch. He shifted to reverse and then to drive and back to reverse again, trying to rock the car out of the ditch, but he had no luck. The car was stuck. With a bitten-off curse, Otto shoved back the voice in his head warning him that time was ticking until the next bomb was dropped. Literally spinning his wheels wouldn't help anyone. Taking a deep, calming breath, Otto got out of his car.

The wind hit him like a punch, the snow painfully hard and sharp. The BB-like pellets stung his face and neck, and he hoped desperately that Sarah was safe inside a Dresden hotel, and not having to fight through this weather. Circling the car, he quieted the panic building inside him and examined the situation, kicking some of the drifted snow clear of the wheels.

It was too deep, though, and the car had become entrenched. If he'd had his shovel, Otto would've had a chance of digging it out, but that wasn't an option. "Damn it, Hugh," he muttered, frustration and the suffocating feeling of urgency pressing on him.

Reaching into his car, he turned off the engine. He'd slid far enough to the side that the placement shouldn't be an issue for anyone else traveling on the road, he thought automatically before catching himself. There wouldn't be anyone else on the road tonight—the explosions had prevented that. What was happening to their town?

Pushed by a building sense of urgency, Otto started jogging toward the station.

CHAPTER 17

At the sound of the barn door closing, Sarah huddled closer to the stall partition, trying to make herself invisible. She put a hand on Mort's collar. Xena wasn't a barker. In fact, Sarah hadn't heard her make any noise at all, except for an occasional, almost inaudible whine. Mort, on the other hand, had been trained to bark. He barked to alert his people of danger and to intimidate and sometimes just because he was excited. Sarah was ready to quiet him, but she knew it would be too late. If he barked, then they were caught…and dead.

The fire and wind howled even louder outside, the sound muted only slightly by the barn walls. It covered the sound of footsteps, and Sarah didn't know if the intruder—or intruders—were still standing by the door or if they were right at the stall, leaning close enough to peer down and see her and the dogs. Bean snorted, a long, loud sound of fear, his muscles shivering with tension. It was unnerving, crouching so close to the huge, skittish creature's hooves. One spook, and Sarah could have a hoofprint on her head.

"What does he want us to do with the horse?" a male voice asked.

Sarah started to shake. If they meant to hurt Bean,

she wouldn't be able to keep hiding. She'd have to do something to prevent it.

"Who cares," another voice came. It sounded familiar, and Sarah wondered if it was a person she knew. How many times had they passed each other in the hallway or on the grounds? She might have greeted him cheerfully, not realizing that he would one day hunt her down…that he might possibly be the one to kill her. "Just leave it. Let's search the place and go."

"We're going to just leave the horse in here? What if it starves to death?" The voice was closer, clearer, and Sarah started making frantic plans in her head. If they spotted her, she could run or fight or…do something. The stall itself didn't have any escape hatch, except for the one sliding door. She'd basically locked herself in a cage. There was no escape if they found her.

"It's not our problem," the second, deeper voice said. "Someone'll find it. Cops and feds'll be all over this place tomorrow."

"Nope. We've wiped out their systems. No phones, radios, cells, wireless… They're not talking to nobody." The first guy sounded almost giddy.

"Let it out, then, if you want." The second man said in a bored voice. "It'll survive on its own. There are wild horses all over the place out here, I've heard."

"Yeah?" He sounded too close, too loud. "That's awesome. It's like the wild, wild West out here."

She needed a plan, or at least a weapon. Why hadn't she grabbed that sledgehammer when she had a chance? That did remind her of her knife, and she very gingerly unzipped the main pocket on the pack. The nylon fabric vibrated with Bob's growls, and Sarah said a silent prayer of gratitude that the thunderous noises outside covered any sound from either the annoyed cat or from her attempts at quietly opening the pack. Finally, there was a hole large enough for her to slip her hand in. She felt around for the knife. It seemed to take forever, and she was afraid that the sliding door would open at any second. Finally, her fingers closed around the cool metal of the knife, and she almost sobbed in gratitude.

"I'll let him out, then." His voice was so clear that he had to be right next to the stall door. Sarah started breathing in quick gulps. "Hey, there's a goat in there, too! Can I let the goat out? Are there wild goats?"

"Yeah, dumb-ass. Haven't you heard of mountain goats?"

"Right. I'll let both of them go, then."

"You do that." At least the second man was on the other side of the barn, judging by the faintness of his voice.

As she pulled the weapon out of the pack, Mort started leaning toward the sliding door. Sarah caught his collar, mentally begging him to stay quiet and still. Xena pressed against her, as if she could hear Sarah's pleading thoughts. Sarah was concentrating so hard on Mort, so worried that he'd start to bark, that she wasn't watching Bean.

When the horse charged toward the door, it startled Sarah so much that she almost shrieked, swallowing down the scream at the last moment before it escaped. Bean, ears pinned, snaked his head toward the door, striking out at it with a front hoof. The slam of metal on metal as the edging on the door hit the frame rang out, louder than the wind or the raging fire outside.

"Shit!" The man's voice was farther from the stall,

and Sarah started to shake, partially in relief and partially from fear. "That thing's crazy!"

Bean struck the door again, the loud bang making Sarah jump.

"It's a demon horse," the guy said. He was still a good distance from the stall, and Sarah began to breathe more slowly. *Good boy, Bean. Keep him away.* "His eyes are glowing red. Hey, Shelton! Check it out. His eyes are all possessed and shit, like that statue at the airport."

"I'm going to be all 'possessed and shit' if you don't help me search and quit messing around with that horse."

The man moved away from the stall, his grumbling about ungrateful devil horses getting fainter and fainter until Sarah could only hear the wind and fire again. Her hand dropped from Mort's collar as the dog relaxed slightly, although she kept a hand on his back, stroking him lightly with her fingers.

Now that her heart wasn't thundering in her ears, Sarah could hear the faint drone of Bob's growls, but she hoped the men couldn't hear or, if they could, they would just assume it was the wind. She patted the pack lightly where a catlike bulge was, but that only increased the growling, so she moved her hand away.

"It's clear," Shelton said, his voice just loud enough for Sarah to make out his words. "She must've been in the house. Let's go back to town. One down; one to go."

"Target practice!" the other man laughed loudly, making both Sarah and Xena start. "Boom!"

The roaring of the wind and flames was deafening for a moment until they shut the door behind them with a bang. Sarah sat in the stall for a long time, even after she heard the sound of what she was guessing was a helicopter. White spotlights lit up the barn, making Bean shift uneasily, his head high in the air. The *whump-whump-whump* that they'd heard before running for the bunker was almost unbearably loud, but it faded gradually until they were left with just the red glow from the fire and the howling wind.

Sarah climbed to her feet, her muscles protesting being held in such a tense, crouched position for so long. Peeking over the solid half-wall, she made sure no one else was there before straightening completely. A part of her remained terrified that the guys were still both there, waiting right outside the stall. She didn't truly believe they were gone until she saw the empty barn.

Urgency flowed through her. She carefully lifted the backpack, sliding her arms through the straps and buckling the one around her waist to keep the pack as stable as possible. Poor Bob. He was such a good cat. If he'd yowled, even once, their hiding place would've been discovered. Sarah's skin prickled with sweat at the thought.

Moving carefully toward Bean, she tried to push down her anxiety. He didn't need her amping up his nerves. The aggressive display had freaked her out a little, though. Before, he'd seemed flighty, but Sarah hadn't expected the charging and striking. He shifted, his ears flicking toward her and then to the sides, as if to take in as many sounds as possible.

"Hey, Bean," she said softly, probably too quietly for even the horse to hear. Having to speak kept her breathing, though. "You feel like getting out of here? I know that your house didn't get blown to bits like ours did, but I'd rather not leave you here alone. What do you say?" After a few tense seconds, he blew out a breath and lowered his head slightly. His ears were still swiveling around, but Sarah couldn't blame him for that. She was jumping at every sound, too.

Moving slowly to his left side, she slid the halter on, buckling it with shaking fingers. As she pushed the stall door open and led Bean out, she glanced at the goat.

"Coming, Hortense?" If she had to lead the goat, too, that was going to take a hand—and a halter—she didn't have. To her relief, Hortense snatched one more bite of hay before following them out of the stall. The dogs surged out last, staying clear of Bean's hooves. Circling around, Mort took the lead again, heading toward the barn doors, while Xena walked close to Sarah's left side.

Bean stared at everything, but he didn't spook or yank away or crash into Sarah or do any of the hundred things that she feared he'd do. Sarah looked at the main barn doors, but her paranoia about someone waiting outside for them was strong—even more than when she was in the stall, scared to look around. Besides, there was a raging snowstorm happening outside. Her gaze turned toward the tunnel entrance.

She wasn't sure if she could even get Bean into the underground passage, but she wanted to try. If she could get them away from the house before going outside, she felt like they would have a greater chance of escaping without being spotted. She didn't really have a plan beyond getting all the animals to town and finding Otto. That was enough for the moment.

It took her a while to find the latch on the doors. They'd been camouflaged to blend into the rest of the wall. If she hadn't just emerged from them a short time before, Sarah wouldn't have even known they were there. She ran her fingers over the rough wood surface for what felt like hours, although she knew it was only minutes. Finally, frustrated, she yanked her gloves off and felt around again.

There! Her fingers touched a square of smoother wood, and that pulled down to reveal a latch. Relief poured over her, and her knees sagged a little, but she stiffened them. It was nowhere near time to collapse in a heap. Sarah still had to get all the animals out and make it to town. As she glanced over her ragtag, scared group around her—except for Hortense, who was nibbling some spilled grain on the ground, as content as she could be—Sarah felt a wave of panic pressing against her. She pushed back, damming up the fear into a tiny box labeled "open later." She needed to be the adult—well, the human—in the room. They were counting on her to keep them safe, so keep them safe she would. Sarah had a moment of thankfulness that she didn't have the puppies with her as well. Bob would've had to share his pack, and Sarah was pretty sure he wouldn't have been happy about that.

Unlatching the door, she pulled both open as wide as they'd go and turned on the light. The opening to the tunnel was wider than most two-horse trailers, so she was hopeful that Bean would be okay walking through it. It was as if Otto and the previous homeowner had seen the future and known that someone was going to have to sneak horses out of the barn at some point, because there weren't any steps. A fairly steep ramp led down into the tunnel. Once she got Bean down that, the rest was easy. It was simply walking.

"Ready, everyone?" Feigning confidence, Sarah started walking down the ramp into the tunnel. Xena and

Mort followed immediately. It took a moment for Bean to follow. First, he stretched his neck toward the tunnel entrance and blew one of his scared snorts. "Don't be silly. It's just a tunnel. It's like loading in a very, very long trailer."

Sarah swore that Bean gave her the side eye.

"Fine, it's a little scarier than that, but not much. There's nothing in there to hurt you, though. I can promise you that." She started forward again, and he followed, shooting through the opening like a ball out of a cannon. Sarah jumped out of the way, nearly tripping over Xena, and braced herself for the massive jerk on the lead line. Once Bean was in the tunnel, though, he stopped abruptly, spinning around to face the entrance he'd just plowed through.

"That's one way to do it, I guess," Sarah said under her breath. Hortense walked in with no drama or worry, and Sarah wished that all the animals had her calm smarts. She pulled the doors closed, loving the solid click of the latch fastening, before heading down the tunnel. Mort trotted ahead, as if scouting the way, and Bean walked willingly enough next to her.

When he reached the T-intersection, Mort turned toward the house, and Sarah called him back. A pang went through her. The house was gone. They could hole up in the bunker, but it didn't feel safe anymore. What if the fire spread downward, and they were trapped in a smoky hole in the ground? The idea made her shiver and her spine prickle with cold sweat. No, they'd go to town, like she'd originally planned. Sure, there were scary guys out to kill her, but they'd figure it out.

Somehow.

By the time Otto reached the police station, he was half-frozen and nearly crazy with worry about Sarah and Theo and Hugh and…well, pretty much the entire town. The only thing keeping him warm and sane was distracting himself by coming up with creative revenge plots to get back at Hugh for stealing his squad-car shovel.

The station was small, but it seemed oddly abandoned. The sound of Otto's boots hitting the floor echoed. Although he told himself it was nothing to worry about, that everyone was at the training in the Springs, the silence still made him uneasy. He jogged toward the communications room, holding his key card to the reader and yanking open the door.

No one was there.

The screens were dark and the chairs were empty, and his stomach gave a painful twist. Pivoting, he headed toward the lieutenant's office. It was abandoned as well. The lights were still on, and Blessard's favorite travel mug was sitting next to his battered keyboard. All Otto's instincts—which had been muttering at him that something was very, very wrong—turned up the volume, shouting at him to get out of the building.

First, though, he strode to the lieutenant's desk and picked up his landline phone. Otto wasn't even shocked at the silence when he put the phone to his ear. He'd expected it to be dead, like all their other communications. Otto left the LT's office and jogged for the stairs, taking several steps in each stride, not slowing down as he hit the release bar on the door at the bottom. Part of him was braced for the garage to be empty, for all the vehicles to be missing, but his SUV was still there where he'd left it that afternoon—what felt like weeks ago, rather than mere hours.

As he drove out of the garage, he plowed through a drift of snow that had piled up against the door. There was a thick layer on the ground now, and it was still falling heavily. The wind was sweeping it into tall drifts, and Otto knew that, if it continued this way for another few hours, the roads would soon be impassible.

Otto barked out a laugh that sounded too loud in the silence of his SUV. What did it matter if the town roads were impassible? No one could get out anyway.

He automatically reached for his radio, intending to try to reach the lieutenant. As his hand touched his portable unit, Otto remembered that it was useless. He was completely cut off from everyone else—city, county, and state.

It was a strange and uncomfortable feeling. Otto was used to the constant chatter of his radio, and nearly constant texts and calls from other officers and his supervisors. The silence now felt wrong—very wrong.

He turned out of the department surface lot onto the street, trying to think what he should do next. His rear tires couldn't find purchase in a snowdrift blocking the exit, and his four-wheel drive kicked in, shooting him forward. Otto kept his speed up as he headed down the street, even though he didn't know where he was going. His instinct was to go find Sarah, but without excavation equipment and dynamite, there was no way Otto was getting out of town. *She's safe*, he reminded himself. *She and Grace are probably enjoying their night at a fancy resort.* His mind knew it, but his gut still wanted to go to Dresden to find her, even if that meant tearing through the obstruction on the pass with his bare hands.

The street was strangely quiet. He glanced down at the dashboard clock and saw that it was barely nine. It wasn't that late. Where was everyone? Despite the accumulating snow, he slowed as he looked around. A number of residents had moved to warmer climes for the winter, but even the houses he knew were occupied—by the Romas family and Sean Bilks and the Chenykes—were dark. The only illumination came from the occasional streetlamp and the security lights around the police station behind him. It was strange and eerie.

He was starting to turn on Main Street, when the night lit up behind him. The deafening blast sent his foot instinctively down on the brake, and the SUV juddered to a halt. He hunched forward, his body folding over the wheel, his arms coming up to cover his head. There was a roar of fire, and he slowly straightened, his arms lowering as the truth sank in. There'd been another explosion.

Slamming his SUV into Park, he jerked open the driver's door and jumped out into the snow. He stared for a moment before jerking himself out of his shock and running toward the station—or what used to be the station. The white light of the immediate explosion had already muted to yellows and oranges as fire engulfed the jagged remains. Flames covered everything, consuming the police department completely. Otto stopped abruptly when blazing heat scorched his face. There was nothing he could do. There was nothing left for him to save. He'd worked in that building, for the Monroe

Police Department, for eight years, ever since he received his law enforcement degree. Now, in a single second, it was gone.

As the immediate shock subsided and reality kicked in again, Otto peered into the snow-clogged sky and spotted the white lights of the helicopter. It was headed east, toward the center of town. Otto rushed back to the SUV and climbed in. As he shifted into Drive, he debated his options. He could chase the helicopter and try to bring it down, but his resources were limited. He had his duty weapon, a Taser, a knife, and a multipurpose tool, none of which would be much use against a helicopter. All of his other guns were at his house, which wasn't accessible right now.

Chasing the helicopter was out. That would be a good way to get himself blown up. So what was his next step? What he needed, Otto decided, was to track down the others. He knew they were still in town. The streets were abandoned, even more than usual during a snowstorm. The explosion should've brought everyone running to help or gawk, but there were no lights on in any of the houses. Despite the mass exodus of Monroe every fall, there were still townspeople who stuck around. Their homes were just as dark as the houses that had been abandoned for the winter.

Where were they? Otto flexed his hands, squeezing the steering wheel and then releasing it as he tried to think logically. Aaron's flunkies had just bombed both mountain passes and the police station. Who knew where they would strike next, but Jules's house was a real possibility. Otto's heart rate sped up at the thought, but he forced himself to think it through. Logan Jovanovic had recognized Grace when he and Aaron had tried to grab Sarah in the viner bathroom. It made sense that the Jovanovics were in on it, as well. It was no secret in town where Jules lived, and everyone knew that Jules and Grace lived together. Only a few people knew that Grace was out of town. That house was a likely target. Theo would know that, and he'd get everyone out.

Tipping his head back against the backrest, Otto squeezed the wheel so hard his hands cramped. "So where did they go?" he asked out loud.

If Sarah had still been living at Jules's when this happened, where would Otto have brought her? He frowned so hard at the idea that his face ached. He'd want her somewhere safe, but they couldn't leave town. Since any building could be the next target, they'd need to go somewhere that couldn't be hit—or wouldn't be. *The bunker*, his brain immediately supplied, but he shook away the idea. If they couldn't leave town, they couldn't get to the bunker.

Otto's bunker, at least.

An idea flared to life in his head, and he shot forward in his SUV. It was a long shot and slightly insane, but he knew where he'd have brought Sarah if this had happened with her in town.

Gordon Schwartz's militia compound.

The tunnel seemed to go on forever. Sarah forged on, though, checking every few minutes to make sure that all of the animals were still tagging along. The monotony of the passageway was a blessing, because Bean could find nothing out of the ordinary to spook at. They reached a ladder that led to a trapdoor in the ceiling. Sarah looked at it longingly before trudging past.

Gradually, the passageway began to look more like a mining tunnel than a hallway. The ceiling grew lower, and Sarah began to worry about Bean. He could fit as long as he kept his head down, but, if anything startled him, he could easily crack his head against the rock above. She shortened the lead line, hoping she'd be able to keep his head down if something jumped out at them.

The space between lightbulbs was getting longer, and Sarah considered pausing so she could pull out her flashlight. She decided to keep walking, needing to get out of the tunnel that was getting increasingly claustrophobic.

A frigid breeze blew through the tunnel, making her shiver and use her free hand to tug her coat zipper higher. Mort trotted ahead of them, his head raised as he sniffed at the air. As realization struck, Sarah's hand froze at her collar. If the wind was getting in, then they had to be close to an exit.

Excitement filled her. Despite the snow and Aaron's goons and all the dangers of being out in the open, Sarah was just so happy to be getting out of the tunnel. The passageway curved to the right, and then the wind really hit them, so cold that Sarah lost her breath. Snow blew into the tunnel, sharp pebbles that stung her face. Ducking her chin into her collar, she walked forward, leading Bean.

Right in front of the exit, the ceiling dropped another foot. Sarah paused, eyeing the level of the rock and comparing it to the height of Bean's withers. If he kept his head down, she was pretty sure he could squeak underneath, but that was a pretty big if, especially with the wind and snow smacking them in the face.

Sarah held her breath and kept the hand holding the lead line low as she walked quickly toward the trouble spot. Bean hesitated after his head and half of his neck were under the lowest point, and Sarah's heart squeezed with anxiety. Giving an encouraging cluck, she tugged on the lead rope. After a moment, he moved reluctantly forward, keeping his head down. As soon as his tail cleared, she blew out all the breath she had been holding, feeling light-headed with relief.

She did another count, making sure all the animals were accounted for. Mort was waiting for them at the entrance, not seeming to feel the wind that was blasting him. Now that they were at the end of the tunnel, she felt a jolt of fear at leaving its secure walls. It was stupid to go out in a blizzard. Maybe they should just stay in the protective shelter of the cave until the snow stopped.

Shoving back her cowardly thoughts, Sarah moved out into the open, gasping as the full force of the wind hit her. If there was any way for her to help Otto and her newfound friends, she couldn't just cower in a cave.

Squinting against the wind, she looked around. They were about a quarter of the way up the ridge to the east of Otto's property. The fire engulfing the remains of his house were a blazing you-are-here sign. The destruction of their home had one upside.

"Glass half full, I guess," Sarah said with a choked laugh.

She was glad that they weren't very far up the side of the mountain, since she'd worried that they'd come out at the very peak, and she'd have to put Bean into climbing gear. There was a trail—or what looked like one, since it could've been anything under the thick layer of snow—that led down toward the road that passed in front of Otto's driveway.

It looked so far away, though, that Sarah wanted to cry. It felt like they'd already walked so far, had too many scares, fought enough dangers. The distant road seemed to be mocking her. She was tempted to sit down in the snow and give up. At the thought, she gave herself a mental shake. Giving up was not an option. The animals were depending on her, and Otto—although he might not know it—was counting on her to help them. Besides, she'd been through worse—much worse.

Pulling her shoulders back, she took the first step onto the snowy trail. "No sense standing here and getting cold." She shivered as the wind tossed a handful of snow down her coat collar. "Well, colder."

Bean followed, surprisingly docile. Sarah wondered if all the experiences of the night had blown the horse's mind, and he just didn't have it in him to bother being scared anymore. Either that, or he was just tired. Whatever the reason for his calmness, Sarah was grateful. If he spooked, he could jump right off the edge of the trail and down the rocky cliff.

Mort, of course, squeezed ahead of them to take the lead, and Xena followed right behind and to the side of Sarah. At first, Sarah worried about Xena getting stepped on, but Bean walked far enough behind that he didn't crowd the dog. Hortense was at the very back of their odd train, and she was obviously not happy about the entire situation. She would stop abruptly, refusing to walk forward. When the group got far enough ahead of her, she would trot to catch up and then start the whole process again.

Sarah decided that she loved her boots even more than she'd initially thought. The snow wasn't deep enough to go over the tops, and her feet were warm and cozy. The sagging, too-large snow pants were somewhat annoying, but she appreciated the warmth and dryness enough that she didn't take them off. The fabric cut the wind, too, so the only parts of her that were cold were her face and neck and fingers.

In fact, she was soon sweating. Lifting her foot to clear the snow with each step was exhausting. Unused to the motion, her thighs ached and burned, and she dreaded how they would feel the next day. At the thought, though, she quit mentally whining. She wasn't sure what would happen tomorrow. Would she be dead, or back in Texas with Aaron's thugs, or mourning Otto or Jules or Grace or—

Abruptly, she cut off her imagination. Instead, she tried to plan. When she reached Monroe, she'd track Otto down. He'd know of a place they could stash Bean and Hortense, and then they could... Her planning petered out there. She wasn't sure how they could stop Aaron and his goons. Would the Monroe police be able to stop them? There were so few officers in town right now, with the winter decrease plus those off at training. Maybe they could call the county sheriff's department, or the state police, or even the FBI. Bombing a town seemed bad enough for the feds to get involved.

As Sarah considered the options, she moved between two pine trees and saw that they'd reached the road. A spurt of elation faded when she realized how much more walking they needed to do before reaching town. Bean stepped forward and blew warm, moist air on the back of her neck.

She turned to eye him appraisingly. "Will you kill me if I ride you?" she asked him. Despite his mellow attitude since they'd left the tunnel, it could be a whole different story—as in a story about a bucking horse at a rodeo—if Sarah got on him…bareback. Without a bridle. She was starting to think it was a very bad idea, but then she looked at the road stretching in front of them. It was just over nine miles. She did not want to walk nine more miles in the snow.

Determined to at least give it a try, Sarah led Bean toward a snow-covered downed pine lying just off the road and lined his left side up to it. She climbed onto the log, and Bean rolled an eye at her before swinging his haunches away from the tree. Hopping off, Sarah realigned the horse and stepped onto the log and threw her right leg over his back before he could move away again.

Once on his back, Sarah went still, trying to be ready for anything—bucking, bolting, rearing, or a little of all three. Instead, he froze, except for the twitching of his muscles. When Sarah realized that she was waiting for him to move, and he was waiting for her to move, she laughed in a small, relieved huff.

Giving him a gentle squeeze with her legs, Sarah shifted her weight to turn him, relaxing a little more when he responded easily. Xena whined anxiously from the ground.

"It's okay, Xena," Sarah said. "I'm still here, just taller. Let's go find Otto."

The dog's scarred ears pricked up, either from her

name or Otto's. Sarah steered Bean down the middle of the road at a brisk walk. Sitting on a warm horse was already better than shuffling through the snow. Turning her head, she did an animal count. Xena was next to Bean, and Hortense had given up on her attempt at passive aggression. Looking resigned, the goat had fallen in behind Bean.

Instead of leading, Mort had turned into Otto's driveway.

"Mort!" Sarah called, her heart breaking a little when the dog looked at her and then in the direction of where the house still smoldered before reluctantly joining their small group. She could sympathize with the poor dog. She, too, wished they were heading home, that there hadn't been an explosion, that Otto was here and fine and Aaron wasn't trying to kill them, but that was just too bad. If wishes were horses…

Glancing down at Bean's mane, Sarah gave a short laugh. Everything else was going to hell, but at least she could ride.

CHAPTER 18

THE DRIVEWAY TO GORDON SCHWARTZ'S COMPOUND WAS bad on a good day, and today was not a good day. Otto was able to get his SUV about three-quarters of the way down the drive before he bottomed out in a snowdrift. He left it there and walked the rest of the way. By the time he finally managed to reach the ten-foot gate topped with barbed wire, Otto was not in the mood to mess around. When pushing the button on the homemade call box didn't bring a response within thirty seconds, Otto climbed the chain-link. At the top, he used the wire-cutter implement on his multi-tool to snip the strands of barbed wire. Swinging his leg over, he climbed down on the other side.

Just like the police station, the compound felt eerily empty. The mental comparison made Otto twitchy, and he scanned the sky, checking for the lights of a helicopter. He couldn't see anything but snow and the solar-powered security lights scattered around the area, so he continued to slog through the heavy drifts. He'd been in the compound a few times, but just on the first and second floors of the main house. He'd never been in the bunker. In fact, no one knew for sure that one existed. It was just assumed that someone as paranoid as Gordon Schwartz would have at least a safe room, if not an extra-large bunker stocked with enough supplies for three years of underground living.

After pounding on the front door with his fist, Otto tried the knob—locked. He made his way around the side of the house, annoyed. If Hugh, Theo, and the others were holed up in Gordon's bunker, they could've at least left Otto a note or a map or something.

As he rounded the corner into the backyard, someone grabbed his arm. Otto swung around, fist already raised and ready, mentally reprimanding himself for letting someone sneak up on him. The wind was loud, but that was no excuse when he was in a militia compound and Aaron and his buddies were in town.

"It's me," Hugh said in a hushed voice, and Otto stopped his arm mid-swing.

"Did Grace call you? Are she and Sarah okay?" All his worries returned in a rush.

"I haven't heard, not since they were leaving town a little after four." Hugh's tone was grim.

Otto's stomach tightened as he thought of all the worst possibilities.

"They're fine." Although still quiet, Hugh sounded like he was making an effort to sound casual. "What about you? Did you run into any trouble?"

"Yes. You took the shovel out of my squad car," Otto grumbled, keeping his voice low.

"What? The town is being invaded, and *that's* what you're worried about?" Hugh led the way to a tiny shack that looked like an old-school outhouse. It even had a crescent moon carved into the door.

As Hugh held the door open, Otto gave him a sideways look.

Hugh snickered. "Go on in. Trust me."

"Trust you like I trusted you to put the shovel back?"

"Why are you still going on about the shovel?"

"There are two vehicles stuck in the snow right now, thanks to you," Otto said, pulling out a small flashlight and turning it on before stepping into the outhouse. Of course the shovel was a small annoyance, but it kept him from focusing on the big problems— like the fact that their town was blowing up around them. In the tiny shed, the seat had been moved to the side, revealing an open trapdoor. Otto looked into the opening, pointing the beam of his flashlight into the hole, revealing a ladder descending into the dark space.

Hugh snorted quietly. "You got two cars stuck in the snow? Nice driving."

"It wouldn't have been a problem." Otto started down the ladder, keeping the flashlight beam pointed down. He didn't like blindly heading feet-first into a stranger's bunker. "If I'd had my shovel."

"Enough about the shovel. Keep moving."

Otto did, although he wasn't about to forget his revenge schemes. He'd just wait until they'd saved the town first—if the bombers left anything to save. The thought sobered him, and he hurried down the remaining rungs, landing on a concrete floor. Moving the beam of his flashlight in a slow circle, he saw he was in a small room with cinder-block walls and a drain on the floor. "What is this? A kill room?"

"Just don't think about it, and you'll be happier." Shining his flashlight ahead of them, Hugh led the way to a metal door that looked positively medieval. Hugh tapped out a quiet pattern, using the butt of his flash-light, and the door swung open.

"Another pig. Great." Gordon Schwartz groaned dramatically, but he stepped back and let Hugh and Otto enter. About twenty people scattered around watched anxiously as they stepped inside. Otto was relieved to see Theo, Jules and her siblings, the lieutenant, Grady, Cleo the dispatcher, Steve the fireman and his four kids, and several other townspeople. When Otto had driven down the dark, empty streets in town, he'd been worried about them. Even Norman Rounds was there, trying to fade into the background, as usual.

This room was much larger and a little more comfortable than the first one they'd entered, with an overhead light fixture, cots, and even some industrial-looking carpeting. Otto would've rather been in his bunker with Sarah. His gut clenched. He hoped she was safe. If Aaron's men were behind the attacks on the town, they'd be looking for Sarah. Even Dresden wouldn't be safe.

"Otto!" Jules jumped off the cot she'd been sitting on and hurried over to hug him. "We've been so worried! Have you heard from Sarah? Are she and Grace okay?"

Her questions fired up all of his worry again, and he could only offer Jules a shake of his head. "Haven't heard anything yet." Sam, standing behind Jules, flinched.

Dee followed her sister, giving Otto a squeeze around the waist. "The puppies are here, and so is Turtle."

"Turtle?" It took Otto a second to remember. "Oh, right. Windmill cat. Thank you for taking care of the pups."

"Of course," Dee said in a tone too serious for her

age. "No one gets left behind. Tio even brought his drone."

"Airplane," Ty corrected quickly, giving his little sister a look.

Dee eyed him right back. "Just because you say it's not a drone doesn't make it true."

"Okay, y'all," Jules interrupted the brewing argument. "You can discuss this later when things stop blowing up."

That brought Otto's mind back to the current situation. "What's the plan?"

"We're going to check on residents and bring them here, right after we make a run to the station armory," the lieutenant said. "When the second pass was shut down and we lost all communication, we evacuated. Grady suggested we come here to regroup."

Otto winced. "The station was hit."

"Hit?" Blessard repeated.

"Gone. They bombed it." The lieutenant took a breath, his face reddening, and Otto knew that a cursing streak was coming. "Kids here."

Blessard clamped his lips together, his face turning almost purple, but he managed to hold in his swearing. "Okay. Good thing we evacuated. Wish the armory wasn't gone."

"Is there any way to call for help?" Jules asked.

"Landline and cell phones are dead," Cleo said. "They blocked our digital radio communication, too. Internet's down—it was at the station, at least." She gave Gordon a questioning look.

"Don't have it. Just another way for the government to watch us." Gordon crossed his arms over his chest.

Otto studied him. "What about a CB or ham radio?" As soon as Gordon looked down, Otto knew he'd guessed right.

Scowling, Gordon was silent for several moments before he said, "Don't have one."

"Oh, for Pete's sake," Hugh said. "Take Cleo to the radio. We don't care that you're unlicensed. Right now, we just need help taking down the guys who are blowing up the town."

"Told you." Gordon still looked sullen. "Don't have one."

"He doesn't," the lieutenant confirmed. "I searched this place when we first arrived." Gordon gave Blessard a surprised glance, as if he hadn't thought a cop would vouch for his honesty.

"I do," Cleo said. "At my house, two miles past the blocked east pass. As soon as the snow stops, I can try to hike there."

"Help won't be able to get here until the snow stops anyway," Theo said, standing next to Jules.

"Nothing getting through the west pass." Otto pulled up the photos on his phone and handed it to Theo. "I didn't see the east pass, but I'm assuming it was hit the same way."

"They'll need to fly in, then," Jules said, leaning in to look at the pictures. "Whoa. What a mess."

"Most helicopter pilots won't fly in this," Hugh said, and Jules gave him a look. "I said 'most.' Those guys dropping the bombs… They don't strike me as being too concerned about standard safety procedures."

"How many helicopters are out there?" Otto asked. If Nan, who lived five miles outside of town, had reported a low-flying helicopter at the same time as Grady, who'd been sitting in his car in the middle of Monroe, then that meant there was probably more than one.

"Two, we think," Theo said absently, studying the photos closely before handing the phone to Jules.

"Two." A jagged stab of fear ripped through Otto. "One hit the passes and the station. The other one flew over Nan's place. It was heading toward my house. The animals." He turned abruptly and headed toward the door.

Hugh caught his arm. "Hang on. How are you going to get there? You don't have any vehicle that isn't stuck in the snow, and you couldn't drive through the pass anyway. The town's exploding, and people are stuck in their homes. We need your help here."

Otto paused reluctantly, hating that Hugh's words made sense. He could hike around the rockslide and follow the back trails to his place, but it would take hours on foot, especially without snowshoes. It was more important to help the town's residents get to safety before the next bomb went off.

"He's right," Theo added, echoing Otto's thoughts. "We should split into teams. Who all are planning to search?"

Theo, Hugh, Jules, and all the kids raised their hands.

"Here are the keys to the store," Grady, planted on one of the cots, tossed the key ring to Otto. "It's no police armory, but you're welcome to everything in the hunting department. I'm not going out there until those bomb-dropping helicopters are gone. You lot are nuts."

"No minors." Theo's voice was firm. Although the younger kids looked disappointed, they didn't argue.

Sam did, however. "I w-want to help."

"I need you here, Sam," Jules said, glancing at Dee, Ty, and Tio. "If we leave the twins unsupervised, they'll destroy this town faster than any bombs could."

Sam, his mouth set mulishly, met his sister's eyes for a long, tense moment before giving a single jerk of his chin in a grudging nod.

Theo's frown deepened. "Jules, you're staying here with them, too."

"No, I'm not."

"Yes, you are."

Gordon snorted. "Good luck, then."

"What do you mean?" Theo demanded, his eyes narrowing on Gordon.

"If three cops showed up and tried getting me to leave my home, I'd tell 'em to"—he glanced at the kids—"suck eggs."

"Good thing you're already here, then," Hugh said.

"Lots of people still in town think more like me than don't." Gordon gestured toward the three cops. "You think the three of you are going to convince Justin Ling to come with you? Or Barry and Wanda Post?" He gave a short laugh. "Like I said, good luck."

"They won't need it, because I'm not staying here, and do you know what else I'm not doing?" Jules's Southern accent was thick, a sure sign that she was annoyed. "I'm not arguing with you about it." She stepped to Otto's side and crossed her arms, giving Theo a *just-try-it* glare.

"Let's go," Otto said gruffly, heading for the door. Gordon was right. They needed Jules. There were plenty of people in Monroe—especially those who stayed all winter—who didn't trust any government figures, including police. Between the three of them, they could protect Jules. Otto was pretty sure Theo knew that, too, but he was too in love to think clearly when it came to Jules's safety.

"Wait." Lieutenant Blessard stopped him. "Take these radios and keep them on in case communications come back up." He handed Theo, Hugh, and Jules each a handheld radio. "Otto, switch yours with me. These are fully charged." Pulling his radio from the holder on his duty belt, Otto handed it over and took the one Blessard offered as the lieutenant continued. "I'll establish base here. Cleo, once the weather clears, you can head to your house."

"I'll go with her," Steve volunteered.

Blessard gave him a tight nod and then turned back to Otto and the others. "Be careful out there."

"Safety first. That's our motto," Hugh said in a joking tone that didn't hide the seriousness underlying his words. They grabbed their coats and gear, and Hugh and Theo leashed Lexi and Viggy.

"Ready?" Otto asked gruffly.

The other four looked at him with serious expressions. "Ready."

"Let's go." He opened the door, wishing he were at home with Sarah instead, snuggled in bed with the dogs and cat piled around them, or at least with her in Dresden so he could keep her safe. The townspeople needed their help, though. Besides, any action was better than hanging out in the bunker doing nothing.

It wasn't until they were out of the fake outhouse with the wind whipping around them that Otto realized they didn't have any way to get around except for walking. Grady's store would only be a mile or so, but the deepening snow would make it feel like more. They trudged down the driveway to the gate.

"Should've gotten the key from Gordon," Otto said, raising his voice so it could be heard over the wind. Getting the two dogs over the fence was going to be a challenge. He turned to retrace his steps back to the bunker, but Hugh stopped him.

"I've got this." He already had his lockpick kit out. In less than a minute, the padlock was open and Hugh was unwinding the chain holding the gates shut. Once they were all out, he left the padlock unfastened, arranging it so that, at first glance, it appeared to be locked.

The wind had blown much of the snow into a huge drift on the south side of the road, so there was a channel on the north side that was just a few inches deep. They fell into a ragged line. Everyone was tense, even the dogs. Otto couldn't stop looking around, especially at the sky, expecting another bomb to fall—on them, this time—at any second.

They didn't speak, moving quietly in mutual unspoken agreement. There was no way to know who could be around the next corner or hiding behind the nearby house. They were half a block from Grady's store when Viggy started to growl.

They all slipped between the print shop and the abandoned building next to it. When Viggy continued to growl low in his throat, Otto looked at the dog. Viggy was staring across the street into the darkness of the empty lot where the diner had stood. As Otto watched, keeping back in the shadows where he'd hopefully be hidden, three figures dressed in winter camouflage and carrying rifles prowled into the street.

"…anyone. They're hiding somewhere. The entire town can't be empty."

"Could be a ghost town," another one said, his voice sounding younger than the first.

"This isn't a ghost town." The third, judging by her higher-pitched voice and her smaller stature, was a woman. "They're hiding somewhere."

"Where?" the younger male asked. "We've searched half the houses in this pissant place. No one. It's like on that show about the virus, after everyone—"

"They're here," the woman said, interrupting him. "Blanchett was told they'd be here."

Told? Who gave Blanchett their location? Otto turned his head and met Theo's gaze. The possibility that someone they knew had sold them out made his gut churn.

"We'll drop a couple more bombs, and everyone'll come scurrying out," the woman promised. "One more down, and then we can head back to civilization."

One more down. Were they talking about Sarah? Rage flared in Otto's chest, and he took a step forward, not knowing if he was going to pound on the three mercenaries who'd laughed about trying to kill her, or if he was going to scale the mountain and run to Dresden to find her and keep her safe. Before he could do either, Theo and Hugh caught him and pulled him back.

He shook them off, his teeth clenched, but they just grabbed him again. As he twisted out of their hold yet again, Otto saw that the three strangers were walking away from them, toward Pound Street. The urge to charge after those monsters who'd talked about killing Sarah so casually was almost unbearably strong.

"Otto. *Otto*," Hugh was hissing in his ear. "Listen.

They don't know she's not in town. They can't get to her if they don't even know where she is. You need to calm down, or else you're going to give everyone here away. Do you want to do that? Do you want to be responsible for our deaths?"

Reason finally penetrated, and Otto stopped fighting the hands restraining him. "I'm okay," he gritted out. Theo made a disbelieving sound, but his grip on Otto loosened. Hugh released him, although his body posture showed that he was ready to grab Otto if he showed any sign of launching himself after Aaron's thugs again.

Glancing at Jules, at how stricken she looked, Otto felt his desperate panic bump up again. As if she could read his thoughts, Jules spoke. "Hugh's right, Otto. She and Grace are probably tucked in one of those boutique hotels in Dresden, snoring away. They'll be fine." Jules attempted to force a smile, but it was more of a frightened grimace.

Not wanting to scare Jules any more than she already was, Otto dipped his head in the semblance of a nod. He couldn't say the words, though, couldn't say he was sure that Sarah would be fine. Aaron had been in jail and monitored, but he'd managed to unleash an army on the town. Sarah might never be safe.

Despite his relief that she wasn't in Monroe, he needed to see her, to run his hands over her, check her for any injuries and feel that she was solid and alive. Then he would relax. Until then, they had a small mercenary army to vanquish—and townspeople to help.

"Let's go." Otto's voice didn't sound like his, even to his own ears. With a final check to make sure the three strangers were out of sight, he slipped out of their hiding spot and moved quickly toward Grady's, the other three close behind him. He went around back, figuring that there would be less chance of them being spotted going into the store than if they entered through the main doors.

Unlocking the back door, he slipped inside. Pulling out his small flashlight, he took a look around the dark stockroom and then held the door for the others. Hugh and Theo came in next and did a quick search before signaling that the room was clear. The encounter with the three mercenaries had disturbed them all, and they were quiet as they moved through the store toward the sporting goods section. They formed a triangle around Jules, with Otto and Hugh in front and Theo behind. The hunting display was wedged in a corner, tucked behind a glass case. The store was silent except for the almost inaudible sound of their feet on the floor. Hugh stepped forward, bending over the counter to check behind it.

Thump. With a low grunt of pain, Hugh reeled back several steps, yanking Lexi back with him. Otto ran forward, swinging around the end of the counter with his gun up and ready. Why hadn't the dogs warned them that someone was in the building?

CHAPTER 19

SARAH HAD NEVER FELT SO COLD. SHE BURIED HER GLOVED hands under Bean's heavy mane and blinked ice crystals off her lashes. The wind continuously pelted her face with what felt more like BBs than snowflakes. Tucking her chin into the collar of her coat, she tried to look on the bright side. All of them were still alive. In fact, despite the cold, the trip down the road hadn't been too bad, more monotonous than scary. Every time they came around a curve to a section of road overlooking Monroe, however, there seemed to be a new fire burning. At last count, there had been four.

The faint scent of smoke reached them, and Bean tossed his head uneasily.

"I know, Beanie," she said softly, rubbing his neck with numb hands. "Not too much longer." She hoped.

When the buried mountain pass came into view, Sarah wanted to cry. They'd come so far, only to be stopped so close to their destination. She was so cold, and every muscle in her body was both sore and exhausted. Mort had a slight limp, and Hortense was about as pissed-off-looking as a goat could be. Bob had stopped his steady, unhappy growling, but Sarah was pretty sure that was just because the cat was so miserable that he couldn't even complain about it anymore. Only Bean and Xena had been still going strong.

As they drew closer to the rockslide, Sarah peered through the driving snow at the fallen boulders and trees. There was a strange shape at the base, a dark-colored square that was too symmetrical. Even with the snow partially covering it, she could tell that it couldn't be natural. She walked Bean toward it. When he got close, he gave one of his long nervous snorts and shied.

Sarah realized what it was—a vehicle. The windshield was so cobwebbed with cracks that it was completely opaque. Her stomach lurched at the thought that someone had been driving on the road when the explosion had occurred. Sliding off Bean, she rushed toward the front of the van. Bean balked, not wanting to walk toward it. She tugged on the lead rope, and he reluctantly followed.

Dreading what she might find inside, she moved to the side. The driver's door window was white from cracks, as well. Except for the broken windows, two flat tires, and a few serious dents, it looked like the van had escaped the worst of the explosion and subsequent rockslide. As she reached for the driver's door handle, she hoped desperately that everyone in the van was okay and that they'd walked to safety.

Please be empty, she thought as she jerked open the door. A body toppled toward her, and she jumped back, inhaling a shriek. A man fell limply out of the driver's seat and landed on his back in the snowy road. Sarah lunged toward the person, her brain spinning. Should she do CPR? She'd never been trained to do it. She didn't even know how to check for a pulse. Even as the thoughts zipped through her mind, she realized that it was too late to help.

Above the glazed, dead eyes staring through her, there was a round hole. The man had been shot in the head. His legs were bent, as if he still sat in the driver's seat, his body as stiff as a mannequin's. Although Sarah didn't know much about forensics, it was obvious that he'd been dead a long time. Sucking in short, loud breaths, Sarah stared at the body in front of her.

What should I do?

She forced herself to move to the other side of the van. There was nothing she could do for the driver. Questions were swirling through her head, which was fuzzy from shock. Who had shot him? Who was he? Why was he killed? Although she really, really did not want to open the front passenger door, she made her hand grip the handle. As the door swung open, she jumped back in anticipation, but no one fell. The woman had fallen the other way, toward the center. Sarah made herself get close enough to see the faraway, filmy stare and the missing back of her skull before she lurched back and vomited.

Even as she heaved, Sarah panicked. Someone had killed these two people. She needed to go, to find Otto. He'd know what to do. Before she could leave, though, she had to check the rest of the van. If someone else was in there, hurt but not dead, she needed to help them.

Spitting out the last of the bile, she heard Xena whine. The dog pressed against the side of Sarah's leg, as if trying to console her. She reached down and stroked Xena's silky-smooth ears, and the contact calmed her slightly. She needed to get this done and get the animals out of there.

Without thinking about it, in case she talked herself

out of it, Sarah circled to the back of the van. The doors were ajar, and her hand trembled as she pulled one of them open. It was empty. Her breath escaped in a relieved *whoosh*, but then it caught again on the next inhale. The back of the van had molded bench seats running lengthwise on both sides. A black grill separated the back from the front, and three sets of open handcuffs lay scattered on the floor. Sarah's heart stopped.

Three sets. Three prisoners.

Aaron. Jeb. Logan.

With a cry, she scrambled backward, tripping over Xena and toppling into the snow. The FBI had been scheduled to pick them up that day. It all made horrible sense. Both victims in their suits, the explosion, even Jeb and Logan's strange abduction attempt. They'd *wanted* to get arrested, she realized. It had all been part of Aaron's plan. She should've known that he wouldn't give up that easily. What Aaron wanted, Aaron took. He wasn't about to let her—and his chance at taking over the Jovanovics—escape from him.

She scrambled to her feet, wanting to run. "Calm down," she muttered, hearing the high note of hysteria in her voice. "Calm down. Be smart."

Xena leaned against her again, her furry body shaking. It helped Sarah to focus.

"Get the animals. Then find Otto."

She looked around. Mort was a few feet away, watching her uncertainly. Hortense was pawing in the snow by the shoulder and eating the weeds she uncovered. Reaching back, Sarah touched the lump in her pack.

"You okay?" she asked Bob, and was rewarded by an annoyed growl.

Bean stood, head high and his eyes wide, a safe distance from the van. Sarah realized that she'd dropped his lead rope when she'd seen the first body. Her stomach squeezed as she remembered how long it had taken for him to approach her and Otto in the pasture. With him spooked and in a strange place, it could take hours to catch him.

Sarah approached on wobbly legs. The snow had gotten much deeper, and the drifts reached almost to her knees. "Hey, Bean," she said softly. "Please don't make this difficult."

He let her get within six feet before shying back. Tamping down the voice in her head that was screaming *Run! Hurry!* Sarah slowed her steps, shuffling through the snow in a creeping crawl that made her want to scream with impatience. She needed to get away from the scene of Aaron's latest crime, away from the bodies of his victims and the possibility that he might come back for her. It was so tempting to lunge for Bean's lead rope, to chase him, but she knew that wasn't the faster way. *Fast is slow*, Chester always used to tell her. *With animals, fast is slow, and slow is fast.*

She crept toward Bean, talking nonsense in a low voice that was as soothing as she could manage. He watched her nervously, his eyes so wide with worry that the whites showed. Slowly, slowly, she got closer. Bean threw up his head with a nervous snort, and she froze. She was so close. If he ran, and she had to do this again... Sarah forced herself to breathe and wait and be still. Bit by bit, Bean's head lowered. Taking a tiny step and then another, Sarah carefully reached out. The lead rope was just out of reach. She shuffled forward, inch by inch, and her gloved fingers brushed the cotton rope.

She grabbed it, the feel of the rope safely caught in her fist making her want to cry with relief. *No time for that.* Although she agreed with the strict voice in her head, she stepped closer and pressed her forehead against Bean's neck. He stood still, turning his head so that he could blow warm air down the back of her coat. She took a moment to breathe.

Soon, panic began creeping in again, and she knew they had to move. She walked Bean into a slight ditch next to the road to get him low enough that she was able to scramble onto his back. It wasn't pretty, but she managed to get on. Once she was up, Sarah looked at the pile of rubble, being very careful not to look at the van or the body next to it.

On one side of the rockslide, the ground dropped off abruptly. On the other side, the rock face rose abruptly, almost as flat and smooth as a wall. As much as Sarah hated to do it, she turned Bean around and they backtracked, following the ridge until the slope gentled. There was the start of a deer trail snaking its way to the top of the rocky mass, and Sarah urged Bean to follow it. As they climbed, Bean's metal shoes slipping occasionally against the smooth granite surface, Sarah prayed that the trail didn't disappear or turn into something unnavigable.

When they reached the top, she briefly celebrated before starting to sweat again. Bean's muscles bunched underneath her as he slid and scrambled down the slope. With just a halter, Sarah wasn't able to control his speed. If he found it easier to rush down the slick trail, then he did just that. They reached a terrifyingly steep portion of the trail, and Sarah looked around for another option. There was none. Either they followed the trail, or they turned around and returned to the van and the murdered FBI agents. Clinging to Bean's mane, she sat back and closed her eyes.

"Okay, sweet boy. I'm trusting you. Let's get to the bottom safely, okay?"

Bean stepped onto the slope.

CHAPTER 20

"DROP YOUR WEAPON!" OTTO SNAPPED AT THE FIGURE huddled behind the counter. Then he blinked as he recognized her. "Grace?"

"What the hell, Gracie?" Hugh whisper-yelled, having followed Otto around the counter. "Quit pointing your gun at her."

Otto realized that the last bit had been for him, and he quickly lowered his weapon. "Sorry, Grace." She gave him a small, shaky smile.

After Hugh helped her stand, Grace reached toward his forehead with a hand that visibly trembled. She paused before making contact. "Hugh. I'm so sorry. I didn't know it was you. There were all those explosions, and then I heard someone creeping around, so I hid, since I figured it was either a looter or...well, someone up to no good. I never guessed it was you. I didn't know you could go without talking for that long. Oh no. There's a red mark already. I bet you'll bruise."

"Shh, Gracie." He pulled her into a long hug. "I'm fine, and that was pretty badass of you. Nice hit. What was that? It wasn't your fist, was it?"

"No." Grace pointed to a crossbow lying on the floor by their feet.

"Did you...hit me with that?" Hugh sounded like

he was about to laugh. "Why didn't you shoot me with it?"

"I don't know how to use it." Starting to sound more annoyed than shaky, Grace pulled away slightly so she could glare at Hugh. "And I didn't hit you with it. I threw it at you."

Hugh made a choking sound.

"Don't you dare laugh." Despite her words, Grace looked as if she was fighting a smile. "If you want someone who knows everything about weapons, then you shouldn't be dating me."

"Please." Hugh snorted. "As if I could date anyone else. You've ruined me for all other women."

"Really?" Her grin broke free. "Good. That means you need to mind your *p*'s and *q*'s. If you drive me away, you won't have any other options."

Instead of getting offended, Hugh chuckled as he hugged Grace against him again. "I love it when you sound like an old-fashioned librarian."

She laughed, too, although she pretended to try to push him away.

As the post-scare adrenaline rush subsided, Otto realized something. "Why aren't you in Dresden?"

"My check-engine light came on." She grimaced, leaning into Hugh. "Sarah let me use the fax machine in Grady's office. Sarah and then Grady left, but I was still waiting for a return fax when the line went dead. After the first explosion, I tried to call Hugh, but my cell didn't have service. I figured it'd be safest to wait here until I could reach someone, but then I heard an explosion that sounded really close by. I started to get pretty freaked out, but the thought of going outside was

scarier—for a while, at least. When I couldn't take waiting for a bomb to drop on my head anymore, I decided
to chance it. I was looking for something I could use to
defend myself when I heard you and hid."

As Grace told her story, Otto's stomach drew into a
tighter and tighter knot. "Where's Sarah?"

"She went home to your place after she let me into
Grady's office." Her eyes widened. "Is she there by herself? Poor Sarah! She must be terrified."

Otto turned, intending to run out of the store and
not stop until he reached his place and saw that Sarah
was unharmed. Blood rushed noisily through his head,
making him deaf to anything the others were saying.
Cleo's voice from earlier echoed through his brain,
saying that helicopters had been spotted in the vicin-
ity of his house. What if Sarah was hurt or trapped or
killed? Bile rose in his throat, making it burn.

Hands on his arms brought him to an unwilling halt.
"*Let go!*"

"Otto." Hugh's voice cut through the red haze that
blanketed Otto's mind. Hugh had hold of his left arm,
and Theo silently gripped his right. "Listen. You need
to do this right. No sense in running out into the snow
and getting shot or freezing to death, especially since
everything you need is right here. Think, buddy. You
don't even have gloves on."

Otto's heart rate slowed slightly as reason sank in.
Hugh was right. He could move a lot faster with the
right gear. "Fine."

"We'll go with you," Grace said, but Otto gave a
short shake of his head.

"No. You'll slow me down." She flinched, and he

knew the words had been too harsh, but it was the truth. He needed to move quickly, without worrying about anyone else keeping up. As much as her friends loved Sarah, they weren't driven by the panicked need to find her like Otto was.

Theo and Hugh released him, and Otto surged forward. He grabbed a hiking pack and snowshoes. The others helped, filling the pack with insulated coveralls, gloves, and a balaclava. Jules ran to grab bottles of water from the cooler, and Otto switched out his boots for warmer ones.

"We'll go as far as the pass," Theo said, tossing in some waterproof matches. When Otto took a breath, ready to argue, Theo's look shut him down. Biting back his objections, Otto gave a short nod.

The guns and ammunition were locked up, and none of the keys Grady had given them worked on the case. Hugh offered to pick the lock, but time was ticking away, and Otto didn't want to stay in the store any longer than he had to. Otto had his loaded 9mm Glock, as well as a spare magazine.

"Are you carrying?" he asked the others.

"Of course," Hugh said.

Theo just jerked his chin up in his typical short nod.

"Yes!" Jules pulled up her coat and hoodie to show the gun in a belt holster at her waist.

Otto blinked in surprise.

"Theo's been teaching me to shoot." Jules allowed her hoodie and coat to drop back into place, covering the gun. "He said I'm a natural."

"She's a good shot," Theo said without looking away from the display. He picked up several folding knives and handed them out. Even though Otto already had his, he accepted another. He had a feeling that it would be a good time to carry a spare.

Unfolding her knife, Grace examined it before closing it again and slipping it into her pocket. "I'm not. I'm terrible. Hugh, tell Otto how terrible I am at shooting." There was an underlying tension to her voice, to all their voices, that told Otto they were eaten up with worry for Sarah. Grace's attempt at joking sounded forced, and he knew she was trying to distract them from the dangers they were all facing.

"She's bad," Hugh agreed.

"I'm not getting better, either," Grace admitted. "Every time we go to the range, I get fewer and fewer holes in the target. It's a little annoying, especially with Straight-Shooter McGee over there." She jerked her thumb at Jules, who gave a tight smile.

Otto felt tension building inside him. He needed to move, or he'd explode. Hooking the snowshoes to his pack, he swung it onto his back and buckled the straps. "Do you have what you want to take?"

Grabbing some crossbow bolts, Grace tucked them in her pocket and slung the bow onto her back. "Ready." Her voice shook slightly, before she straightened her shoulders and lifted her chin. "I'm feeling very Katniss right now." Hugh gave her a tender smile and squeezed her arm.

As they made their way through the back room again, Otto's unease grew. He glanced at Theo and Hugh. By the tense way they were walking and scanning the area, Otto could tell they were as on edge as he was. He pushed open the back door with relief. Although being inside the store was technically safer than being outside, it had felt small and crowded, with too many blind corners.

The wind was finally starting to subside, allowing the snow to fall straight down rather than driving sideways. The flakes lit up in the glow from the security light. Otto frowned as he looked across the illuminated, snow-covered lot and then back at the small sodium bulb above the back door.

The light stretched too far for that weak bulb. Turning, he backed away from the building until he could see the cloudy sky. Bright lights, small but quickly growing, pierced through the snow.

"'Copter incoming!" Otto barked, waving for the others to run away from the building and then falling in behind them. "Head for Mrs. Epple's house!" Even when she went to Florida for the winter, the woman never locked her doors.

Jules glanced back, a confused look on her face, and then slowed so Theo and Viggy could take the lead. Jumping a decorative, two-foot-high border, they cut across the backyard of a cedar-sided ranch-style house. Theo opened the door and held it, but Jules gave him a shove into the house.

"Now is not the time to be chivalrous!" she said sharply, following him inside. "I don't know where I'm going!"

The rest of them stampeded into Mrs. Epple's house, running through her kitchen and antique-filled living room. Otto peered through the lacy curtains, searching for the helicopter. It wasn't hard to find.

Not only were the lights blinding, but the sound of

the engine and the rotors cutting through the air were thunderous, even here. Theo—who'd taken up position on the other side of the window, with Viggy bristling with excitement next to him—pointed outside. "Three at two o'clock."

Across the room, Hugh called in a low voice, "I've got two on this side."

"Four," Grace corrected. "There are a couple more slinking along the back of the coffee shop."

"Good catch, Gracie," Hugh said.

Theo glanced at Otto. "Take out the helicopter, and Jules and I will deal with the rest."

"Wait, what?" Jules asked from one window over. She was kneeling on a floral chaise, using the back as a gun rest as she aimed out the opened window. Theo slid their window open.

A shock of cold air hit Otto in the face. "Let's do this."

Lining up his sights, Otto aimed for the tail rotor of the helicopter. It was a small target, but the most vulnerable part of the aircraft. If he managed to hit it, he could bring the helicopter down unless the pilot was unbelievably skilled. Once he started shooting, though, he'd attract the attention of the people on the ground, so he'd have to be fast.

He squeezed the trigger, slow and easy, barely hearing the blast. The helicopter didn't waver. Otto aimed again, focused on his task, and everything else faded into the background except for his target. The helicopter started turning to face them, the spotlights flickering in Otto's peripheral vision. He was losing his chance. Forcing the adrenaline down, he aimed and then pulled the trigger again.

The tail rotor shattered. "Hit!" Theo called triumphantly.

"Focus on the bad guys, darlin'!" Jules yelled back, her voice higher than usual.

As the helicopter began to spin, Otto turned toward the mercenaries on the ground. The spotlights flashed and then went dark and then flashed again as the helicopter spun out of control, messing up Otto's vision. He thought about taking out his flashlight, but that would just give the guys outside a lit-up target to aim at.

Blinking hard, he cleared his vision and focused on one of the figures in winter camouflage. He pulled the trigger, and the man went down. Otto couldn't think about how he'd just shot someone, possibly even killed them. Right now, he needed to concentrate on getting everyone in that room out alive.

Jules yelped.

Theo's head whipped around at the sound. "Jules! You hit?" He rushed over to her.

"Just a graze," she replied, but she sounded breathless.

"Okay?" Otto asked.

"Yeah. It's minor." Despite that, Theo still sounded murderous.

Refocusing out the window, Otto took aim again, this time on a figure mostly hidden by the branches of a snow-covered pine tree. Otto fired, and the sniper dropped, just as the helicopter crashed into the roof of Grady's store.

"Get down!" Theo warned, and Otto dropped to the floor and scooted away from the window, covering his head with his arms. The world exploded in a way that was becoming too familiar, the night lighting up right before the thunderous explosion. The glass blew out of the window, shards raining down on the hardwood floor.

Otto's ears felt as if they'd been stuffed with cotton balls. Everything was muffled and slow-moving. Lifting his head, he checked out Theo, Jules, and Viggy. The three were huddled together, but all looked conscious and unharmed, so he turned toward Grace, Lexi, and Hugh. In the dim light, with his night vision destroyed by the blinding explosion, he couldn't see if they were hurt.

"Okay?" he called. The word echoed in his head, but he wasn't sure if it had come out loud enough, so he said it again.

"We're good!" Hugh said, and Otto felt his tensed muscles relax slightly. "Or we would be if you'd stop screaming at us."

That was such a smart-ass Hugh answer that Otto felt a rush of relief. It only lasted a moment, though, before Otto remembered Sarah was alone and there was a small army outside. Duck-walking back to the window, Otto held his gun at the ready as he peered outside. The burning store and helicopter lit everything as brightly as daylight—a hell-scape daylight. He scanned the area, but all he could see were the fallen men lying unmoving in the snow.

"Looks clear on this side." Theo echoed Otto's thoughts. "How are things to the north?"

"Four down over here. We're clear." Hugh paused for a second, and then asked, "Unless you see anyone, eagle-eye Gracie?"

"No." There was a slight shake to her voice. "No one moving, at least."

Her words reminded Otto of what he'd just done, but he pushed away the memory to deal with later. Right now, he had to go find Sarah. There was still one more helicopter and who knew how many more of Aaron's mercenaries. The town was still under siege, and no one could get in to help until the snow let up—even if Steve and Cleo did manage to get a message through to the outside world.

"Theo, you lead," Otto said, straightening up to a standing position. Glass crunched under his boots as he moved toward the door. "I'll take the rear."

With a short nod, Theo picked up Viggy, slinging him over his shoulder. Otto turned to Hugh. "You okay with Lexi, or do you want me to get her?"

"We're good." With his unbroken arm, Hugh swung Lexi up off the glass-strewn floor. She wriggled and tried to lick his face. "Thanks, Lex. Okay! Enough! I think the puppies are more restrained and well-behaved than you."

"And you, probably," Grace said as she fell in behind him. Her voice sounded almost back to normal, although Otto knew that was just a front. They'd all have to deal with the events of the night…if they survived it.

Theo, gun in one hand and steadying his dog with the other, checked the area out front. He stepped outside, and Otto felt the tension in his muscles ratchet up. There were no gunshots, though, just the roar of the flames and the occasional pop of a small explosion. Otto now wished he'd given Hugh time to break into the gun-and-ammo case. It was a waste that everything would get destroyed when they'd likely need the weapons before the night was over.

Once outside, Theo lowered Viggy to the ground and then moved fast. The others poured out of the house and took off after him, running as quickly as they could through the snow. The dogs loved it, bounding along in rabbit hops. Otto, on the other hand, was tense and watchful, expecting people in camouflage to come out shooting at any moment.

It bothered him that they couldn't stop long enough to check if any of the mercenaries were still alive. It was one thing to shoot in self-defense, but the idea of leaving survivors bleeding in the snow twisted up his insides. Again, he was forced to push that thought away and focus on keeping everyone in his group alive and getting to Sarah.

The snow was still falling heavily, muffling the sounds they made as they ran through the yards. Theo led them on a zigzag route toward Gordon's compound, keeping close to trees and buildings as much as possible to give them cover.

Something was coming toward them. Otto opened his mouth to give a warning, just as Theo's hand came up in a "stop" gesture. They were in the middle of an unfenced yard without any nearby concealment. It was the worst possible position for a fight. Otto, Theo, and Hugh surrounded Grace, Jules, and the dogs, and Jules immediately aimed her pistol through the small space between Otto and Theo.

The shapes kept moving toward them, and Otto brought his Glock up with both hands, lining the sights up to the biggest form in the center. Something was wrong, though. Whatever they were appeared both too large and too small to be Aaron's soldiers.

One of them broke away and sprinted toward them. As it grew closer, Otto recognized him. Shock rippled through him. "Hold your fire!"

"Is that Mort?" Hugh asked.

"Yeah." His surprise changed to a tentative thread of hope. If Mort was here and okay, then there was a chance that Sarah might be, too. Holstering his gun, Otto stretched out his hands and crouched, greeting Mort with a rough scratch of his scruff. He ran his hands over the dog, verifying that Mort really was in front of him, warm and familiar and blessedly alive. The delicate tendril of hope strengthened, and Otto's heart beat faster. Mort was here. Mort was fine. *Please let Sarah be with him.* Viggy whined with eagerness, and Mort danced over to his old buddy.

His heart crashing against his rib cage in hope and excitement, Otto started to jog toward the other forms moving through the snow, unable to believe what he was seeing. As he recognized Bean and Xena and then the woman riding the horse, Otto's jog turned into a run. She was there. He wasn't quite sure how, but Otto didn't care. His Sarah was alive and right in front of him, and he couldn't reach her fast enough.

"Sarah?" His yell came out as a croak, all of his oxygen fueling his legs as he plowed through the snow toward her.

"Otto!" Sarah threw her leg over Bean's back and started to slide to the ground. Otto caught her before her boots could touch the snow. Once his arms wrapped around her and he pulled her in to his chest, it became real. He was holding Sarah. All of the nightmare scenarios he'd been imagining—her bleeding or caught or blown to pieces—lost their power to haunt him. She was here, and he would keep her safe.

"Sarah." He pressed his cheek against the top of her head, squeezing her even more tightly. "I was so worried." At the understatement, his laugh bubbled out, filled with sheer joy and amazement and gratitude. She clutched him just as hard, her face pressed into his chest.

He didn't want to let her go for even a second, but he needed to see her and make sure that she wasn't hurt. Lowering Sarah to her feet, he looked her over, checking for any bullet holes or missing limbs or, really, even the faintest scratch. She looked perfect. Her cheeks and nose were pink from the cold, but none of her exposed skin looked like it was in danger of frostbite. He pushed back an irrational urge to strip her naked and check every inch of her for possible damage. His hands smoothed over her cheeks, and she smiled at him. He couldn't seem to stop touching her. In fact, he was pretty sure he'd never be able to stop. Unable to hold back any longer, his mouth crashed down on hers.

She kissed him back just as desperately, just as eagerly. The night had been endless, and Otto felt as if they'd been separated for so long. As they kissed, warmth filled him, and his worst fears loosened their hold, slipping away until all he knew was relief and bliss.

Pulling back, he broke the kiss and met her eyes. He loved that dazed and happy look she got when he kissed or touched her. A part of him hadn't believed he'd ever see it again. The thought of a life without Sarah felt like a kick to the belly.

"I love you," he said without thinking or planning or even knowing the words were going to fall out of his mouth. He didn't care about the possible rejection or embarrassment. She needed to hear it, because she could've died, and then she would've never known how he felt about her. "I love you so much."

Her gloved hands came up to cup his face, mirroring his. "I love you, too, Otto."

He had to kiss her again. When he finally raised his head, he felt almost dizzy with happiness. Clearing his throat, he somehow found his voice. "Are you okay?"

"Yes." She smiled at him, and everything inside him warmed, but then her expression turned sad. "I need to tell you—"

Something tugged on his sleeve—hard. He glanced down and blinked.

"Hortense?" His heart lurched. Not only was Sarah alive and uninjured, but she'd rescued all of his animals. He loved her so much it hurt.

"I couldn't leave her there." The goat started chewing on his coat sleeve. Normally, he wouldn't let her, but right now he was just so happy to see them that he let her go to town.

Otto marveled that Sarah had brought the horse, the goat, and the dogs all the way from his house and over the blocked pass. His love was impressive, and braver than anyone he'd known. He looked at Bean. The horse appeared calmer than Otto had ever seen him. "You rode him bareback with a halter?"

"Well, we didn't really have time to tack up, since we were running for our lives and all," Sarah said. "Listen, Otto…"

Jules and Grace interrupted before she could finish. They took turns hugging Sarah.

"Glad you're safe, Sarah," Theo said, giving her a brief but genuine smile. "We need to keep moving, though."

"Aaron's behind this," Sarah blurted out. "He, Logan, and Jeb escaped the transport van. They shot two FBI agents. The van and their...bodies are on the other side of the rockslide."

Silence fell over the group. The pieces clicked into place in Otto's mind. The conversation they'd overheard on their way to Grady's made more sense now.

"How'd they—" Hugh started to ask, but Theo interrupted him.

"We have to go," he warned. "We've been standing here talking too long already."

Otto fully agreed, but now they had a new problem. The dogs and possibly even the goat could join them in the bunker, but there was no way to get Bean down there. He tried to think of anyone in town who had a barn or even a shed of some sort where they could keep the horse temporarily. His mind was a blank, though. All his brain kept repeating was *Sarah is okay. Sarah is here, and she's okay, and she loves me*.

"Schwartz has a workshop in back of his house," Theo said, seeming to read Otto's mind. "It's not really set up for horses, but it'd probably work in a pinch. He raises rabbits, too, so he should have hay."

"Amazing, isn't it?" Hugh said in a low voice. "Gordon Schwartz, savior of the town. Who would've thought?"

It is amazing, Otto thought. "We'll head back to the bunker."

"Theo, Jules, and I'll keep searching for people," Hugh said. "Gracie, it's bunker time for you."

"But—"

"No." Hugh, Theo, and Jules spoke in unison, interrupting Grace.

"You and Sarah are their targets," Theo said.

Grace's shoulders slumped slightly before she turned to Sarah with a small, forced smile. "Guess we're bunker buddies, then."

Sarah linked her arm through Grace's, squeezing it affectionately against her side. As Jules, Theo, and Hugh turned to leave, Grace said quietly, "Hugh."

He turned back toward her, and Grace reached out, grabbing a handful of his coat. Yanking him toward her, she kissed him. It didn't last very long, but both were obviously breathing hard at the end. Otto glanced away, feeling like a voyeur.

"You're savage," Hugh said quietly. "I love that about you."

"And I love you," Grace responded. "Which is why, if you die out there, I swear I'll resuscitate you just to kill you again. Got it?"

"Got it."

The two groups separated with quiet goodbyes and admonitions to be careful. Otto followed the two women toward Gordon's place, leading Bean and keeping an eye out for danger. He was also sneaking quick glances at Sarah. His brain couldn't wrap around the knowledge that she was actually here, that she actually loved him. His gaze couldn't stay off her. Even in the oversized winter clothes and backpack, she looked beautiful.

Now Sarah was safe and within reach, but Aaron was still out there.

They had to keep her safe—and save the town.

CHAPTER 21

SARAH COULDN'T STOP LOOKING AT OTTO. AS THEY WALKED through the snow, silent except for the slight crunch of snow underneath their boots—or paws or hooves— Sarah kept sneaking peeks at Otto over her shoulder. Having him so close, knowing that he loved her, made the bombs, the bodies, the long ride through the blizzard, Aaron—all of it—seem like a fading nightmare.

She glanced back at him again, smiling when she caught his gaze. The corners of his mouth tipped up in his gradual way, and her heart almost hurt from joy at seeing that again. Until that point, Sarah hadn't realized how scared she'd been that something had happened to him. Now, she couldn't stop glancing over her shoulder, just to check to make sure he was still there.

Out of habit, she kept doing an animal count. Hortense was doing a better job at keeping up, although whether that was because Otto was there or because she knew she was headed for someplace warm and dry for the night, Sarah didn't know. Xena seemed a bit shyer with Grace there, and was walking so close behind Sarah that her paws brushed the backs of Sarah's boots.

They were all on edge, staying silent, their gazes roaming the area in a steady scan as they walked in a tight group. Grace had something on her back. In the dim light, it took Sarah a few minutes to figure out what it was.

"Is that...a crossbow?" Sarah whispered.

"Yes." A strange expression crossed Grace's face. "I don't know how to use it yet, though, so I'm not much help."

Otto cleared his throat quietly. "You were a lot of help as a spotter, Grace."

"What happened?" Sarah asked, looking at Grace's unhappy profile and then back at an equally grim Otto.

Neither answered, keeping their eyes on anything but her. She fell silent, deciding to ask Otto when they were alone. They walked in tense silence for a few more minutes until they came to a tall, menacing-looking gate. When they stopped, Sarah realized how incredibly tired she was. The thought of taking even one more step was overwhelming.

Otto removed the lock and unwound the chain. Once they'd slipped through the gate, he rearranged it to look as if the gate was secured again.

Otto, leading Bean, put a hand on Sarah's back, urging her forward. Xena followed, but Mort lagged behind, limping badly. After handing Bean's lead rope to Sarah, Otto returned to Mort, lifting the large dog like he weighed nothing. Sarah and Grace waited until Otto had caught up, and then they continued their trek through the snow. The security lights were muted by the still-falling snow, and Sarah peered through the dimness, looking for the building housing the workshop.

When they reached an outhouse, Otto carried Mort inside.

Confused, Sarah and Grace stared at each other, and

then inside the tiny shed. In the dim light, Sarah watched as Otto swung the seat to the side and opened the trap door beneath it, all while holding Mort with one strong arm. He looked at Sarah. "This ladder leads into the bunker. It'll be safer in there."

"I want to help put Bean and Hortense away." She couldn't admit that, now that she was with Otto again, she didn't want to be separated, even for a short time. "We've been through a lot together."

He hesitated, but finally nodded and gestured toward Grace.

"Wait," Sarah said, unbuckling the waist strap of the backpack and slipping it off her shoulders. She fished out a folding knife and flashlight before holding the pack out toward Grace, careful not to jostle the cat. "Can you take Bob down?"

"Bob?"

"Otto's cat."

"Oh." Grace gave a small choke of a laugh as she pulled off her crossbow before easing her arms through the straps. "I thought you'd named your favorite pack or something." She swung the crossbow over her shoulder and visibly braced herself. Looking like she was scared out of her mind and trying to hide it, Grace started to descend the ladder, quickly disappearing into the darkness below.

"You brought Bob, too?" Otto asked quietly.

"Yes. I didn't think he'd follow like the others, so I put the poor guy in the pack pocket. He's pretty unhappy about it."

Otto was quiet as he studied her for a long moment. "Thank you." His voice sounded rusty. "I'll be right back." He used one hand on the ladder and the other to steady Mort over his shoulder as he followed Grace through the opening. In just a few seconds, Sarah was all by herself, hanging on to Bean's lead rope with a white-knuckled grip.

"Dummy," she whispered to herself, not able to take her eyes off the spot where Otto had disappeared. "You were on your own for much longer, and you did just fine. Don't lose it now."

The wind hummed around them, and Xena pressed against the backs of her legs. Sarah didn't want to admit to herself that she was just as comforted by the contact as the dog was.

Otto's head popped through the hole, and Sarah jumped.

"Come here, Xena," he said quietly, but she hunched lower and looked away from him, as if she could disappear that way.

"I think she's coming with us," Sarah said, her voice shaking slightly.

Even in the low light, she could see Otto's gaze sharpen as he looked at her. "That's fine. We'll bring her down with us once we get the other two settled. Are you cold?"

"I'll live. Don't you want to bring Hortense down there?"

"No." He boosted himself out of the hole, closed the trapdoor, and swung the seat over it, hiding the entrance. "Bean needs the company."

"Right." She handed him the lead rope after Otto closed the outhouse—fake outhouse—door. "I forgot that they're usually roomies."

They walked in silence for a few moments before Otto asked, "What happened?"

"They blew up your house," she said, her stomach twisting as she remembered the black skeleton enveloped by orange and red flames. "I'm sorry."

Otto didn't respond for several moments, and Sarah felt tears sting her eyes. It had been such a beautiful house. Finally, he spoke, his voice rough. "You saved them all."

"I couldn't get to the chickens." Sarah bit her lip. "I probably should've gone outside and at least let them out, but I was scared Aaron's men hadn't left or were waiting right outside the barn to grab me."

"No, they're safest in their coop," Otto assured her. "There's plenty of food and the waterer's heated, so they'll be fine for a few days while we get all this"—he waved a hand, encompassing the entire horrible situation in one gesture—"under control."

"I'm sorry," she said again. "This is my fault. If I hadn't come here—"

Otto put a hand on the back of her neck, and she went silent. "It's not your fault," he said. "And I'm very glad you came here."

"You are?" She just couldn't believe that, even with the reassuring weight of his hand on her. "Everything's on fire, and your house is gone."

"Sarah." He stopped by the big workshop door and turned toward her. "Buildings and mountain passes can be rebuilt. As long as you're safe, I'm grateful."

She blinked, overwhelmed. "Oh."

Otto gave her that slow smile again and opened the door. It rattled as it went up, making Sarah jump. Otto turned on a small flashlight and led Bean into the shop. After hesitating in the entrance for a brief moment, Bean plodded after him. *Poor guy*, Sarah thought as she walked in behind them, Xena right next to her. Bean must be even more exhausted than she was. Hortense followed them in. Grabbing the hanging rope, Sarah lowered the door.

It was too loud, seeming to ring through the night, and it made her cringe. She breathed out in relief once it was down. The shop was rough, with a dirt floor and unfinished walls. Just a workbench on one wall changed it from a "shed" to a "workshop," but it would work for Bean and Hortense. As Theo had predicted, there was a small stack of alfalfa hay bales stacked against one wall. Hortense immediately walked over and helped herself to a bite.

Grabbing an empty bucket, Sarah brought it to the spigot next to the workbench and filled it with water. Xena followed, getting a drink as it flowed in. Otto unclipped the lead rope from Bean's halter and opened one of the hay bales, cutting the twine holding it together before pocketing his knife.

Sarah moved the full bucket over by the hay and then stepped away as both Bean and Hortense crowded in to drink. Xena waited until the other two had finished before taking her second turn at the bucket. Leaning her shoulder against the wall, Sarah watched them, feeling both exhausted and triumphant. She'd gotten all the animals to Otto safely. Now they just needed to save the town from her brother.

"I wish they could join us in the bunker where it's warmer," she said as Otto walked over to her.

"They'd hate it down there." He gave her a small, tired smile. "Horses and goats like it colder than we do. As long as they have protection from the elements and hay in front of them, they'll be happy."

With that worry soothed, Sarah's thoughts jumped back to their messed-up situation. "What's the plan?"

Otto pulled off his gloves and rubbed a hand over his face. "Still need to come up with one."

Sarah couldn't resist. She took his bare hand in hers. "We'll figure it out. You're safe. The rest is easy."

His smile was tired but still gorgeous. "That's exactly what I was thinking. You're safe. That's all that matters." He hesitated, watching her intently. "I really do love you."

The words sent a warm thrill through her. It was one thing for him to say it in the heat of the moment, right after he'd realized that she was alive and unhurt. For him to tell her now, in the relative safety of the workshop, meant that he hadn't said it merely because emotions were running high. The way he looked at her, his gaze steady and unwavering, erased all doubts. He meant what he said.

Squeezing his hand, she looked back at him, trying to project that same confidence. So much of her life had been about hiding what she felt, about presenting a calm front, pretending that the ever-present danger and fear didn't bother her. Now, she wanted to do the opposite. She wanted Otto to see how she felt, to believe her as she believed him.

"I love you, too."

Otto smiled, and she knew that it had worked. He'd seen that she meant the words with everything inside her.

Leaning down, he kissed her lightly. She caught the back of his head and held him there, needing more than just a peck. She hadn't been sure if she would ever see him again, hadn't known if he was even alive. A simple, gentle kiss was not nearly enough.

Otto seemed to agree. He intensified the kiss, pressing more firmly against her as his lips parted. She met his tongue with hers, and he groaned deep in his chest. Otto kissed her harder, deeper, almost wildly, as if he needed to dive into her or he would die. Sarah knew she felt that way. Kissing him wasn't just something she wanted. She needed it, needed him, with a bone-deep instinct that made her clutch his hand and the back of his head, desperate for him not to pull away.

His arm wrapped around her, tugging her close, their joined hands locked between their bodies. Their kisses grew frantic. Even though she now knew Otto was alive, all of her earlier fears, all the shocks and horrors she'd encountered welled up inside her, pressing to get out. He was the only one who could make her feel like everything would turn out okay, despite the terrible things that had happened.

She couldn't get close enough to him, but she didn't want to let go of his hand in order to clutch him more tightly to her. From the way he was holding her, she knew he felt the same way. The workshop, the animals, the snowstorm, the whole nightmare of a night faded, and there was only Otto—his huge, hard body and his amazingly gentle hands. Too soon, he pulled away, breathing hard.

"We should get into the bunker," he said, his voice rough and reluctant.

Although she hated to stop kissing him, Sarah knew he was right. With a sigh, she pulled his head down. His mouth was tempting, but she knew it'd be even harder to stop a second time. Instead, she gave him a peck on the nose that made him smile. Seeing that was almost as belly-melting as his kisses.

Giving her a final hug, Otto released her. Sarah felt a surge of anger for Aaron. He never could let her be. He was determined to ruin every ounce of happiness she managed to find. This time, though, he wouldn't win. She was hanging on to Otto with everything she had.

Xena pressed against Sarah's side, as if making sure she wouldn't be left behind. Reaching down, she stroked the dog's head reassuringly.

Otto moved to the human-sized door, rather than raise the overhead one again. Silently opening the door, he looked around and then motioned for Sarah to come out. She braced herself for the wind, but the night was still. Although a little snow still fell, it was in soft, large flakes, rather than the hard ice pellets that had stung her face the entire ride to town. Sarah looked around at the way the security lights softly lit the property, showing the snowy blanket that covered everything. It was beautiful, like a Christmas card.

Their footsteps were silent in the soft layer of snow, so the only sound was the occasional *swish* of rubbing fabric as they walked. Shouldn't there be other sounds? Sarah found herself walking faster. The snow-covered surroundings and too-silent night seemed suddenly eerie, rather than peaceful.

They were crossing an open section, and she picked up the pace so that she was right behind Otto. It felt too exposed, like anyone could see them. The shadows around them suddenly had a thousand eyes, all focused on Sarah. There was a strange buzz in the distance, so faint that Sarah wondered if she was imagining it. After all, her imagination seemed to be operating at full force at the moment.

One of the shadows detached from a clump of trees and headed toward them. Sarah sucked in a breath, ready to warn Otto, but he'd already drawn his gun. He knew. The figure got closer, not seeming at all intimidated by the weapon pointed at him. Sarah's muscles tensed and her heart started pounding.

"Sarah, get back to the workshop," Otto barked, the quietness of his words not diminishing the command.

Sarah moved to obey, but she only took a step back before the approaching man's voice reached her. Her body went wobbly with relief.

"Otto." It was Lieutenant Blessard.

"Why are you out of the bunker? Has it been breached?"

A shock of fear hit Sarah at the thought, but the lieutenant shook his head. "When you didn't return to the bunker, I thought you might need help. Blanchett's people are headed this way."

The relief of a moment ago was gone again. How had Aaron found them? He had to be tracking them, but how?

"We need all our trained guys back here. Sarah, come with me back to the bunker. Otto, take the dog and find Theo and Hugh. The people in town can wait. They'll be safe. Blanchett knows the women are here." He looked grim. "This is where he's going to focus all his firepower."

The continuous buzzing sound was getting louder, and it finally struck Sarah what the sound was—snowmobiles. Her heart beat quickly in her chest, and she tried to slow her breathing. Hyperventilating wouldn't help anyone.

"Otto." Blessard closed his fingers around Sarah's arm and tugged. "Go!" Xena gave a low growl, and Sarah looked at Otto. Blessard was his lieutenant, not hers. She trusted Otto, and she'd only take commands from him.

"They're too close." Otto grabbed her hand, pulling her arm out of Blessard's grip, and sprinted through the snow toward the workshop. Sarah, with Xena right behind her, ran with him, but the snow was deep enough to make each step a huge effort. It was a familiar nightmare—trying to sprint away from danger but only managing a slog.

"Do you think they'll find the bunker?" Sarah asked, her voice as soft as she could make it. Her words still sounded too loud.

"It's hidden well," Otto said, although Sarah noticed that wasn't exactly a no.

"What if I lead them away?" Her voice shook, but she still forced out the words. Aaron was her monster. She'd brought him to this wonderful little town that had been nothing but kind to her. It was her responsibility to deal with the army he'd brought to Monroe.

"No." It was a growl more than a word.

The workshop was getting closer, but they were taking too long. Biting back a sound of fear, Sarah continued fighting through the snow. Even if they couldn't reach the building, they could hide in the trees scattered around. Anything would be better than this full exposure, their dark forms standing out starkly against the white ground, with no camouflage in sight.

There was a low grunt behind them, and Sarah turned her head just in time to see Blessard trip and fall, his body hitting the snow full-length from his face to his toes.

"Keep heading to those trees," Otto commanded as he released her, rushing back to help the lieutenant to his feet. As he stood, Blessard gave a pained yelp, his body sagging sideways.

"I did something to my ankle." His words ended in a groan as his right side collapsed again, almost dragging Otto to the ground. Sarah moved to Blessard's right and pulled his arm around her shoulders.

"Sarah." Otto's glance was filled with worry—but also admiration. "Run. I'll help him."

"We'll both help him." It was harder than she expected. Every step was difficult. Every move from Blessard threatened to bring him down—and her with him. She wondered if he had a concussion as well, because his balance seemed to be affected. If the earlier run had seemed nightmarish, this was even worse. Their progress changed from feet to inches, and the buzzing was getting ever louder. The snowmobiles would be on them at any second, and they were still a good distance from the cover of the trees. Otto turned so he was facing them.

"Let go," Otto said, and Sarah obeyed automatically, releasing Blessard's arm. Before the lieutenant could crumple to the ground, Otto hoisted him up over his shoulder. "Run."

She ran. Without Blessard's weight pulling her off-balance, she felt like she was flying, even despite the deep drifts. Several single headlights appeared over the ridge, reflecting off the snow until an entire army appeared about to run them down. With a final blast of effort, Sarah dove for cover behind a short, bushy pine tree growing crookedly next to the barn. Xena quickly huddled next to her, and Otto carefully moved Blessard off his shoulder, settling him on the snowy ground.

They crouched behind the tree, peering through the prickly branches at the cluster of five snowmobiles in the yard. Sarah counted eight people dressed in winter camouflage before the engines were turned off and the lights extinguished.

It took a few moments for Sarah's night vision to kick in after the glare of those headlights. As she blinked frantically in the full darkness, she closed her fist on Otto's coat. Shapes slowly came back into focus, and the night wasn't completely black anymore.

"What? Wa's going on?" The lieutenant's voice was slurred and much, much too loud. Otto quickly clapped a hand over Blessard's mouth and met Sarah's worried gaze. The lieutenant definitely had a head injury. Sarah fought down panic. Everything was going wrong.

Otto looked away, peering through the tree branches, and Sarah followed his gaze. A pair of mercenaries, rifles slung across their backs, headed their way. Sarah stiffened, pulling out her knife and unfolding it, keeping it carefully pointed away from Otto and Blessard. She was terrified of doing something stupid like losing her balance and accidentally stabbing one of them.

To her surprise, Otto put his gun away. Sarah was tempted to poke him and ask him what the freak he thought he was doing, but she didn't want to distract him. The pair of mercenaries plowed through the snow, heading right toward their pine tree. Sarah was terrified that they had been spotted, but she tried to reassure her panicky brain that Aaron's goons would've already been shooting if that had been the case.

"Gunnersen?" Blessard groaned, the word muffled by Otto's hand. Sarah felt her heart rate kick up even more, and she squeezed the rigid knife handle until it bit through her gloves and into her fingers.

The first guy was about six feet ahead of the other, and he was closing in rapidly. Sarah shivered as he drew nearer, putting a reassuring hand on Xena's head when the dog started panting nervously. She kept glancing at Otto, waiting for him to draw his gun again, but he didn't reach for the weapon.

Instead, Otto moved his hand off Blessard's mouth and did something with his hands in the snow. It wasn't until he launched the snowball that Sarah figured out what he was doing. It hit the trunk of an aspen tree twenty feet away with a dull thud.

Both mercenaries twisted around toward the sound. Otto lunged, grabbing the closer man and pulling him back behind the tree, an arm locked around his neck. Otto did something so fast that Sarah couldn't see, and then the man was lying in the snow next to her, his eyes fixed in a startled expression.

It was Jeb. Sarah couldn't look away from his distant stare. She'd spent years in his unwanted company, and now he was dead.

"Jeb?" A male voice yanked her out of her horrified daze. It was the second guy who'd called, she realized. He must've discovered that his buddy was gone. Jeb. He must've realized that *Jeb* was gone. The mercenary ran toward their hiding space, his rifle off his back and in his hands, but Otto still didn't pull his gun.

As the man got close, Otto charged, knocking the barrel of his rifle up and driving him back. The guy tripped, landing on his back in the snow, Otto on top of him. In just seconds, that man lay as still as Jeb.

"Nice work," Blessard said, his words sounding clearer but still too loud.

Otto gave him a sharp glance, his finger to his lips in the universal sign for *quiet*.

"Leave me and Sarah here," Blessard said, lowering his voice to a harsh whisper. He seemed much more coherent than earlier, and Sarah hoped he'd stay that way. His concussed ranting had almost gotten them killed. "We need backup. If you can't reach Theo and Hugh in time, get to the people in the bunker. The others might not be trained fighters, but at least they can help— the adults, at least. I'm sure Gordon has an arsenal in there. Get people, get weapons, and then get your ass back here. Take the dog. You've been training her, right? Guess this'll be a trial by fire."

Otto stared at him. "I'm not leaving either of you."

"Otto."

"No."

"This is an order." Blessard's voice had a hard snap to it that made Sarah flinch, but Otto's even gaze didn't waver.

"I'm not leaving either of you."

A shout in the distance made all of them snap their heads around so they could peer through the branches. The lieutenant was suddenly on his feet, his gun drawn and pointed right at her. Sarah stared, unable to comprehend what she was seeing. Blessard was a cop, one of the good guys. She knew how to recognize evil in people—at least, she thought she could, but the lieutenant's betrayal shocked her to the core. What was happening?

"Don't move." Blessard backed up several steps, his movements smooth, while still keeping the pistol aimed at Sarah. The twisted ankle, the concussion—he'd faked everything. A small sound escaped before she could swallow it back, and Otto shifted toward her. "Don't move, or I will shoot her."

"Why are you doing this?" Otto sounded as if he'd been punched in the stomach.

"We're not equipped to fight these people," the lieutenant said. He seemed weary, but there was a thread of steel in his words. Somehow, Sarah knew they weren't going to be able to talk him out of this. "It's Monroe in the winter. We're barely equipped to handle a license-plate theft. The Blanchetts' and the Jovanovics' battle isn't with us. If we give them the two women, they'll leave. If we don't, they'll destroy the whole town."

"We can beat them." Otto's voice was rough, urgent, and his gaze flicked back and forth between Sarah and his lieutenant. "You don't need to do this."

"Yes, I do." The lines on Blessard's face deepened, and his mouth pulled down in a tense frown. "This isn't one person with a few hired guns. This is the Blanchetts and the Jovanovics. It's an *army*. If they fail tonight, they'll keep coming. Monroe will be besieged until these women are back in their custody or nothing is left of Monroe. This is my town. I'll do what I need to in order to save it. Sarah, come here."

"Don't do this, Lieutenant," Otto growled.

Blessard's jaw muscles tightened, but he didn't look away from Sarah. "I don't think your brother would care if I put a hole in you first, as long as it wasn't anywhere too life-threatening. Be smart and listen. Come here."

Her vision narrowed until all she could see was the gun he was holding. Her body wasn't trembling anymore—at least, she couldn't feel it. Sarah wondered if she'd gotten so scared that something had snapped in her head, because she was simply numb. She rose from her crouch, almost falling when Xena pressed against her legs.

"Not the dog," Blessard ordered. "Either the dog stays with Otto, or I shoot it."

Sarah's frantic gaze found Otto, and he reached out to catch Xena's collar. His expression was terrifying. She'd never seen him look so coldly furious. Whining softly, Xena strained against his hold, trying to get closer to Sarah.

"Sarah, move this way." Blessard continued to walk slowly backward, and Sarah took a step toward him and then another. Her mind spun as she tried to think of a plan, a way out of this. A tiny part of her wondered if the lieutenant was right. Was she worth it? If the town was saved from annihilation, wasn't that worth the loss of her freedom?

Then, she remembered Grace.

The Jovanovics wanted to kill Grace. If Blessard got his way, Grace wouldn't just be trapped in a marriage with nasty Logan Jovanovic. Grace would be dead. Even if Sarah had been willing to give herself up to save the town, she wasn't about to sacrifice Grace. She took a step closer to Blessard.

Think! She needed a plan, but her thoughts were slipping past so quickly she couldn't grab on to any of them.

Slowly, they moved away from Otto and closer to where the snowmobiles were parked. Sarah felt horribly exposed out in the open, and she braced herself, expecting a fist or a bullet to hit her at any second. The lieutenant's face tightened with displeasure as he took quick glances around, never looking away long enough to give her a chance to run.

Suddenly, he raised the gun in the air and fired, the explosive *crack* ringing through the night. The moment the gun was no longer aimed at her, it felt as if a rope holding her back had snapped. Without hesitating, she lunged forward, slamming against the lieutenant's chest and taking both of them to the ground.

Blessard let out a grunt as she landed on top of him, but he quickly recovered, rolling them over so that Sarah was on the bottom. Terror surged through her as he loomed over her, his body pressing her into the snow. She struggled, but he held her down, his teeth bared with determination.

His expression blanked, and his eyes went wide and then sagged closed. As his head dropped forward, he went limp, flattening her and pushing her even more deeply into the snowdrift. Panic filled her as snow toppled over her face and his suffocating weight made it hard to breathe.

Then he was gone, and she was being hauled out of the snow and into Otto's arms.

"Is he dead?" she asked, her voice shaking as she clutched handfuls of his coat.

"No. Just unconscious." He moved her away from

him. "We need to hurry. He fired that shot to call your brother's men here."

The reality of their situation crashed down on her again, and her body sagged. Otto caught her before she toppled back in the snow, but she pulled out of his hold. There wasn't time for her to have a freak-out. She needed to *move*.

Sarah's legs began to work again, and she ran next to Otto, Xena following closely behind her. Yanking his radio off his belt, Otto hurled it to the side. Sarah was baffled for a moment until it hit her—Blessard must have been using it to track them. Somehow, he'd led Aaron's army right to them. It felt wrong to stay out in the open, rather than sprinting for the cover of the trees, but she trusted Otto. He'd get them out of this. As they ran across the open area toward the snowmobiles, the snow grabbed at Sarah's boots, trying to slow her down. Blessard's gunshot must've succeeded in alerting the other mercenaries, since all six were running toward Otto and Sarah. Otto straddled one of the snowmobiles and started the engine, and Sarah jumped on behind him. She turned toward Xena, but she just backed away from the sled, cowering.

Jumping off, Otto grabbed the dog, scooping her up as if she weighed eight pounds rather than eighty. As he turned toward the snowmobile again, Sarah moved up closer to the front, grabbing the handlebars. She'd never ridden a snowmobile, and panic filled her brain, shrieking that she couldn't do this. Forcing herself to shove back the terror, she looked down at the controls. She was smart. She could figure it out. She *had* to figure it out, or she and Otto and Xena were dead.

There were no pedals at her feet, so she assumed the accelerator and brake were by her hands. As soon as she felt Otto's—and Xena's—weight drop onto the seat behind her, she pushed the lever under her right thumb and the snowmobile jumped ahead. Startled, she released it, and the sled slowed abruptly, jerking her forward.

Sarah pressed it again, prepared this time as it shot forward. It accelerated quickly, and everything blurred as cold air hit her unprotected eyes. The snowmobile's runners skipped over the uneven drifts, bouncing its passengers, and Sarah had to force herself not to slow down. Even though she felt completely terrified and out of control, this wasn't the time to take it slow.

She could hear a popping sound over the engine, and her worst fears were confirmed when Otto shouted, "Zigzag! They're shooting!"

Sarah tried, turning the handlebars and leaning first left and then right and then left again. They flew up a small hill, twisting from side to side. As they crested it, Otto shouted.

"Trap!"

She instinctively turned, just as the runner snagged on the edge of a tarp lying on the ground, hidden and all but buried beneath snow, pulling it askew and revealing a deep pit in front of them. Hauling on the right handlebar, Sarah leaned as much as she could into the turn as the left runner slid out over empty space that had been hidden by the tarp. Her brain was screaming with horror as she pulled on the right grip with all her might, terrified that she'd eluded Aaron's thugs just to drop the three of them into an enormous hole in the ground. Snow sprayed in an arc as the snowmobile banked. The left skid caught the ground at the edge of the hole, and they shot forward onto solid ground.

Sarah dragged in a desperate breath as she accelerated, flying away from the hole that had nearly killed them. "What was *that*?" she yelled, almost dizzy with relief and terror at what had almost happened.

"Booby trap! Gordon has them everywhere on the property!" Otto shouted back, and Sarah mentally and thoroughly cursed Gordon's intense paranoia. There was no time to slow down and recover, even though her whole body trembled from the close call. Aaron's goons were still chasing them—and shooting. She began her zigzag pattern again, twisting back and forth until the boundary fence came into view. She slowed, uncertain.

"Ram it!" Otto yelled right by her ear, and she jammed her thumb down on the gas. The sled shot forward, unexpectedly fast, and Sarah was tossed back into Xena. The dog gave a small yelp.

"Sorry!" Sarah shouted, all her focus on trying to steer, to keep the powerful machine under control. She stared at the gate as it got closer, terrified to drive into it but determined to get away. Hunching lower, she pressed down so hard on the accelerator that her hand shook with tension.

Something was wrong, though. Instead of speeding up, the sled started to slow, the engine making a rough skip every few seconds until it sputtered and cut out.

"No!" Sarah pushed on the gas, but it was no use. The snowmobile was dead, only inertia keeping them skidding across the snow. Gradually, they slowed until they were barely moving at all.

"Switch!" Otto ordered, and Sarah automatically

obeyed, swinging off and then on again behind Xena, locking her arms around the trembling dog before Xena could even think about jumping off. Sarah looked behind them, seeing the bobbing lights as the other snowmobiles grew closer. She clutched Xena more tightly, burying her face in the dog's hard shoulder as Otto tried to restart the engine.

There was nothing, just empty clicks.

"Let's go," he said, swinging off and helping her dismount at the same time. Xena jumped into the snow behind them. Grabbing hands, they ran toward the fence. What had seemed so close when they were speeding toward it now looked painfully far away. The snow was even deeper here, swallowing Sarah's boots and making each step pull at her sore quads. The nightmarish feeling returned. She was running as fast as she could, but it was still too slow.

The snowmobiles were loud now, buzzing like a swarm of bees, the lights so close and bright that they lit up the boundary fence. It was like a glowing target, one that Sarah knew she would never reach in time.

"Go!" she shouted at Otto, trying to pull her hand free. "Don't wait for me! Take Xena and go!"

He didn't respond, just hung grimly on to her hand, hauling her after him. Instead of continuing toward the fence, though, he turned left. Sarah didn't know why, but she hoped desperately that it was part of some genius plan that would save them. She glanced over her shoulder. The sleds were almost on top of them. A small part of her terror-filled mind wondered why they weren't shooting anymore. The mercenaries must've had a great shot by now.

Otto abruptly stopped and turned, pushing Sarah behind him. He drew his gun, crouching down and aiming. Sarah reached in her pocket, pulling out her knife and opening it. This was it, she knew. Their last stand. She hoped that Aaron would call off his men and free the town once she and Otto were killed. At least then some good would come out of their deaths. Her free hand clenched in Otto's coat again. She didn't want to die, and she really, really didn't want Otto to die.

Two of the snowmobiles circled around them, swinging to the left and right. She turned, keeping her back to Otto's, so she could watch them. The engines were still too loud to hear anything, but she could see that all three—two men on one sled and a woman on the other—were laughing, mocking her and Otto's desperate attempt to flee.

The sleds continued around, about to pass each other, when they both disappeared. There was a deafening crash, and Sarah realized that they'd fallen into one of Gordon's booby traps. A mix of horror and sheer relief poured through her.

She turned just as Otto fired, the hot casing flying back and catching in her coat collar, burning her neck. She brushed it away, barely feeling the pain, as one of the other snowmobile riders slumped over.

The rider toppled into the snow, and the empty sled careened toward them. It was no longer accelerating, but the smooth runners slipped across the fresh snow with nothing to slow the snowmobile down. Sarah scrambled to get out of the path, but it was traveling too fast—it was going to hit them.

Otto gave her and Xena a hard shove, sending them

rolling through the snow until they sank partway into a deep drift—seconds before the snowmobile flew by. It raced past, one runner just inches from her face.

Otto wasn't so lucky. The corner clipped him, sending him spinning.

"Otto!" Sarah screamed as he toppled into the snow. She fought to regain her feet, feeling like she was swimming through the drift. The snow was dry and fine, refusing to let her go. Instead, it swallowed her hands as she tried to push to her feet. It felt like even the snow was on Aaron's side.

Fear for Otto gave her strength, and she heaved her body forward, lurching out of the drift. Sobs caught in her throat as she fought her way through the snow toward Otto's fallen body. When she finally reached him, he was lying facedown, snow drifting to cover the back of his head. She tried to roll him over, but just succeeded in making his huge form sink deeper, so she turned his head to the side, brushing away the flakes.

He blinked, looking dazed. Blood streamed from a jagged red gash along his hairline.

"Get up, get up, get up," she chanted through chattering teeth, shoving the snow away from his face.

"What?" he mumbled, his eyes hazy and unfocused.

The roar of another engine closing in on her made Sarah look up. The last snowmobile stopped ten feet from them in a spray of snow. The driver grinned, and Sarah's breath caught in terror—it was Logan. She'd thought that leaving Texas meant escaping him as well as Aaron, but she was beginning to think that she would never be free of either of them. They were determined to ruin her newfound happiness.

The man riding behind him stood on the seat, dragging her attention away from Logan's mocking face. She jerked back as he raised his rifle.

Otto's gun! she thought, frantically hunting around them for the pistol. She couldn't find it, and she realized she'd dropped her knife at some point. She dug in Otto's coat pocket, her hand closing around cold metal.

Thank God!

Pulling it out, her heart sank when she saw it was his multi-tool. There was probably a blade, but she didn't have time to pull out all the implements to find it. She threw the tool at the two men on the snowmobile. It flew over their heads harmlessly, but they both ducked, giving Sarah an extra few seconds. She reached into Otto's pocket again, and this time she pulled out a knife.

Logan laughed at her—cruel, sneering laughter. "Thought you got away, didn't you? Poor little Alice."

Opening the knife with trembling fingers, she plowed through the snow toward the two men.

Logan's voice went from mocking to cold in an instant. "Enough of this. Kill her."

The man standing behind Logan aimed his rifle. Her whole body shook, but she kept plowing forward. With each step, she sank in over her knees, but she continued her charge, bracing for the impact of a bullet ripping through her. At least it would give Otto a few more seconds to recover. If he survived, that was all that mattered.

There was a roar behind her, and the amusement disappeared from the men's faces. Xena was a blur as she raced toward the mercenaries, and the one holding the rifle shifted his aim to the dog.

"No!" Sarah yelled. There was nothing she could do, no way to reach the gunman in time before he could squeeze the trigger. Gripping the blade of the knife, she cocked back and threw it as hard as she could. The knife flew through the air, end over end, and sank deep into the side of the gunman's neck. He screamed, dropping the gun as his hands reached for the knife, scrabbling to pull out the blade. Blood poured from the wound, and Sarah couldn't look away, not until the man toppled off the seat and fell into the snow, where he lay unmoving.

"You're still dead, bitch," Logan snarled, lunging for the fallen rifle. As he stood, swinging the barrel toward Sarah, Xena hit him square in the chest. With a shout, he fell onto his back in the snow. Xena stood on top of him, snarling in his face. His gaze locked with the dog's as he slowly raised the rifle he still gripped in his right hand.

Sarah felt rage building in her chest, expanding until it was almost impossible to breathe. It was one thing for Logan to terrorize her, but she was not going to allow him to hurt Otto or Xena. With a wordless yell, she charged. Grabbing the rifle with both hands, she pushed it down, using her body weight to pin his arm—and the gun—to the snowy ground. Logan cursed, and Xena growled, snapping at his face with her teeth bared.

Lifting the gun, Sarah slammed it down again, over and over as Logan swore and screamed until his fingers finally loosened. She yanked the rifle out of his grip, slightly startled when it came free. Stumbling back a step, she quickly regained her balance and raised the butt of the rifle to her shoulder. She'd never held one before, and it felt strange in her grip, too long and bulky.

Logan gave her a grin that was mostly a snarl. "You

going to shoot me, princess?" He spat out the last word. "You don't have the balls."

Her whole body trembled so severely that she knew he could see her shake, and she hated that he knew she was terrified. Her finger found the trigger guard and slipped inside.

"Put the gun down," he snapped, and she jerked back, startled by the loud command. Xena growled and barked sharply in his face, but he didn't look away from Sarah. His smirk was tense. "It won't work anyway. The safety's on."

Her gaze flickered down at the gun, just for a fraction of a second before she caught herself falling for Logan's bluff. It was long enough, though. He struck, wrapping his hands around Xena's thick neck and rolling them to the side.

"No!" Sarah shouted, knowing he would kill Xena without any remorse. The dog yelped, and Sarah felt a calm settle over her. Her hands stopped shaking; she knew what she needed to do. Aiming the gun at the back of Logan's head, she pulled the trigger.

The recoil jolted her, but it was the realization of what she'd just done that made her stumble back. The smell of smoke filled her nose, and her ears rang from the loud bang. She forced herself to look at Logan. She needed to know if she'd missed, if he was still a threat.

Instantly, she looked away. He wasn't a threat anymore.

Xena scrambled to her feet and ran to her, pressing her trembling body against Sarah's legs. Carefully, Sarah lowered the gun, placing it next to her on top of a drift. The rifle sank and the snow sifted on top of it, making it almost seem like it had disappeared.

"What?" At Otto's voice, Sarah looked behind her to see him struggling to sit up. She fought her way through the snow toward him, pausing briefly to turn off the snowmobile. Silence settled over them, broken only by her rough breathing. She tried to calm down as she reached Otto. Her heaving breaths were too close to sobs, and this wasn't the time to cry.

"Otto?" Crouching next to him, she saw how much blood streaked the side of his face, and her stomach lurched.

"What's...?" he slurred, blinking at her like he was having trouble focusing.

Sarah fought down panic. How could she get an injured Otto back to the bunker? She pushed the thought away. *One thing at a time*, she thought, trying to remember the little she'd read about first aid. *First, stop the bleeding*.

It was a relief to have something to focus on, to have a plan, no matter how basic. Gently holding his face, she tilted it so that she could see the cut more clearly. In the dim light, the blood looked black, and it seemed like it was everywhere. She swiped at the area below the cut with her glove, but the material wasn't absorbent, so it just smeared blood across his forehead.

She took a mental inventory of what she was wearing, trying to figure out what would work best for bandaging, and plopped down in the snow. As she yanked off one of her boots, Otto stared at her, swaying a little.

"Wha...what are you doing?" He sounded a little less drunk, although Sarah knew that could've just been wishful thinking on her part. She pulled off one of her knee-high wool socks and held it up.

"Bandage," she said, tugging her boot back on. Just in that short time she'd had it off, the cold had darted through her remaining sock and chilled her foot.

"Bandage?" He frowned. "Are you hurt?"

"It's for you." Her voice shook slightly as she reached to wrap the sock around his head and tie it tightly in the back. It covered most of the still-oozing gash, and she hoped it would at least slow the bleeding until they could get back to the bunker where someone a lot more competent than she was could look at it. "Sorry. It's probably not the most sanitary."

He smiled and gave her forearm a squeeze. "It's fine. Help me up?"

With Sarah's assistance, he managed to haul himself to his feet. Once there, he swayed slightly, and she held her hands out as if to catch him. His jaw muscles tightening, he managed to steady himself. Although he still looked dazed, his eyes gradually cleared, and he seemed to take in the situation without needing an explanation. He looked furious and grim and sad, but all he said was a simple "Good job, Sarah."

She blinked at him, shock and residual horror making everything hazy. "Thank you?" Relief that Otto was awake and standing—that she was alive and that Xena was unhurt—rushed through her, making her voice break.

Otto cupped her face in his hands and looked at her carefully. "You okay?"

It took her a moment to answer. "Yes. You're okay, and Xena's okay. That means I'm okay." When he continued to eye her, she covered his hands with her own. "I mean it, Otto. I did what I needed to do. It's done."

After another long look, he seemed to accept that. "Let's go." Otto's hand on her back was gentle. Sarah leaned into the contact, and Xena pressed into her side. She'd seen and done some terrible things over the past twelve hours, but Otto and Xena were worth it. For them, she'd do anything.

CHAPTER 22

OTTO STARTED THE SNOWMOBILE.

"C'mon, Xena," Sarah said, scooting back to clear a spot on the seat. "Up."

The dog tucked her tail, looking unhappy, but she obediently hopped onto the sled. Sarah wrapped her arms around Xena as Otto slowly accelerated, turning the sled around and heading back toward Gordon's house. He kept the snowmobile's speed low, for which Sarah was grateful. Without the adrenaline of the chase, the wind whipping by them felt even colder.

It seemed like an eternity before the workshop and house came into view. Sarah had never been so tired in her entire life. Her head kept bobbing forward, only the cold and the fear of toppling off the side of the sled keeping her in place. Otto slowed as they approached the place where Blessard had fallen. Sarah was torn. Even though she knew they couldn't leave him out here to freeze to death, he'd betrayed them. She didn't want to even look at the lieutenant, much less drag him into the bunker with them.

Sarah didn't hear the sound at first, with the buzz of the snowmobile filling her head. Gradually, though, it got louder—the *thump-thump* she was going to hear in her nightmares. Her arms tightened around Xena as she looked up, scanning the sky, terrified of what she would see.

"Otto!" she yelled when she spotted the bright lights of the helicopter hovering above them.

With a terse nod, he sped up and turned south. *Hurry, hurry, hurry!* Sarah thought desperately. If the helicopter would only follow them, then Gordon's property might not be bombed. The bunker would likely withstand a blast, just like Otto's had, but the workshop certainly would not. She clutched Xena tighter, willing the snow-mobile to go faster.

Wind whipped around them as the helicopter flew lower. Otto wove back and forth, heading across the yard and toward a wooded area east of the house. There was a loud, fast *thump-thump-thump*, and the snow kicked up around them.

Someone in the helicopter was shooting at them.

As the realization hit, Sarah hunched over Xena, trying to cover as much of the dog as possible. Otto turned abruptly, swerving and dodging in no discernable pattern. The small part of Sarah's brain that hadn't been consumed by terror assumed that Otto was in defensive mode now, and evading bullets was his only goal.

Sarah peered around Xena and Otto, blinking as wind and kicked-up snow immediately made her eyes water. If they could get into the trees, that would provide some cover. They could cross the property and ram through the boundary fence, leading the helicopter away. It wasn't a good long-term plan, but it would keep everyone safe for a little while, at least.

There was a movement in front of them, catching Sarah's attention. The door of the outhouse bunker entrance swung open. *No! Go back inside!* her brain screamed as a tiny figure appeared. There was only one person that small who'd been in the bunker.

Dee.

Dread and horror squeezed all the air out of Sarah's lungs as she saw Dee walk out of safety and into danger, holding something bulky in her arms.

"Dee!" Sarah screamed, not knowing if she was yelling at the little girl or warning Otto. Dee didn't react, but Otto shouted, "I see her!"

He turned, hard to the right, making a tight half-circle and flying back the way they'd come. Instead of heading toward the workshop, he steered the sled back to the open expanse they'd just left—away from Dee. He zigzagged back and forth, trying to dodge the bullets, and Sarah leaned into each turn. A strange calmness settled over her. There was no way to get out of this now. She couldn't throw a knife at a helicopter and bring it down.

The helicopter circled around in front of them, the light shining directly on them like a spotlight. It felt like they were in the laser sights of a gun. There was no way that the shooter could miss them now, no matter how many turns Otto made. At least they'd led Aaron's men away from Dee and the animals and the rest of the people in the bunker. Hopefully, they'd be okay.

Something flew over them, barely clearing their heads. Otto stiffened, and Sarah stared at it—whatever it was. It appeared to be a tiny plane, but that didn't make any sense. Sarah was sure that her fear and the dim lighting was messing with her perception.

"What is that?" Sarah yelled.

"Not sure!" Otto didn't slow but continued driving toward the object. It rose higher, flying directly toward the huge black beast of a helicopter. Otto banked left, turning again, giving them a tiny bit of breathing room before the helicopter caught up with them again. The tiny plane-like object trailed behind. When Otto steered right, the helicopter followed. The small flying object lifted higher, allowing the bulk of the helicopter to pass under it. As soon as it passed the main rotor, the little plane darted down—right into the tail rotor. There was a loud clattering sound, like a bolt caught in a high-powered fan, and Sarah hunched instinctively again. The helicopter sounded different, and she risked a look up and back. The remains of the tiny plane fell from the tail, where the rotor hung, useless and mangled. The helicopter started to turn, spinning in place like a top. It swung in crazy loops, heading toward the ground—and getting closer and closer to them.

The wind whipped the snow into a blinding blizzard around them. Sarah squeezed her eyes closed and tucked her head down. The snowmobile shot forward.

"Hold on!" Otto shouted, his words barely audible over the noise. The helicopter sounded so close that Sarah didn't want to look. She knew it was almost on top of them.

The sled flew, skimming over the snow so fast it felt like they were hovering above the ground. Sarah turned her head. She had to look. It had to be worse to feel the helicopter coming down on top of them without seeing it.

It wasn't. Seeing the huge shape spinning over them, its main rotor moving so fast it was just a circular blur, was horribly, indescribably worse than just imagining it. Sarah screamed—at least, she thought she did, sound lost over the roaring wind and the engine and the thumping blades.

The helicopter spun in drunken circles right above them, dropping lower and lower until Sarah ducked, feeling as if it was close enough to graze the top of her head. The noise was terrible—shrieking and groaning and thumping—as the machine tumbled toward the earth.

The snowmobile went faster and faster, flying weightlessly across the snow as the helicopter turned in endless circles right above their heads. It tipped, the tail touching down first, hitting the ground right behind them with a boom loud enough to rival the bombs. It swiveled on the ground, whipping around toward them as it toppled over onto its side, the main rotor digging into the earth as it tried to keep spinning. The helicopter turned, the broken tail swinging toward them like a shattered baseball bat, and Sarah screamed again, not able to look away. The snowmobile engine shrieked as Otto pushed it to its highest speed.

They flew. There was no other way for Sarah to describe it. Like a stone from a slingshot, they crested a small hill and rocketed through the air, snow flying around them. The runners hit the ground with a bounce, and the sled shot forward again, earthbound this time.

Gasping for breath, Sarah looked at Otto's back and Xena and her own snow-covered self. How could they still be alive? How were they not crushed by the downed helicopter? It had been so close to them—how had it missed?

Twisting around, Sarah looked behind her at the

wreckage. The helicopter was on its side, the main rotor detached, flung far across the yard.

"Otto!" Sarah shouted, delight rising in her as she realized that they'd survived. Death had been so close, so sure, but they'd somehow managed to outrun it. Keeping one arm locked around Xena, she grabbed a handful of Otto's coat. "You're amazing! I love you and your driving skills!"

He slowed, looping around so that they were facing the downed helicopter. As soon as they stopped, Sarah kneeled on the seat, reaching over Xena to hug Otto's shoulders. He wrapped his arms over hers.

"I can't believe it," she cried, staring at the wreckage as she squeezed him tighter. "Did I mention that you're an *excellent* driver?"

His laugh boomed out, shaking his body, and Sarah clung to him, basking in the feel of him, of his joy and sheer *alive*-ness. So many times, she'd thought they were going to die, but they'd made it through. All of them had survived the horrible, endless night.

The helicopter cabin opened, and someone stumbled out, slogging through the snow toward them. Another person was slumped over the controls, either unconscious or dead. As Sarah watched, she saw the man who'd emerged from the helicopter reach into his jacket and pull out a pistol.

"Gun!" Sarah shouted, releasing Otto. She sat back down and wrapped her arms around Xena. As Otto sped up, Sarah twisted around to look at the man. He stopped and lifted the gun, and Sarah could finally see him clearly.

It was Aaron.

Blood streaked his face, but he was smiling as he aimed. Her own *brother* was about to shoot her with a smile on his face. Otto pushed down on the accelerator, but it wasn't going to be fast enough. Sarah knew they were still within range of Aaron's gun. He loved target shooting, and he was good at it. Her brother was not going to miss. Sarah felt a shot of pure fury jolt through her. She and Otto had gone through so much, survived despite the craziest odds, and now she was going to die because her brother was a dickhead?

Oh, hell, no.

"Fuck you, Aaron!" she yelled. "Fuck you and your stupid rules and your stupid fucking face! I'm going to live! I'm going to live, and it's not going to be with you in your prison!"

That startled him. She saw his head jerk up before he took aim again. It wasn't enough of a hesitation, though. They were still too close to the crazy man with a gun—and good aim.

There was a roar. Sarah didn't know how else to describe it. It sounded like a whole bunch of very angry people, all shouting together. When she saw the crowd stampeding toward Aaron, Sarah laughed with amazement and delight. That was, in fact, exactly what it was.

Jules and Theo and Viggy, Hugh and Lexi and Grace—with her crossbow—were rushing toward Aaron. Mort and Gordon and Steve were also there, and Ty and Tio and Sam and even little Dee bringing up the rear. They trampled through the snow, the dogs surging ahead, all three barking with the excitement of the chase.

"Look!" she yelled to Otto, slapping him excitedly on the shoulder. "It's the villagers! And they're pissed!"

Otto slowed the sled abruptly, circling around to head back toward the downed helicopter. Aaron, his face switching from smug glee to horror, turned and started to run across the snowy field. The crowd of people followed, quickly closing the distance between them and a fleeing Aaron.

As Otto steered the snowmobile toward her brother, Sarah whooped. "I love this town!"

Aaron hit a deep drift and stumbled, floundering through the knee-high snow. Aaron had just made it through and was beginning to speed up again when Viggy reached him. The dog's mouth closed on Aaron's right forearm and jerked it down. The gun toppled out of his grip as Viggy pulled Aaron to the ground, the dog's tail waving wildly with excitement. The crowd closed around Aaron.

"Hurry!" Sarah said, bouncing in the seat with impatience as they headed back toward the action. "We're missing it!"

"Bloodthirsty," Otto called back to her, but from the tiny bit of his profile that she could see, it was obvious that he was grinning. Reaching up, she squeezed his arm. It was the closest she could come to a hug on a moving snowmobile with a big dog between them.

By the time they'd pulled up to the crowd, Aaron was lying on his belly with his arm cranked behind him and Theo's knee on his back.

Sarah jumped off the snowmobile and wobbled as her legs threatened to collapse underneath her. Otto stood and grabbed her arms to steady her. She gave him a shaky smile. "We made it."

"Yeah." That slow smile was extra precious now. "We did."

"Thank you, Theo. I'll take him now. Okay, everyone. Back up! Give us some room."

The sound of Lieutenant Blessard's voice chilled Sarah's blood, and she froze, her relieved smile slipping off her face. Her gaze met Otto's, and the horror in his expression reflected her own.

"No!" she and Otto chorused. He moved faster than her, his long strides plowing through the snow more quickly than she could manage. Blessard had moved everyone else back. He stood apart from the small crowd, holding Aaron's arm—Aaron's *uncuffed* arm. Her brother turned to look at her, and he smiled…a cold, cruel, bone-chilling smile.

"Blessard is dirty!" Otto shouted, sprinting toward the lieutenant. "He's Blanchett's man!"

Theo and Hugh looked stunned for a split second before they were lunging for Blessard. It was too late. Aaron grabbed the lieutenant's gun from the holster. Yanking it out, he aimed it at Sarah.

Everyone stopped moving.

"Alice." Aaron's voice broke the silence. Despite his bloody, messed-up appearance, his voice sounded just the same as it always had. "Come here."

She couldn't. She wouldn't. After having a taste of freedom, there was no way she could return to whatever hell he had planned for her. Swallowing hard, she stared at the gun in his hand and forced out one word. "No."

"No?" He smirked, and Sarah's stomach twisted. She'd forgotten that Aaron always got his way. Xena growled softly, and Sarah put a hand on the dog's head to quiet her. There was no reason that Xena had to die today, too. Bracing herself for the shot, she stared at her brother, refusing to close her eyes. If he wanted to kill her, then he was going to have to look her right in the face when he did it.

When he suddenly moved, she flinched, but there was no *bang*, no impact, no pain. He hadn't shot her. Her immediate relief evaporated when she saw where Aaron was pointing the gun now: right at Otto.

"Don't!" The word was ripped from her as she stumbled forward. "I'll go with you." She'd rather die than return to Aaron, but she'd do anything to let Otto live.

"Sarah, no! Run!" Otto shouted hoarsely, his gaze fixed on her rather than the gun pointed at his head.

She just shook her head and mouthed *I love you* as she walked toward Aaron. The look in Otto's eyes was so haunted that she had to look away. She stared at Aaron as she got closer, letting him see all the hatred she held for him in her expression. A strange look flashed over his face for just a moment before his sneer returned.

As soon as she got close enough, he yanked her forward, turning her so that her back was against his front and his arm was hooked around her neck. He pressed the gun to her temple. Xena barked and snarled, making Aaron scramble back several steps, pulling Sarah with him. The painful pressure on her throat, the struggle to breathe, was horribly familiar. How silly she'd been to think she could escape this. She let out a hopeless, airless sob, and Xena charged.

"Xena, no!" Sarah cried, terrified that Aaron would shoot the dog. Otto caught Xena by the collar. His arm strained from the effort of holding her back.

"Let's go." Without waiting for a response, Aaron moved sideways toward the snowmobile, dragging Sarah along with him.

"Think about what you're doing," Gordon said, surprising her. "This is how you *fall*." He stared at Sarah, and she blinked at him, trying to figure out what was going on. Why was Gordon giving life advice to her brother? "First thing to do when you get yourself into a *hole* is stop digging."

Fall? Hole? The way he'd emphasized the words caught Sarah's attention, but why was Gordon talking about holes, of all things, right now?

Realization hit her so suddenly that her body jerked.

"Watch it," Aaron growled, pressing the muzzle harder against her skull.

"Don't, Xena!" she shouted, and Aaron dragged her backward several steps. He stopped when he saw that Otto still had a grip on the dog's collar, and Xena wasn't even pulling against him.

"Whatever you're doing, knock it off," Aaron growled, tightening his arm. For a few terrifying seconds, Sarah couldn't breathe. She tried to ignore the pressure on her lungs as she met Otto's eyes.

"Wait." Otto took a step forward. "Let's talk about this."

Aaron jerked Sarah back, farther away from Otto. "Come a step closer, and I will shoot her."

Otto hesitated before moving forward again a single step, causing Theo to grab his arm to hold him back.

"I said, stay there!" As he stepped back, Aaron pulled the gun from Sarah's temple and pointed it at Otto.

"No!" She bit Aaron's forearm hard, clamping her teeth into his flesh. His bellow of pain gave her grim satisfaction. Releasing her grip, she twisted in his loosened hold until she was facing him. "If I'm dying, then so are you." She threw herself forward, using her weight to drive him backward that final, critical step.

"What—?" His foot hit empty air, and his face flattened with shock. He started to topple backward, pulling Sarah with him, and she squeezed her eyes closed and pictured Otto's beautiful face. Aaron released her, his arms flailing out to the sides to catch his balance, but it was too late. They were already falling.

Until Sarah wasn't. Something caught the back of her coat, and she jerked to a stop, dangling above the booby trap. Aaron tumbled down, falling twenty feet before he hit the ground with a solid crunch. She watched as his body bounced, his head snapping forward and back, and then he was still. Deathly still.

She was hauled up, and her view was broken. Frantic hands turned her around and pulled her into a hard, wonderfully familiar chest. Otto clutched her close, breathing roughly but not saying a word. Wrapping her arms around him, this amazingly gentle man she'd thought she'd never see again, she held him just as tightly, just as quietly. She didn't mind his silence.

After all, that was kind of Otto's thing.

She smiled, closing her eyes. They'd done it. They'd all survived, and now could live happily ever—

Whump-whump-whump.

Her head jerked up as she searched the sky frantically. "Another one? I thought we got them all!"

"Two was only an estimate," Theo said as he and Hugh grimly handcuffed a struggling Lieutenant Blessard. "Everyone back in the bunker!"

"No need." Norman Rounds's bland voice stopped everyone in their tracks. "It's the FBI."

"The FBI?" Theo repeated. "How do you know? And how would they know we needed help?"

"Because I called them."

"How?" Theo demanded. "All our communications are down."

"I used Gordon's ham radio."

Hugh swore. "I knew you had a ham radio! I knew it!"

"Norman!" Gordon said, turning a dark shade of red. "That is a secret of the brotherhood. I can't believe we trusted you!"

"I can't believe you had a ham radio and didn't let us use it to call for help!" Hugh shouted.

"The feds aren't *help*!" Gordon yelled back. "They're just as evil as the rest of them—more, even!"

Everyone started arguing as the helicopter got louder. Fighting the urge to bolt, Sarah watched the chopper carefully as it closed in. It did look bigger. The light placement was different, and it was a lighter color. She didn't completely relax, however, until it landed in the field next to the workshop and a half-dozen people wearing jackets with *FBI* on the backs poured out of it.

Finally, she leaned against Otto, and he wrapped his arms around her. She felt safe and warm for the first time that night. This was it. Her life in Texas was over. Now, she was truly free.

CHAPTER 23

"I KNEW IT WAS A DRONE." JULES WAS OBVIOUSLY TRYING TO sound annoyed, but she wasn't succeeding. "What did I say about y'all building a drone?"

"It's a model airplane," Ty protested.

"Well, a model airplane with a few additional features." Tio was honest to a fault.

"W-what's the difference betw-w-ween a model airplane and a drone?" Sam asked.

"Size, mainly." Tio scratched his nose. "And those few additional features."

"So a drone, then?" Jules clutched her head with both hands. "I can't believe I'm even considering this after y'all sent your little sister out onto a battlefield with it!"

A chorus of protests from Ty, Tio, and Sam quieted when Jules waved her arms. "I know she snuck out." She sent an admonishing look toward Dee, who was sitting on the floor, petting Xena with one hand and Mort with the other, while Turtle was curled in her lap. In pet heaven, Dee didn't even catch the silent scolding. "But the only reason she was able to sneak out was because Sam was preoccupied with keeping the two of you from doing the *exact* same thing."

Ty put on his most innocent expression. "Everyone was arguing about what to do after y'all heard the helicopter. If we'd waited for someone else to come up with a plan, Sarah and Otto would've died. Besides, how were we supposed to know Dee'd do that? We didn't even know she could fly it."

"Well, she had watched us a lot," Tio said. "She picks things up pretty quickly, too, so—"

"T!" Ty cut him off. "Not helping."

Sarah exchanged a look with Otto. They were sitting next to each other at the dining room table in Jules's house, holding hands. Bob was sleeping on Sam's chest. The cat had adopted Sam and followed him around like a dog whenever he was home. Sarah wasn't sure that she and Otto would get Bob back when they moved home.

The thought of home sent a pang through her. Although it was wonderful to be in the midst of the warm chaos and company of their family, she missed having alone time with Otto.

Theo walked in, wearing his uniform, and crossed to Jules to give her a kiss. He, like Otto, looked exhausted. It had been two weeks since Aaron and the Jovanovics had sicced their private army on the town, but there was still a lot of cleanup to do. She'd barely seen Otto, even though they were both staying at Jules's house until the pass was cleared. They were planning on living in the bunker until spring, when construction on a new house could start.

The chief and the officers who'd been at training in the Springs had been helicoptered in, and they'd set up a temporary police station in the empty office building across from the viner. Lieutenant Blessard's betrayal had rocked the small force—and the town—and everyone was still reeling. It helped that most of the TV crews that had descended on Monroe after the attack were gone. Monroe was slowly starting to get back to...well, not exactly normal, but it was getting closer.

"Theo," Jules said, refocusing after the peck turned into something longer and more intense. "Is building a drone legal? The boys want to build another drone, and I'm pretty sure that's a bad idea, even if Dee did use it to bring down the helicopter and save the day—or maybe *because* she brought down a helicopter? Why do I get the feeling that parenting isn't this hard in normal families?"

Theo hugged her against his side as he looked at Tio. "Will it weigh more than half a pound?"

"Maybe?" Tio said, looking at Theo expectantly.

"If it does, you'll need to register it with the FAA."

Jules gave Tio a stern look. "You will not be registering a drone with the FAA."

"Then I'll make it under a half pound." Tio gave a small nod.

Ty grinned. "Dude! A mini-drone! So awesome."

"Should I allow this?" Jules glanced around the kitchen, as if looking for advice from any quarter, and Sarah raised her hands in a shrug. She was biased, since she was hugely grateful to Tio for creating his drone and to Dee for flying it into the tail rotor of the helicopter and saving their lives. Also, she agreed with Ty. A mini-drone would be awesome.

"Good news," Theo said, distracting Jules. "West pass is open."

They all cheered, and Sarah squeezed Otto's hand hard with excitement. They could finally go home. As the kitchen filled with happy chatter, Otto stood and leaned over to speak in Sarah's ear. "Want to take a walk?"

She was about to mention that it was very, very cold outside, but Otto looked unusually excited about something. Curiosity had her agreeing, and they headed for the front entry where they pulled on their winter gear.

The first step onto the front porch took Sarah's breath away, and she regretted agreeing to a walk. Turning to Otto, she planned to ask if they could just stay inside, when he grabbed her hands.

"The pass is open," he said.

She waited a moment before answering. "Yes…?"

"That means… Would you… Uh, do you want to—" He broke off, and she stared at him. Otto hadn't been this incoherent since the first—and second—and maybe third—time they'd met. He looked down for a moment and then met her gaze again, his jaw set with determination. "Let's get married."

Shock was quickly swept aside by a rush of joy. "Okay. Yes."

"Now."

"Now?" She blinked. "As in *now* now?"

"Yes. The pass is open. It's not supposed to snow for a while. Let's go to Vegas."

"Vegas?" Sarah knew she sounded like a not-very-bright parrot, but those were not the words that she'd expected to come out of always-patient Otto's mouth. Not *married*, not *now*, and certainly not *Vegas*.

"Yes. I love you. I want to be married to you as soon as possible." He paused, looking uncertain. "Unless you want a big wedding?"

"God, no." A big wedding was not one of her dreams. It would only bring back memories of when she thought she'd be stuck marrying Logan Jovanovic.

That would've been a big wedding. A huge wedding. A huge, miserable mistake of a wedding. She shook off the thought. That hadn't happened, and now she had her wonderful, gentle, kind Otto right here, proposing to her, asking her to go to Vegas to get married. "Yes. Okay. Let's go. Now." She laughed, her happiness spilling out all over. "But what about Bean and Hortense and the others?"

"Gordon said he'll keep watching them. He's built some stalls, fenced off a paddock for them, and bought more hay."

"Wow. How generous."

Otto scowled. "He knows he has to make up for lying about his ham radio. Besides, he's jumped bail. He's in a legal mess, and he needs our help to get out of it."

"He did let everyone stay in his bunker," Sarah said, feeling a little bad for Gordon. "Plus, that booby trap saved us." She blocked out the image of Aaron's broken body.

"I know," Otto said. "But he can take care of my animals for a little longer. The dogs and Bob can stay here. When we get back, I'll begin working with Xena again. The chief gave me the go-ahead to start training."

She squeezed his hands with excitement. "K9 training?"

"Yep. She's been so much more confident the past couple of weeks," he said proudly. "Xena's going to be Monroe's next K9 officer."

"That's great!" Sarah hugged him, squeezing hard. After everything that had happened, it was hard to believe that things could ever get better, but they had—so much better.

The sound of an engine made her reluctantly pull away from Otto. Hugh's new pickup bumped over the driveway and pulled up to the porch. Grace climbed out of the passenger seat.

"Brrr!" Grace gave an exaggerated shiver before pulling the puppies' carrier out of the cab. "What are you two doing outside? It's freezing out here!"

Too excited to hold it in, Sarah blurted out, "We're going to Vegas to get married!"

"Congratulations!" Handing the carrier over to Hugh, Grace hurried up the steps and hugged Sarah. "When?"

"Now."

"Now?"

At the echo of their previous conversation, Sarah laughed. "Yes, now. The pass is open, so we're leaving while Gordon is still willing to watch Bean and Hortense."

"That's great." Hugh shook Otto's hand and gave Sarah a one-armed hug as the puppies yipped in their carrier. At four weeks old, the pups were getting big—and even more adorable.

"We could go, too." Hugh gave Grace a hungry look. "Have a double wedding."

She made a big show of pretending to consider it and then shook her head. "I'm having too much fun dating you."

"C'mon, then, girlfriend." Hugh ushered Grace into the house. "Let's leave the lovebirds alone."

"Are you eighty?" Grace asked before Hugh closed the door. "Because sometimes you sound like you're eighty."

Sarah turned back to Otto. "I love you, and I'd like to go to Vegas and marry you and live in Monroe forever, and let's leave right now before it snows again and more people with guns and bombs and helicopters try to kill us, okay?"

He didn't smile his slow smile that time. Instead, it was a full-out, beaming grin. "I like that plan." When he leaned down and kissed her, Sarah could still feel his smile, and it was the best feeling in the world.

EPILOGUE

COURTNEY YOUNG PRESSED THE BUTTON ON THE BLENDER with a short, angry jab. Yet another cook had quit, forcing her to fend for herself. When she'd married her wealthy husband, she'd thought she'd never have to cook for herself again. She couldn't even go to a juice bar, since the doctor had warned her not to wear makeup until the latest cosmetic surgery had healed. It had been years since she'd left the house without makeup, and she wasn't about to humiliate herself like that for a smoothie.

She lifted her manicured finger off the button and the grinding sound stopped, leaving just the cable news anchor's voice filling the kitchen. *"...scene taken right out of an action movie, this tiny mountain town was..."*

Courtney picked up the remote with an annoyed huff. Why would they think anyone would be interested in what was happening in some "tiny mountain town"? Turning toward the TV mounted on the wall, she lifted the remote, her finger on the power button.

Shock left her motionless, her arm outstretched. The news camera panned over the small town's main street as the voice-over continued. A woman in a waitress uniform stood outside a drab-looking VFW, smiling up at a uniformed police officer. She glanced over at the camera and froze for a brief moment before ducking her head and rushing inside the building. The cop glared at the camera.

Courtney's gaze remained fixed on the television long after the story was over and the anchor had moved on to a Supreme Court decision. Finally, she turned off the TV and carefully placed the remote on the counter. Picking up her cell phone, she found the number of the latest in a long string of private investigators.

Tapping the number, she held the phone to her ear and gave the tiniest smile.

"Time's up, Juliet."

*Keep reading for a sneak peek of the next book in
Katie Ruggle's Rocky Mountain K9 Unit series*

THROUGH
THE FIRE

THE MATCH FLIPPED END OVER END, THE SPINNING FLAME creating a small pocket of light in the dim house. It landed in a pool of lighter fluid, and flames rippled outward with such speed that Alex took a startled step back, away from the quickly spreading fire. Arson was one of the few crimes she'd never had to commit before, but the lure was understandable. The dancing flames were mesmerizing, and the potential damage significant. Lighting a fire was a powerful feeling, one she could get addicted to.

A little reluctant to leave and not see the end result of that one lit match, she slowly opened the back door, never looking away from the growing fire as it licked around the blanket-wrapped corpse.

"Sorry, sweetie." A flicker of guilt sparked and died just as quickly. "It was nothing personal. You just had what I needed." She patted the messenger bag looped over her shoulder. This moment had been a long time coming. She'd sacrificed so much to get here, and she was finally, *finally* close to getting her revenge. "I'll make a much better Elena Dahl than you ever would, anyway."

With a final glance back, Alex walked outside, blinking at the bright early-morning light reflecting off the snow. She walked with confidence, cutting through the secluded backyard. Long ago, she'd discovered that acting like she was supposed to be somewhere was the easiest way to get away with anything. The coming weeks would be the ultimate test of that. Besides, there was no one in this godforsaken semi–ghost town to see her slip away from the gradually growing light and into the waiting tree line.

It was time to visit her new home.

CHAPTER 1

Kᴵᴛ ʜᴀᴛᴇᴅ ʙᴇɪɴɢ ʟᴀᴛᴇ.

The thought of being late to her very first day of work was especially horrifying, and her muscles tensed as she shot another glance at her SUV's dashboard clock. She only had seventeen—*sixteen*, she mentally corrected as the digital numbers changed—minutes to find her new house, unhitch the rental trailer containing all her worldly possessions, and get to the police station on time. She swore under her breath as the pickup in front of her slowed to inch around a curve.

It wasn't looking promising.

Justice shifted in the back seat, giving a low groan as he settled into a new position. Flicking a look at the bloodhound in her rearview mirror, Kit couldn't keep from smiling. With his long ears and floppy jowls, Justice always looked adorably rumpled.

Quickly turning her attention back to the twisting road, she saw the achingly slow truck's signal light begin to flash.

"Hallelujah," she muttered, easing to a crawl as the pickup turned. For the past twenty miles, she'd been stuck behind the wheezing old vehicle, which had only sped up from its painfully slow pace whenever a passing lane appeared. She'd left the hotel in Denver before six that morning, assuming that would give her enough time to get to work before seven, but she hadn't anticipated congested traffic or the snow-glazed roads.

At least the turtle-like speed allowed her to take in the views. This was only her second time in Colorado; the first was when she'd come to Monroe for her interview in late summer. The scenery was beautiful in a terrifying way, with shoulder-less roads edged by sheer drops and hairpin turns slicked with ice. A thick layer of snow covered everything except the road, piled off to the sides in dramatic, towering walls that narrowed the highway into claustrophobic corridors. The feeling surprised her. She figured being in such a small town in the wilderness would seem open and freeing, but the mountains and snow piles and even the twists and turns in the road seemed to press in on her, heavy and oddly menacing.

"It's just different from what we're used to," she told Justice, needing to hear a reassuring voice, even if it was her own. Her SUV topped a rise, and Monroe appeared before her, nestled in a valley and looking cozy enough to be the center of a snow globe. The sight of the adorable hamlet settled her nerves a little. How could anything bad ever happen in such a picture-perfect postcard of a place? Working here was going to be relaxing to the point of boredom. "This'll be good—much better than Wisconsin. We just have to get used to it. Right, Justice?"

Justice grunted, and Kit chose to take that as agreement.

Just as she passed a small sign reading *Welcome to Monroe, elevation 7,888 feet*, her GPS spoke up, telling her to turn right in half a mile. She obeyed, swinging her SUV wide so the trailer didn't cut the turn and catch on a curb. She shouldn't have worried. There was no curb. There was barely a street. Under the layer of packed snow, the road was painfully narrow and either gravel or so worn that most of the asphalt had given up, leaving only a potholed mess. She felt a pang for the townhome she'd left behind.

"Stop it," she ordered before she could jump into a full-fledged pity party. "This *will* be better. Justice will have a yard, and there won't be any shared walls, so you won't have to listen to the neighbors fighting over who put the empty milk carton back in the fridge. You're going to love it here."

As she rounded a bend in the road, the house came into view. She pulled up in front of the cedar-sided cabin and let out a long, relieved breath. It was perfect. She'd seen pictures, but photos could hide a lot of flaws. Tidy and well-maintained, the small house looked exactly as she'd hoped it would. The drive and walkway to the front porch had even been cleared. There were a few other homes around, but they were definitely far enough away that she wouldn't hear any neighbors arguing unless they made a serious ruckus.

"See, Justice? There's that big fenced yard I was telling you about."

Her relief didn't last long when she caught a glimpse of the clock again. Even if she was extremely speedy, she was definitely going to be late to her first day at her new job. She muttered various creative swear words under her breath as she pulled her SUV and the trailer past the end of the driveway.

As she started backing up, turning the trailer into the driveway, she noticed another vehicle in the street behind her and quickly slammed on her brakes. Craning her head out of her open window, she saw a dark-haired, bearded man behind the wheel of an elderly pickup. Her swearing was less muffled that time. It was hard enough backing such a small, wiggly trailer without an audience—an audience most likely impatient for her to get out of the way so he could squeeze past her SUV and get wherever he was going.

She looked at the snow mounded on either side of the skinny road. There was no way the pickup could go around, not without getting stuck in the four-foot drifts. With a resigned sigh, she started backing up again. The pickup was far enough away that she wasn't in any danger of hitting him with the trailer. The only danger was humiliation if it took her a half hour to get the trailer into the driveway straight.

Turning the steering wheel, she watched as the back of the trailer lined up with the driveway. Slowly, she started backing it in.

"It couldn't be this easy, could it?" she asked Justice, hope blooming in her chest, marveling at the way the trailer was obediently rolling up the driveway. Even as she spoke, the trailer turned too far, leaving it cockeyed and headed for the snowbank. Kit hit the brake before she got the trailer stuck in her new yard. "Of course it can't. This is my life, after all. Everything has to be as embarrassingly painful as possible."

With a sigh, she shifted her SUV into Park and got out, heading for the driver's side of the waiting pickup. The man rolled down his window, and she did a stutter-step when she got her first up-close view of him. He was the most beautiful person she'd ever seen.

Taking his features one by one, he wouldn't sound that attractive—short, dark brown hair, matching beard, hazel eyes—but there was something about him that knocked her sideways. He was rugged yet refined, with sharp cheekbones, full mouth, and a strong jaw and chin evident even underneath the beard. His lashes were long and lush enough to make pageant contestants jealous. His model-like beauty was emphasized by the contrasting mountain roughness of his untrimmed beard and utilitarian clothes, making him look like an actor playing the role of a backwoods lumberjack.

He was startlingly attractive—and unexpectedly intimidating.

Kit blinked a few times to reorient herself and remember what she was going to say. Years of working with cops and other first responders had inured her to burly, masculine men…at least that's what she'd thought. This guy had taken her off guard, however. His unbelievably gorgeous face and silent regard were giving her a flashback to high school, and all the long-forgotten insecurities of a flat-chested, dorky teen tried to elbow their way back into her brain. She nipped those feelings in the bud. There was no way she was going to let anyone make her relive the misery of her teen years.

That thought and a sharp, cold gust of wind snapped her back to reality, and she realized she'd just been standing there staring for much too long. She held back a groan. What a way to make an impression on one of her new neighbors—or fellow townspeople, at least.

"Hi," she said, trying to make her smile seem casually friendly despite her strange reaction to him. She had a trailer to park and a new job to start. There wasn't time to get distracted by a guy, no matter how pretty he was. "This is probably going to take me a few minutes. Can you back up and get where you're going a different way? Otherwise, I can drive around the block to let you get by."

His glance moved from the trailer's torqued position and back to her face. "I don't understand the problem."

She blinked. "Just what I said. It'll probably be a few minutes before the road will be clear. I'll need to pull forward to straighten the trailer before backing it into the driveway again." That was assuming she'd manage to keep it straight on the second attempt, which she highly doubted, especially with him sitting there watching her.

He looked at the trailer again. "Why did you do that?"

"Do what?"

"Turn the trailer like that? Why didn't you just back it in straight?"

Great. Hot mountain man's going to be an ass.

Kit bit back a rude answer and sent the man a steady look. She had to give it to him—he had a great poker face. Even though she knew he was being sarcastic, there wasn't anything in his posture or expression that gave him away. He even rumpled his forehead as if honestly puzzled by her inability to back the trailer into the driveway on the first try. What was next—a crack about women drivers? "I'm working on doing just that, but this small trailer's a bit tricky. Just give me a few minutes, and I'll be out of your way—unless you want to back up and use someone else's driveway to turn around in."

"What's tricky about it?"

She took a silent breath, trying to hold on to her impassive expression. Being a cop for eight years should've allowed her to perfect the look, but her emotions always showed too easily. Honestly, she didn't need some incredibly-hot-but-snarky guy to mansplain this to her as she prepared to humiliate herself in front of him...again. At least he didn't seem to be in any hurry. He could sit there and mock her, but she wouldn't have to waste time driving around the block to let him though. "Okay. I'm going to go give it another attempt. If you're going to stay, just know that my ability to back a bumper-pull trailer is inversely proportional to the number of judge-y people staring at me."

His head cocked, and his full mouth turned up at the corners in a smile that was so unexpectedly sweet that Kit couldn't breathe for a solid four seconds. "Inversely proportional? You like math?"

The question threw her even more off balance. "Sure, I guess? I mean, I like it more than backing in this trailer."

His smile widened, showing off white, mostly straight teeth. The front two overlapped a tiny bit, and she found that small flaw surprisingly endearing. "It's the same thing."

"What?" Still confused, she frowned at him. "No, it's not."

"Yes, it is. Everything is math."

"Uh...okay." Another gust of wind caught her, reminding her that she was still standing in the street, trying to figure out what this beautiful stranger was talking about, becoming later and later for work with every second that passed. She took a step away from the pickup and the odd, distractingly handsome mountain man. "I'm going to go do math, then." She hitched her thumb toward the trailer. "Hopefully, I'll remember enough high school algebra to get my trailer out of the way so you can get on with your day."

"Not algebra." The wrinkles in his forehead deepened as his smile changed, turning more quizzical than delighted.

"Right, of course. Geometry, then." She headed back to her SUV, shaking her head slightly as she got into the driver's seat, trying to brush off the strange encounter so she could get the trailer into the driveway and both of them could get on with their lives. As she glanced in the side-view mirror, she jumped.

The stranger had followed her, standing right next to her back bumper, and he was *enormous*. Adrenaline nipped at her, and she mentally scolded herself for letting down her guard. She'd turned her back on a stranger, and she knew better than that. Just because a guy was hot didn't mean he wasn't a threat. As if sensing her tension, Justice sat up and peered out the window. When he caught sight of the stranger, his tail thumped against the seat. Ferocious, Justice was not.

Kit put a hand on the door latch, ready to get out of the car if the man came any closer, but he'd stopped. The tension in her muscles eased a tiny bit when he kept some distance between them, and she stuck her head out the window to give him a questioning look. Justice sniffed the air through the partially open window and then licked the glass with his broad tongue.

"I don't believe that you're going about this in the most efficient way," the mountain man said. "You need help."

She frowned, pretty sure he'd just insulted her. "What does that mean?"

"I'll do the math, and you can drive. Together, problem solved." He swept his arm to the side in a dramatic wave that erased her lingering tension, making it impossible to be intimidated by him. With his enormous bulk and shaggy beard, she hadn't expected him to be so wonderfully *dorky*. Any lingering insecurities dredged up earlier were flushed away. She'd be willing to bet a lot of money that this guy hadn't been one of the popular kids in high school either. This guy had been getting stuffed in lockers just like Kit.

She eyed his broad shoulders. At least, he'd been stuffed in lockers until he'd hit a growth spurt.

A smile tugged at her mouth as she lifted her hands in defeat and pulled forward, straightening the trailer before shifting into reverse again. After turning a circle on the seat, Justice lay down with a groan and closed his eyes.

"Turn the wheel eighteen degrees to the left," the man called, and she darted a glance at him in the mirror. She'd expected him just to give her a few hand signals, but apparently he was going to micromanage this process. With a small shrug, she did as he suggested—or as close as she could manage. From his exasperated look, that wasn't exact enough for him. "I said eighteen degrees, not twenty-six."

Instead of annoying her, she found the mild scolding amusing, and she gave him an apologetic wave as she straightened the wheel slightly. It must've been acceptable to Mr. Tall, Hairy, and Exacting, because he gave a slight nod.

"Now continue backing for four feet and eleven inches."

Four feet and eleven inches, Kit repeated in her head with a mental eye roll as she eased the trailer back. The directions struck her as funny, but she held back her laughter. The man seemed so earnest, and she didn't want him to think she was making fun of him. He was being nice enough to help her out, after all.

"Stop!"

Startled by his shout, she slammed on the brake. Adrenaline was rushing through her again as she leaned out the window, frantically trying to see behind the trailer. "What? Was I going to hit something?"

"No." He turned his puzzled gaze to hers. "You were about to go too far."

She stared at him, annoyed by the remaining anxiety threading through her body. "Did I actually go five feet instead?" Immediately, she felt bad for mocking him, especially when he gave her such a warm smile.

"No. You're perfect." Above the top edges of his beard, his cheeks darkened as he cleared his throat and looked away. "Perfectly positioned, I mean."

"Of course." A hundred teasing responses rose in her head, but she restrained herself and just stayed silent, waiting for the next instruction.

Staring at the snow-covered road, he rubbed at the back of his neck, and Kit had a feeling he was flustered. That was a novel experience for her. Even as a kid, she'd always been considered one of the guys. It was rare that she induced speechlessness in a man—especially one as gorgeous as this one—and she was reluctantly flattered by his reaction.

Then her gaze moved to the dashboard clock, and the time made her stomach sink. She was going to be so horrendously late. "What's next?" Her voice was too loud, making him glance at her, startled.

"Right." He took a deep breath, the air expanding his broad chest even more, and he looked between the trailer and her SUV, his gaze calculating. "Straighten the wheel, and reverse another three feet, two inches."

Kit eased up on the brake and allowed the SUV to back up. Prepared this time, his urgent "Stop!" didn't startle her.

"Turn the wheel six degrees to the right."

Kit was quite impressed with her self-control, since she managed to keep a straight face throughout the process, even when his extremely specific directions included half inches. She had to admit that his math-inspired technique worked. The trailer ended up in a perfect spot: right next to the walkway and leaving just enough room on the other side for her to park her SUV once she got home. Setting the parking brake, she hopped out and went back to unhitch the trailer, but the stranger was already on it.

Kit dug a good-sized rock that was bordering the walkway out of the snow and wedged it behind one of the tires as a wheel chock. As she straightened, she noticed the man was eyeing her with approval. She flushed, thinking that he'd been focused on her bent-over backside, but he gestured at the rock, instead.

"Good idea," he said, and she felt stupidly disappointed that he hadn't been admiring her rear end—and then she felt silly for being so shallow.

"Thank you." She reached out to shake his hand. There was an odd pause where she wondered if he was going to accept the gesture, and then he took off his right glove and clasped her hand in his. It was warm and pleasantly rough, and his huge hand completely swallowed hers. That enveloping hold made her feel disconcertingly small and safe, and she hurried to speak to distract herself. "This would've taken longer without your help."

"Yes." Now that he had her hand, he wasn't releasing it, and things started to feel awkward again. "It would've taken considerably longer."

Once again, Kit wasn't sure whether to be offended or amused, but she settled on amusement. After all, the man wasn't wrong. Letting out a huff of laughter, she gently tugged her hand back. "I'm Kit Jernigan."

Finally releasing his grip, he gave a small nod but remained quiet rather than give his name.

With another small laugh, Kit headed back to the driver's seat of her SUV. The guy had just saved her a bunch of time and aggravation. The least she could do, she figured, was let him keep his anonymity. She'd return to cop-mode soon enough.

Opening the car door, she looked over her shoulder at the man, who was still standing where she'd left him. "I hate to math and run, but I'm already late for my first day at my new job. Thank you again, though."

With another short lift of his chin, he watched as she pulled out of the driveway and turned away from his pickup. Before she reached the next intersection, she couldn't resist another glance in the rearview mirror. He'd moved next to his truck, but he was still watching her, and Kit jerked her gaze back to the road.

"What a strange guy...whoever he is." She realized that she was smiling. "Just between us, Justice, I kind of like him—even if he is too pretty for his own good." The dog, who'd been snoozing for most of the trailer-parking process, opened his eyes and thumped his tail against the seat in what Kit took as agreement.

Blowing out a hard breath, Kit focused on getting back to the police station. It was still her first day at a new job in a strange town, but her encounter with the nameless man had given her a fizzy sense of hopeful anticipation.

If all her neighbors were as interesting and helpful as her mystery mountain man had been, maybe her new life in Monroe wouldn't be so terrible after all.

CHAPTER 2

SOMEONE HAD BLOWN UP THE POLICE DEPARTMENT.

It was bad enough starting a new job in a strange town, but it was even worse to find a charred shell of a building where the department was supposed to be. Kit glanced at the printout of the most recent email from her new chief, but the address listed hadn't changed from the last time she'd been there: 101 Pickard Street, Monroe, Colorado. It was the same as what was printed on the Monroe Police Department sign—the sign directing her into the empty parking lot that butted up against the blackened skeleton that had, not too long ago, been the building in which she'd had her interview…the place where she was supposed to start her first day of work.

Justice whined from the back seat, and she reached back to pet his silky, floppy ears. "I know, buddy. As soon as I find where the not-exploded police station is, we can finally get out of this car."

Pulling away from the curb, Kit headed back toward the town's main street. There had been a halfhearted effort made to plow, but several inches of packed snow still covered the roads, making her grateful for her SUV's all-wheel drive. She slowly headed toward downtown, figuring that Monroe was small enough that any random townsperson would know where the police department had moved. She just needed to find that person.

Like everyone else in the country, she'd heard the news about the drug lord's attack on this tiny mountain town just a few weeks ago, but she was shocked by the extent of the damage. She'd interviewed with the Monroe police chief over three months ago, when the tiny town was still intact and bustling with tourists. Monroe had seemed like a perfect escape then, with quaint shops lining the downtown area and quiet streets dotted with cedar-sided cabins. Set in a valley and surrounded by snow-peaked mountains with bright yellow aspen trees dotting the slopes, the town could've been used as a movie set.

Now, as she drove slowly through that same downtown, the difference was shocking.

The general store was gone, as was the diner, both just blackened holes in the line of shops. Most of the other places had closed signs in the windows, and the streets and sidewalks were empty. It still looked like a movie set, just one with a post-apocalyptic plotline now—probably involving zombies.

Despite the cold, Kit rolled down her window several inches so she could hear what was going on outside her car. It was a habit she'd developed while patrolling, and now, even though she wasn't technically on duty, she felt uneasy with the windows up. The silence was eerie.

The town was too quiet for seven on a weekday morning. People should've been heading to work and getting their kids to school, but there was no one in sight. The only sound was her SUV engine and the crunch of snow under her tires.

As she passed a shuttered restaurant, the VFW parking lot came into view, and she sat straighter. A dozen or so cars—including two squad cars—were scattered throughout the lot.

"Look, Justice," she said, glancing in the rearview mirror to see that the bloodhound was sitting up, ears perked as he looked out the window. "Actual people—well, cars, at least. I was beginning to think that we'd stumbled into a horror movie."

She pulled into the lot, backing into a space next to one of the squad cars. A Belgian Malinois in the back stood up and started barking, and Justice's tail thumped against the seat. He'd never met another dog he didn't like.

Kit smiled as she got out of her SUV. After driving through the creepy, bombed out town, it was reassuring to see the dog in the squad car. Being part of the K9 unit was her life—at least, it had been. She didn't feel so much like the last remaining survivor on earth anymore.

Carefully, she made her way across the snowy, icy lot to the VFW entrance. As she stepped inside, she removed her sunglasses and stayed in the entry for a minute, allowing her eyes to adjust from the bright sunlight reflecting off the snow outside to the dim interior. It smelled like every VFW she'd ever been in—a mixture of musty old building, years of cigarette smoke, and home-style food.

She followed the sounds of chatter and the scent of bacon into a dining area that looked as if it had been converted into some sort of restaurant. Remembering the destroyed diner down the street, she wondered if this was where they'd relocated. The place was fairly full, and the sight of people after her tour through this weird, empty town was encouraging. Scanning the patrons, her gaze immediately caught on a table with three uniformed cops, and she headed in their direction.

People quieted as she moved through the dining area, weaving between tables, and the cops spotted her quickly. All three were men, and she wondered if there were many women on this small-town force. She hoped so. Although she'd been in the minority at her last department, they'd had a great group of female cops. The thought of being one of only a few women in a sea of guys was daunting.

None of the cops watching her were smiling. Automatically, her shoulders drew back and she raised her chin a little, striding confidently to their table. If she was one of a few or—God forbid—the only woman at her new department, it was especially important to show them right off the bat that she could hold her own.

As she got closer, the guys got bigger, and she swallowed a groan. At a few inches over five feet, she was going to be dwarfed by them. She made a mental note to find whatever gym this town had as soon as possible and get a membership there so she could resume her workouts. She might not be able to grow any taller, but she could always get stronger.

By the time she reached the cops' table, the diner was quiet except for the occasional clink of a coffee mug hitting a saucer and the sizzle of food cooking on the grill in the kitchen. With a mental grimace, she realized that she was going to become the crowd's morning entertainment. *Welcome to small-town life*.

"Hi." She held out her hand to the closest cop, who happened to be the biggest one. "I'm Kit Jernigan. I accepted a job with the Monroe PD. Today's my first day."

He studied her for a moment before accepting her outstretched hand. He looked reserved and wary, but not hostile, and Kit took that as a good sign. "Otto Gunnersen."

Turning to the man sitting next to Otto, she offered her hand again.

This one had a shaved head, and he introduced himself as Hugh Murdoch as they shook hands. He studied her with a slight upward twist of his mouth, and she kept her expression bland, hoping he wouldn't turn out to be an asshole. Smirking was rarely a sign of a pleasant personality. Not really wanting to hear what smart-ass comment was going to come out of his mouth, she quickly turned to the last cop, the one with dark hair and eyes and a hard cast to his face.

He waited the longest before shaking her hand, but she refused to flinch, just holding his gaze while keeping her hand extended. Finally, he accepted it, giving a firm shake. "Theo Bosco. Have a seat."

She remained standing, knowing that these three would make her grueling hiring interview seem like friendly chit-chat. "It's my first day, so I should check in with the chief. I just stopped in to get directions to the police station—the *new* location."

"Right across the street," Hugh said, typing something on his phone as he used his foot to slide out the chair across from him. "Sit. I've sent a text to the chief to let him know you're with us. Roll call's in a half hour, and Theo and I will be starting our shift then. We'll show you where to go—well, the two of us will. Otto's on nights, so he's done."

Resigned to her fate, Kit took the chair they offered, and a pretty server hurried over. The other diners had gradually started talking again, and the noise level in the place returned to its earlier volume.

"Good morning. Coffee?" At Kit's nod, the waitress poured her a cup and then moved to the other side of the table to top off all the others' mugs. Kit watched as she worked, wondering why the waitress seemed so nervous. Even when she was in uniform, Kit knew her appearance wasn't intimidating—not like these three burly cops— but the waitress kept giving her anxious glances.

Once everyone's coffee mug was full, she stopped next to Theo's chair. When he rested a hand on her lower back, she seemed to relax slightly, giving him a sweet smile before turning back to Kit. "Would you like a menu?"

"Coffee's fine, thanks." She gave the server a smile, figuring that would be the end of the conversation, but the woman lingered.

"Are you a reporter? I hate to ask, but everyone is going to harass me all day if I can't answer their questions about you." The server's words were rushed and thick with a Southern drawl. Her nerves were obvious, even if her fingers hadn't been clamped so tightly around the coffee pot's handle that her knuckles had turned white. "Most of the news crews left last week, but we don't see many other strangers around here, especially now." Her laugh was quick and jittery. "Monroe isn't really a tourist destination at the moment."

Theo gave Kit a look she couldn't interpret before turning to the waitress. "Jules," he said soothingly, rubbing her back in small circles, "she's not a reporter."

"The newspeople were everywhere last week," Hugh explained to Kit. "Like a plague of camera-toting locusts. You couldn't go anywhere without having a microphone jammed in your face and some well-coiffed person demanding to know how you felt about the town exploding. It was like twenty-four-hour mandatory counseling."

Otto grunted in what sounded like agreement, but Theo raised his eyebrows. "Seriously, Hugh? *Well-coiffed*?"

"What?" Leaning back in his chair, Hugh gave a slight, pained wince. It was so quick that Kit wondered if she'd imagined it. "Are you mocking my excellent vocabulary?"

"Yes." Even though he was looking at Hugh, Theo continued rubbing Jules's back.

When Hugh started to respond, Otto cleared his throat gently.

"Right," Hugh said. "Back on track. Jules, meet Monroe's newest K9 officer, Kit Jernigan."

Jules jerked slightly, and Kit was pretty sure she would've taken a step back if Theo's hand hadn't been there. Kit studied the woman carefully, wondering why that information had scared the waitress. If appearances were correct, Jules was dating Theo and was friends with the other two, so the presence of one more cop shouldn't have been frightening. For some reason, though, it was. Although she tried to hide it, Jules was visibly nervous.

"Nice to meet you." Kit tried to keep her tone low-key and friendly, but Jules still looked like she thought Kit was about to leap out of her chair and grab her.

"Hi." Jules attempted a smile, but it trembled at the edges before collapsing completely. "Welcome to

Monroe—what's left of it, at least." She turned her head, glancing behind her. "I'd better get back to work."

As she started to move away, Theo caught the hand not clutching the coffeepot. "Jules."

She smiled at him, but gently slipped free and headed for the kitchen. Theo watched her go before turning back to Kit. He didn't look happy. "Where are you from?" he demanded.

She had been expecting this. "Gold Mill, Wisconsin."

"PD or county?"

"Police."

"How long?"

"Eight years."

"All with the same department?"

"Yes."

"Why'd you leave?"

For the first time in their rapid-fire exchange, Kit hesitated. After numerous interviews, she should've been used to the question, but it still managed to throw her off guard, kicking up the same cloud of bitterness and grief it always did. It took a few seconds before she recovered enough to pull out her stock answer. "There was an incident that created some bad feelings. It was time for a fresh start."

From the look on Theo's face, he'd noticed her hesitation, and Kit knew the topic would come up again. Next time, he wouldn't let her get by on vague generalities. "Why here?"

"Gold Mill has about eighty thousand people and a huge opioid problem. After dealing with that for eight years, I was...tired." She almost laughed at the understatement. "When I interviewed with the chief in early

September, Monroe seemed like a nice place, a peaceful place, somewhere I could be part of the community that I served. Plus, I like snowboarding, and it's much more fun here than the tiny hills we consider ski resorts in the Midwest." She attempted a quick smile at the last bit, but none of the other three returned it, so it quickly faded.

Her apprehension from driving around the bombed-out town had faded when she'd entered the VFW, but now it returned in a rush. These were her fellow officers, the people who were going to have her back when she was in a life-threatening situation—or they were supposed to be, at least. By the way they were staring at her, they'd just as soon toss her off the nearest cliff than work with her. She'd expected it to take a while before she integrated into the department, but she hadn't thought there'd be such instant resistance.

"Yeah, peaceful." Hugh huffed a laugh as he shifted in his chair and winced again. This time, Kit knew she hadn't imagined it.

"Are you okay?" she asked, and all humor immediately disappeared from his face. "Are you in pain?"

"I'm fine." The words came out with a sharp snap.

Otto turned his head toward Hugh. "What's wrong? Is it your arm?"

"No. My arm's fine."

"The cast just came off two days ago." By his concerned frown, it didn't look like Otto believed his partner's denial. "Shouldn't you have it in a sling?"

Hugh let his head fall back in an exaggerated motion. "It's fine. Want me to prove it?" He smirked at Otto. "I could punch you in the nuts, and then you could tell me if you think it's healed enough."

Although Otto didn't look too concerned about the threat, he stopped grousing and turned to Kit. She braced herself for more questions. Of the three, this one made Kit the wariest, maybe because he'd been so quiet this far, except for fussing over Hugh's arm. "You're K9?"

"Yes." She was much happier to be talking about dogs than what had happened at her old department. "For the past six years. After working with a K9 partner, I could never go back."

Otto didn't smile, but he looked slightly less serious, so Kit decided it was close enough. "Bet it was hard to leave your dog."

"I didn't." She grinned, still thrilled that everything had worked out as it had—even despite the apocalyptic state of her new town. She'd found Justice at a rescue a year ago, and she'd done all of his training, so she would've been heartbroken to leave him behind. "My bloodhound came with me. Chief Bayard agreed he'd be an asset, so I bought him from my old department." They'd given her a really good deal, which hadn't surprised her. No one she'd worked with had been too impressed with Justice. Training him had been a long, slow slog, but it had been worth it.

All three cops eyed her with renewed interest. "Patrol?" Theo asked.

"No." The memory of that complete fail made her grimace. "He doesn't have the drive. He's an amazing tracker, though."

"We don't have any trackers," Hugh said, rubbing his arm. Kit was pretty sure that he wasn't aware he was doing it. He seemed to be a show-no-weakness kind of guy.

"We do now," she said, trying to keep her voice light. It'd take time before they accepted her, she knew that. But sitting through this tense mini-interview with her new partners made her realize just how much it was going to suck until they did. Quickly shoving away the thought, she reminded herself that it couldn't be any worse than the past six months at her old department.

Hugh made a noncommittal sound just as Theo glanced at the entrance. "Incoming."

Resisting the urge to duck at his warning—which she felt she couldn't be blamed for, considering the current state of the town—Kit followed his gaze to the door. A tall, beautiful woman in a down coat, skinny jeans, and amazing boots that Kit instantly coveted walked in. After giving their table a quick, guilty glance, she made a beeline for the kitchen, tipping her head forward so that her hair—glossy and ink-black—fell forward to hide her face.

"Gra-cie," Hugh called out in a singsong, but she didn't turn or even look at him.

Theo snorted. "What'd you do to piss off Grace?"

"Nothing." Hugh stood up, his lips tightening slightly as he got to his feet. Although Kit recognized the pain that flashed across his face for a microsecond, she didn't mention it this time. He hadn't seemed to appreciate it when she asked about his arm earlier, and she didn't want to compound her mistake. "Everything was bubbles and puppies when I saw her last night. Something's up."

As Hugh started to weave his way through the tables toward Grace, Jules came out of the kitchen, and Grace nearly ran toward her.

Theo gave a long, drawn-out groan. "Jules is involved?" He got up and followed Hugh.

Glancing toward Otto, Kit saw he was tapping at his phone, frowning.

"What's going on?" she asked, feeling lost. It hit her how much she'd have to figure out—a new job, a new town, all these new people—and she was suddenly overwhelmed. In Gold Mill, even though it was a much bigger community than Monroe, she knew people, knew the players on both the shady and the bright sides, knew who to go to for information, knew where to find the suspects when they bolted, knew which people to check on to make sure they had food and heat, knew who to trust and who to listen to with a high degree of skepticism. The amount that she'd need to learn about Monroe and its citizens seemed momentous.

"Guess we'll see." Despite Otto's calm, even tone, the line between his eyebrows deepened as he glanced at his phone again.

Figuring she wasn't going to get any information out of him, she turned her attention to the other four. After a short, intense conversation with Grace, Jules peeled away and delivered the food she was carrying to a family sitting at a table in the corner. Although Theo stopped several feet away, he still seemed to be looming over her. As she passed him on her way back to the kitchen, she smiled, standing up on her tiptoes to kiss his cheek, not seeming at all intimidated by the looming. They exchanged a few quick words that Kit couldn't make out before Jules patted his arm and hurried away. After watching her for a few broody seconds, Theo started back toward their table.

Hugh, it appeared, was having a much more exciting time of it. He and the very stylish-looking woman— Grace, he'd called her—were having a low-voiced argument that involved a lot of dramatic gestures and facial expressions. Watching them, Kit was positive that they were together—or had been very recently. No one argued that passionately unless there was some chemistry involved.

Kit turned her attention back to their table as Theo sat in his recently vacated seat. He looked even crankier than he had before the mini-drama. When Otto raised his eyebrows in question, Theo gave an irritated shrug.

"She's going to fill me in later."

"About what?" Otto asked.

"News."

"What kind of news?"

Theo's frown deepened as he took a drink of coffee. He even drank angrily, Kit noticed, trying not to smile. "She didn't say." Glancing at Hugh and Grace, Theo scowled. "Doesn't look like Hugh knows, either."

"Sarah knows." Otto held up his cell phone for a moment, face-out, and Kit saw a screen full of texts. "Says she'll tell me about it when she gets home from work this afternoon." He dropped the phone back into his pocket.

"Work?" Theo asked Otto, although his gaze found Jules and followed her around the dining area. "The general store is gone. Where's she working?"

"Grady's house. She's helping him with his insurance paperwork," Otto said absently as Hugh returned, dropping into his chair with an exaggerated scowl that Kit suspected hid a wince of pain. She glanced over to the door to see Grace leaving the dining area.

"That woman is incredibly stubborn."

Theo gave Hugh an incredulous look. "You're just learning this now?"

"She needs to be," Otto said mildly. "You'd steam-roll anyone who wasn't."

With a gasp, Hugh clutched his chest as if mortally wounded by Otto's words. When no one else reacted, Hugh dropped his hand and shrugged affirmatively. "That's probably true. Did either of you get any information?"

"No." Theo had mellowed slightly, but the reminder made him scowl again. "She said later."

Hugh grunted. "I didn't even get that promise. All I got was a 'mind your business.' Obviously, she's forgotten that *everything* is my business—everything interesting, at least. My curiosity is hungry and must be fed. Otto? Anything from the lovely Sarah?"

Otto shook his head silently.

"It has to be a new arri—" Hugh cut off so quickly that Kit was pretty sure someone had kicked him under the table. He turned to eye Kit with a thoughtful gleam in his gaze, one that made her want to scoot back a little, to keep from being sucked into his shenanigans. Her younger sister, Casey, had a look very similar to that, and it had gotten Kit into a lot of trouble when she was little—a lot of fun, maybe, but mostly a lot of trouble. From Hugh's expression, Kit guessed he was even more of an imp than Casey had been.

He smiled, and her suspicions quadrupled. "Let's go, greenie."

Although she had to press her tongue against the back of her teeth to keep herself from telling him that she was *not* green, that she'd had eight years of experience in a much bigger and busier town than this bombed-out little hamlet, Kit managed to stay silent as she stood.

"Where are we going?" The suspicion in Theo's voice confirmed it. Hugh was planning something that would get them into trouble. So much for having a quiet first day consisting of filling out forms and getting measured for her uniform.

The way Hugh widened his eyes in a look of innocence made Kit brace herself and Theo groan. "We're giving our newest officer a tour of the town, of course. We could start at Jules's place. See if any…old friends happened to stop by for a visit."

"If you wait until this afternoon, Sarah will tell me what's going on," Otto said.

"I've always been bad at waiting." Hugh headed for the door, and Kit followed, a sinking feeling in her stomach. Bending the rules was sometimes necessary when it was the right thing to do, but she had planned to stay out of trouble at her new job—at least on her first day. The problem was that she didn't know enough about the situation or Hugh to make a judgment. She glanced over her shoulder at Theo, hoping he'd be the voice of reason.

Instead of trying to rein in his partner, though, Theo was wearing a look of grim determination. With a silent sigh, Kit ignored her instincts and followed Hugh out of the diner. It looked like she needed to start trusting her new partners. Hopefully, they wouldn't get her killed… at least not on her first day.

The red-tailed hawk was back, and Wes was pretty sure she was laughing at him.

She landed on the railing of the fire tower's observation deck, turning her head sideways and fixing one eye on Wes through the wall of glass that made up the south side of the tower room. He took a slow sideways step, his arm lifting ever so slowly as he reached for the camera sitting on the rolling workstation. If he hadn't been worried that the sound of his voice would startle the hawk, he would've used the voice command to move the wheeled table—and the camera—closer to him.

The red-tailed hawk was pathologically camera shy, but Wes was determined. The bird had been basically taunting him all summer and fall, posing like a *Vogue* model until Wes lifted his Canon. As soon as the perfect shot was a second away, the hawk took off—every single time.

Today looked like it was the day. He even had the right lens on. His fingers closed around the camera, and the hawk didn't startle or fly away. Instead, she stayed stock-still, watching him. Forcing himself to keep his movements slow and smooth, he raised the camera and peered at the blurry shape through the viewfinder. Far behind it, the town of Monroe, with its blackened buildings covered in a fresh layer of white snow, nestled in the valley. It would've looked like a Christmas card if it hadn't been for the plume of smoke rising from the southwest side of town.

The camera's auto-focus kicked in, but it was too late. Shot forgotten, Wes returned the camera to the table and grabbed his binoculars, barely noticing as the startled hawk flew away. Scanning the area, he searched for the smoke he'd spotted through his camera lens. Although Colorado's traditional wildland fire season was technically over, he still kept watch over Monroe and the forested acres that surrounded the tiny town.

Peering through the binoculars, he found the grayish-white plume again. Without looking away, he reached out again—for his radio, this time. The town had already had a rough few weeks. The last thing it needed was another disaster.

Too bad that's exactly what it had.

In the spirit of celebrating the heroes who touched our lives, Sourcebooks is pleased to introduce you to the furry friends who make every day just a little bit brighter.

Bruce is a pit-Lab mix who has it all figured out. He came to live with Senior Production Editor Rachel in 2014 and has spent his time organizing her extensive library and meeting the neighborhood squirrels. You may recognize him from the front-inside cover of *Survive the Night*!

True to her name, **Kitten** is a full-grown cat with a youthful spirit and very small body mass. She's fond of travel and spent much of her time traipsing through London's canal boat community and chasing foxes before moving to America in 2015.

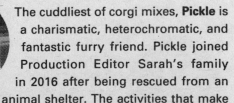

The cuddliest of corgi mixes, **Pickle** is a charismatic, heterochromatic, and fantastic furry friend. Pickle joined Production Editor Sarah's family in 2016 after being rescued from an animal shelter. The activities that make Pickle the happiest are: sleeping, eating, chasing ducks by the pond behind the house, and sleeping even more.

Resident lizard slayer by day, and devoted guard dog at night, **Zoey** has an attitude that rivals many of the great divas in celebrity history. Adopted by Katie's agent in May 2015, this rottweiler/poodle mix (really!) loves to star in her mom's Instagram feed. She will willingly pose with all her mom's new books, if she is paid commission in treats.

Max is the mightiest of hunters and is as brave as her namesake. Reigning over National Accounts Manager Liz's household since summer 2015, she loves to lounge by the window in the sunniest of spots or come down for a snuggle so long as no one—i.e., the other cat—is watching.

Kya is a chatty, sassy middle-aged calico. She has lived with Editorial Assistant Jessica since summer 2015 and loves to snuggle and chase anything that resembles a string. She also likes to ignore the toys her mom buys for her in favor of stealing all the hair ties she can get her paws on.

Pike is a handsome two-and-a-half-year-old half-whippet and some type of shepherd mix. Adopted at ten weeks old from a local rescue, he now lives with Web Designer Kandi. His body and legs are really long, so when he wags his tail, his whole body wiggles.

Io is a flat-coated retriever living with Art Director Adrienne, and is a natural at playing fetch. True to the rest of her household, Io is an amazing goofball. She takes long walks with Adrienne every day and helps her owner clear her head and always keep smiling.

Podrick loves showing his affection by giving nose licks and head bumps—but watch out! If you pet him the wrong way, he might think you're trying to play. Podrick came to live with Editorial Assistant Emily in July 2015.

Roland (a.k.a. **Rollie**) has a fine literary pedigree: he was named after Steven King's Dark Tower series! He's a two-and-a-half-year-old pit-Lab mix and joined Editorial Assistant Taylor's home when he was eight months old. He's a big sack of love and a terrible guard dog. His favorite pastimes include swimming, cuddling, befriending anyone in uniform, and destroying cardboard boxes.

Loki is the furry little God of Mischief. When he isn't nibbling on Christmas trees or napping wherever he pleases, he likes to help *unfold* the laundry and play "catch me if you can!" Associate Director of Production Tina adopted Loki from a rescue shelter and life has never been HOPPIER!

ABOUT THE AUTHOR

When she's not writing, Katie Ruggle rides horses, shoots guns, and trains her three dogs. A police academy graduate, Katie readily admits she's a forensic nerd. While she still misses her off-grid home in the Rocky Mountains, she now lives in a 150-year-old Minnesota farmhouse near her family.

ALSO BY KATIE RUGGLE